CRITICS PRAISE KIMBERLY RAYE AND
SLIPPERY WHEN WET!

"Kimberly Raye's NASCAR romance *Slippery When Wet* combines sensuality and humor as she pits two race car drivers against each other on and off the track circuit…A perfect pick-me-up read as winter approaches (or any other time a reader needs some good perking up)—sexy, funny, and just downright fun!"

—Merrimon Book Reviews

"Extremely exciting and fun to read…I will definitely watch for other works written by this author."

—Fresh Fiction

"This fast-moving and sexy addition to Raye's NASCAR series has a nice, if unexpected, ending."

—*Romantic Times BOOKreviews*

"Kimberly Raye has brought her sizzling writing style to the genre of NASCAR romance, where men pit their machines—and lives—against each other. In this case, it is every man and woman for his or her self. The action is thrilling, and the romance is one of smoldering awareness that finally burst into red-hot flames."

—Romance Reviews Today

"The story line is fast-paced, especially when the lead couple competes with each other."

—*...eview*

Other *Love Spell* books by Kimberly Raye:

SLIPPERY WHEN WET

KIMBERLY RAYE

IN THE MIDNIGHT HOUR

LOVE SPELL

NEW YORK CITY

LOVE SPELL®

July 2009

Published by

Dorchester Publishing Co., Inc.
200 Madison Avenue
New York, NY 10016

ISBN 10: 0-505-52772-3
ISBN 13: 978-0-505-52772-1
E-ISBN: 978-1-4285-0707-4

Visit us on the web at www.dorchesterpub.com.

To my wonderful son, Joshua Joseph Rangel.
Mommy loves you!

My heartfelt thanks to Jan Freed,
an extraordinary and gifted writer who's never too busy
to help out a desperate friend.

And an extra special thank you to Dana Green,
for sharing her knowledge of the Lafayette and USL area.

IN THE MIDNIGHT HOUR

Prologue

It was a bed just made for sin.

The instant the thought rooted in Veronica Parrish's mind, she should have turned and hightailed it out of the antique shop.

She wasn't the least bit interested in sinning.

More like sleeping. A good, solid night's rest.

But as she stared at the mahogany four-poster bed with the legion of satyrs carved into the headboard, she knew in her heart she'd get very little sleep in this bed.

Right. It wasn't as if she had time for sinning. With two jobs and school, she barely found the opportunity to eat and sleep. Not that she needed to eat. At five feet six and one hundred and thirty-nine and a half pounds—she had a digital scale—she could have skipped a few meals, or at least traded her favorite pizza for one of those salads they sold in the campus deli. As for sleep . . . She stifled a yawn. Now, *that* she needed.

She abandoned the small but elegant brass bed she'd been eyeing, scooted past the clerk, and wound her way around furniture and crates to the king-size bed in the far corner of the back room.

"Good choice," the clerk said, coming up behind her. "It just came in a few days ago from an estate liquidation. I haven't even had the chance to get it cleaned up and moved to the front yet. It's a beauty, dust and all, though, isn't it?"

"Yes." Her breath caught as she reached out. Her fingertips trailed over the smooth mahogany of one hand-carved bedpost and wiped away the silver coating. Instantly, the wood seemed to warm to her touch and a strange tingle shot through her.

"This piece dates back to the 1830s." The clerk stood behind her, an anxious look on his face, a spot of mustard on his cheek from his interrupted lunch.

She glanced at her watch. She had all of fifteen minutes to decide on a bed. It was now or never with her schedule. Early mornings alternated between Landry & Landry, the accounting firm where she worked part-time, and classes at the University of Southwestern Louisiana, where she pursued her accounting degree. Evenings she spent at the school's Dupré Library, moonlighting as an assistant before going home to her small efficiency. She had no time for shopping or indecision.

This monstrosity would take up half her apartment. Too big. Too expensive, she realized when she glanced at the price tag. She'd already budgeted a decent amount of money and set her sights on a smaller bed, like the nice brass bed she'd been looking at earlier. Tasteful, comfortable.

Boring, a voice whispered, and she stiffened.

Okay, maybe so; but boring, at least in Ronnie's book, was better than bold and outrageous, and that's exactly what this bed was.

Her gaze drank in the huge headboard, the carved satyrs that seemed to stare back at her, through her. Four massive posters surged toward the ceiling. It was a man's bed, with a distinct presence and undeniable strength. Overwhelming, dominating.

Comforting. She could imagine curling into the mattress surrounded by so much wood and . . . well, strength. She touched one bedpost again, felt the strange current whisper through her body, as if calling to her.

Take me home.

But it wasn't a call, it was more of a command, as if the bed had a will all its own and was anxious for her to make up her mind.

Right.

She snatched her hand away as a nervous giggle bubbled on her lips. She was getting carried away. Lack of sleep was making her giddy. She'd pulled too many all-nighters studying, catching quick catnaps on the worn sofa in the back lounge at the library, and now she was starting to get punchy. She needed a bed in the worst way. Her own had died last week when her neighbor's chubby three-year-old twins had used it for a trampoline. A few jumps and the springs had given, the frame had cracked, and the bed had breathed its last breath.

Now or never.

Again, her gaze traced the solid frame, the carved posts, the satyr-sculpted headboard. Definitely made for sin. She frowned. It was the sort of creation to make one think of passionate kisses and erotic fantasies, which was exactly why she didn't need it. Veronica Parrish didn't have time for such foolishness. She had to stay focused on graduating in two months. She'd worked too hard to let anything distract her.

Earth to Ronnie! It's just a bed. It's not as if you're about to purchase a Chippendale's dancer and take him home to do a little research for your human sexuality class. It's a piece of furniture, for Pete's sake.

"It's expertly crafted," the clerk interjected, obviously trying to sway her. "Solid wood. No particle board here, that's for sure."

Her attention strayed back to the price tag. "It's a bit more than I intended."

"If it's money you're watching, I've got a cherry wood double in the far corner. Simple and tasteful, and at least half the price of this. Or there's that little brass number. Either one would probably be more appropriate for your needs."

Appropriate. Exactly what she needed. She always made the nice, rational, appropriate choices in her life. Never took any chances, never acted on her feelings.

It was a man's world, after all, and if a woman wanted to make it she had to think like a man. With her head instead of her heart.

Ronnie reached out again, her fingertips brushing the wood.

The strange tingling started again, spread through her body, seeking all the strategic points—the sensitive shell of each ear, the hollow of her throat, her tender nipples, her navel, the backs of her knees, the arch of each foot. The sensations were highly unsettling. Extremely impractical. Wildly unladylike.

And this was *not* the sort of bed a strictly career-minded woman, especially the daughter of Covenant, Louisiana's ultra-conservative mayor, should be forking over her hardearned money for.

That's what her father would say if he were here.

Her mother would call it scandalous.

Both would call her a political liability, just the way they'd done when she'd announced her intention to pursue an accounting degree at a college one hundred and fifty miles away.

Not that they didn't like accountants. If Veronica had been their son, they would have kissed her off and wished her well.

Men made great accountants, but women . . . Well, they made good wives and mothers and great Jell-O molds, at least according to her father and his political platform, which emphasized a return to the traditional roles of men and women and family.

He would have steered her toward the brass bed, or a white wicker number, something more . . . ladylike. Meek and mild, rather than bold and outrageous. A woman's bed instead of a man's.

"I'll take this one," she said as a smile curved her lips. "*This* one."

Chapter One

Valentine Tremaine loved women.

There was just something about the softness of a woman's skin, the shine of her hair, the warm, musky scent that was hers and hers alone, the way she walked and talked and smiled and did other, more *relevant* things.

Ah, women . . .

Creatures sent straight from heaven. God's supreme effort to outdo all the Devil's pleasurable vices. There was no food as delectable. No whiskey as warm and soothing. No drug as addicting.

Ah, yes. Women . . .

They came in every size and shape; short and tall, petite and buxom, shy as a summer shower and bold as a clap of thunder, and Val adored them all regardless.

Like his father and all the Tremaine men before him, he had no special preference when it came to females. They were all attractive in their own unique way, all intoxicating in their similarities, whether a raven-haired beauty, a golden-tressed angel, or a redheaded temptress. He'd had his share of all three, and many, many in between.

Not that he was a man to brag, or to take the gift of a woman's body for granted. Val took nothing for granted, and that reason alone made his appeal phenomenal.

He loved women, and they loved him.

And so he wasn't the least surprised by his immediate and rather lusty response when this particular woman crawled into his bed. Women had shared his bed for years, and his passion feverish and intense, had never failed him.

...ed that she didn't so much as glance in his ...y when he'd been anticipating her stretched ...since the moment she'd first walked into the ...very night for the past week since Fate had brought ...ogether and this sweet woman had come to his rescue in that dusty old antique shop.

He was definitely in the mood to show her a little gratitude. Perhaps a lot, he amended after a quick glance down at that very prominent, very appreciative part of him.

From his usual casual repose on the bed, he'd watched her pull off her baggy T-shirt, slide off her shoes, and peel off her pants. She'd exchanged them for an even larger T-shirt that swallowed up her curves and her big, beautiful breasts, making her look rather young and vulnerable.

She was far from it, of course. By his estimation, she couldn't be a day younger than twenty-five, and no doubt very experienced in the arts of love. It wasn't just her delectable body that clued him in. It was the way she moved, so graceful and sexy, putting away her things, fixing herself some supper, making the most mundane chore exciting. As if she knew he watched.

Undoubtedly she did, he told himself when she'd set about pulling her long, flame-colored hair into a ponytail. The motion had lifted her large breasts, pushed them against the cotton of her shirt, and Val had nearly groaned aloud.

But he'd held his tongue, opting to save his energy for a much more pleasurable activity once she joined him.

And tonight would be the night. The past week she'd fallen asleep at her desk where she retired every night, a stack of books in front of her. She studied vigorously for several hours before sleep caught up to her. Then she would rest her head on her folded arms and close her eyes.

He'd watched her well into the night, until the clock struck midnight and he was able to go to her. He'd been so tempted to touch her. So many times he'd reached out, but, alas, he'd forced himself away, opting to tuck a blanket around her to chase away the night's chill.

He wasn't sure why. He could have done all he wanted with her. A woman of her sensuality would have come alive in his arms, and he ached so badly. He'd spent the past century and a half cooped up in one rotting house after another, with no one to warm his bed, to warm him. Ah, he'd come close a few weeks ago in a storage shed on the outskirts of town. Of course, it had been during the day and he'd been little more than a figment of the woman's imagination, a whisper in her ear, an invisible touch along her pale skin. But he'd been there, and she'd felt him.

A fat lot of good it had done. The woman, a lawyer's assistant who'd been cataloguing estate items, had turned out to be engaged. Upon learning such a crucial piece of information, Val had stopped the dalliance immediately. No matter how desperate, he had his principles. Which was why, with this beautiful, *available* woman at his fingertips, he'd merely bid her sleep well the past week.

No more. Tonight she would come to him, call to him, and his deprivation would end.

For all his fantasies, his bold dreams of the evening ahead, nothing quite prepared him for what transpired next.

She settled herself in the center of *his* huge bed, on *his* white sheets, and didn't so much as spare him a glance.

Not that she could see him, mind you. He'd long ago come to terms with the fact that he wasn't exactly the man he used to be. He was more now, or less, depending on how one surveyed the situation. He chose the former, of course, and so it irritated the hell out of him that she didn't pay him any mind. She might not be able to see him, but she could *feel* him, by God!

Things quickly went from bad to worse when she turned away to reach for something on the nightstand.

Being a lover of the female species and extensively experienced in giving and receiving sexual favors, Val, through his numerous liaisons, had grown to appreciate the different tastes and desires of a woman when it came to his bed.

But this . . .

Irritated, he watched as she retrieved a pizza and a can of soda. She flung back the lid, popped the soda tab, and reached for a large slice soggy with cheese and sauce. After a huge bite and an endless moment with her eyes closed, her mouth moving slowly, sensuously as she chewed, she finally swallowed.

And so did Val. Hard.

Then with a smile, she took a sip of soda and reached for the remote control.

The television clicked on, sending a dance of colorful shadows through the dim bedroom. And so began the newest phase in the one hundred and fifty years of Valentine Tremaine's death—or new and improved life, as Val chose to see it.

But he was starting to have his doubts, especially since he found himself for the first time in bed with a woman who had no interest in him whatsoever.

"*Valentine.*" He whispered the name into her ear, catching a succulent whiff of strawberries and cream. "*Say it*, chérie."

She slapped at the air as if warding off a bothersome fly. He started to speak louder, but caught himself. He wasn't of the mind to frighten, but to seduce.

Unfortunately, she didn't seem the least bit interested. She simply sat there, eating and drinking and watching the news. While Val ached and burned and watched her.

And where he'd always considered himself a patient man, he soon discovered he was a very, very impatient spirit.

Ronnie shoved the last of the pizza slice into her mouth. Ignoring a rush of megasized guilt, she reached for another. So she'd jog to class the rest of the week. The month, even. A year of exercise would be worth the next few minutes of fast food ecstasy—

The solid *whack* of cardboard hitting cardboard thundered

through her head. The lid slammed shut just inches shy of her fingers. Her gaze riveted on the closed box. Uneasiness zigzagged down her spine and her heart stopped for one long, silent moment.

The clock ticked away, the sound magnified in the sudden hush as she stared at the pizza box as if it had metamorphosed into a living, breathing thing.

And Brad Pitt's beating down the door for a date!

Her lips curved into a shaky smile and she managed to take a jagged breath. A gust of air, she told herself, her gaze darting to the French doors. *Closed* doors, because she'd turned on the air conditioner. Her attention shot to the vent in a nearby wall. The pink ribbon tied to one slat hung limply. The air conditioner had cycled off minutes ago.

Carefully, she lifted the lid the tiniest bit and peered beneath. Just three-quarters of a pizza pie. She giggled. Like she'd expected to find anything else. Opening the box, she started to retrieve another slice.

The cardboard whacked closed again, as if a solid hand forced the lid back into place.

"This can't be happening." She closed her eyes, forcing herself to take a deep, calming breath. Okay, so it *had* happened, but there was an explanation for it. There was always an explanation. *Think calm, cool, rational. Think* instead of feel, her motto for the past eight years.

She took a deep breath, opened her eyes, and tried the box again.

The lid lifted easily and laughter trembled from her lips. Somehow, someway a draft had worked its way into the room and closed the box. Her imagination—her sleep-deprived, exhausted imagination—had done the rest. Fancy not being able to lift a measley cardboard lid. She was simply tired and overworked.

But tonight would remedy all of that. She'd left the library early, after having fallen asleep during a fifteen-minute break that lasted a full hour. Delta, the night librarian, had taken pity on her and sent her home with strict instructions to rest.

"You keep working yourself to death, you're going to get old before your time, sugar."

"I'm already old." Or at least older. At twenty-six, she had at least four years on most of the other seniors at USL. While an accounting degree only took four years, Ronnie didn't have the luxury of going full-time. She'd had to work full-time during the summers and part-time throughout college to meet school and living expenses.

"You're one step out of the womb, sugar," Delta had told her. "Take a look at me." The woman had frowned, emphasizing her sun-browned face carved with dozens of laugh lines. "Sixty-four years' worth of wrinkles—and all from catching catnaps in the library lounge when I should have been in my own bed sound asleep."

That had been enough to send Ronnie straight home.

Her first class was at eight in the morning, and although she still had to jot down a few extra notes on her term paper topic for Professor Guidry's human sexuality class, she could drag herself up an hour early to do it. She refused to think of anything tonight but a little R&R.

Determined to ignore the nagging guilt that prompted her toward her book satchel, she stabbed the remote control button and found a music video channel. Humming with the song, she retrieved another slice of pizza. No stress-induced hallucination was going to rob her of the pleasure of a double cheese and pepperoni.

She hadn't had a really good pizza pie since she'd left her hometown of Covenant and her friend Jenny, the daughter of the town's one and only pizza parlor owner. Friends since kindergarten, Ronnie and Jenny had gone through school and puberty together, despite Ronnie's father, who'd never approved of the friendship. Jenny had been a wild child, the product of a divorce, and a bad influence, according to Mayor Parrish.

Oddly enough, Jenny was the one married and settled in Covenant with a husband and two toddlers, while Ronnie was here, a hundred and fifty miles away in Lafayette, still single, sitting in a messy efficiency she didn't have the time or the energy to clean, nursing a pizza smack dab in the middle of a bed that belonged in one of those Enhance Your Love Life catalogues advertised in the back of *Cosmo* or *Vogue*.

If only her folks could see her now.

She nibbled on her pizza slice. Her mother would turn every shade of red. Her father would probably have a heart attack. He'd definitely issue a statement claiming Ronnie's behavior was due to an accidental drop on the head as a child rather than her upbringing.

Not that Ronnie had to worry about either. They wouldn't see her, because traditional Mayor Parrish and his lovely wife wouldn't visit their nontraditional daughter. Ronnie had traded marriage and a family for late-night study sessions and student loans, her role as dutiful daughter for that of political liability.

And, of course, she'd made the choice publicly. In front of a church full of people gathered to watch her marry the man of her father's dreams, Raymond Cormier, the town's chief of police and one of her father's staunch supporters.

She took another bite of pizza and flipped through a couple of television channels, finally settling on an old black-and-white movie.

On-screen, Shirley Temple hugged her long-lost father. A sense of loneliness washed through Ronnie.

Despite her differing views and their bitter parting, she missed her parents. There was a lot to be said for living at home. She'd had three solid meals a day, no bills hanging over her head, and two people who loved her, even if they were painfully conservative. At least she hadn't been alone.

Then again, there was also a heck of a lot to be said for independence, regardless of all its responsibilities and worries. She ate and slept when she wanted. Wore sweatshirts, jeans, and sneakers instead of the awful, "feminine" dresses her Aunt Mabel had made for her. Did whatever she felt like doing.

Smiling, she placed the half-eaten slice of pizza back in the box and stretched out on the bed. Her T-shirt rode her hips. Soft cotton cushioned the backs of her bare legs. Yes, independence had its good points. This was *her* apartment, *her* bed—in all its bold, outrageous glory—and she was going to sleep like a rock tonight.

Her gaze went to the pizza box and the same sense of unease she'd felt earlier came crawling back through her. Just a draft, she told herself.

She heard the soft buzzing sound again, like a faint whispering. Whispering? More like a fly or a gnat. She slapped at the air, then gathered up the pizza box and refrigerated the leftover slices. Out of sight, out of mind, she told herself. She checked the double deadbolts on her apartment door, flicked off the lights, and climbed into bed, ready to relax and watch a little TV. But she couldn't seem to get comfortable. The pillow wasn't right. The sheet twisted this way, her leg felt uncomfortable that way, and every time her gaze strayed to the spot just to her left where the pizza box had been sitting, a shiver worked its way through her.

Even watching the latest video from a group of bare-chested hunks didn't take her mind off the pizza box episode.

Correction—it wasn't an episode. Just one of those things easily explained if she'd been a physicist or rocket scientist instead of an accounting major.

Finally, unable to relax, much less sleep, she flicked off the television, turned on the nightstand lamp, and retrieved her book bag. She would write out her paper topic right now. Homework never failed to put her to sleep. In a half hour she'd have her topic ready to hand in, and she'd be sound asleep. One hour max.

"Take that, Guidry," she said, smiling to herself as she finished penning her brilliant idea. She was busy jotting down some extra thoughts—better to have too much information when Guidry called for topics than too little—when her eyes started to droop.

Her fingers went limp, the pen sliding from her grasp as she snuggled back into the pillow. *Ahh . . .* This was much better than being hunched over her desk. *Mmm . . .* Her first night in her new bed. She smiled as her eyes drifted shut.

The bed was so soft, so warm, so . . . ticklish?

She forced one eye open to stare at her bare arm. There was nothing there, yet she felt a soft whisper across her skin, a feather-light stroke as soft and understated as the glide of silk over smooth marble.

Her skin prickled, goosebumps danced along her arm, and Ronnie had the sudden and inexplicable feeling that she wasn't alone. The same feeling she'd had with the pizza box earlier. As if something, or someone, were there with her, beside her, touching the box, touching her . . .

Geez, she *was* sleep deprived.

She pulled the sheet up over her bare legs to her waist. The textbook she'd been perusing for possible topics was open, facedown on her chest, the weight oddly soothing.

Her eyes closed again. The softness of the mattress lulled her body into complete relaxation and her chest rose and fell in a steady rhythm for the next fifteen minutes. Until her cuckoo clock struck midnight and the loud noise launched an all-out offensive against General Sandman.

She had to get up, she thought, vaguely aware of the textbook weighing down her chest, her notes scattered next to her. She had to at least put away her things and set her alarm. Packing lunch and picking out clothes could wait until morning. But there wouldn't be a morning if she didn't set the blasted alarm.

She knew that, yet for some reason it didn't hold any urgency. Her entire life centered around a carefully planned schedule— the only way she had time for school and two jobs—but at that moment, nothing seemed as important as keeping her eyes closed and relaxing in the hazy bliss that surrounded her.

The last cuckoo grated on her nerves, then the room fell into blessed silence.

Peace enveloped her, soothing her aching muscles and weary mind. Blackness welcomed her like a long-lost friend, and then she was floating, drifting, sleeping.

The weight on her chest suddenly lifted, the release of pressure luring her back to the fringes of reality, the hum of the air conditioner, the tick-tock of the clock, the strange uneasiness, not as pronounced as before, that crawled through her. Something wasn't right. She knew it even before she felt the strange movement.

Ronnie forced one eye open to see the sheet drift down to puddle around her ankles, exposing her bare legs. Then the edge of her T-shirt lifted, glided upward, baring a pair of silky white panties, several inches of pale skin, her navel, more skin, the underside of her breasts. Her nipples tightened. The material snagged on the stiff peaks.

Her breath caught, her chest rose, and her nipples strained against the fabric. It was a highly unsettling sensation. Erotic, forbidden.

Impossible!

Her other eye opened and she watched in stunned amazement as the material lifted, easing over her nipples, exposing the throbbing, rosy tips. The edge of the shirt bunched as if invisible fingers tugged at the thin covering—

She clamped her eyes shut.

The pizza.

Her mother had always told her junk food would rot her brain—traditionalist families were sticklers for good, wholesome home cooking. That's what was happening. Her brain was rotting, because this couldn't—no way in hell, heaven, or the in between—be real! The sheet couldn't move on its own, nor could her shirt. No way. Uh, uh. Forget it.

She chanced another peek and shock bolted through her. Her T-shirt was no longer moving at the will of invisible fingers. They were *real* fingers. Long, lean, tanned fingers attached to a strong hand and muscled forearm dusted with sand-colored hair—

Impossible.

She clamped her eyes shut. This couldn't be happening. There couldn't be a man in her bed. She'd locked the door and checked the French doors, and there wasn't any place to hide in her small apartment. Except under the bed, but she'd checked that herself, an old habit she'd developed since moving out on her own. She was completely, totally, indisputably alone.

Alone.

After such a lengthy sermon of reassurance, she might have believed her assertion but for one thing. She could feel the pressure just above her left breast where the material tugged higher, higher, the motion caused by the strong male hand she'd glimpsed a moment ago.

But there couldn't be a man in her bed. Other than the pressure on her skin, she didn't feel a presence beside her. Surely the bed would dip beneath his weight? Most certainly she would be able to feel his body heat, the warmth of his legs next to hers, hear his breathing, the thump of his heart. *Something.*

"Impossible," she muttered and the tug on her T-shirt stopped.

Her eyes flew open to see—

Nothing. Just the frantic heave of her bare chest, the empty sheets surrounding her, the dark shadows lingering just beyond the reach of lamplight. There was no one in bed with her, and no one had crawled out. She'd opened her eyes too fast for that. There'd been no squeak of bedsprings. No rustling of covers. No telltale indentation next to her. Nothing.

No one.

Yet . . .

An enticing scent wafted through her nostrils, teased her senses. A rich, musky fragrance tinged with the faint hint of leather and apples that made her want to drink in another deep draft.

Nah, she decided when she inhaled again and smelled only cheese and tomato sauce. No strange aroma. Just a hallucination warning her of potential brain rot if she didn't start eating right.

No more junk food, she vowed, tugging her shirt down and yanking the sheet up. A hallucination. A junk food-induced dream.

A sort of pleasant dream, she admitted several minutes later, her body still buzzing from the sensation of fabric gliding, hands moving, nipples tightening.

Okay, so maybe there was something to be said for junk food late at night. No wonder her mother had warned her against it. Anything to keep Ronnie from having a little fun.

She took a deep breath; her body prickled and she marveled at the sensation. She'd never had such a "pleasant" dream before. Her nighttime fantasies usually involved a computer with a high-powered spreadsheet program that could calculate taxes faster than she could blink. Oh, and she also had the one where she pictured herself in a custom-tailored business suit in a posh office—the high-powered computer at her fingertips, of course—head of her very own CPA firm. Her dreams had never involved a man with tanned arms and strong hands, doing forbidden things to her. Men were distracting. She didn't have time for sex, and especially not love, and so she kept her mind strictly tuned to school and work. Usually. Until now.

The junk food, she assured herself.

And Guidry's class.

And, of course, this bed.

With all three corrupting her, it was no wonder her dreams had taken a turn for the worse.

Or the better.

She smiled to herself, pushing away the fear and panic. She

was a grown woman and they were just dreams. It wasn't as if she would have to face Mr. Dream Man the morning after, and spend precious hours worrying over a relationship, or over an "accident" that would chain her to a crib and a husband and rob her of her career.

She worked hard. She'd earned a few harmless dreams.

She would start by making pizza a mandatory late-night snack while she studied for Guidry's class. And she'd buy a few six-packs of soda in case the extra sugar rush was needed for this particular fantasy. And she would do her snacking and studying in bed, of course.

Ah, pizza and cola. Imagine what a pint of Häagen-Dazs could do!

On that titillating thought, she drifted into a deep sleep, not the least bit alarmed when the sheet started to glide down again and her T-shirt to inch its way up. Her body responded, arching against the seeking hands, straining into the moist heat of a firm mouth.

Just a dream, of course, her conscience reassured her time and time again. Just a dream.

This is more like it, Val thought, feeling the woman respond beneath his expert hands. *Mon Dieu,* she was hotblooded. He licked a blazing trail up her stomach, up the slope of her breast until his mouth closed over one puckered tip.

She was so sweet and warm, her nipple hard and greedy against his tongue. He suckled her long and deep, tasting her, relishing the feel of a woman's response to him. It had been so long. Too long.

Her moan sent an echoing thrum through him, making him harder, more eager to bury himself deep inside the blissful warmth of her body. She was the culmination of endless nights spent dreaming and now she was real. Here with him, under him, begging him.

And she was a *virgin*.

The realization hit him with the same force as the bullet that had robbed him of his mortal life.

Shocked, he stared down at the ripe, soft woman. His fingertips teased her nipple and, sure enough, he felt the surge of emotion that swelled inside her. Desire. Anticipation. *Wonder*.

Merde! A virgin.

He stared at her face and willed her to meet his gaze.

Her lids lifted and amber eyes the color of fine whiskey glittered back at him. They widened as if shocked at the sight of him, the expression quickly fading into that of pure pleasure.

"A dream," she mumbled to herself, her eyelids fluttering closed.

He trailed a hand up the inside of her thigh, peeling back the scrap of lace that served as the twentieth century's version of bloomers. There was certainly something to be said for modern times, but Val had no energy to rejoice over the changes. He was intent on a higher purpose, a soft, warm, wet purpose, and the truth.

His hands returned to her thighs, urging them apart to give him full view of her femininity. With a trembling hand, he touched the soft, slick folds and a rush of warmth spilled over his knuckles. She arched into him. He touched her again, stroking, probing until she came up off the bed, a breathy moan sailing past her lips as a wave of ecstasy crashed over her and she came completely undone. *And at nothing more than the brief touch of his hand!*

Nom de Dieu! A *virgin*.

He jerked away from her, stumbling from the bed to the French doors. He needed some air. Cool, relaxing air. He threw open one door. A wave of summer heat washed over him, through him, and he burned all the hotter.

There was no relief, he realized, anguish driving him to his knees. No relief at all, because Valentine Tremaine didn't touch virgins.

He left the spoiling of innocence, the breeching of maidenheads up to those men interested in more than a night's pleasure. Val had no use for clingy, naïve, inexperienced women who expected the world. He sought an equal in his bed. A woman who revered freedom and relished independence as much as he did. Virgins robbed a man of both, not to mention his livelihood. His life, too, as Val well knew.

Never again, he vowed to himself, even with one as comely, as sensuous as this woman. *Never again.*

Crossing the room, he stood next to her. She lay on the bed, her eyes closed, her head thrown back into the pillow. Flame-colored hair spilled around her head, across the white pillowcase. Her T-shirt was bunched beneath her arms. Her chest rose and fell to a frantic rhythm, her breasts soft and creamy and swollen, her turgid nipples the color of fine wine. A fiery thatch of red curls formed a triangle at the base of her thighs, hiding the most intimate delights of her body.

By all that was holy, she was a sight! Every inch of her made for a man's hands, mouth, body.

Not his, of course. But then, Valentine Tremaine wasn't a man anymore.

Not that he didn't ache as badly as one with a near-naked woman in front of him. He did. Worse, even, because now in his present state, his feelings were magnified. That's what she'd felt—the presence of his energy rather than a body, though that energy still maintained the same shape and form, the spirit a shadow of the physical self, and much more potent to the senses.

Val had stirred her from the inside out. He'd stroked her feelings with his own, caressed her body with the sheer force of his will disguised as his hands and lips. Most certainly she would see a man if she looked at him now, since the night was at its darkest, the veil between the worlds its thinnest. But he was more. And he burned more fiercely, craved more desperately.

Ah, but not for her. Never for her.

Her eyelids fluttered and she gazed at him through passion-glazed eyes. There was an instant of confusion, panic, then the feelings eased as she smiled and mumbled, "Just a dream."

Her heavy gaze drank in his face, burning a path over his shoulders, his chest, down to the prominent erection waging war on his tenuous control.

There she lingered, studying the jutting proof of his desire as if she'd never seen a man before.

A *virgin*, he reminded himself, his fists clenched tight at his sides. *Pure. Untouched. Unschooled.*

But he reacted to her as if she'd been the most talented whore at a Bourbon Street brothel. His breathing quickened. Anticipation sizzled back and forth along his nerve endings. Hunger gnawed deep inside his belly.

Just when he knew he was going to explode if she stared at him an instant longer, her eyes drifted shut and she sighed.

"Ah, pizza," she mumbled. "Double pepperoni."

It was a long time later, after several deep, agonizing breaths, before Val felt calm enough to return to bed. He sank into the mattress just as the clock struck three a.m. It was time to forget the woman, to rest and reenergize.

For all his determination to leave her be, he couldn't resist reaching out one last time. His fingers brushed one ripe nipple, traced the underside of her satiny breast, and came to rest against the furious thump of her heart.

Despite the century and a half of unsatisfied lust shaking his control, a strange tenderness came over him.

A virgin.

He fingered one satiny lock of her flaming hair. "*Sleep well, Rouquin,*" he murmured and reluctantly withdrew his hand.

Then he settled himself beside her for an agonizing night. Much the same as the night before, and every night since Val had drawn his last mortal breath.

The difference was, at least he'd been alone, his bed collecting dust in a storage shed owned by the Historical Society of

New Orleans. Then he'd gone on to spend some time in a re-stored antebellum mansion converted to a museum, still alone and untouched. Then some rich historian had purchased the bed, only to die shortly after. Val had still been alone, his bed collecting more dust in a storage warehouse while a dozen or so children fought for the rights to their papa's estate. Finally, everything had been sold a short time ago and Val had wound up in an antique shop. Still alone and celibate, despite his close brush with ecstasy just days before the sale.

The lawyer's assistant, a sweet blonde with long legs and a nice bottom, had been tagging items at the warehouse when she'd spotted his bed. She'd promptly kicked off her shoes and stretched out. Delighted, Val had incited a few erotic daydreams to put her in the mood. She'd been moaning and panting and so very ready, and then her fiancé had arrived, and he'd been none too happy to find his woman taking her pleasure without him.

Had it not been for the warehouse security guard, Val's treasured bed would have been firewood on the spot—the fiancé had picked up an antique ax and nearly taken off a bedpost. If the jealous man had succeeded, Val would have been pushed to the other side, into a fate much worse than eternal peace. Ready or not.

Not.

In the meantime, he'd unknowingly traded solitude for a soft, tempting, sexy *virgin*.

He wondered if maybe he'd finally given up the ghost and crossed over into hell. Or perhaps this was the final act to push him over the edge, to drive him into the Afterlife. Yes, that was it. He'd spent too long here and the Powers That Be were tired of indulging him.

But Val still had unfinished business, and he didn't care how hellish they made his time here, he wasn't leaving until he'd found some answers.

The virgin chose that moment to turn over, her breathing still raspy from her climax, her body glowing with a fine sheen of perspiration as she rolled near him, into him, and he all but climaxed at the sheer contact.

A lesser man would have conceded. But Val was more than a man, and he wasn't about to budge, not even if he'd had twenty virgins taunting him.

All right, perhaps twenty. But as it stood, he had only one. And one, he swore to himself, he could definitely resist.

He settled himself down and reached for the textbook he'd lifted from her chest earlier. A few descriptive pictures snagged his interest and he smiled. Then frowned.

Obviously his little *vierge* was trying to educate herself.

The smile returned. Perhaps he could help her with her education. Yes, he thought to himself as he reached for her pen and notes. He could, indeed, help her on this subject, and maybe, just maybe she could help him.

As much as Val wanted her in his bed, there was one thing he wanted even more. He wanted the truth.

Chapter Two

"Ronnie! Are you all right?" Several sharp knocks followed the voice.

Ronnie buried her head beneath the pillow. "Just five more minutes," she begged. Five measly minutes.

"*Veronica! Rise and shine or you'll miss the school bus.*"

Ugh. "*I hate school, Momma. My dresses are sooo long and ugly, and my hair is sooo long and blah, and I'm the biggest geek in the entire junior high. Let me skip today. Please?*"

"*Nonsense. Your dresses are respectable and ladylike and your hair is your glory. You're a prime example of a proper young lady, Veronica. You represent this family.*"

"*By looking homely.*"

"*Traditional, dear.*"

Bam! Bam! Bam!

"Coming, Mama," Ronnie grumbled into her pillow. "Traditional, homely, what's the difference?"

She forced one eye open, only to clamp it shut, instantly blinded by the stream of sunlight through the French doors.

Whoa. There were no French doors in her bedroom back home. Just pink frilly curtains and lace-edged blinds and—

She smiled into her pillow. She wasn't at home. She was in her own place, in her own bed, and she wasn't in junior high anymore. There was a God!

And the Devil himself was beating down her door.

Bam! Bam! Bam!

"Ronnie?" The knock turned to a pound, like the Energizer bunny that kept going and going and—"If you're alive and able to move, please open up!"

"I'm coming." She forced herself up onto her elbows.

"Ronnie? I mean it. If you're alive, you'd better get to this door right now. Otherwise, I'll assume the worst."

"Coming!" she yelled, but her voice was little more than a croak. She groped for the soda leftover from last night. Her fingers curled around the can. She took a long swig and waited for the instant rush of caffeine.

Oh no. She'd bought caffeine free. *Ugh.*

"Last chance. I'm going to get the super if you don't open up, and if you're not dead, you're going to wish you were. He hates missing a minute of 'Wake Up, New Orleans.'"

Wait a second. She fought for her wits as the last minute of reality swirled in her fuzzy brain. Danny pounding on her door. Sunlight. *"Wake Up, New Orleans"* . . . *No!*

She blinked at the clock and her heart stopped beating as the time registered. *Seven fifty-five.*

It couldn't be! She had an eight a.m. class, the campus was a fifteen-minute walk—driving was out since it would take thirty minutes to find a blasted parking space—and she needed to dress and wash her face and—

She blinked, fixing her gaze on the slim black hands of her alarm clock. It was seven fifty-six now. She'd wasted an entire minute trying to focus.

"Ronnie!" It was Danny's worried voice again. "I'm going to get Mr. Sams. I'm turning. Here I go—"

"No!" She flung her legs over the side of the bed, her mind instantly alert with the rush of nervous dread through her system. Nervous dread could kick caffeine's butt anytime. "I'm coming!"

"You've got five seconds to open this door. Otherwise I'll know something's wrong. Five, four, . . ."

She shoved her nightshirt down and stood up. Her feet made instant contact with the pair of silky panties she'd been wearing the night before.

"Three . . ."

Cool air filtered under her T-shirt to stroke her bare bottom as last night's dream rushed at her full force.

"Two."

She went rigid, every nerve in her body tingling at the remembrance. Her insides tightened to the rhythm of the ferocious climax she'd had.

Holy Moly. She took a deep breath. Had she really . . . ? Had *he* really . . . ?

"One."

Whoa, girl. There was no *he*. He was a dream, brought on by stress and deprived hormones, and enough junk food to keep a dentist and a heart specialist in business for a long, long time.

Her gaze dropped to the crushed panties and her face turned at least a dozen shades of red. It was one thing to have a fantasy, to watch it unfold, and quite another to actually participate. Unconsciously, unwillingly. She'd undoubtedly pulled her own panties off, touched herself, induced her own body's response. Geez . . .

She had all of four heartbeats to nurse another wave of embarrassment before the door shook and Mr. Sams's grumbling voice reached her ear.

"Dammit, boy. They's talking to the quarterback for the New Orleans Saints this morning, and I'm missing it. This had better be good or I'm crackin' some heads." Metal clanged, deadbolts clicked, and the doorknob trembled.

"No!" she shouted, snatching up her panties and forcing her legs to move. She hit the door a second before it gave way and slid the chain into place. "I—I'll be right there," she murmured against the wood. Calm, cool, rational . . . *Get a grip.*

"Are you all right?" Danny's concerned voice carried from the other side. "I've been knocking for at least ten minutes!"

"I'm fine. I just overslept." The explanation met with a colorful expletive from Mr. Sams and an astonished "You?" from Danny.

"Just give me a few minutes and I'll be right out."

Ronnie spent the next ten minutes moving at the speed of light. She washed her face, combed her hair, yanked on clean clothes, downed a can of soda, and gathered up her book bag, and all without any more freaking out.

As she reached for the textbook on her nightstand, her gaze snagged on the piece of paper tucked inside. Relief washed through her and she sent up a silent wave of thanks to a host of dead saints that she'd had the good sense to write down her paper topic the night before. Otherwise she'd be in deep . . . what Mr. Sams had said.

"Man-o-man, are you sick?" Danny was right beside her the moment she walked out of the apartment. "You better have one heck of an excuse for worrying me like that." He followed her down the hall and out the front door.

"I overslept."

"Come again?"

"You heard me." She stifled a yawn and popped a Hershey's Kiss into her mouth, determined to get her caffeine rush one way or another. "I overslept. I didn't get to bed until midnight."

"I didn't fall into the sack 'til two a.m. and here I am, fresh as a daisy. 'Course, I have been taking this new vitamin supplement, Excite and Energize."

"Two a.m.?" She hefted her book bag over one shoulder and raised an eyebrow at him. "Big date?"

His expression went from worried to disappointed as he followed her down the front steps of the restored eighteenth-century townhouse now home to half a dozen small apartments including hers, and out into the early morning sunshine. "Wanda had a calculus test today."

With black hair and dark brown eyes, Danny Boudreaux looked like David Copperfield, with wire-rim spectacles and a bright future as a mechanical engineer. He was dark, intense, and very, very smart.

If only one Wanda Deluca, cheerleader/nutrition major/five feet eight inches of *hot* female, saw half the things in Danny that Ronnie did, he'd be in heaven. As it was, he was merely Wanda's tutor. A living hell, as far as he was concerned.

"Wanda was up studying until two a.m.? And I thought textbooks gave her hives." Ronnie turned on to the sidewalk and started for the corner.

"Actually, we didn't get started until midnight. She can't hit the books until after cheerleading practice. Then she had to shower and eat, do her yoga, and watch Letterman. I went over to her place after that."

A pang of sympathy shot through Ronnie and she wished a head full of split ends on Wanda's shiny blonde mane. "She made you wait up until she went through her nightly ritual *and* watched Letterman?"

"It's a nightly group thing she does with her friends, but it wasn't really her fault. I sort of offered to wait."

"She takes advantage of you, and you let her."

Danny shrugged, "She needs me."

"She needs a swift kick in her panties. If she wants to study, then, by all means, help her. But stop bending to her schedule. You set the time and the place. You're the one doing her a favor." She adjusted the book bag on her shoulder and ignored the urge to check her watch. She was already late. No sense worrying over Guidry's reaction and spoiling her walk to campus.

Even as she told herself that, she picked up her pace. "Why don't you just ask her out?"

"*Wanda*? As if she'd go."

"You'll never know until you try."

"I know this much. I'm not her type. She goes for all brawn and no brain."

"You've got brawn," Ronnie said when they hit a crosswalk and stopped. As they stood waiting for the light to change, she eyed him. "Okay, so you're more brain, but you're not bad in the bod department. You're a little slim, but you're really well built, and you take care of what you've got with all those vitamins you're always taking. Wanda could do a lot worse."

"Too bad she hasn't realized that yet."

"She will, especially if you give her a little encouragement. Let her know you're interested."

"Look who's giving love advice. When's the last time you had a date?"

She fought back a wave of heat at the memory of last night. That had been anything but a date. Just a dream. A harmless dream.

A *wet dream*, a deep, sultry, *man's* voice in her head corrected.

Ronnie wiped at the bead of sweat that slid down her temple, grateful when the walk sign flashed on. She started across the intersection. Her gaze snagged on a young man heading toward them. He was as big and muscular as a football player. A black T-shirt emblazoned with a pink silhouette of Elvis and the words *Hunk-a-hunk-a-burnin'-love* in matching script stretched across his massive chest.

Ronnie was not accustomed to attracting anyone's attention. With her baggy clothes and blah appearance, most men glanced past her. Mr. Hunk-a-hunk looked at her face.

". . . Ronnie?"

"Uh, yeah?"

"The date," he prodded. "When's the last time you had one?"

Ronnie turned her attention back to her friend. "Three years ago, I think, but I'm not the one complaining."

"Three *years*," he said with a shake of his head. "And I thought I was hard up."

"I'm not hard up, thank you very much." Not after last night.

"Face reality, Ron. I could give you pickup lessons, and my sex life is just this side of nonexistent."

She sighed and stopped for another crosswalk. "I don't have the time or the energy for love."

"I'm not talking love. I'm talking sex. A little one-on-one tackle."

"With my schedule, it's hard enough to find time to sleep." The light changed and she darted across the intersection.

Danny's long legs ate up the distance behind her. "It only takes fifteen minutes."

She shot him a sideways glance. *Fifteen minutes?* Her dream had lasted longer than that.

"Okay, so maybe twenty, twenty-five, depending."

"On what?" she asked.

He shot her a sideways grin. "You tell me. You're the one taking Guidry's class."

She frowned. "You know I only took his class because I needed another elective to graduate, and it was the only one offered this early in the morning."

"That's what they all say."

"I'm serious, Danny. Besides, the last thing Guidry teaches is 'a little one-on-one tackle.'"

"Sure. So tell me," he went on, "what cataclysmic event caused the always punctual Ronnie Parrish to sleep late. Your alarm clock explode?"

A smile played at her lips. "I slept in my new bed for the first time since the store delivered it."

His eyebrows raised expectantly. "That comfortable, huh?"

She cleared her suddenly dry throat. "Comfortable isn't exactly the word I would use." *Earth-shattering. Mind-boggling. Spectacular.* "But I guess you could say that."

"Wow," he said, a dreamy look on his face. "There must be nothing like a new mattress. I've been sleeping on the same old lumpy one I've had since I was five years old."

Mattresses were the last thing on Ronnie's mind. Her scalp tingled as she felt the gentle tug of fingers on her hair. And in her mind, she heard the sultry voice, the deep baritone rumbling through her head as it had followed her into oblivion.

"*Sleep well, Rouquin. Sleep well.*"

Rouquin. She'd heard the term so many times. A girl didn't grow up with bright red hair in southern Louisiana and not get called Red a time or two. But no one had ever said the name quite the way her dream man had. Maybe it was the deep tone of his voice, or the way he growled the R just enough to send a shiver through her that rocked her control as much as his touch did.

Mmm . . . His touch.

Her breasts suddenly throbbed, her thighs tingled, and a yearning for something she couldn't name filled her.

She took a deep breath, ordered her body to behave itself, and shot another glance at her watch. Waving goodbye to Danny, she launched into a full-blown run across campus.

Guidry was just going to the chalkboard when Ronnie slinked into his class a good thirty minutes late. Thankfully, his back was turned and he was preoccupied with a very detailed drawing of the female ovaries.

"Kind of you to join us, Miss Parrish."

Ronnie stalled halfway into her seat. Her book bag hit the floor with a solid *thunk* that seemed to echo like a cannon blast.

"Uh, yes, sir."

He speared her with a beady, black glare, pulled a pen from his coat pocket, and reached for his grade book. The scratch of pen on paper grated across Ronnie's nerves and she winced. A demerit. She knew it even though she couldn't see the big red check mark by her name.

"How many times do I have to stress that this class, though an elective for the majority of you, is just as important as any other science course. I would wager that none of you would dare be late to Laramie's quantum physics or Bechnell's mechanical engineering." He placed the pen back in the pocket of his immaculate white lab coat. "I expect each one of you to treat this course with the same respect and appreciation that you give your other classes. Understood?" Four dozen heads nodded in unison and Ronnie sank into her seat.

A group reprimand wasn't so bad—

"And as for you, Miss Parrish . . ."

Ronnie braced herself. So much for the worst being over.

"Since you hold this class in such little esteem that you can't find your way out of bed in time to join us at eight sharp, then I assume it's because you are so knowledgeable in our area of study. In that case, I ask your expert direction in labeling the specifics of today's subject." He gestured toward the model sitting on the podium and motioned her forward. "Front and center, Miss Parrish, or I'll add another demerit to your already growing résumé."

Eight years of college and she'd never been late to a class. Where was the justice in the world? Surely she'd gained a few brownie points. She helped old people cross the street. She loved animals and cried during long-distance commercials. She was a good person. Fair. Considerate.

"We're waiting, Miss Parrish."

She took a deep breath, pushing aside her self-pity, and walked to the front of the classroom. Okay, so Guidry was overreacting a little. But she had come late to his class, and so he had a right. She would simply do what he asked, as payback for disrupting him, and then she could get on with her day.

No problem.

Every eye riveted on her as she picked up the plastic model, mentally reciting the specifics. This was easy. She knew the required anatomy better than the forty-something ice cream flavors in the campus sweets shop. So Guidry thought she took his class for granted? Well, she would show him she didn't take any course for granted. She studied and prepared her buns off for each of them—

The thought stalled as she glanced down at the full-scale likeness of a man's penis, and every anatomical fact she new flew south for the winter.

She didn't see well-shaped, industrial-designed plastic. She saw strong, throbbing flesh jutting from a thatch of sand-colored hair as a vision from last night blazed in her mind.

"Don't be shy." Guidry's voice pushed past the sudden ringing in her ears. He stood off to the side of the room, clipboard in hand, pen poised ready to mark a dozen demerits at the slightest mistake. "Please project your answers so we can all benefit from your expertise."

"I . . ." She swallowed, her fingers trailing down the cold plastic that felt more like warm, pulsing flesh with each stroke.

What was happening to her? She'd stared at models before and never felt any reaction.

Not now, she vowed. *Just get a grip.*

"Um, the penis," she tried to swallow the apple-sized lump in her throat, "consists of two parallel cylindrical bodies. They are the, uh, *corpora cavernosa* and the . . ." The answer stalled on the tip of her tongue as her fingers swept down the model in a directive motion that she felt along the length of her spine.

Impossible!

Even as her mind fought against the sensation, her body flushed hot, then cold. Her knees started to tremble and her nipples tightened.

"We're waiting, Miss Parrish."

Concentrate. She took a deep, calming breath.

A bad move. Very bad.

She didn't smell the usual chalk and disinfectant. Instead, her senses reeled under the intoxicating mingling of leather and aroused male, tinged with apples and a faint crispness. The same scent she'd whiffed the night before.

As if!

She was losing it. She was finally cracking up under all the pressure of school and making ends meet. It was bound to happen. No one, even someone as determined as she, could give one hundred percent all the time and not risk their mental health.

Now she was having a full-blown breakdown. Right here, right now, in front of a classroom of her peers and the critical Professor Mark Guidry.

No. She wouldn't go down without a fight. She'd worked too long, too hard . . .

Long and *hard* weren't exactly the adjectives she should be thinking of right now, she decided, her gaze going to the object in her hands.

Plastic, she told herself. It wasn't a real man's penis. Certainly not *his* penis . . .

Concentrate. She took another deep breath and cleared her throat.

"The parallel body is the *corpus spongiosum*. The urethra passes here." She pointed to a specific area, but she didn't see the anatomically correct model of manhood. No, in her mind she was back in her bed, staring at the six feet plus of hunky naked male standing not two feet away.

Her gaze traveled from his jutting strength, upward over a funnel of sandy hair, then a rippled belly, to a broad chest. Her attention lingered on one dark male nipple peeking trough the forest of silky hair. She drank in the sight of strong shoulders, a tanned throat, her study halting when she reached the most sensual pair of lips she'd ever seen.

Lips that had closed greedily over her own nipple.

She swatted away a trickle of sweat.

"And the root area here," she said with a shaky voice, continuing her description, "is attached to the pubic bone by the, um . . . that would be the . . . the *crura*, I think. . . ."

The words died, her left brain completely giving up as her mind's eye riveted on a pair of deep Caribbean eyes. They glittered a vivid aqua, like the sea on a hot summer day. Mesmerizing. Inviting. Promising relief from the heat burning her up from the inside out.

Sweat beaded on her upper lip and she gasped for a breath of air. It was so hot in the lecture hall. Stifling. She couldn't breathe, much less remember whatever it was she was supposed to be doing.

Labeling. That was it. Wasn't it?

"This," she trailed her finger along the head of the plastic model, and felt the touch on the insides of her own thighs. *His* touch, his fingertips sweeping upward, toward the part of her that ached and burned and . . . "This is the . . ." The correct scientific name dissolved on her tongue and she did the unthinkable in Guidry's class. She blushed, from the tips of her toes to the end of each and every hair on her head.

"I know what it is." She searched for the right answer, her grip tightening. "It's the—I mean, well, I think it's the—"

"Enough!" The loud command startled her from her erotic memories of last night and yanked her back to the present. She jumped. The model slipped from her hand and crashed to the table. Pieces scattered and sailed over the edge.

"Unbelievable!" Professor Guidry rushed toward her, scooping up parts of the model while gesturing wildly for her to return to her seat. "You have managed to turn a scientific lesson into a peep show!"

He blew out a disgusted breath and began fitting pieces back together as if it were his own penis Ronnie had just demolished.

"I realize not everyone is comfortable with the human body, but it is perfectly natural for us to examine it." He bit out the words to a host of snickers and giggles. "To study it just as we would any other scientific phenomenon." He ducked behind the podium to retrieve the head, which had rolled beneath a nearby projector.

Ronnie took the opportunity to hightail it back to her desk while he tried to fish the piece out from under the metal projector cart.

"That was priceless," the girl next to Ronnie declared as she slid into her seat. "I've never seen Iron Ball lose his cool."

Ronnie gave a halfhearted smile. Neither had she. Iron Ball Guidry was the poster boy for uptight scientific professionals, from his pristine white lab coat to his creased slacks and spit-polished loafers with the little tassles.

"What do you suppose sex is like with Iron Ball Guidry?" the woman to her left whispered to a friend directly in front of her.

"Are you kidding?" the second woman asked over her shoulder. "Like going to the gynecologist, only not half as exciting. 'Please lie down on the table, miss.'" The girl did her best Guidry imitation. "'Now spread your legs. A little wider, please, I don't have bifocals, you know. Okay, now tilt your pelvis. Yes, just like that. Now I'm going to insert my Superman into your Wonder Woman and you're going to feel the first level of stimulation. This is called the *preorgasmic phase.*'"

Ronnie felt the giggle rise to her lips, then her gaze hooked on Professor Guidry, who was still crawling on the floor, gathering plastic parts, and the sound died in her throat. He looked so shaken at her having shattered the model.

He deserved it. He'd deliberately tried to embarrass her, and all because she'd been unintentionally late to his class.

Even so, the laughter wouldn't come. Not when she'd just earned herself a demerit the size of Texas. Could he actually fail her for breaking his precious penis?

Luckily the class ended, and Ronnie didn't have time to worry over the answer. She bolted from her seat and joined the crowd heading for the doorway.

"Just a minute," came the sharp voice from behind the podium. Guidry got to his feet, brushing at invisible dust bunnies and smoothing his lab coat. "Paper topics, people. On my desk before you leave or I'll assume you don't plan on writing a term paper and will grade you appropriately."

"For the record, Miss Parrish," Guidry said when she reached the podium and handed him her neatly folded paper, "I will not tolerate tardiness in this course. I am well aware of the rumors around campus. Everyone feels that human sexuality is something inborn. An easy A. Well, this course is as scientific, as educational as any other course at this university, and I'll have my students treat it as such. I have no misgivings about failing someone, especially after the sort of juvenile behavior I witnessed today."

"I'm sorry, sir. I really am."

He wasn't the least moved by the apology. "Furthermore, I expect full participation and effort from every student. I hope you've put a lot of thought into your term paper topic. The paper will count for sixty percent of the overall course grade, and after your recent performance, you will need every percentage point to pass this course."

"I really am sorry, Professor. I would never make light of your course. I didn't mean to be late. You see, I work two jobs and—"

"I worked two jobs during college and graduate school, Miss Parrish, as do a lot of students, and we all live to tell about it, I assure you. I suggest you get your priorities straight. Exhaustion is not an acceptable excuse."

"Maybe not, but it's the truth."

"Nor is there an acceptable excuse for your childish babbling and blushing today."

"I didn't mean to babble or blush. It's just that . . ."

"Yes?"

"Well, I . . ." She couldn't say it. She couldn't tell a stranger, even if he did happen to be the resident expert on human sexuality, about her dream.

Her classmates' speculations on the professor's love life echoed through her head. As stuffy and uptight as Guidry was, he probably didn't even have dreams.

Wet dreams, came the deep, sultry voice in her head.

Those either. She could kiss goodbye any chance of the professor understanding how she felt.

Felt? She shouldn't be feeling anything. It had just been a dream, for heaven's sake! A few hours of harmless fun quickly forgotten once she opened her eyes. A few fantasies were fine, as long as she kept them in proper perspective and out of her real life.

On that note, she gathered up her book bag and marched to her next class. She managed to shove the images of last night away for safekeeping while she went through the motions of a typical, busy day. She sat through lectures, studied, reported for receptionist duty at Landry & Landry, then spent eight hours shelving books at the library.

It was when she was on her way home that her dream man pushed his way back into her mind, haunting her on the short walk, a sort of foreplay for the night ahead. When Ronnie reached her apartment, she wasted little time in getting ready for bed. She was tired, in desperate need of sleep, but most of all, she was ready for a little more harmless fun. With a shiver of anticipation, she crawled beneath the sheets, closed her eyes, and waited for the enticing dream.

One that never came.

Chapter Three

This must be her.

He stared through the windshield of his '59 T-Bird bright and early Saturday morning and watched the same woman he'd nearly bumped into yesterday descend the steps of the townhouse. She matched the description the guy at the antique store had given him. Not to mention this was the right address.

It was her.

Now all he had to do was sit back and watch, learn her routine. Then he could make his move.

His hands flexed around the steering wheel. He'd never been a patient man, which could have been part of the "problem," his doctor had told him. Closing his eyes, he concentrated on the deep breathing exercises to help him relax. Relaxation was the key. No stress. No pressure.

His eyes opened. Once he took care of things here, he would certainly feel less pressure and he could get on with fixing the "problem," before it was too late. No way was he going to sit by and lose the one thing in the world that mattered to him the most. His woman.

He wasn't about to let anything come between them, and that meant he had to eliminate the competition, so to speak. What was a man if he couldn't fight for what was his? If he couldn't show his woman that he and only he could keep her satisfied?

Eliminate. That was the ultimate goal.

But first he had to watch.

This Saturday played out like any other. Ronnie rolled out of bed at seven a.m. and hurried to the campus library to report for duty. She checked out books, helped several students and a few irate professors find specific titles, and shelved cartload after cartload of returned books.

What made today different, however, was that Ronnie, rather than counting the hours until quitting time, welcomed the work. She needed all the distractions she could get to keep her mind off the truth.

No dream.

She'd spent an endless Friday night tossing and turning, *waiting,* but nothing had happened. When she'd closed her eyes, she hadn't met up with her dream man. Instead, she'd alternated between visions of Guidry marking a big fat F on her term paper and ripping the diploma from her hands, and her own funeral soon afterward. The tombstone appropriately read:

HERE LIES VERONICA PARRISH
SO VIRGINAL, PROPER AND SWEET.
SHE FAILED HUMAN SEXUALITY,
AND NOW SHE'S SIX FEET DEEP!

Being busy at the library helped. Unfortunately, it didn't occupy her thoughts completely. Disappointment followed her around all day, dogging her like a hungry puppy.

Was she so repulsive she couldn't get a man even in her own dreams?

She shook her head. Now where had that thought come from? She wasn't repulsive. She was just . . . busy. Focused. Too fixated on her career to worry about fussing over makeup and clothes to help attract a man. She didn't want to attract a man, to find herself chucking hard work and ambition for marriage and family. She'd come too far, sacrificed too much to land right back where she'd started and hear her father say, "If you had only listened to me."

She'd made her choice, and she intended to see it through.

Still, she couldn't help but glance at her reflection in an abstract painting as she pushed a load of books past the Arts section. She looked so . . . *blah*. With her hair pulled back, her face void of color, she was pale, washed out—

Her gaze shifted to the corner of the painting and she caught the reflection of Mr. Hunk-a-hunk-a-burnin'-love she'd seen at the crosswalk the day before. He'd changed his T-shirt and now the words *Jailhouse Rock* glittered in bright green neon— the guy definitely had a thing for Elvis.

Mr. Jailhouse sat at one of the library tables, a book in his hand, his attention fixed on her. She turned around, but by then he'd shifted and looked away, leaving her to wonder if she'd just imagined his attention.

Probably.

As homely as she looked—all those traditional years back in Covenant had taught her great camouflage techniques when it came to clothes and make-up—nobody in his right mind would pay her any attention, especially a semicute jock.

By the time Ronnie shelved the last book on her cart, she'd convinced herself she needed a little pampering. Not to catch a man, mind you. Just to boost her own ego and relax a little. Why, she'd been so worked up about Guidry and her grade that she'd been too uptight to even fall asleep, much less dream.

No more.

Tonight she would push everything from her mind—Guidry, graduation, work, the twins, whom she'd promised to watch tomorrow morning—*everything*. She refused to worry. It was Saturday night, time to kick back and let loose, and that's exactly what Ronnie intended to do.

The minute she walked into her apartment, she peeled off her jeans and T-shirt and retrieved the bottle of champagne

Danny had given her as a house-warming gift last year when she'd moved from the dorm into the efficiency. It wasn't expensive stuff, but a year in her fruit bin had to have helped. Age was the key to good liquor, wasn't it?

She grabbed a couple of candles, situated them around the tub, and lit the wicks. Soft light cast flickering shadows across the surface of the steaming water. Ronnie hit the lights, slipped out of her underwear, and slid into the water. Champagne, candles—by the time she finished her bath, she would feel clean and pretty and relaxed enough for a little sleep and a romantic interlude.

With a dream man.

A no-strings-attached figment of her imagination.

All the better.

She reached for the champagne bottle, took a huge swallow, and sputtered. The bitter liquid burned its way down her throat and she grimaced. Maybe she'd settle for just the bath and candles to do the stress-relieving trick.

Corking the bottle, she placed it on the floor by the tub, settled back down into the warm water, and closed her eyes.

Mmmmm, she could get used to this.

Val would *never* get used to this. To her and her seductive antics. Last night she'd spent eight long, endless hours rolling this way and that, lifting her full, luscious breasts just so, sighing a tad too often and too deeply, easing her leg ever so casually over to his side of the bed.

He refused to accept that she didn't know he was there. She knew. Deep down, her subconscious knew, no matter that her conscious mind refused to acknowledge him. She sensed him, his presence, his incredible hunger, and she was responding to him.

Merde! Of all the rotten luck.

Here he was trying to preserve her innocence, and his own peace of mind, all the while she was driving him insane, trying to lure him into her bed—*his* bed—between her innocent thighs. . . .

No! Not now. Not ever again. He had another, more important matter to focus on, the question that had haunted him for a century and a half. He didn't need a virgin distracting him, robbing him of his peace, before he'd had the chance to relish a sweet, restful moment.

No matter how beautiful she was. How soft her hair. How silky her skin. How tasty her wine-colored nipples that peeked past the surface of the bathwater . . .

He swallowed and tried to force his gaze away from the picture she made, lounging so serenely in the claw-footed tub. He closed his eyes, but she was still there, the memory of her so warm and eager pushing and pulling at his control.

She sighed and the sound whispered through his head, drawing his undivided attention. A smile tilted her full lips as she reached for the bar of soap and began lathering herself. First her arms, then her legs, then one firm, round breast—

Enough! He could take no more. He was on his feet, crossing the distance to her before he could stop himself.

Val wondered as he closed the last few feet between them, the smell of rose-scented soap and ripe female stirring his senses, if maybe he wasn't about to make the same mistake twice.

Ronnie heard the ripple of water a second before she felt the pressure on her fingers. Her grip on the soap loosened and the slippery bar flew out of her hands. Her heart slammed into her throat and her eyes snapped open, fully expecting to see a rapist leering at her. A murderer ready to chop off her head—

Nothing. Her gaze jerked around the empty bathroom, to the medicine cabinet where the bar of soap had left a slimy white trail down the glass before clattering into the sink.

The bathroom was empty. That meant . . .

Her gaze pushed into the darkened bedroom and she damned

herself for her silly candlelight plan. She should have left every light blazing.

She stood and, with trembling fingers, reached for a fluffy white towel. Wrapping the cotton tight around her, she tucked it securely under one arm and stepped out of the tub. Picking up a candle and a nearby can of hairspray—her Mace was in her purse on the kitchen counter—she tiptoed out into the bedroom.

The few feet to the light switch were the longest of Ronnie's life. She fully expected to be conked on the head, stabbed, shot—a dozen scenarios raced through her head, none of them pretty, since they all ended with her lying naked and dead on the floor.

As frightened as she was, she couldn't help but think about how mortified her mother would be that her baby girl had been found not only dead but *naked*, viewed in all her womanly glory by every officer who happened on the scene. Then there were the paramedics and, of course, Mr. Sams, her nosiest neighbor and the super, who would open up her door the moment the stench alerted him that something wasn't right.

It was bad enough to be dead, but naked, too? With her too large breasts, overly rounded hips, not-so-flat tummy? She tugged the towel more securely around her. No way were they ripping this towel from her hands. She would go to her grave clutching white cotton.

She took a deep, calming breath and forced her feet the last few inches to the light switch. She reached out, and a seventy-five-watt bulb blazed overhead, chasing away the shadows and leaving no part of the efficiency hidden.

Her gaze streaked through the room, pausing at the space between the refrigerator and stove, just large enough for a medium-sized man. Nothing. Her attention shot to the door, still double-bolted from the inside. Then to the French doors. Both locked, the glass intact. The apartment was completely empty.

Hopefully.

Her gaze lingered on the bed. With its massive frame, it was large enough to conceal a pretty big intruder. But surely she would have seen someone crawl beneath it? Heard the slide of clothing against the hardwood floor? Felt the strange awareness that she wasn't alone?

She glanced down at the goose bumps chasing up and down her arms. Scared as she was, she wasn't taking any chances—she had to check everywhere.

Quietly, she retrieved a knife from the utensil drawer. With the knife in one hand and the hairspray still clutched in the other—she could always do his hair after she filleted him—she approached the bed.

A long, tense moment later, Ronnie sat on the edge of the mattress and gave a shaky, relieved smile. Her imagination. She hadn't actually felt anyone tug at the soap; she'd tossed it. She'd been so relaxed, maybe halfway asleep, and something, maybe the chug of the refrigerator or the air conditioner cycling on, had jarred her. She'd jumped and the soap had taken a hike toward the mirror.

That had to be it, because her apartment was completely empty. Unless she had a ghost living with her . . .

She laughed. A ghost who hated soap. It made perfect sense, except for the all-important fact that Ronnie didn't believe in ghosts, or, bogeymen, or things that went bump in the night. She'd never been afraid of the dark. Never spotted a UFO or any little green men, although she did enjoy watching *The X-Files* now and then.

Spiders did give her the chills, though, and snakes made her queasy, but otherwise she considered herself a pretty brave soul. A well-adjusted person. Normal. Sane.

Drunk, she thought as her gaze snagged on the bottle of champagne still sitting by the tub. That was it. She was sloshed and she'd imagined the strange pull on the bar of soap.

From one drink?

Well, she'd never been much of a drinker. A few sips of forbidden beer at one of Jenny's slumber parties. Three or four of her aunt Mabel's rum balls at the annual church bazaar.

Drunk? More like tipsy.

Maybe.

Probably.

Satisfied that she'd found the real reason for the flying soap, she summoned her courage and headed back to the bathroom. Water gurgled down the drain as the tub emptied and Ronnie extinguished the candles. Discarding the towel, she pulled on a pair of panties and a nightgown, flicked off the lights, and slid between the sheets.

She closed her eyes, mentally goading herself to relax, but her heart still pumped furiously from her temporary scare. Even fifteen minutes later, she was still too worked up to fall asleep. She gave up the effort and flicked on the television. Two newscasts and a full hour of a psychic hotline infomercial later, she finally relaxed enough to doze off.

So much for wild and wicked dreams, she thought as she drifted into a peaceful slumber filled with visions of her aunt Mabel scarfing down rum balls. Might as well make the best of it, she figured, sidling up to her aunt and helping herself to one of the confections.

As she chewed, savoring the flavor and salving her ego with the fact that food, especially dessert, was the equivalent of sex for many women, she could have sworn she heard a deep, male chuckle and the all-too-familiar hypnotic voice murmer, "*Sleep well*, Rouquin."

Why the heck did he have to keep saying that?

"But I want Cocoa Pebbles," Randy, the more vocal of her neighbor Suzanne's twins, declared the next morning. "They're my favorite."

"Last week Fruity Pebbles were your favorite," Ronnie told him. "That's why Aunt Ronnie rushed out and bought you some. See?" She smiled and held up the box.

Randy threw his spoon into the untouched bowl of cereal. Milk and cereal splattered and he sulked.

"Now, now, Randy. That's not nice. Be a good boy and eat your cereal."

"I want Cocoa Pebbles."

"Me, too," declared Brandy. Following her brother's lead, she slammed her spoon into her bowl of cereal. Milk flew, cereal went *splat*, and Ronnie reached for the Tylenol.

"But last week—" Ronnie started, only to snap her mouth shut when the kids pounded their chubby fists on her kitchen table and screamed for Cocoa Pebbles.

She spent the next hour trying to convince them the chocolate milk she poured over the Fruity Pebbles technically made them Cocoa Pebbles.

Sort of.

"I hope they weren't any trouble," Suzanne said when she arrived a few hours later to find Ronnie clearing dishes and wiping up puddles of milk. Randy and Brandy stood in front of the television waving their hands in the air in a perfect imitation of the huge purple dinosaur on the screen, an activity that had only recently consumed them.

"Come on, angels," Suzanne said. "Give Ronnie a kiss and let's go."

The angels, complete with sticky hands and a few cereal crispies in their hair, rushed at Ronnie. Four chubby arms wrapped around her neck and, despite the hectic morning, Ronnie smiled.

And then she frowned.

She was doing this for the money, she told herself for the umpteenth time as she pocketed the five bucks Suzanne handed her. Forget hugs and adoring smiles. She was interested in cold, hard *dinero*.

Yeah, right. A whole five bucks. You're really raking it in.

Bite the bullet, old girl, and admit the truth.

Okay, five bucks wasn't much, but it was all Suzanne—a single mother with two growing kids—could afford. And though Ronnie's father might call Suzanne a poor example of motherhood and a ripple in the earthquake currently cracking the foundation of the traditional American family, Ronnie couldn't help but feel for the woman. Root for her. Suzanne loved her kids, and that's what made a good parent.

She closed the door and turned back to the chaos that had once been her apartment. While she might root for her neighbor, she couldn't help but be extremely grateful that the twins were Suzanne's little bundles of joy and not her own. There was definitely something to be said for birth control.

Not that Ronnie didn't like kids. She loved them, but she wanted a career first. Then later, much later, she vowed as she crawled under the table and scooped up handfuls of soggy cereal, once her career was established, she could focus on finding a husband. One better than good, old-fashioned, take-care-of-the-little-woman Raymond she'd nearly married eight years ago. A guy who did his share of the cooking and cleaning and child-rearing, and who wouldn't feel threatened by her job. Nontraditional all the way.

Hey, lady, you want fries with that load of bull?

How was she ever going to attract Mr. Terrific if she couldn't even get a guy to smile at her? While she might not want to snag a man now, she needed to at least know how.

Hence the value of her dreams.

Experience was the best teacher, and Ronnie intended to gain a little experience.

A half hour later, she trekked across campus to the library and spent much of the next eight hours in the P section shelving leftovers from a freshman English assignment on Edgar Allen Poe, and planning her strategy.

She'd been nervous last night, scared after the soap incident, and so her dream man had stayed away. Maybe in order to duplicate the dream, she needed to duplicate the circumstances leading up to the dream.

Her plan decided, she stopped on the way home from the library, picked up a double pepperoni with extra cheese, a six-pack of diet soda, and a pint of Decadent Fudge Dream for good measure.

Instead of inspiring dreams, however, her feast resulted in an endless night of tossing and turning, heartburn, and a major caffeine headache.

"What's wrong with you?" Danny asked her bright and early Monday morning as they headed for campus. She'd already snapped at him for knocking too loud and cried when she'd dropped her key at a nearby intersection. "I know it's Monday and you're tired after working the entire weekend, but today . . . you're cranky. High-strung. Hey, this isn't one of those female things, is it?"

She glared at him.

"Then what's bothering you? Tell Uncle Danny."

She shrugged. "That thing with Guidry." Liar. But how could she blurt out, even to her best friend, that her dream man had stood her up not once, but three times now.

"Don't worry about Guidry. He blows a lot of smoke, but he's harmless." Danny leveled a stare at her when they reached the crosswalk. "You're a terrible liar. There's something else bothering you besides an uptight professor."

"Stress." She sighed. "Just a lot of stress."

"You thrive on stress. You live for it. The more pressure, the harder you work."

"This is a different kind of stress."

"Different?" He looked puzzled for about an eighth of a second. Then a grin spread from ear to ear. "*That* kind of stress. Well, it's no wonder. Three years is a long time. That is what you said, right? Three years since you . . . well, you know."

"Three years since my last date, and it wasn't really a date. Just a study session. We collaborated on a paper."

"So how long has it been since . . . you know?" She didn't answer and he elbowed her. "Come on."

"Twenty-six years," she finally blurted after a lengthy silence.

"But you're twenty-six . . ." His words died away and his eyes widened. "You mean you've never—"

"Don't say it." She held up a hand. "It's bad enough, but if you say it my love life is bound to go from bad to worse."

"How much worse could it get?"

"Look who's talking, Mr. Wanda-doesn't-know-I'm-alive Boudreaux."

"At least I'm trying, and as pure as I may look, I'm not exactly a virgin."

"What does 'not exactly' mean?"

"It means that I've done the nasty before." He shrugged. "Once anyway."

"The nasty?"

"You know—the wild thing, the booty bump, the body smack, the—"

"Now I understand why it was only once."

"So I'm not the smoothest guy. I'm trying, which is more than I can say for you. Geez, I knew you didn't play the field, but I never thought you were a—" At her pointed look, he clamped his mouth shut on the word. "I mean, you're a great girl. Smart. And you've got—"

"Don't say great personality. Please."

"Well, you do."

"Thanks a lot."

"There's nothing wrong with a good personality."

"That's great personality, and there is if that personality isn't stuffed into Cindy Crawford's body."

"Cindy Crawford can't hold a candle to you. You're about to

graduate with a 4.0 GPA. You've got a great future in accounting, and you're cute."

"Cute, as in, if you lost about fifteen pounds you'd be pretty."

"You're not fat."

"But I'm not skinny."

He threw up his hands. "I give up. Look," he said, turning to her. "There's no reason you can't meet a really great guy. You just have to get out and look."

"For your information, I don't want to meet a really great guy right now. I'd just like to know how, so that when I do decide it's time, I'm armed and ready."

"What's wrong with meeting someone now?"

"I'm too busy. I'm graduating in two months."

"You hope you're graduating in two months."

"Very funny. I am graduating. Guidry can't fail me when I ace his term paper, and I will. I've got the best topic in the class, and I've already done a ton of research. I'll get my diploma, then it's full-time at some prestigious accounting firm, maybe even Burns & Anderson in New Orleans, and hello to the rest of my life. I'll take the CPA exam next year, then start my own firm."

"At that pace, you'll wind up being a thirty-four-year-old virgin instead of a twenty-six-year-old one."

"Thanks a lot."

"You need to go for the gusto while you're young. Get a little experience. You don't have to marry the guy, or even like him. Just play the field."

"I can't exactly play the field if I don't know the rules. How to walk and talk and act . . ."

"To attract a guy, all you have to do is breathe." He eyed her oversized T-shirt. "And maybe wear something a little more clingy. A bodysuit or something."

"How about I parade around in a wet T-shirt?"

"That would do it."

She shook her head. "Women aren't just a pair of boobs, you know. We've got brains, too."

"Yeah, but it's not your brains we fantasize about." When she glared, he added, "I know there's more to a woman than her bra size. If I were picking a study partner, I'd rather know her IQ, but if I'm looking for a little mindless fun, it's only natural I'd be influenced by a pair of double D's." When she punched his arm, he shrugged. "I'm just telling it like it is. Go on and ignore me if you're happy with a life of celibacy. But from the rigid set to your shoulders and the way you're PMSing all over the place, I don't think you are."

"First off, you wouldn't know PMS if it jumped up and bit you, mister. And second, I *am* content." *Or I used to be*, she added silently.

But then she'd never known what she'd been missing out on until her dream man had paid a little visit and given Ronnie Parrish her very first orgasm.

And that was the trouble. Now that her body had had a little taste of heaven, it wanted more. It wanted *him*.

Chapter Four

"I was very pleased with the term paper topics and have made suggestions on each proposal. Please keep my advice in mind and get to work. Projects will be due in eight weeks, on the last day of class." Guidry slapped a stack of papers on the corner of his desk. "Please pick up your topic on the way out—and good luck."

The class had thinned out by the time Ronnie reached Guidry's desk. She grabbed the papers and located her name in the top corner. Pulling her paper free, she stared down at the words and her heart literally stopped beating.

"This—this isn't my topic," she said, shock beating at her senses as she reread the words.

"Come again?" Professor Guidry pulled off his glasses and wiped at the lenses.

"I said this isn't my topic."

"That is your name in the corner?"

"Well, yes."

"And your handwriting?"

"Yes, but this isn't the topic I wrote down. I planned to write about society's stereotype of boys and girls and its influence on social development." She had firsthand experience with that one.

"Quite a good topic. My personal field of interest is in sociology and its effect on sexual development."

"I know. That's how I came up with the topic. I've even done a notebook full of research already. But this . . ." She stared down at the paper. "I can't do this."

"I've already approved it."

Panic twisted at her gut and forced the air from her lungs. "But it's not mine."

He shoved the glasses back on and glared at her. "Your little joke has backfired, Miss Parrish. You thought to make light of this class on Friday, and insult my intelligence by turning in that paper topic. But I'm calling your bluff. That's the topic you turned in, the topic I approved, and that's what you will write about. Unless you prefer I give you your F now." He reached for his grade book.

"An F?" Her mouth dropped open. "But—but I have to pass this class. I need the credit to graduate."

He snapped the book shut and shoved it into his briefcase. "Then I suggest you get to work."

"But . . ." She stared at the sheet of paper and tried to swallow past her heart, which had jammed into her throat.

Fifty Steps to Ultimate Sexual Fulfillment.

The words were scribbled in her handwriting, with her name on the header. But they weren't her words. She didn't know one step on the way to sexual fulfillment, much less fifty.

Okay, so maybe one, she amended, the dream rushing full-force through her brain. But one dream, even one as good as the one she'd had, wasn't enough to write a twenty-page-minimum term paper, complete with a bibliography of sources. And where would a person even start to get sources for something like this? *Playboy? Penthouse?* The boys' locker room?

"Surely you can see there's been some mistake? I would never . . . I mean, I couldn't . . ." She searched for words to describe the turmoil rushing through her. "I can't do a paper on this."

"You can and you will, Miss Parrish."

Her gaze went from the dreaded topic to Professor Guidry, who looked about as reasonable as the IRS rep who'd visited one of her tax lectures last semester.

Not that he looked like the fifty-something auditor. No thinning hair or paunchy middle. Guidry was tall, at least six-two, and not a day over thirty. One of the youngest professors at USL, she'd read in some article the campus newspaper had done on him. But he looked forty, with his glasses and navy tie, and acted fifty, with the chip on his shoulder the size of a boulder.

If he loosened up, lost the glasses and the anal look that forever carved his features, he wouldn't be so bad. He had classic Creole coloring and a head full of thick black hair that would have curled around his ears if given the chance. As it was, Guidry slicked back every strand with some atrocious hair gel. No hair fell forward into his nearly black eyes to clutter his thinking, or to give even a touch of softness to his stern face.

Okay, so it would take more than contact lenses and a new hairdo. Guidry needed a makeover from the inside out, starting with a new heart to replace the one he had. Or didn't have.

"Sir." Her lips trembled as she fought back the tears blurring her vision. "Please. I just can't do this topic."

Her pleading met with a black glare. "You should have thought about that before you tried to make light of this course and this assignment. You know, I expected more from a mature woman like yourself, Miss Parrish. You're a senior, not to mention you're an older senior, by university standards, and you've got several years on most of the freshmen in this class. I am severely disappointed. I don't care for practical jokes, particularly when they're directed at my life's work."

"But I didn't—"

"You did, and how you must deal with the repercussions. This is the topic you submitted, this is the one I approved. End of discussion, Miss Parrish. Good day."

He shoved his clipboard and lecture notes into his briefcase and left her staring after him, her head spinning and her hands trembling around the paper.

Fifty Steps to Ultimate Sexual Fulfillment.

What did a twenty-six-year-old virgin know about sexual fulfillment? Sure, she'd kissed a few guys, and she'd nearly married one, but Raymond had always acted the perfect gentleman. Other than chaste kisses, a little hand-holding, and a few lustful stares, he'd been content to wait for the honeymoon to start planting seeds for his family. *Their* family.

The realization of what Ronnie had been about to get herself into had hit her as she'd stood so virginal and proper at the altar nearly eight years ago.

Her future had flashed before her eyes as the minister had read the sacred vows that would forever tie her to Raymond Cormier, a man she didn't love even though he was one of her father's most devout supporters. Ronnie had opened her mouth to say "I do" and instead had blurted out, "No."

Forever was . . . well, it was *forever.*

She'd already spent her entire life being the dutiful daughter, learning to cook, playing piano, and always acting the little lady—so sweet and proper and demure. She wasn't about to spend till-death-do-us-part being the dutiful wife—making dinner instead of money, having babies instead of a career.

Women could do more, be more, want more, and Ronnie did. She wanted a career, and that meant she had to ace this class.

She took a deep breath. *You can do this. You've beaten the odds, hung in for eight long, money-scarce years. Just toughen up and do it.*

Straightening her shoulders, Ronnie marched from the lecture hall, down the corridor—and straight into Mr. Jailhouse Rock, only he'd changed into Mr. Heartbreak Hotel.

"Uh, excuse me," she said, grasping at the books that threatened to tumble from her arms. *Here's your chance. If you're going to write that paper, you'd better start gaining a little experience with the opposite sex.*

Ronnie pasted on her best smile and pushed her chest up and out. "Fancy meeting you again."

"What?" He didn't even glance at her chest.

"I've seen you before. At the intersection, and the library." She tried batting her eyelashes. "You looked at me."

"Did I?" he asked, shifting from one foot to the other, as if anxious to get away.

"So, do you go to school here? Are you a Ragin' Cajun?"

"A what?"

"A football player."

"Football?" His head jerked up. "Uh, yeah. I play a little ball. Here. Yeah, right here."

"I knew you were a jock." And a cute one, and probably very experienced. The cute ones usually were. "I'm an accounting major." She expected a response. Instead, he shifted again and stared past her.

Get out while the getting is good. Delta's favorite saying raced through her mind. This was useless, futile. She'd spent the past eight years learning about cost accounting and tax credits instead of cultivating her womanly skills.

She'd buried them beneath her ambition. Too deep to dig them up now—

No. She could do this. She was a doer.

She ignored the nerves beating at her senses. *Stay calm and say something. . . .* "You have really great eyes."

"Uh, contacts. Gotta go."

"Maybe we could have coffee."

"Never touch the stuff when I'm in training."

"But football season's over—"

"Later." He darted past her and disappeared around the corner. No backwards glance. No "Nice talking to you." Nothing except the frantic slide of boots on the walkway as he practically tripped over his feet to get away from her.

Fifty Steps to Ultimate Sexual Fulfillment.

She was in trouble. Big, big trouble.

Ronnie's weekdays usually passed in a hustling blur, but not today. The hours crawled by slower than molasses on ice cream. Monday was lecture day in her other two classes. So she spent the next couple of hours taking notes in a freezing lecture hall and watching the clock. Then the two Landrys of Landry & Landry were out of the office for a meeting and the phones were unusually slow. The campus library was practically a morgue.

Ronnie spent the entire day going over and over in her mind what had happened that morning with Guidry and her failed attempt at bagging herself a date for some measley coffee.

By the time she walked into her apartment building just after eleven that night, she had a major headache and an upset stomach.

"Ronnie. Oh, thank God you're here." Mr. Weatherby, the old man who lived down the hall, rushed toward her, a fluffy orange cat in his arms. "Pringles is sick and I have to run to the all-night animal hospital to pick up some medication for her. Can you look after her until I get back?"

Just what she needed to top off her day. The cat from hell.

Was someone Upstairs trying to tell her something?

That maybe her father had been right and she should have stuck to making babies and keeping house instead of a career?

The cat made a sick mewing noise and Mr. Weatherby stroked the feline's head. "There, there, sweetheart. Daddy knows it hurts but he's going to get you some medicine to make it all better. You can stay with Aunt Ronnie in the meantime." He stared hopefully.

Ronnie sighed, dropped her book bag at the door, and held out her arms. "Oh, all right."

"Thank you so much, dear." Mr. Weatherby beamed. "I should be back within the hour."

Fifteen minutes later, Ronnie had settled down on her bed, the almost full bottle of champagne from last night cradled in her lap. Desperate times called for desperate measures, and she was a doer, after all. No sense moaning and groaning. *Just do it.* She tilted the bottle to her lips.

The alcohol burned down her throat and she pursed her lips. Another long swig, then another. The third drink wasn't nearly as bad as the first. And on the fourth, a tingling warmth stole through her. The bittersweetness lingered on her tongue and she sighed.

"I'm in deep doo-doo, Pringles." She stroked the ailing cat and took another drink of champagne. She was a doer, but even doers deserved to wallow once in a while. "I should just go ahead and let Guidry fail me. My life is over anyway. There's no way I can write that ridiculous paper."

Ridiculous. Crazy. Insane. Yes, she had to have been insane when she wrote down that silly topic, and she *had* written it. It was her handwriting, all right. She'd analyzed the paper over and over during her boring shift at the library. The trouble was, she couldn't remember writing anything so ludicrous. She'd finished writing up her nice, sane, rational topic on kids, then fallen asleep and had the dream—

That was it. It had to be. That had been the night she'd had the somewhat erotic dream—okay, very erotic. Somehow, some-way, she'd transferred what she'd been feeling to her paper topic. She'd written the ridiculous topic in the heat of the moment.

Temporary insanity. Unfortunately the defense wouldn't work with Guidry. He was dead set on punishing her. Nailing her to the wall.

"What am I going to do?" She downed another long swallow of champagne and hiccuped. "I need a fresh, authentic paper with fresh and authentic sources. I need . . ."

A man, some experience of her own, then she'd know more than one step toward sexual fulfillment. As it was, she'd be turning in a paragraph.

"Why me?" she cried, the word ending on another hiccup. The cat half-purred, half-moaned and Ronnie stroked the animal's orange fur. "I'm a good person. I give to the Salvation Army at Christmas, I brake for animals, I baby-sit the Hades twins every time Suzanne asks." She hiccuped again. "I hold the door open for people. Why, just the other day I let this kid cut the line in front of me at the grocery store and he even had more items than me." Another hiccup. "I don't deserve this. Do I, Pringles?"

The cat gave another half-purr, half-moan and rested her head on Ronnie's knee.

"I'm a good smartian." She licked her lips and tried the word again. "Sa-ma-ri-tan. Yeah, that's what I am. This stuff shouldn't happen to me." She leaned over and gazed into Pringles's glittering eyes. "What do you think, Pringles? You think Aunt Ronnie deserves all of this?"

The cat batted a paw at Ronnie's face. Claws scratched across her cheek and she jerked back. "Thanks a lot, Pringles. Just wait until you're feeling better. You can go beg at Suzanne's door for a saucer of milk, because my carton is closed to you, mister— Oops." The champagne bottle slipped from her fingers. Golden liquid spilled out over the hardwood floor while the bottle clattered and rolled beneath the bed. She threw up her hands. "What else could happen?"

"The damned thing could get stuck," she muttered two minutes later as she crawled beneath the bed, her arm stretching for the bottle, which had rolled several feet deep. "That's what else could happen."

The cat half-purred, half-moaned again, obviously upset at being pushed off Ronnie's lap so she could chase a champagne bottle. A soft thud echoed and Ronnie peered over her shoulder to see four carrot-red paws poised on the floor near her leg. Pringles ducked her head and green eyes gleamed in the darkness.

"Hold your horses. I'm almost done," she grumbled to the cat as she stretched her arm. Her fingertips brushed smooth glass. "Almost . . . Ouch!"

Claws sizzled across her bare leg; Ronnie jumped and her head banged against the bedframe. Wood creaked, paper rustled, and something gave way above her.

"What the . . . ?"

She scrambled from under the bed, slapping at her face as if a dozen creepy crawlers had rained down on her. After a frantic look at her hands and legs, she took a deep calming breath. Okay, no spiders. At least not on her. But she'd definitely felt something. Retrieving a flashlight, she peered back under the bed.

No spiders under there either. Just a mountain of what looked like letters. Letters? Raising the flashlight beam, she saw the spot beneath the bed where her head had hit. A piece of wood had slid to the side to reveal a now empty compartment. Curiosity chased away her fear and she crept back beneath the bed and gathered up the papers.

A few minutes later, after sopping up the spilled champagne, she settled herself on the bed, her newfound treasures in hand. Her thigh burned where Pringles had scratched four nasty red welts, and she glared at the cat.

"Bad, Pringles."

Pringles, now curled up on Ronnie's pillow, didn't so much as bat an eye. Obviously, the cat felt she'd done her duty in getting Ronnie back up on the bed with her.

Ronnie picked up one of the letters and studied its yellowed edges.

It was obviously very old. Carefully, she unfolded the ends and spread the sheets open. Her gaze snagged on the top corner of the first page and shock bolted through her.

August 9, 1842.
1842!

It couldn't be.

She was no expert, but as she stared at the deteriorating edges, the fading script, her gut instinct told her she'd made a prize find. A letter over one hundred and fifty years old! Make that several letters, she decided as she set about opening each one. The dates spanned a sixteen-year period, from 1832 to 1848.

But it wasn't the dates that drew Ronnie's attention. It was the salutation. The authors were all different, but the letters were written to the same man, about the same man.

And what a man!

Valentino had nothing on this guy. He was legendary. A lover of gigantic proportions, in technique and in stature, she quickly realized as she drank in the letters.

Her face heated. Her body throbbed. Thankfully, she had to pause after the first few letters to hand Pringles over to Mr. Weatherby.

Bolting the door behind them, she retrieved a cold soda and downed half the can before settling herself cross-legged on the bed. She took several deep breaths, then reached for another letter.

. . . way you touched me last night. I've never known a man with such strong, shameless hands. And then when you kissed my . . . The letters went on and on in graphic detail, each one written by a different woman.

Now here was a guy who knew fifty steps to ultimate sexual fulfillment. He probably knew a hundred!

She leaned back against the pillow, a letter clutched in her hand as she stared dreamily into space, doing her best to picture what this lover of all lovers would look like.

Handsome, definitely. But black hair or brown? Green- or blue- or brown-eyed? Short or tall?

Not that it mattered. She didn't want him for his body. She wanted his experience. His expertise.

"If I only had you here, my sweet Valentine," she mused, using the salutation each letter started with, "this paper would be a piece of cake. My troubles would be over."

"My thoughts exactly," a deep male voice grumbled beside her.

Ronnie's eyes snapped open and her gaze swiveled to the right. Shock bolted through her when she saw the man stretched out on the sheets not six inches away from her.

Long, thick hair the color of summer wheat framed a chiseled face with high cheekbones and a sculpted nose. A sensuous mouth slanted at the corners in a sexy grin that said this man knew all her secrets. Bluer than blue eyes clashed with hers for a long moment and Ronnie felt her self-defenses stripped away, along with her clothing and her common sense. He didn't just know all her secrets. He *was* her secret.

The man from her dream.

Her gaze dropped, drinking in tanned, tight, muscled flesh that went on and on and . . .

Make that the very *naked* man from her dream.

"What . . ." she swallowed, searching for words that couldn't quite make it past the shock gripping her senses. "What—what are you doing in my bed?"

Deep laughter sent a wave of shivers through her. "*You've got that wrong,* chérie." He leaned toward her, closing the scant distance that separated them. "*What, pray tell, are you doing in my bed?*"

Chapter Five

So much for being hospitable, Val thought as he stared at the woman who'd fainted dead away—and just when things were starting to get interesting.

Tonight she wore a T-shirt and a pair of bloomers—shorts, he'd heard her call them—that were very short, indeed. Another delight of modern times. His gaze swept the delicious length of her long, long legs before moving back to her face, to her closed eyelids, her flushed cheeks, her pink lips parted just enough to make his groin tighten.

"Wake up, Rouquin," he murmured. His fingers were clenched at his sides to keep from touching her.

One touch and Val would want another. And another, and touching was not part of his plan.

"Rise and shine, Veronique!" His voice grew in strength, a deep baritone that thundered off the walls. She didn't so much as budge, even when he launched into a chorus of the outlandish song drifting from the television. A blonde-haired woman dressed as a cross between a stable boy and a voodoo queen, with too much makeup and not enough meat on her bones, danced across the screen as she sang about virgins and being touched for the very first time.

Not this virgin, he vowed, and not by him.

His efforts to wake her failed and he moved on to a more active course of action. He reached for the nearly empty champagne bottle.

Not for himself, of course. Val was beyond the effects of alcohol. The champagne was for the lovely Veronique. A wake-up call, so to speak.

He leaned over her and tipped the bottle. He watched as a trickle of champagne splashed over her chin, dribbled down her throat, to dampen the material of her shirt.

Her nipples pebbled, responding to the sensation, begging for more. Val, never a man to refuse a lady's request, gladly obliged. He drip-dropped the champagne over her breasts, watching the material dampen to a deep golden hue and cling to her rosy nipples. His mouth went dry and it was all he could do not to lean down and suckle her through the soaked fabric.

Ah, but he'd resigned himself not to touch, and so he let the champagne do his touching for him.

He lifted the edge of her shirt and drizzled more champagne on her bare stomach. The golden liquid pooled in her navel, slid decadently toward the waistband of her shorts . . .

She moaned and wiggled and he knew she was on her way back to consciousness. A few more drops of champagne and she lifted her pelvis just enough to bring other things to mind and make him lick his lips.

Desire warred with determination, wreaking havoc on his spirit. But ultimately, the latter had to win, for Val couldn't, *wouldn't* touch one so pure.

Soon, he promised himself. His meddling the other night was the rainbow on the horizon, the relief calling to him. If all went as expected, Val would have the answer he so desperately sought, and the sweet Veronica would have her education. Then he would have a very willing *woman* in his bed, a bon voyage present to send him over to the Afterlife.

"*Wake up,* chérie," he sang again, coaxing her back to the here and now. He trailed the cool bottle down the outside of one bare leg, up the inside of her knee, her thigh, her—

"Yikes!" She bolted upright and scrambled backward. Her gaze darted frantically, from the champagne bottle resting on the bed between her parted legs, to him.

He winked. "*Did you have a nice nap?*"

"Ohmigod! Y-you can't be . . . ," she stammered. "Y-you aren't what I think . . . No way are y-you . . . I-I'm dead, aren't I?"

He breathed a deep sigh and leaned away from her. "*Alas, I am the one who is dead. One hundred and fifty years, to be exact.*"

"*Dead?*" She seemed to grapple for words, for understanding, and he couldn't blame her. Before he'd become one, he'd never believed in ghosts either. "B-but if you're dead and you're here, that . . . that means you're a . . . a . . ."

He arched one eyebrow. "*A ghost?*"

"A *naked* ghost."

He glanced down, a smile curving his lips. Strong fingers grabbed the edge of the sheet. White cotton slithered over his tanned legs to settle at his waist. "*Better, mais oui?*"

"Yes. I mean, no." Ronnie shook her head and blinked, as if that would be enough to make him disappear. "This can't be happening. I—I don't believe in ghosts."

"*Do you not? You're talking to me, seeing me, feeling me, Veronique. Grounds enough for belief.*"

She clamped her eyes shut and shook her head. *Get a grip. You know this can't be happening. He can't be a ghost, so he must be . . .*

Her eyes flew open and before she could think better of it, she reached out. Trembling fingertips feathered over a rock-hard abdomen. His muscles tightened, contracted. A soft groan passed his lips and she snatched her hand away and scrambled backward as if she'd touched the Devil himself. "How did you get in here?"

"*You brought me here.*"

"Like hell." Her gaze darted past him, gauging the distance to the door. "If you get up and leave right now, I won't press charges. We'll just pretend this never happened—"

"*I am a ghost.*"

She shook her head. "What do you want? Money? My purse

is on the table. I don't have anything of value except some antique earrings from my Aunt Mabel, but they're really hideous." A hysterical laugh bubbled on her lips. "But then you probably don't care what they look like. All you want is my money—"

"*I do not want your money.*"

"Then . . ." Panic beat at her brain, scattering the haziness of the champagne. "Oh my God, you're here to . . . You're going to . . ."

"*Relax. Alas, as beautiful as you are, I'll not touch one hair on your head. I am not an intruder, Veronique. Not a robber or a rapist. I'm a ghost.*" As he said the words, he held up his hand against the light.

Veronica blinked. It couldn't be . . . She could see the faint hint of the lightbulb through his hand.

"*You're not going to swoon again, are you? I'm afraid I have used nearly all the champagne.*"

"But I felt you. I-I felt warm skin and hard muscle and—"

"*It is not a body you feel, but my energy. It is strongest between midnight and three a.m., when the veil between the worlds is its thinnest.*"

She took a deep breath and tried to keep the room from spinning. "Worlds?"

"*The mortal world and the spirit world. You see me clearly now,*" he went on, "*feel my presence at its strongest, as if I am real, but even when you can't feel me, I'm always here. Still in your world, but not of your world. Watching you, Veronique Parrish.*"

"My name's Veronica."

"*I know. Veronique.*" The name rumbled from deep in his throat, a rich sound tinged with the faintest accent.

"You—you're French." Not that his being French had anything to do with anything. The thought simply struck her out of the blue, testimony that she wasn't thinking quite right. A strange, naked man in her bed and all she could think was that he was French.

She fought for logical thought. "H-how do you know my name?"

"*I know everything about you, chérie. You go to school and work two jobs and you spend most nights in that awful chair, lost in your studies. So committed and focused and in desperate need of a little relaxation. That's what drew me to you in the antique, store. I read the desperation in your eyes, so similar to my own.*"

"You were at the antique store?"

He stroked one mahogany bedpost. "*I am wherever this bed is. It is my link.*"

"But I didn't see you."

"*You wouldn't because I am far from mortal, my schedule opposite what it used to be. My spirit is at its weakest during the daylight hours. That is when I rest and rejuvenate, a sort of sleep. I conduct my primary activities at night.*" A wicked grin curved his sensuous lips. "*Then again, chérie, perhaps my schedule hasn't changed so much after all.*"

She shook her head, trying to push away the alcohol-induced fog and grasp the reality of what he was saying. A ghost. A haunted bed. *Impossible.*

"*Don't be troubled. It's all very simple, really. This is my bed, my connection to this world. You purchased it and brought me into your home.*"

"If that's the case, then you've been here for days. How come I haven't seen you before—okay, so I've seen you, but that was a—"

"*—dream?*" He shook his head. "*Guess again, Rouquin.*"

The word echoed in her head and her heart stalled in her chest. *Real.* Oh, no. "You, um . . . that was you."

He winked. "*And you.*"

Heat burned her cheeks. "W-why didn't you say anything before?"

"*You never called my name before, though not for lack of effort on my part.*"

She thought back to the night with the pizza box, when she'd heard the faint buzzing, like a whisper. It had been a whisper. *Him.* He'd been whispering his name. Oh, God. His name. Her gaze swiveled to the letters. "Y-you're Valentine Tremaine. *The* Valentine Tremaine from the letters. The man who used to . . ." Words failed her as a dozen erotic images flashed in her mind.

His smile widened. *"At your service."* His deep voice slid into her ears to chase away the shock gripping her senses and send an altogether different sensation spiraling through her.

Lust, pure and simple.

She trembled at the force of the emotion and he smiled, as if he knew.

"I do know," he said. *"I know all of your deepest, darkest secrets. You have a very passionate nature, Veronique."* Her gaze locked with his and a vivid image pushed into her mind.

The sheets sliding down, her nightgown sliding up, strong hands reaching for her, a warm mouth suckling her, a man's body pressing into hers . . .

Heat pooled low in her belly, spreading outward, sending a hot flush creeping over her skin. Her nipples pebbled, throbbed. Her breath came in short, frantic gasps before she managed to gather what little control she had.

"I truly never thought you could be so pure," he said. *"It was quite a shock, I must admit, especially at your age."*

"You're a ghost," she blurted. "A ghost."

His gaze narrowed. *"And you're a virgin, of all the damned rotten luck."*

Through her shock, his words registered and a hysterical laugh burst from her mouth. "I take it you don't like virgins?"

"I prefer experienced women. But, alas, all is not lost. I can help you with your problem, chérie. I am quite skilled in the arts of love."

She shook her head, a smile playing at her lips. "A ghost—a French ghost—offering me love advice. I'm drunk, right?" Tipsy, maybe, but rolling-on-the-floor drunk? "Or maybe I've got a brain-draining infection from where Pringles scratched me?" She glanced at the burning red welts on her leg.

Strong, tanned fingers invaded her line of sight, feathered over the raw flesh in a soothing stroke she felt clear to her toes. *Real*, yet there was something different. . . .

A strange tingling that wiped away any lingering doubts that Valentine Tremaine was anything but what he said.

A *ghost*. The ghost of the man from the letters. A man renowned for his exploits, an expert in the art of love, according to the dozens of women who'd written to him.

"*You see, I am most qualified to help with your paper.*" He grinned. "*I must say, the times have certainly changed. What you consider academia nowadays was taught in the brothels back when I was a boy.*"

"How do you know about . . . ?" The words faded as the wheels in her brain started spinning, gathering information and piecing it together. She shook her head. "No, it can't be."

As she stared at him, at the sheepish expression on his face, she knew it was. Anger rolled up through her, pushing aside embarrassment and disbelief. "You," she blurted. "It was you. You did it. You changed my topic—my nice, sane, thoroughly researchable topic—to that ridiculous fifty positions to ultimate sexual fulfillment."

"*That's fifty steps, lovely.*" He winked. "*There are more than fifty positions, not that I will be demonstrating any of them while your maidenhead is still intact. But I will help you with the steps if you do a little favor for me.*"

"I . . ." The words stumbled into one another, causing a traffic jam in her throat. She reached for the half-empty champagne bottle. A drink. She needed a drink.

She touched the opening to her full lips, took a long swallow as champagne dribbled down her chin. Not that it mattered. She was already soaking wet courtesy of the resident poltergeist—

"*Not a poltergeist, love. A ghost.*"

"A low-down, dirty, conniving, sleazy, slimy, topic-changing ghost!" Her voice rose in pitch with each word, until she was practically screeching. "You *changed* my topic." The truth shook her even more fiercely than his presence. She jumped off the bed, bolting to her feet. "How could you do such a thing?" she cried, anger and frustration whirling into a volatile mix. "You've ruined my life!"

"*I ruined nothing.*" He got to his feet on the opposite side of the bed and had the nerve to look completely innocent. Baffled, even. "*I thought you would be happy. At the very least, grateful. I'm offering my assistance.*"

"Assistance? Why couldn't you have kept your meddling hands to yourself?"

A wicked gleam lit his eyes. "*If memory serves, you enjoyed my meddling hands your first night in my bed.*"

"It's *my* bed," she blazed, "and I thought you were a dream. Not a . . . a *ghost!*"

I'm very disappointed in you, Miss Parrish. Guidry's words echoed through her head, stoking her temper.

Her fingers curled around the champagne bottle and before she could stop to think that she was an all-around nonviolent person, she hurled it at him.

He groaned as the bottle passed clear through his shoulder and shattered on the wall behind him.

"*What was that for?*" Pain chased shock across his handsome features and guilt curled up inside her, followed by a surge of empowerment.

Anger.

"For being a low-down, dirty, conniving . . ." She hurled a nearby textbook at him. He ducked, pages slapped the wall, and Ronnie reached for something else to throw. Her fingers curled around a nearby paperweight. ". . . sleazy, slimy, topic-changing . . ." Her arm sailed through the air. ". . . *ghost!* You've screwed up eight years of hard works!"

"*But I'm here, ready, willing, and—Ouch!*" He rubbed at the spot on his arm where the paperweight passed through.

"Did that hurt?" She grabbed a nearby stapler.

"*Oui.*"

"Good!"

"*You aren't having your monthly, are you—Merde!*" he growled, as the stapler sailed through the hard wall of his chest, slammed into the sheetrock behind him, and spewed staples.

"What is it with men, huh? Not all women's problems are related to PMS! We've got stress like everybody else."

"*Did you not listen?*" he bit out. "*I said I'm going to help you, do you not understand? One minute you're whining like a bébé, 'Help,' and the next—Sonofa—*"

"How's this for help?" She hurled another book at him. "And this, and this, and *this*."

He ducked the lamp she launched at him.

"*Think about it,*" he growled, face contorted with barely checked anger and a strange glimmer in his eyes. As if he fought the urge to lunge across the bed and wrap his fingers around her throat.

Or kiss her until her toes curled.

"Think, *Veronique. You need me.*" Then he put his back to her. His image shimmered and faded just as a thick notebook sailed from her hands and slapped the far wall.

You need me, the deep voice whispered through her head.

Hadn't she said as much not more than a few minutes ago, before he'd appeared and she'd realized she'd laid down good money for a haunted bed?

But that had been different. Just a figure of speech, farfetched hopes, a crazy fantasy.

"I don't need anybody." Her arm sagged, her fist still curled around a tennis shoe she'd scooped off the floor. "Least of all a meddling ghost."

Veronica Parrish had spent the past eight years on her own,

making her own way, working toward her own future. If she needed better grades, she studied harder, if she needed more money, she took on an extra job. If the oil in her car needed changing, she did it herself. She took out her own trash and fixed her own leaky faucet. Since she'd made her choice and left home, she'd grown accustomed to taking care of herself. She wasn't used to relying on others, asking for help, *needing* anyone.

Fifty Steps to Ultimate Sexual Fulfillment. The topic replayed in her head, batting at her defenses and making her stomach churn with dread.

You need me.

Need was an awfully strong word. Okay, so she could use his help, but damned if she was going to admit even that much right now, with her head pounding and her heart pumping and the room spinning. . . . Ugh, she'd definitely had too much to drink.

The only thing she needed was to crawl into bed, *her* bed, close her eyes, and sleep away the past ten minutes.

She dropped the tennis shoe and turned toward her dresser. Retrieving a nightgown, she started to yank her T-shirt over her head, and her hands stalled, her senses instantly alert to the slight trembling in the air. Her imagination or . . .

She let the edges of the shirt fall back into place. Despite the fact that she'd been undressing right in the middle of the room for the past week and he'd undoubtedly seen her. That had been different.

She hadn't known of his existence then.

But now . . .

Her body instantly clued to several important facts. A strange, prickling awareness that chased goose bumps up and down her flesh. An expectancy in the pit of her stomach. A deep-seated knowledge that while she couldn't see him, he was there.

Watching.

Images from the dream flashed through her mind. Geez, he'd seen much more than her naked body. He'd seen her aroused and on fire. Seen her burst into flames. *Caused* it, with his smoldering looks and his expert touch.

Her cheeks heated and she stumbled toward the bathroom. As the door closed behind her, she could have sworn she heard a sigh of relief.

Or disappointment.

As mad as she was, a wave of compassion swept through her.

One hundred and fifty *years* of celibacy.

Twenty-six and she was already cranky. She couldn't begin to comprehend the frustration that set in when one passed a century.

It is its own form of hell, his raw voice echoed through her head. *But you can ease the frustration and give me peace. I will lend my expertise, you will help me, and all of our problems will be solved.*

Help him? Now what could a twenty-six-year-old virgin possibly do for the ghost of a legendary lover?

She tried to come up with some possibilities as she crawled into bed, *her* bed, and pulled the covers up tight to her neck, but the champagne quickly lulled her into a deep sleep. No thoughts. No worries. Just him.

A wicked, gorgeous man who smiled and teased and touched her just so . . .

Hmmm . . . Maybe needing someone wouldn't be so bad after all.

After all, he wasn't really a *he*. He was a ghost.

She was dreaming about him again.

As maddening as the knowledge was, it filled Val with a strange sense of satisfaction. Joy.

He was standing clear across the room, away from her body, her thoughts, yet she still dreamed of him, of her own accord.

The knowledge stirred a powerful ache in his groin, and the vision she made . . . ah, the vision . . .

The long nightgown she'd donned now tangled at her waist, revealing her long legs and silk-covered bottom. His gaze moved upward, to her luscious breasts hidden beneath the buttoned-up gown. One small pearl had worked its way undone at her throat, giving him a glimpse of her tanned neck. But just a glimpse. Her lips were parted, her eyes closed, flame-colored lashes fanning her silky cheeks.

He'd certainly bedded more attractive women.

Her eyes were set a bit too far apart, her lips were too full, her face a tad too round. There was nothing classic about her beauty. No aristocratic features, such as high cheekbones or a sculpted nose that marked good breeding.

Ah, but when those tiger eyes were open . . . they were so expressive, whether glaring daggers at him or burning with skepticism. Her lips were full and moist when she drank champagne, her face smooth and flushed when she dreamt of him.

Like now.

Valentine strode back toward the bed and sat down on the edge. Her warmth reached out to him, her scent filtered through his head to tease his senses. He couldn't help himself. He reached out, trailed a fingertip along her smooth cheek. She was so soft, so warm, so . . . *innocent*, he reminded himself.

He snatched his hand back and contented himself with drinking in the sweet scent of strawberries and fragrant female, soothing in itself to a man who'd been so lonely for so long.

Too long without company, without peace.

Without the truth.

One hundred and fifty years, and he was no closer to answering the question that burdened his soul than he'd been when he'd taken his last breath. Being a ghost didn't exactly facilitate the search for answers. His spirit was linked to the bed, doomed to haunt whatever dwelling the bed resided in. First, he'd been isolated in a strange shed, then in the museum, then in storage again, this time the warehouse. His spirit couldn't leave the dwelling where his bed resided and so he'd never had a chance to search for answers on his own, never had access to anyone who might be willing to help.

But now . . .

"You need me, chérie, and I need you," he whispered into her ear. She arched toward him, greedy for another touch, another dream, but Val wasn't going to indulge her. Not yet. Not until she'd agreed to his terms and the first lesson began. Then he would proceed with the utmost care, because Val had no intention of forfeiting his chance at eternal peace.

No matter how tempting.

"Tomorrow night," he promised. *"Tomorrow night."*

Chapter Six

Maybe she'd just imagined the entire thing.

Ronnie considered the possibility the next evening as she started her shift at the library. With each book she shelved, the notion seemed more likely, particularly since she'd found no evidence that the ghost of Valentine Tremaine had made an appearance at all. The apartment looked spotless, as if the angry tirade still vivid in her memory had never happened.

Had she really gone ballistic in front of a ghost?

There wasn't a bit of supporting evidence. Not a book out of place, a shard of glass from the shattered champagne bottle. Only a large trash bag sitting in the corner. She'd meant to look inside, but she'd been running so late for class she hadn't had the time or energy to plow through it.

She'd seen no proof of his existence.

But she'd felt it. A strange sense of . . . *something*. A presence. A *ghost*.

Maybe. And maybe George Clooney would drop down on one knee and pop the question any time now. And even more unlikely, she'd accept.

Okay, so maybe she would. After all, George Clooney . . .

She'd definitely had too much to drink last night. Liquor-induced hallucinations and lots of wishful thinking. She needed a way to ace Guidry's class, so she'd invented some fictitious form—and what a form—of help after reading the provocative love letters.

His image pushed into her mind—long, whiskey-blond hair, tanned skin, a killer smile, and bluer than blue eyes that stripped her bare and enjoyed every moment.

Valentine. Definitely an appropriate name for a lover of such gigantic proportions. In stature as well as deed. Her face heated as she rememembered the sight of him, six feet plus of naked male, heavily muscled, with the same whiskey-colored silk sprinkling his chest, swirling down his abdomen, surrounding his . . .

Tomorrow night. Words whispered in the dead of night. Real or imagined?

Ronnie blew out a deep breath. Imagined. Just like the ghost himself, because Ronnie Parrish didn't believe in anything she couldn't see and touch and explain. No mysterious forces working in the universe, no unexplained phenomena. For everything there was a nice, sane explanation if one looked long and hard enough.

Wasn't there?

She wanted to think so. The trouble was she'd seen and touched Val last night and, while she couldn't explain his existence, she couldn't quite disprove it either.

"Do you believe in ghosts?" she asked Danny as they sat in the campus café, sharing a pizza and a pitcher of soda later that afternoon.

Danny stopped in mid chew and eyed her suspiciously. "This coming from the woman who blew the whistle on the tooth fairy to my twelve-year-old niece during her last visit?"

"That was an accident. How was I to know a junior high kid who'd stopped believing in Santa Claus still carried a torch for the tooth fairy?" She took a sip of diet soda. "So do you?" she pressed.

"Is this your roundabout way of saying you saw a ghost? A real, house-haunting Casper?"

"Of course not." She busied herself brushing crumbs off her lap. "I mean, I thought I might have heard a little noise last night, that's all."

His face lit with excitement. "Like chains rattling?"

"Um, not really."

"Moaning?"

Only her own, she thought, remembering last night's dream. "Nuh-uh."

"Screaming?"

"You've been watching too many of those late-night horror flicks."

"Well, if it wasn't moaning or screaming or rattling chains, what was it doing?"

She leveled a stare at him. "He was talking to me."

"*He?*" He arched an eyebrow at her. "I'd say you're definitely hard up for some action."

"Thanks a lot."

"I've got a friend in the chess club, Herbert Michaels. He's not that great looking, but he's a grad student, perfect GPA, and his first year's earning potential is off the charts. I know he'd die to go out with you. To go out with anybody."

"As exciting as this guy sounds, as financially promising, I think I'll pass."

"You sure as shootin' won't at the rate you're going." She glared and he grinned. "Sorry, you walked right into that one. So have you figured out the first position yet?"

"It's *step*, Mr. Smarty-pants. Fifty *steps* to ultimate sexual fulfillment, and I'm working on it."

Tonight. Hopefully. If Valentine Tremaine turned out to be real and his proposition more than wishful thinking.

Not that Ronnie *needed* him, mind you. She didn't need any man to be successful. But want him . . . Now, that was a different story altogether.

Ronnie wasn't leaving her future up to chance. While Valentine Tremaine might be Plan A, Ronnie intended to have a backup plan, just in case she'd had much more to drink than she thought, and he had been a hallucination. After she'd finished up at the library, she stopped at an after-hours grocery and loaded up on plenty of caffeine for an all-night session of brainstorming ways to approach the Guidry paper. She also bought a copy of *Playgirl* which she discreetly slipped into a thick copy of *Good Housekeeping*.

Later, when she was rounding the corner of her apartment building, groceries in hand, she spotted Professor Guidry exiting his apartment across the street. He climbed into his drab brown Volvo and Ronnie entertained the fleeting thought—maybe a better Plan B—of throwing herself in front of his car. She'd be out of commission and he'd be apologetic for hitting her.

Or would he?

Let me be the first to sign your cast, Miss Parrish—with a big fat F since you won't be able to finish my class or write your paper or graduate.

The idea quickly dropped to the C slot.

She was not going to fail Guidry's class, no matter if she had to visit every adult bookstore in the city, take out a subscription to *Playboy*, or let Danny fix her up with every nerdy grad student at USL.

Her thoughts went to the letters, to the very experienced man who'd inspired them, the cocky self-assured ghost who'd propositioned her.

With trembling fingers, she turned the key in her apartment door, walked inside, and flipped on the light. She swept a gaze at her surroundings, and the breath she'd been holding rushed out in a loud *whoosh*.

Just an unmade bed, a kitchen table covered with textbooks, and the leftover cup from the coffee she'd downed that morning.

No naked ghosts.

Disappointment welled inside her and she fought it back down. "So you go to Plan B." She turned to the groceries, unpacked her *Good Housekeeping* with its hidden cargo, and slapped it on the counter. Tomorrow morning she'd call Danny, accept his matchmaking offer, then comb the local video store.

An evening with 9½ Weeks should beef up her sexual education.

She pulled a pint of melting ice cream from the sack and started for the refrigerator. Of course, if she got really desperate, she could hit the hard-core section of the store for *Louise Does Louisiana* or some other ridiculous-sounding title—

"You're late. It's a quarter after midnight."

The familiar voice shattered her thoughts. She whirled, the ice cream splattered on the linoleum, and her heart beat ninety to nothing as she stood face to face with six feet plus of hunky ghost.

"You *are* real." She couldn't help herself. She reached out. Warm, pulsing skin met her fingertips and she let her hand linger, absorbing the strange, vibrating heat.

"That's because I am."

Their gazes locked for the space of a heartbeat and heat flared in his eyes. So hot and bright that Ronnie swallowed. She let go. "I mean, you feel like a real *man.*"

"It's the midnight hour, chérie." His gaze caught and held hers again. Heat flared in the dark depths of his eyes, and an answering warmth spread through her. She forced her attention away, noticing for the first time that he wasn't standing in front of her in all his naked glory. He wore a flowing white shirt, fitted black breeches, and knee-high black boots.

"You have clothes," she blurted.

He glanced down and adjusted his shirt. *"They are a damned sight uncomfortable—one hundred and fifty years without them tends to spoil a man."*

"Why are you wearing clothes?"

"I could take them off—"

"No, I mean, clothes are good." Liar. "Just surprising. I didn't know ghosts could actually wear clothes. I mean," she swallowed. She was babbling, she knew, but one tended to resort to mindless chatter when confronted with something from out of this world. From another world. The *spirit* world. "Where would a ghost get clothes? I mean, do you guys have malls or something?"

"The clothes, like everything else, are a form of energy."

"Well, um, you've got really great taste in energy."

"Merci." He winked and bent down. Strong, tanned fingers closed around the dropped ice cream carton. Chocolate oozed from inside.

She watched him scoop up the splattered dessert, his fingers working meticulously, and she realized in an instant that he'd cleaned up the apartment the night before. Despite the fact that she'd given him hell.

Real.

Relief snagged through her and the words were out before she could stop them. "Thank you." Thank you? He flashed her a grin as he cleaned the mess and she shook her head. First she complimented his energy and now she pledged her undying gratitude. She was definitely headed for a breakdown sometime soon. "What am I saying? It's your fault I'm in this mess in the first place. You should be thanking me, buster."

"And why, pray tell?"

"For not calling in an exorcist and having you exorcised right out of my bed."

"My bed." He handed her the oozing mess.

"I bought it."

"Possession," he drawled, his husky voice emphasizing the word, *"is nine-tenths of the law."*

"I don't think this is what our lawmakers had in mind." She dropped the ruined dessert into the sink.

"Ah, but it fits." He chuckled and indicated a dollop of ice cream on her hand. *"What is this?"*

"Chocolate Brownie Delight." She licked the chocolate from her skin as he watched, his eyes an even deeper shade of electric blue.

"I should have known from the wondrous smell."

"You can smell?"

"*Everything.*" He inhaled, his chest heaving, his head falling back as a contented smile crossed his face. "*Strawberries,*" he finally murmured. "*Ripe strawberries with the faintest hint of cream.*"

"I had strawberry shortcake for dessert, but that was hours ago—"

"*Heightened,*" he said. "*As are all my senses. I can see, smell, hear, touch, taste . . .*" He shook his head, as if pushing away the sudden thoughts that darkened his eyes. "*Which brings me to the matter of your schooling.*" Before he could go on, a knock sounded on the door.

"Ronnie, dear!" came Mr. Weatherby's frantic voice. "Pringles has had a setback and is sick again. I really need you!"

"Pringles," she groaned. "Oh, no."

A grin spread across Valentine Tremaine's handsome face. "*Duty calls.*"

"Ronnie? Are you there?"

"No," she blurted, her head whipping in the direction of the door. "I mean . . ." She glanced behind her in time to see Val's image shimmer and fade.

Shimmer and fade?

She blinked and he was gone. *Gone.* "Wait!"

"I'm not going anywhere, not with a sick cat on my hands," Mr. Weatherby assured her. "Open up, dear."

Thirty seconds later, after two dead bolts and a chain lock, Ronnie held Pringles in her arms and watched her neighbor disappear down the hallway, headed for an all-night pharmacy.

"You've ruined my life, you know that, Pringles?"

"*And how is that?*" Val's deep voice startled Ronnie and she jumped. Pringles screeched.

Ronnie whirled to find Val grinning at her. "Where did you go?"

"*Nowhere.*"

"But you disappeared—" she started, but her words were cut off by another knock on the door.

"Ronnie, it's me!" Danny called from outside. "Open up!"

"Wait!" she called out to him, then turned to Val. "This place usually isn't this busy—" she started, but he'd already started to shimmer. A frantic blink to adjust her eyes, and he disappeared completely.

If he'd been real in the first place, that skeptic, I-still-can't-believe-this part of her maintained. Maybe she wasn't heading for a breakdown. Maybe she'd already had one, and the hallucinations were just an aftereffect. Ghosts. Ghosts who wore clothes. Ghosts who disappeared in the blink of an eye.

"Doesn't anybody sleep around here?" She threw open the door and shoved Pringles into Danny's arms. "It's after midnight. What are you doing here?"

He shrugged. "Wanda had a headache tonight so she canceled our study session."

"And?"

"I've started taking early evening naps so I'm raring to go by the time Letterman's over. Forty-five minutes of shut-eye and ten cups of coffee and a double dose of Excite and Energize."

"Let me guess. You're too wired to sleep?"

He nodded. "And hungry. Mike hasn't been to the store." She knew that Mike, Danny's computer genius roommate, was the designated shopper. "We're out of everything except the green stuff that grows in the fridge, and as much as I like health food, that's stretching it a bit. You're fifteen minutes closer than the Stop & Shop, and you've got a TV." He sat Pringles on a nearby chair and headed for the kitchenette. "Anything good in the fridge?"

No. The word was there on the tip of her tongue. Just tell him no, toss him out, and get on with things. With Val.

"I'm really starved and Alex is hosting the collegiate championships on *Jeopardy* in about a half hour."

She shrugged. "Doritos in the cabinet, sandwich stuff in the fridge." Sucker, her conscience chided.

While Danny made himself a sandwich, Ronnie scoured the

apartment, peeked under the bed, looked in the corners. Just to be sure. She wanted to give herself every benefit of the doubt before she declared herself absolutely insane.

"Something wrong?"

"Uh, no. I just, um, misplaced a book." She opened a closet and peered inside.

"I'll help you look," Danny offered.

"No." She closed the closet. "I'll find it later."

"Maybe you just imagined him," she said to herself after she'd gone into the bathroom to change her ice cream-splattered shirt. She stared into the mirror, noted the shadows under her eyes. Tired. She was overworked. No wonder she was dreaming up such outlandish things.

"Who is Danny?"

The deep voice brought her whirling around to find Val standing inches behind her, so tall and good-looking, filling up her tiny bathroom.

"You *are* real."

"I thought we already established that." He frowned. *"Now who is this Danny sitting in your living room, eating from your refrigerator?"*

"He's a friend."

His mouth drew tight. *"A boyfriend?"*

"Just a friend. A guy pal. Someone I hang out with. A guy, but a safe guy."

"Safe?"

"As in nonthreatening, as in I don't have to worry about him putting moves on me or me putting moves on him. There's no chemistry between us. Just friendship. Safe." She planted her hands on her hips and did some frowning of her own. "You disappeared," she said accusingly. "One minute I was staring at you and the next, poof! Gone."

"Out of sight, but not out of mind, chérie. I was still there, you just couldn't see me. It wouldn't do to have your neighbors get a look at me. Some people get quite spooked."

"My neighbors? You mean I'm not the only one who can see you? Anybody else could?"

"Only those with an open mind, who believe in ghosts."

"Can you do that shimmering thing anytime you want?"

He nodded. *"One of the many wonders of being what I am."*

Handsome and sexy and charming and . . . a *ghost*.

The ghost who'd propositioned her last night.

"You mentioned something about a favor—"

"Ronnie, are you all right in there?" Danny's voice cut into her sentence, followed by a soft knock on the bathroom door.

"Um, fine. I'll be out in a minute." She turned back to Val. "What is it you want from me?"

"I haunt my bed for a reason." His smile dissolved as if she'd reminded him of something he wanted to forget. *"Not all people turn into ghosts when they pass on. Some cross over to the other side, but others remain in this realm, unwilling to give up the ghost because of some question that haunts them, some truth they've yet to uncover, some deed unfinished. Perhaps they're sad or guilty or just curious. The point is, they are tied to this world until they can finish their business here. Then they can cross over and be at rest."*

"So what's your business?"

"I have a question. I need to know what became of a certain woman."

It was Ronnie's turn to frown. "An old girlfriend?"

"Just a woman—"

"Are you sure you're all right?" Danny's voice cut in. "You've been in there an awful long time."

"Fine," she growled. "Just women's business. So what about the woman?" she asked Val.

"She was rumored to be pregnant."

"Yours?"

"Yes. No." He shook his head. *"I don't know. We shared only one night together. A night I have no memory of."*

"Why can't you remember?"

He shook his head. *"Too much whiskey, perhaps."*

"Doesn't alcohol dull the libido? You don't strike me as a man with a dull anything, especially a libido, if what's in those letters bears any truth."

"They are all true, and you're right I never indulged too much, never to the point of forgetting a sweet face, a delicious scent, until that night—"

"You want an aspirin or something?" Danny asked.

"Uh, no," she called out.

"'Cause I don't mind getting you something. Wanda has the very same trouble sometimes. Headaches. Cramps. The whole time-of-the-month thing."

"It's not my time of the month," she blurted.

"But you said—"

"Can't a girl sit in her bathroom in peace?"

"Well, excuse me. A guy doesn't act sensitive, and he's out of luck. He acts sensitive, and he's still out of luck. I wish you women would make up your minds. . . ."

"Help me, Veronique," Val urged, drawing her attention as he stepped closer, *"and I will help you."*

Help, not need.

Funny, but when he put things in that perspective, it didn't seem as . . . as distasteful as it had before.

Help, as in a mutually beneficial business arrangement. Fifty-fifty.

"A woman, huh?" At his nod, she said, "I guess it can't be that much different from tracing a family tree." Not that she'd ever traced hers, but there were books that told how to go about the process. "When do we get started?"

"Started on what?" came Danny's voice from the other side of the door.

"Nothing," she called out. "I was singing."

"You were talking."

"My singing just sounds like talking."

"What's going on, Ronnie?"

"Go watch TV," she told him.

"Not until you open up." He pounded on the door again. "I mean it."

"*You should go*," Val told her. "*And so should I.*"

"No," she blurted as he started to shimmer, then fade. "Please don't leave—"

"I'm not going anywhere," Danny declared.

She hauled open the door to find her friend hovering on the other side. "I wasn't talking to you."

His gaze swept the interior of the bathroom. "Then who were you talking to?"

"No one. I told you, I was singing." She hummed and blurted out a few bars of her favorite song. "See?"

He gave her the once-over. "I know talking when I hear it."

"Talking, singing, both forms of communication."

"Is something wrong with you?"

"I'm just tired."

He stared at her long and hard, before letting the subject go with a shake of his head. He settled into a chair and fixed his gaze on the TV, Pringles on his lap, while Ronnie stretched out across her bed, closed her eyes, and replayed the conversation with Val. The proposition.

She smiled. While Valentine's help was for a higher purpose—to help her pass—it would also fulfill more personal needs.

The dream flashed in her mind, the feel of his hands on her body, the heat pooling in her stomach.

Geez, she had it bad. She was attracted to a *ghost*.

Mmm . . . As crazy as the idea sounded, it also excited her. Sacrificing her time and effort on a man when she should be concentrating, on her future was one thing. But this . . . this was different. Val was different. He wasn't a man.

He was a ghost.

Handsome, sexy, and risk-free. She didn't have to worry about falling in love, about being lured away from the path she'd chosen for herself by love, sex, or a combination of both. He was simply a ghost. Here one minute, gone the next. *Safe.* As safe as Danny, but definitely more exciting.

Val helped her, she helped him. He crossed over to the Afterlife, she aced Guidry's class and graduated, and moved on to the rest of her career-driven life.

No getting sidetracked with a messy relationship.

She sighed and rolled over to stare at the ceiling.

"*Close your eyes*, Rouquin," the voice whispered, and her head jerked to the side to find Danny fixated on the television. She turned the other direction and drank in the empty expanse of bed to her left. She didn't see Val.

But she felt him.

"What about the lessons?" she whispered.

"*We'll start tomorrow night. Sleep well.*"

"Now how am I supposed to sleep well knowing that?"

"Did you say something?" Danny shot her a glance.

"Uh, I said I'm sleeping. I'm sleeping well."

"Great, you need it. You're acting punchy. Look, I'll let myself out in a little while. Alex is about to do Double Jeopardy." He grinned, excitement flashing in his brown eyes. "The category is ancient Egyptian rivers."

"My personal favorite." She closed her eyes. Not to sleep, but to think, anticipate, *feel* the warmth and heat so temptingly close. Val . . .

Tomorrow night.

Chapter Seven

"This isn't exactly what I had in mind." Ronnie slid the top button into place and glanced in the floor-length mirror.

The ugly brown dress—an eighteenth birthday present from her Aunt Mabel and one of the few mementos Ronnie had kept from her past life—buttoned from neck to ankles, the sleeves long, concealing everything but Ronnie's head, hands, and feet. She'd always hated the dress, but she'd loved her aunt, who'd passed on shortly afterward.

A housedress, her aunt had called it. Undoubtedly because it was large enough to fit a nice two-bedroom, two-bath, maybe even with a double-car garage.

"I'm just the student, mind you, but it seems to me *undress*ing would be more appropriate to my paper topic. Or at least some skimpy lingerie. Something sexy. We're talking about attracting the opposite sex, not repelling it."

"*Exactly, and sex appeal is not about what a woman wears. It's about the way she feels inside. Feeling sexy is the first step to ultimate sexual fulfillment. What you think here—*" Val tapped his forehead "*—sets the stage to attract the opposite sex. If you feel attractive, men will sense it. It will lure them quicker than an eyeful of cleavage.*"

"Have you been flipping the television to Dr. Ruth while I'm asleep?" She shook her head. "What am I saying? You're the Doctor of Delight, according to those letters. You certainly don't need a sex therapist to tell you the score."

He frowned. "*Do you always talk so much?*"

"Actually," she smiled, "it's one of the things I do best. That, and I'm a whiz at receivables."

"That's admirable, chérie, but neither is likely to help you pass your love course, and you're wasting precious time. Back to the subject. Now close your eyes."

She obeyed. The warmth at her back grew stronger as he moved closer. The dream flashed in her mind, the sheets drifting down, his hot, wet mouth trailing over her skin. She shivered. "Are you going to kiss me?"

"You're jumping ahead, and even if you weren't, I still would not kiss you."

Her eyes popped open. "But we have a deal—"

"Which involves my tutoring you, not kissing you. I will tell you everything you need to know." He indicated the fresh notebook she'd left on the kitchen table. *"And you will write everything down."*

"But my paper requires more than just a theory. I need documentation to support what I'm proposing."

"The love letters are written proof that my methods work."

And how. Several graphic scenarios flashed in her head and she blushed. "True, but they're old. I have to prove that your methods work today, in the nineties. For that I need current experiments."

"So conduct an experiment."

"How can I if you don't kiss me?"

"Not an experiment with you as the subject, dear. I'll tutor you and you find your own subject."

"Me go after a man?"

"That would be the obvious choice, unless you're a bit more daring than I imagined." His warm chuckled chased goose bumps down her arm.

"A man will do just fine." *This* man, her dream-obsessed hormones insisted.

The trouble was, he wasn't a man.

Val was just a ghost. Albeit a good-looking, charming, tantalizing, sexy ghost, but still a spirit, and Ronnie needed the real thing.

The dream rushed through her mind, the hot mouth working at her nipple, the purposeful fingertips tantalizing her bare flesh. If a ghost could stir so many feelings inside her, a real man would be even better. And he wouldn't fade once three a.m. hit.

And that was the problem in a nutshell.

Val was Val. A ghost. Just this side of her imagination. *Safe.*

But she needed real.

Or did she?

A smile tugged at her lips as an idea hit her. She could be the subject, or rather a creation of her own mind. A Madame X. She could document Madame X's journey into the realm of sexual fulfillment. But she would still need experiments.

Her gaze zeroed in on Val. Although he looked determined now, Madame X could change his mind.

"What are you thinking?" Val eyed her suspiciously.

"Don't you know?"

He stared at her a full minute more before shrugging. *"Sometimes. When your defenses are down."*

"And they're up now?"

He nodded and she smiled. The last thing she needed was him noseying around in her thoughts all the time.

"So what is going on in that stubborn little mind of yours?"

"Just that you're right. I do need a man. If you can make me flush hot and cold, imagine what a real hunk can do." She shivered in anticipation.

Val frowned and snapped, *"Are you ready to begin?"*

"Shoot."

"Don't tempt me."

"Why so touchy all of a sudden?"

"I'm not touchy," he muttered, so low she wondered if she'd just imagined it. *"That's the problem."*

As in, he *wanted* to touch her.

Of course he did. He'd endured a century and a half of celibacy. He probably salivated at the sight of one of those exercise shows, drooled while glancing through the Victoria's Secret catalogue. He didn't stand a chance with Madame X, the poor guy.

Ghost, she reminded herself as she snapped her eyes shut. "Now what?"

"Think of the first time you exploded beneath a man's touch."

"But I've never—"

"Mais oui, you have, Rouquin. In your dreams."

Yes, the dream.

"Remember." His deep voice rumbled in her ears, stirring her senses the way his hands had brought her to such sweet ecstasy. *"Are you remembering?"*

"Yes."

"Good. Now tell me exactly where you are."

"I'm in my bed."

"My bed," he whispered.

"My bed," she countered, and though she couldn't see his smile, she felt it. The tension that emanated from him eased for the space of two heartbeats and his warm chuckle slid along her nerve endings before the sound faded.

"So you're in the bed," he murmured. *"Tell me what you smell."*

She took a deep breath. Oddly enough, she didn't smell the musty aroma of mothballs from the old brown dress. A sweet, seductive scent spiraled through her nostrils and made her chest heave.

"Tell me," he urged.

"Leather and apples and something . . . a freshness, like water . . . cool water on a hot day." She took several deep breaths and the mingling of scents wafted through her head. "It makes my nose tingle and my heart beat faster. Makes me breathe a little deeper, as if I can't get enough."

"Now tell me what you feel."

"The soft mattress at my back," she murmured. "A cool, cotton sheet slithering down my bare legs." She shivered, goose bumps chasing up and down the legs in question.

"*What else, love?*"

"Incredibly hot fingertips brushing my cheeks, my collarbone, my breasts. I . . ." Her breath caught as she felt the sensations, the memory as intense as the dream itself. "I feel a moist heat on my—" she swallowed and summoned her courage "—my nipple." She gasped at the memory of the fierce suckling. "I-I can feel it Right here. Right now."

"*Can you, chérie? Can you feel the sweet heat stealing through your body, stirring an ache deep in your belly? A hunger?*"

She nodded.

"*Tell me what you want.*"

Nothing. The denial poised on the tip of her tongue. Veronica Parrish wanted nothing except an accounting degree and a successful career.

Usually.

But at that moment, she wanted something entirely different, and, for the first time, she couldn't deny what she felt, no matter how much she suddenly wanted to.

"*Tell me,*" he urged, his voice so compelling it overrode her defenses.

"To be touched," she admitted, licking her lips. "To be tasted, just like in the dream. I want it so much. I . . ." Her words drowned in his sharp intake of breath. Banked tension held his body tight.

His voice, usually so deep and smooth and seductive, came out raw and ragged. "*Open your eyes.*"

Her gaze collided with his in the mirror and she saw the heat in his eyes, the desire so fierce it took her breath away.

"*Look at yourself.*"

Her gaze went to the woman staring back at her, and this time she didn't notice the ugly dress, but the woman beneath it. Her eyes appeared heavy-lidded, her lips parted, the bottom slightly more prominent and slick from the slow glide of her tongue a moment ago. She looked as if she'd just rolled out of bed after a night of . . .

Dreams. Delicious, intoxicating, erotic dreams.

"See how your mouth quivers, how the blush colors your cheeks. Feel how your nipples press achingly against the dress. You're beautiful, Veronique," he said, his voice suddenly hoarse. "Desirable. Sexy."

And for the first time in her life, Ronnie felt sexy, and it was okay. For the first time in years she stopped worrying about burying her sexuality where it couldn't interfere with her career plans. The knowledge made her stand a bit taller and forced her gaze to meet his.

"You must recognize the passion in your soul before you can share that passion with someone. You're a woman, an Eve in the Garden, a gift to mankind. The most precious, passionate, delectable gift a man could receive."

Desire blazed in his eyes and she felt the tension rolling off him, as if he fought hard to keep from reaching out.

She turned to face him. "So now are we going to kiss?"

"Mmm," he murmured as his head dipped toward her. He stopped a fraction shy and she parted her lips, begging him forward.

Bam. Bam. Bam.

"Ronnie! Are you home? I really need you!"

Muscles rippled, his mouth drew into a firm, stubborn line, and Val pulled away.

Disappointment spiraled through Ronnie, a strange sensation to a woman who'd spent eight long years avoiding men and romantic entanglements because they were too distracting.

But then, Val wasn't a man.

Her lips parted and she leaned in. If he wouldn't kiss her, she would just have to kiss him—

Another fierce knock and the moment shattered.

"I *really* need you," Suzanne called out.

"I'll be right back," Ronnie told Val. "Don't go away."

Ronnie cracked open the door to find Suzanne, the twins,

and Suzanne's date for the evening, a lawyer with a Mercedes, to quote her neighbor.

"My sitter canceled," Suzanne said, shoving one of the twins into Ronnie's arms as she pushed inside the apartment without waiting for an invitation. "Reggie here has theater tickets."

"It's twelve-thirty at night."

"It was a midnight show. *Midnight in Manhattan.* Get it? Anyhow, we've missed the performance, but Reggie's boss is hosting an after-premier party that we can just about make if you'll agree to watch the kids for an hour. I'll pay double and I brought videos and the kids adore you—"

"I was really busy." Ronnie hefted a fidgeting Brandy to one hip. "*Really* busy."

She saw Suzanne's gaze dart around the apartment, to the now empty spot where Val had been standing, so very close to kissing her.

Kissing her.

A wave of regret rolled through her, steeling her determination not to be suckered in as a midnight baby-sitter. *No.* No way. No can do. No matter how Brandy was hugging her and giving tiny fish kisses to her neck.

"You know how much the kids adore you."

"But I'm working on a research project."

Suzanne's worried expression faded into a smile. "And here I thought you meant *busy* busy. The kids will be little angels while you study. Right, baby?" she asked Randy, who nodded fervently as Suzanne dropped him onto the sofa.

"Ann-gels," Brandy declared, obviously through making fishy lips. She squirmed and slid from Ronnie's grasp to follow her brother.

"I have to get up really early. I have to be at the library by seven."

"The kids will be asleep before you can count to ten."

"But . . ."

"But?" Suzanne's desperate gaze collided with Ronnie's.

"An hour, you said?" There went a continuation of tonight's lesson.

"Two hours tops." Suzanne handed her a piece of paper. "Here's the phone number where we'll be, but don't call unless it's life or death." She kissed the twins and gave Ronnie a bright smile. "I owe you for this. You're divine."

"More like stupid," Ronnie grumbled as she collapsed on the sofa between Randy and Brandy as they argued over what video to watch.

"Sweeping Bwooty," Brandy declared.

"Hairclees," Randy said, pointing to the Hercules video.

"What do you say we take turns?" Ronnie's question met with tears from Brandy and a kick from Randy. "Turns it is," Ronnie declared.

They would watch a little TV, the twins would fall asleep, and Ronnie could get back to Val, wherever he was.

Her gaze scanned the apartment more than once, and although she couldn't see him, she felt him. Nearby. Watching.

It was both highly unsettling and extremely erotic, despite the huge, ugly brown housedress she was wearing. She felt every movement of her body beneath, the press of her skin against the coarse material, the rasp of fabric against her sensitized flesh—

She forced the thoughts away, turned to the kids, and slipped into her babysitter mode.

Ronnie counted to ten as they started watching *Sleeping Beauty.* She hit the thousands halfway through the movie, and gave up altogether by the time the credits started to roll and the kids started begging for more popcorn.

"Nobody move," she ordered as she unfolded herself from a tangle of chubby arms and legs and went to refill the popcorn bowl.

She left the kids with their eyes glued to the next movie while she rummaged for another package of microwave popcorn. She'd just popped the bag into the microwave and punched the button when she turned and saw Val leaning so casually against her kitchen cabinets.

"You like kids," A grin tugged at his lips as if the knowledge pleased him.

"Usually, but at the moment, I'm not so sure," she muttered under her breath. "They've got rotten timing."

He grinned. *"I'd say they had perfect timing. You were about to toss the lesson plan aside. The kiss doesn't come until after we've mastered the first ten steps."*

"Then you'll kiss me?"

His grin disappeared. *"No."* He shook his head. *"I can't, Veronique."*

"Because you hate virgins."

"Actually, I admire them, but that's beside the point. There are certain rules I must abide by, or face the consequences. While I might want a taste of your sweet lips, I will not indulge." Because Valentine Tremaine feared it wouldn't stop at one kiss. She was too tempting as it was, even in that godawful brown dress, and he'd barely touched her.

Kissing would lead to more touching and then . . .

Val would find himself making the same mistake all over again, and the price for such a thing was much too high. He'd paid with his life so long ago.

This time, Valentine Tremaine would pay with his soul.

He gathered his determination and fought back a wave of erotic images. *"I'm not kissing you,"* he stated. *"I am not."* Then he turned and faded into the shadows, her voice following him.

"We'll see about that."

"Hello. This is Veronica Parrish. I'm busy right now, but if you'll leave a name and phone number, I'll get back with you shortly." Beeeeeeeeeeep.

"Hell's bells, even your message is boring." Jenny's voice carried over the speaker and Ronnie snatched up the phone.

"Hey, Jen. What's up?"

"Can't you spice up the recording a little? Maybe use some background music or some snappy dialogue, or make your voice sound the tiniest bit intriguing?"

"It's just a message."

"That mirrors you. Busy, no-nonsense, workaholic, sex-deprived you."

"Is there a point to this call, or are you just trying to remind me of how full and meaningful my life is?"

"You're hopeless, and speaking of hopeless, I simply can't make it to Lafayette for our lunch date this Saturday. Matt has a softball game he can't miss and my mom's too busy to watch the girls and a two-hour road trip with them would have me throwing myself from the car before we even got there."

"Geez, Jenny, you make domestic bliss sound like sheer heaven."

"It has its high points, but traveling with two toddlers isn't one of them."

"I'll remember that when my turn comes."

"You'll be old and senile by the time that happens."

"Don't say it."

"Say what?"

"That I need to get a life."

"A love life," Jenny corrected.

"I'm trying."

Ronnie couldn't miss Jenny's sharp intake of breath. "As in you've met someone?" Her excitement crackled over the wire.

No. Just tell her no and end it here. "Sort of." Hey, what happened to no? She was too worked up over last night, over her near kiss with Val, and she had to share her excitement with someone.

"Either you did or you didn't," Jenny said.

"I sort of did."

"You're killing me, here."

"He's just not your average guy."

"This is good."

Actually, it was great, but Ronnie refrained from blurting that fact out. As anxious as Jenny was for Ronnie to go for the gusto, she wouldn't be too keen to know the gusto consisted of a ghost, albeit a hunky one.

"So what about lunch?" Ronnie asked, determined to turn the subject onto something else, before Jenny asked any more questions Ronnie couldn't answer.

"I was hoping you could drive out here."

"I can't. Why don't we postpone it until next weekend. Can you drive out then?"

"That'll work. So when do I get to meet this guy?" So much for changing the subject. "Can you bring him to lunch with us?"

Only if we meet between midnight and three a.m., Ronnie thought to herself. "Actually, he doesn't get out much. I doubt he'd enjoy it."

"We'll have Italian. He'll love it."

"He's allergic to tomatoes."

"Mexican."

"Can't handle the smell of jalapeños."

"Cajun."

"Breaks out if he even gets a whiff of cayenne pepper."

"Greek."

"Olive oil gives him hives."

"I'll brown-bag tuna sandwiches and we'll meet at your place. No, don't tell me. He's allergic to paper bags."

"Tuna."

"Sounds like you don't want me to meet him." When Ronnie started to protest, Jenny cut in, "Look, if you're not totally comfortable with the situation yet, I can wait. I'm just glad you're seeing someone."

"Thanks, Jenny. Talk to you later."

* * *

"What happened to you?" Danny asked her when she met him on the front stoop a few minutes later for their morning walk to class.

"I got held up. Jenny called."

"Did she have good news?"

"Just that she can't make it for lunch on Saturday, which is for the best since I'm really busy anyway." She caught Danny's curious gaze. "Why are you looking at me like that?"

"Something's up. Don't tell me. You aced the tax test on Friday."

"How would I know that? I haven't been to class yet."

"You took Guidry hostage yesterday and threatened all sorts of vile means of torture until he changed your paper topic."

"As appealing as that sounds, no. But I have got quite a way with a vegetable peeler. Maybe I'll pay him a visit tonight."

"Well, something happened, because you look . . . different." He gave her a once-over. "Did you change your hair?"

She fingered her usual ponytail and shook her head. "I washed it, but I do that every morning."

"You're wearing makeup."

"Yesterday's remains. I woke up late again."

He shook his head and studied her. "I don't know what it is, but you look . . . I don't know." He shook his head. "Content. Happy."

Sexy. The deep, seductive voice whispered through her head.

Veronica Parrish? Sexy?

Well, things had taken a turn for the bizarre. She had a haunted bed. A Casanova of a ghost. Madame X was on the job, as far as Guidry's paper was concerned. Anything was possible.

She smiled. "Actually I feel sort of happy." She drank in a deep breath. "It's a beautiful morning, don't you think?" She stepped onto the sidewalk and started down the street.

"Uh, yeah." Danny followed her. "It's great if you go for that sort of thing." He stifled a yawn. "I'm more of a night person myself."

"Wanda keep you up late?"

"In more ways than one."

She laughed and hooked her arm through his. "Why don't you just tell her how you feel?"

"It's not that easy."

She yanked his arm and brought him to a halt.

"What are you doing?" he asked as she brought him around to face her.

"A little experiment. Now close your eyes." At his stubborn expression, she added. "Trust me, all right?"

His eyelids drifted shut. "Now what?"

"Now think of your favorite fantasy."

"*What?*"

"I know it sounds hokey, but do it anyway." She studied his face. "And nothing that involves a job with some big engineering company." His eyes snapped open and she grinned. "I know because my fantasies usually run along the same line. I'm talking lustful fantasies."

Danny did as instructed and Ronnie watched as pleasure chased disbelief across his features.

"Have you got one in mind?" He nodded.

"Now take a deep, deep breath and tell me what you smell." He smiled. "Wanda."

"If this is going to work, you have to be a little more specific. You have to really be in the moment, tuned in to *everything*. Now take a deep breath and give me details."

His nostrils flared. "Peach-scented body wash. Peach shampoo. She likes peaches."

"Good. Now what do you feel?"

He grinned. "Wanda." The expression faded as he seemed to search for more. "The heat of her body because she's so close, sitting next to me. The soft silk of her hair on my bare arm as she leans forward to look at the textbook."

"Your favorite fantasy is of the two of you studying? Geez, Danny, you've got to get a little more creative."

"Hey." He frowned. "It's my fantasy, all right? Besides, we move on to more than studying. That's just how it starts."

"Okay, okay. I'm sorry. Don't lose the image." She studied his face to make sure his eyes were still closed before rummaging in her book bag. "The two of you are studying, you smell her, feel her . . ." Her voice lowered a notch as she found what she was looking for and asked him, "Now tell me, what do you want?"

"Wanda," he said, the name little more than a throaty growl.

Ronnie held up the compact mirror and said, "Okay. Now open your eyes."

He did, and stared at his reflection, at the desire gleaming hot and bright in his eyes.

"It *is* that easy," she told him. "You're just as desirable as the next guy. I see it and I guarantee she'll see it. Just tell her."

"Easy," Danny told himself as he paced in front of the campus pizza parlor and tried to work up his nerve to go inside, where Wanda Deluca sat having lunch with several other cheerleaders and a couple of football jocks. His hand went to the doorknob and he faltered.

He really should wait until after lunch. Bothering somebody right in the middle of eating could disrupt their digestion and cause heartburn. He'd hate to cause her any discomfort. Besides, she was busy with her friends—

Balls, Boudreaux. You've got 'em, don't you? So get on in there and use 'em.

He closed his eyes, summoning the fantasy, the smell and feel and heat of the moment. "Easy," he reminded himself as he summoned his courage and yanked open the swinging door.

"Wanda," he said when he reached her table.

Green eyes shifted to meet his. Long blonde hair brushed the shoulders of her white USL T-shirt. Peach-tinted lips parted in a smile and his confidence level shifted a notch higher.

"Hi, Danny. I was just thinking about you."

"You were?"

"Mel Gibson's on *Letterman* tonight, so I have to see the entire show. I should be done by midnight. Then I can come over."

Oh.

He became acutely aware of a dozen interested eyes zeroed in on him.

"That's all right, isn't it?" she asked.

No. "Yeah, sure." He shifted from one foot to the other. "Listen, could I talk to you for a sec?"

"Sure." She excused herself and followed him to the rear of the place, by the jukebox, two video games, and the pay phone.

"Listen, Wanda." He leaned one elbow on a video game, his body effectively blocking her escape. "I need to tell you something."

"Yes?"

"You, see, I . . . That is, I want . . ." His mouth went suddenly dry as her scent filled his nostrils. She was so close, inches away as she leaned in to hear what he had to say. Peaches assaulted his senses and his nostrils flared.

"Yes?" she prompted, drawing him back from a sudden, sharp image of her naked, rubbing a wedge of peach over her pale skin.

"Well," he cleared his suddenly dry throat. "I, um, want you . . ."

"You want me . . . ?" she prompted, eyes wide, expectant.

"I want you . . ." Naked and panting. Over me, under me, surrounding me.

A bead of sweat slid from his temple and he quickly dashed it away.

"I, uh, want you . . ." *Just say it.* "To pass," he blurted. "I—I really want you to pass tomorrow's chem test."

Loser!

"Thanks, Danny." Her smile widened and his gaze hooked on her mouth, on the fullness of her lips.

Man-o-man, she had the greatest lips. Another image straight out of one of his more graphic fantasies pushed into his head, of those full lips sucking at a ripe peach. His blood rushed faster, his heart pounded forward like a runaway train.

"You know, nobody's ever cared about my grades before," she went on, the sudden softness to her voice dispelling the erotic image. "All my mama ever cared about was whether or not I had on enough eye makeup. You never know when you'll meet Mr. Right, she always said. Gotta look your best." At his questioning gaze, she added, "My mom did some modeling when she was young and sort of fell into the habit of relying on her looks to get her what she wanted out of life. First a job in Paris. Then my dad. Then three other husbands, all since moved on to prettier, younger women. But I guess you don't need to hear all this."

"No, I want to."

"Hey, Wanda!" The shout came from a redhead sitting at the table. "We're heading out. You coming?"

"If you haven't eaten, maybe we could get a bite togeth—" he started, clamping his mouth together when she shouted out, "I'll be there in a sec!" to the redhead.

Her gaze went back to Danny. "I'm sorry. What did you say?"

You. Me. Now. Together.

He couldn't quite spit the words out. "That I really need to eat."

"Try the pepperoni," she advised. "And thanks for caring. I'll see you tonight. Oh, and don't forget that I'll be late. I can't miss Mel."

"Yeah, see ya."

"Is there anything else?" she asked when he made no move to let her pass.

"Uh, no," he stammered out. "I guess that about covers it. Um, it's awful hot out. Make sure you drink plenty of liquids during practice so you don't dehydrate."

"You're sweet, Danny."

Sweet? Man-o-man, he'd sunk even lower than pathetic. *Sweet.* That was the kiss of death, coming from a hot babe.

Dehydrate? What the hell was wrong with him? He had the attention—both eyes, he might add—of a beautiful woman, *the* beautiful woman, and all he could manage was a piece of his grandma's advice?

No wonder Wanda thought he was sweet. He *was* sweet— too sweet to tell her what was really on his mind, to drag her into his arms and kiss the daylights out of her, for fear she'd reject him. Or worse, pity him.

Then settle for sweet.

Like hell. He was going to make a move. Soon. He just had to think of one, to work up his nerve and come up with a sure-fire method of wooing Wanda.

He was a smart guy. A sweet, smart guy, true, but he had brains nonetheless. If man could send another man to the moon, then anything was possible. Including Wanda Deluca falling into Danny Boudreaux's bed.

He just had to come up with a plan. A strategy. One that didn't involve him losing his ability to speak at the sight of her green eyes, or peach-slick lips, or that body. . . .

Okay, maybe he needed more than a plan. Shock treatment. A heavy dose of nerve pills. A bucket of ice water.

Maybe all three.

Chapter Eight

"Tracing your family tree?" Delta asked as she walked by the main circulation desk shortly before closing time and saw Ronnie checking out a stack of genealogy books.

"Helping out a friend. He's trying to find out about his great-great-great-grandmother, so I thought I'd do a little research on the subject."

In the interest of her own grades, of course. No way did she feel the sudden need to sit up all night with a load of genealogy books just because she'd read the desperation in Val's gaze. Okay, so maybe the desperation was a teeny, tiny part of it. But helping Val also qualified as helping herself.

"Ronnie, sugar." Delta gave her a nudge, startling her out of her thoughts. "Check out those two."

Ronnie shifted her attention to the two attractive men who'd walked in the door. They wore Dockers and white button-down shirts and she knew they were business majors. Handsome business majors, but brunets.

So? Brunets were hot. Her first boyfriend in the third grade had been a brunet; her fiancé, Raymond, had had the blackest hair she'd ever seen—one of his few redeeming qualities; and she adored a host of movie stars, all brunets.

Brunets were her thing—up until a few days ago when she'd set eyes on Val and his mane of hair in all its long, whiskey-colored glory.

Her attention shifted to one of the men, still a brunet but his hair was lighter, with pale gold streaks from the sun. Mmm, now here was a cutie. Strong hands grasped a book bag as he made his way to the row of computer terminals.

"I don't think they're ready to check out yet."

"No, I meant *check* them out. Cute, huh? Especially the tall one."

When Ronnie turned a grin on the older woman, Delta shrugged. "There might be enough snow on the roof to warrant a snowplow, sugar, but there's still a fire blazing in the cookstove. While I might be old enough to be their mother—" At Ronnie's raised eyebrow, she added, "Make that their grandmother, I can still appreciate the scenery."

"What about Professor Gibbons?" She indicated the seventy-something-year-old man perched in his usual corner in the magazine section reading an issue of *Creole Cuisine*. With a shock of snow-white hair on his head and a matching beard, he looked more like Santa Claus than a retired political science professor. He wore his usual white dress shirt and slacks, with bright red suspenders and a matching bow tie. "He's awful cute, if you ask me."

"You want me to stare at an ancient, dried-up, old cypress when I can eye a couple of healthy, sturdy oak trees?"

"He likes you."

"I've known Cassius Gibbons for twenty years—he headed his department here up until he retired—and the only thing he likes are those food magazines he's always looking at. I swear, the man should have been a cook instead of a political science teacher."

"So take him up on his dinner invitation. He did offer to cook for you, right?"

"He's old."

"He's cute." Since Delta's husband had died three years ago, the woman had realized her own mortality, and she'd waged war on it. No more birthdays, she'd told Ronnie. She simply wasn't getting a day older or a minute closer to kicking the bucket.

It was a great theory. The trouble with theories, though, was that they didn't always prove true when put to the test.

Speaking of tests . . . While she might not intend to get intimate with anyone other than her stubborn houseguest, Madame X really did need to put Val's theories, at least the nonphysical ones, to the test.

Now was as good a time as any, she told herself as the tall cutie approached the circulation desk. Here was a guy who could get most any girl. The type of guy who never gave average-looking Ronnie a second glance.

Not that she cared. She much preferred it that way.

Usually. But this was in the interest of science.

She closed her eyes and summoned her dream. The sweet scent of leather and apples and that unnameable something filled her nostrils. Cool sheets slithered down her legs. A warm mouth touched her throat and slid lower, to her throbbing nipple. . . .

Ronnie licked her lips and opened her eyes, and stared at the tall man with the sun-kissed brown hair. As if he sensed her gaze, his head snapped up. His eyes met hers and he smiled.

A full-blown, I'd-like-to-get-together smile.

Ronnie did the only thing she could think of at that moment. She gave a loud whoop, hugged Delta, grabbed her backpack, and started for home to tell Val the good news.

"It worked! It really worked!" Her excited voice bounced off the walls of the apartment when she walked in just minutes before midnight.

"What worked?"

"The internally attractive thing. I saw a megacute guy, closed my eyes, pictured the dream and how I felt in it, then *bam.* I looked at him, just *looked* at him, and he smiled at me."

His eyes narrowed. *"What guy?"*

"Somebody I picked out for an experiment."

"How cute?"

"Really cute, but that's beside the point. It worked." She

whipped out her notebook. "I have to write this down. Madame X nabs her first victim."

"Madame X?"

"The woman I'm profiling for the paper. I'm going to do a journal of Madame X's Fifty Steps to Ultimate Sexual Fulfillment."

"Who is this Madame X?"

"Me—a fictitious me." Madame X might be on the prowl for available men; Ronnie, however, wanted only an available ghost.

A very angry looking ghost.

"What's wrong with you?"

"You were out looking at men."

"Just one man, and so what? You told me to experiment."

"Of course I did, but I didn't mean . . . Merde, I didn't mean for you to rush right out and stare at the first man you came across." The air charged with tension as his voice rumbled in her ears. "This simply will not do. You must exercise more caution."

"If I didn't know better, I'd say you're jealous."

He speared her with a glare. "Moi? Do not be ridiculous." He said the words, but his expression didn't ease. If anything, he looked fiercer. "I simply do not want you giving encouragement to some poor simpleton whom you are not the least bit interested in. You must be more careful. What if some man were to become infatuated with you? A man you had no real interest in? I will not have you put in danger while under my tutelage."

"Danger?"

"Have you not seen Fatal Attraction?" He shook his head. "Bon Dieu, it can be disastrous to attract the wrong person's interest, not to mention a man will be inclined to think you are simply out looking for a good time."

She grinned. "'Looking for a good time'?"

"On the prowl. Hungry for a man. Walking the walk, talking the talk."

"I know what it means. But how do you know what it means?

I don't think the phrase was coined back in the nineteenth century. Come to think of it, *Fatal Attraction* wasn't around back then either."

His expression eased as he explained, "*I watch a great deal of television. It has been my one link to the outside world. When I was stuck in that stuffy old museum, the night security guard used to bring his television to work. It is a wonderful invention. A godsend.*"

"Yeah," She motioned to the TV screen. "Half-naked babes dancing to rock music videos. I'm sure the good Lord had plenty to do with that. And cable. I bet he's getting a great big commission on cable."

"*I realize that television can be exploitive, but it is also very empowering. In my time, few women would have been allowed to bare their bodies in such a way, and those who did would have been instantly dubbed whores. But now . . . There is such freedom. If a woman wants to show her body, she can without being looked down upon.*"

"Most men I know," Ronnie said, "at least those traditionalists back in Covenant, think that's why society is going to hell in a handbasket."

"*I am not most men.*"

He wasn't a man at all, but for a brief moment, Ronnie forgot that. She saw only him, smelted only him, felt only him, and he felt so . . . real.

"You're from the past, but you're not stuck in the past," she said, marveling that a man from yesteryear could be so up with the times. "You see women as people, not as the inferior sex."

"*Inferior? Pas du tout. Women are by far the superior sex. I admire them.*"

She thought of the love letters, and admiration gave way to a prickling heat she could neither soothe nor explain. "Now that's a new word for it."

He grinned. "*It sounds like you are the one who is jealous now.*"

"*Moi?*" She copied his look of outrage, then shrugged. "It's just hard to imagine you being with so many women."

"*I wasn't with them all at the same time, chérie. Except for that one time with a set of triplets . . .*" He caught the pillow she tossed at him and gave her a full-blown smile.

White teeth flashed, his lips curved just so, and his eyes danced with a blue fire that scorched her nerve endings and made her blood *zing* through her veins.

"So what's next?" she asked, eager to ignore the strange feelings stirring inside her. More than simple physical attraction. She was starting to *like* Val. His sense of humor, his teasing, his charm—

Lust, she told herself, plain and simple.

She forced her attention to learning the finer points of flirting with a man using her eyes, her body language. Val taught her how to accidentally brush her hand against a man's, how to lick her lips just enough to get his attention—small gestures that communicated *I want you.*

By the time they finished, she'd successfully mastered steps two through ten . . . and she definitely wanted him.

They stood facing each other, so close. A whisper away. She felt the heat rolling off his body, read the hunger in his dark gaze and it called to something deep, deep inside. A wantonness, a desperation.

She took a deep breath, gazed at him from beneath lowered lashes, and trailed her tongue across her bottom lip provocatively.

His eyes burned brighter, hotter, and the air charged around them. Score one for Madame X.

"How was that?" she managed, her voice suddenly breathless.

"*Perfect.*"

"Really?"

"*Unfortunately,*" he muttered, closing his eyes as if by blocking the sight of her, he could break the spell surrounding them. Ignore the want.

He was determined, she had to give him that.

"You had better document tonight's lesson." He turned away, but Madame X wasn't about to give up so easily.

She caught one of his hands. "We could keep going."

"No, we couldn't."

"Sure we could. We've got over an hour and I'm not the least bit tired and—"

"We're stopping." He tugged free of her grip. *"Now. Before I do something I'll regret."*

"But that's what I was hoping for."

He stared at her for a full moment before a grin tugged at his lips. *"You'll be the death of me."*

"You're already dead."

"Write."

"Yes, boss. Speaking of writing . . ." she began to say as she retrieved her pen. While Madame X might be far from satisfied, Ronnie wasn't about to push her luck and kill the smile on Val's face. She was starting to like his smiles almost as much as her dreams.

"I need more information if you want me to find out about Claire," she went on. She grabbed one of the genealogy books she'd brought home from the library and flipped to a page she'd previously marked. "This is a sample page of information needed to do a thorough search on someone. Fill out as much as you can."

Ronnie took a deep breath, forced her attention to her notebook, and concentrated on writing about Madame X learning the finer points of flirtation while Val pondered the questions in the book in front of him. More than once, she felt his gaze on her.

"What?" she finally asked when her nerves refused to settle down. "Is my hair messed up? My shirt on inside out? Do I have ink on my chin?"

"No."

"Then why are you staring?"

"I was merely thinking that you don't look like a virgin."

"I usually wear a shirt with a big red V, but it was dirty today." She'd meant to draw a smile out of him, but his serious expression didn't crack. "You've really got a hangup about this virgin business, don't you?"

"Claire was a virgin." His words were quiet, strained. "And the only daughter of the town minister. He was none too happy when he found out she was pregnant."

"I'll bet."

"He came after me." His gaze caught and held hers. "To see that I paid for that one night with his daughter." He shook his head. "If only I could remember."

"It's all right, Val." Her hand closed over his. Heat pulsed beneath her fingertips, his skin so warm and real.

A ghost, she reminded herself. Not a man.

"I need to know," he said.

"You will." She tried for a smile to lighten the suddenly tense mood. "We'll both come out of this with all the answers we need." And a few we didn't bargain for, a small part of her whispered. That same part that wanted to touch him again, not for education's sake, but for her own.

Which was all right, because she'd decided to blow off a little sexual steam and Val was the perfect one to do it with. If only he would cooperate.

A thought struck her. "For the record, how many women have you slept with? I counted one hundred and sixteen letters."

He stared at the hand she'd touched, flexed his fingers before shaking his head, as if to shake away the feeling. His fingers curled and he turned his attention to the genealogy book.

"Come on. Tell me," she pressed.

"Enough."

"Enough as in . . . one hundred and fifty? Two hundred? A thousand?"

"Enough not to answer that question."

Wrong thing to say to a woman who didn't take no for an

answer. "You're my tutor. How am I supposed to know whether or not you're qualified if you don't give me a full list of references?"

He stared pointedly at her. *"Do you really want to know, Veronique?"*

No. "Yes."

His mouth seemed to work at an answer before he shrugged. *"Three hundred and sixty-nine."* A bitter laugh burst past his lips. *"All for a worthy, if not futile, cause."*

"What do you mean?"

He shook his head. *"Nothing."*

The number echoed in her head. "Wow. I can't imagine knowing three hundred and sixty-nine men, much less having sex with them. How did you keep count? Notches carved into your bedpost? A sign-up sheet? What?"

"This." He tapped his temple. *"I kept count here."*

She cast a skeptical glance at him. "You mean to tell me you *remember* three hundred and sixty-nine women?"

He nodded.

"Names."

Another nod.

"Faces."

"Yes."

"And I've got some swampland in Arizona."

"I remember each and every woman, and there is plenty of swampland here in Louisiana. Why would you want swampland in Arizona?"

"Forget it. It's a figure of speech." She folded her arms, leaned back in the kitchen chair, and eyed him. "And if you've got such a great memory, prove it. Name ten women from your past."

He grinned. *"Is that all?"*

"I'm waiting."

"Okay, there was . . ." His mouth opened, and his grin faded as words seemed to fail him. *"Her name was . . ."*

"Come on. Spit it out," she prodded.

"*I know this.*" His forehead wrinkled as he seemed to search his memory.

She smiled. "You can't do it, can you?"

"*Of course I can.*" He glared at her. "*It's just a little difficult to concentrate with you sitting there half-naked like that.*"

She glanced down at the hem of her nightshirt, which reached all the way to her knees, the sleeves that ended at her wrists, the throat buttoned up to the top. "I'm fully clothed."

He slapped the book closed. "*It's practically see-through.*"

She fingered the red plaid material. "It's flannel. No one can see through flannel, not even Superman. It's worse than Kryptonite."

"*And much too clingy.*"

"But it's *flannel.*"

"*All of this yacking is pointless.*"

"*Yacking?*" She matched his glare. "Forged what I said about you being different. You just earned your male chauvinist merit badge."

He smiled at that, as if pleased that he'd displeased her.

Pleased to be fighting? *Men.* Who needs 'em?

You do, her hormones insisted, but Ronnie wasn't listening. She was writing, her energy focused on taking objective notes about the lesson that had just transpired rather than worrying over why Val ran hot one minute, cold the next.

The jerk.

A long while later, she finished up her notes and settled back to wait for him to finish his genealogy work. She tried to keep her eyes open, but she'd had such a long day and, despite the anger making her nerves pulse, exhaustion finally won out.

She wasn't aware of anything after her eyes closed, except the feel of strong, muscular arms sliding around her, lifting her. Then the mattress met her back and she snuggled into the sheets.

"*Sleep well,* Rouquin" followed her into the consuming darkness.

* * *

"It's all right." Her sweet voice echoed through Val's head and he remembered the feel of her hand. For those few moments, as she'd said the words, touched him, it *had* been all right.

Just a few words, the slight pressure of her fingers, and he'd felt a blessed moment's peace from the questions that had nagged him for a century and a half.

Madness!

He should feel anything but peace in her presence. A virgin. How easy it would be to repeat the tragic past and forfeit an eternity of peace.

Too easy, he thought, staring down at her as she slept. The conscious woman avoided direct eye contact and hid behind her ugly, baggy clothes, but asleep her defenses were down. She turned this way, arched that way, parted her lips enough to send a pulsing ache straight to his groin.

He wanted her. Despite who she was. Because of it.

No. He wouldn't take her to bed and doom his soul to an eternity of restless wandering, for that's what waited for him if he bedded Veronica Parrish before he'd answered the question that haunted his soul.

Val learned from his mistakes, and this time he was determined to find peace. Soon. If only his damned body didn't demand its own peace.

A piece of her.

Hell, all of her. Riding him, pulsing around him, drawing him deep, deep, deeper—

No!

Where the man was weak, the spirit would stand strong. He would simply combine a few lessons and get his tutoring over with as quickly as possible, and send sweet Veronica off to try out her newfound education on some unsuspecting man.

He would do it, despite how much the idea bothered him. Despite the all-important fact that for the first time in over a century and a half, Valentine Tremaine couldn't remember even one of the numerous women he'd bedded.

He knew only one name now. The name of the woman he wanted to bed. The first woman he'd ever met who was as intelligent as she was desirable, who could cut him to the quick with her tongue and turn around and melt him with a single, sympathetic glance.

The woman now sound asleep in his bed.

Norman watched as the lights clicked off in the second-floor apartment. He jotted down the time, popped his notebook into the glove compartment, and gunned the engine of the T-Bird. Damn, but the woman kept late hours, even for a student.

He stiffed a yawn and wiped at his tired eyes. The hours were killing him. His gaze strayed to the ax sitting on the seat next to him. Soon, he told himself. But first he had to keep this up a little while longer, until he knew every move Veronica Parrish made. Knowing her routine was the key to success, and Norman came from a long line of successful people. His mother was Cynthia Terribone, a city councilwoman, and his father was John Terribone, owner of the biggest crawfish restaurant in Acadiana.

He felt a pang of regret for what he was doing. No sane, responsible son of two well-respected community members should be racing around in the middle of the night, contemplating what he was contemplating. Hell, he'd thought it was crazy when the doc had first made the suggestion.

"You have to let your aggression out, Norman. Keeping your feelings, your anger and disappointment and jealousy, bottled up will only make your condition all the more serious. To heal, you must face the source of your problem."

Norman had chuckled, just the way he'd done when Norma Renee had suggested they visit the doc in the first place. After all, he didn't have a "problem." Not just no, but hell no.

He did have a problem. Admitting that was the first step in fixing it, or so the doc had said, and so after a few visits, Norman had come around and finally admitted it to himself. It had been the same with the aggression venting. The more he'd thought about it, the more he realized the doc might be on to something.

Just sitting out in his car with the ax helped him feel better. Thinking about what he was going to do with the ax . . . well, that actually made him smile. Not that Norman had ever been a violent person. Hey, he was opposed to the death penalty as much as the next God-fearing Republican.

But a guy had to do what a guy had to do, and this acting-out thing might be just what he needed to relieve his stress.

That's what it all boiled down to. Stress. No faulty wiring or missing parts. Doc had reassured him that on day one.

"Pick an object and act out your aggression." The picking had been the easy part after what had happened. It was the getting to the object that posed the biggest challenge.

Big, but not impossible. Where there was a will . . . , as the saying went, and Norman was determined. Desperate.

That's what his sort of problem did to a guy. It dug down deep in his bones and made him do things he wouldn't normally consider. Like stalking a woman, carrying an ax in his car, and planning some serious damage once he got close enough.

But a guy had to do what a guy had to do. . . .

"Like this?" Wanda finished the chemistry equation and turned hopeful eyes on Danny.

"You're getting pretty good at this."

"Thanks to you." She yawned. "I think I've had enough for one night."

"One more," he urged, stifling his own yawn. He needed sleep, despite his double dose of Excite and Energize that morning. But even more, he needed Wanda. "Just to be sure."

She blew out a deep breath and went to work on another equation. Her long blonde hair fell forward, brushing his arm, and he closed his eyes, relishing the soft feel.

He took a deep breath. The scent of peaches mingled with

her favorite perfume filled his nostrils. She chose that moment to brush her hair back from her face. Golden strands swept his skin, stroking, caressing. His chest tightened as he took another deep breath. And another.

An image slid into his mind. Wanda wearing nothing but a come-hither smile and all that long, golden hair.

With a determined look, she walks over to him, unfastens his jeans, and straddles the monstrous erection that bursts free. *Man-o-man.*

A sigh trembles from her lips as she slides down, down, *down* until he thinks he will die. She's so warm and wet—

"Did you say something?" Her soft voice pushed into his thoughts and his eyes popped open.

"I, uh, said I need to take my dog to the, um, vet. Yeah, the vet." *Real smooth, Slick.*

"I didn't know you had a dog."

"Uh, yeah and he's, um, really sick right now. Summer flu."

"Dogs get the flu?"

"Um, sure they do." Did they? Maybe. Probably. "I really should go. The doc's waiting." He unfolded himself from the chair, his book bag carefully concealing his lap.

"But it's after two in the morning."

"He's an all-night vet. Emergencies, you know. Well, see ya." He beat a fast exit from the dorm room before Wanda could notice that lies weren't the only thing he was spouting.

He was this close to exploding right there in his pants and showing her he had more, much more, on his mind than chemistry.

Would that be so bad? Maybe then you'd stop acting like a pimply faced teenager and tell the lady what you want.

But it went beyond what he wanted. Wanda was the one thing he needed, and the need clouded his usual cool, calm, 4.0 thinking. Made him ramble on about all-night vets and sent him straight home to an ice-cold shower and a restless night of hot, wet dreams.

Love sucked.

Literally, he thought when he woke from one dream, in particular, of Wanda doing more with her sweet, peachy lips than just smiling at him.

Fantasies. That's all they were, but fantasies were better than nothing, and that was what Danny knew he'd be left with if he bared his soul and laid out his feelings for Wanda.

She would laugh and tell him he was dreaming.

She would laugh some more and tell him he was pathetic.

Or worse, she would smile that beautiful smile and tell him she was sorry, she just didn't see him as anything more than a study buddy.

The big kiss-off.

No, the fantasies were better. No crash. No burn.

If only they were enough.

Chapter Nine

Between school and work, the next few days passed in a blur, as did most of Ronnie's weekdays. She caught a quick nap when she arrived home just after ten at night before spending midnight to three a.m. with Val, learning the ropes of the sexually active.

She'd put off trying any of her newly learned techniques on some unsuspecting someone, however. Not because of Val's *Fatal Attraction* warning, but because she was too tired and too busy, even more so since she was researching the life and times of Claire Wilbur for the resident ghost.

Her search started with several phone calls regarding certain documents that might help in her search. First she called the Clerk of Courts for the Lafayette area, only to find out she needed to call Vital Statistics in New Orleans, to find out she needed to contact the Louisiana State Archives in Baton Rouge. By Friday, she'd found out that the archives housed all birth and death certificates, marriage and divorce decrees, census reports, and other relevant records for Orleans Parish—present-day New Orleans and the surrounding area—from 1790 until the mid 1900s.

She could request a copy of Claire's birth certificate by mail and wait the required three to four weeks, or she could take a half day off from the library on Saturday, and drive over to Baton Rouge first thing in the morning.

Driving the two hours seemed the better plan, particularly since she didn't know what she might encounter. What if Claire didn't have a death certificate on record? What if it listed a surviving child? If Ronnie were there in person, she could research more information, depending on her findings.

Her mind made up, she finished her shift on Friday evening and collapsed into bed as soon as she walked into her apartment. As usual, Val woke her at midnight for their lesson.

"Not tonight." She buried her head beneath the pillow. "I have a headache."

"Then I shall mix you up some tea." He started for the kitchen.

"Make it coffee," she called after him. "Black, and I'll be running circles around you in a few minutes."

At the first taste of the thick, bitter brew, she grimaced. "It's horrible."

"Let me put some sugar in it."

"No, I need horrible." She held her nose and took a huge gulp of the god-awful stuff. Caffeine torpedoed to her brain and by the fourth cup, she could actually open her eyes without the room blurring. "Much better. So what's on the agenda tonight?"

"Tonight we move on to kissing."

Finally. She closed her eyes and puckered. "I'm ready."

"Not quite." He thrust a notebook and pen into her hands. *"Now you're ready, chérie."*

"I thought we were kissing."

"We're writing about kissing." He started to pace. *"Now, there are several types of kisses. The closed-mouth peck, the butterfly kiss, the nibbling kiss, the . . ."* He stopped pacing to stare at her. *"You're not writing this down."*

"Actually, I was hoping for a little demonstration." More like praying. Fervently, desperately praying. Her gaze hooked on his mouth, on the slightly prominent thrust of his bottom lip. He had great lips for a man. Sensuous lips. "I work better with actual hands-on, er, make that lips-on demonstrations."

The idea obviously didn't sit too well, because he seemed to think about it, then frowned and glared. He started to pace and dictate various kisses, hardly sparing her another glance.

Just her luck, she thought as she climbed into bed much later, after Val had faded and disappeared into whatever spot he occupied, leaving Ronnie with a major case of desperate hormones and only her dreams for company. A fat lot of good they did her. She kept having the same one, and no matter how pleasant, she was ready for more. For him.

Geez, she'd finally decided to indulge herself, only to find out her intended had a cast iron-resolve. A ghost with will power and a No Virgin policy.

And Val thought he had rotten luck?

Okay, so Val's luck was definitely worse than Ronnie's.

She admitted that as she stood in the basement of the Louisiana State Archives building in Baton Rouge and stared at the death certificate on the microfiche screen. After doing her research on Claire, she'd decided to look up a few records on Val. Namely, his death certificate.

Murdered. Val had been *murdered*.

She felt as if someone had landed a sucker punch to her gut.

A voice chimed in, reminding her that this had happened one hundred and fifty years ago. Practically ancient history. Everyone had to die sometime, and murder was an everyday occurrence. The newspapers were filled with it.

The fact did little to console her. This wasn't some unknown someone she'd read about in the newspaper. This was Val.

A ghost, she reassured herself. Just a ghost.

But one hundred and fifty years ago he'd been real. A living, breathing man. Until . . .

"Murdered. You were *murdered*." She walked into the apartment late that night, after eight hours of shelving books, and speared him with an accusing gaze.

He sat in her recliner, long legs stretched out in front of him, booted ankles crossed. He looked so handsome, so vital, so *real*. . . .

She shook away the disturbing thought and focused on the anger roiling inside her. "Why didn't you tell me?"

The television set flipped off as he shifted his attention from the screen to her. *"You never asked, chérie."*

She hadn't. From the moment Val had first appeared to her, she hadn't asked a thing about his past, about the man he'd been before . . . *before.* He'd started out as a dream, progressed to a ghost, and Ronnie had been determined to stop things there.

The more she knew of him, the more real he seemed.

The more distracting and all the more dangerous.

Don't ask, she told herself. *Just leave things alone, keep your mouth shut, and stick to your own problems. School, work, and the future.* "What happened?" Was that her sad, concerned voice? Geez, it was. Worse, it mirrored what she felt inside.

"Do you really want to know?"

"No, but I need to know."

He stared at her long and hard before unfolding from the chair and pacing to the French doors. The handle clicked, glass swung aside, and Val stared at the street below.

"It was a night just like this one. Clear. Hot. I was alone in my bed at Heaven's Gate."

"Heaven's Gate?"

"My plantation. At one time, it was the biggest in all of Louisiana. It's gone now, burned to the ground before the turn of the century. That bit of information was listed on the plaque naming my bed and its owner at the museum where I spent several years." He closed his eyes. *"It's been so long, but I still remember Heaven's Gate as if I'd just ridden across the grounds or sat down to dinner in the dining room. In my mind it's still so clear. So beautiful."*

"I'm sure it was."

A sad smile curved his lips. *"My father put his life's blood into that house. He came over from France in 1800, to make his fortune and keep my mother in the manner she was accustomed to. She was French royalty and she'd gone against her family, fled her* home, to marry my father. He'd been a scholar, from a titled family, highly educated, and financially secure, but a far cry from royalty. My maman made him feel like a king and so he wanted to build a castle, and he did. The main house was beautiful, with twenty bedrooms and a grand ballroom."

Ronnie closed her eyes, and in her mind she could picture what it might have looked like. Rich brocade drapes, marble fireplaces, intricate friezework.

"Heaven's Gate seemed so huge and empty after my parents passed on and my sisters married," he went on. "I became master of a thriving plantation. I grew tobacco aplenty, but that was the only thing these hands could cultivate." He shook his head as if trying to push away something better forgotten.

Ronnie couldn't say she blamed him. He'd been murdered in his bed, according to the death certificate. This bed. "Oh my God," she blurted out as the realization hit her. "I've been sleeping in a dead person's bed!" She rubbed her arms, eager to dispel a sudden feeling of complete paranoia.

Val flashed her a grin. "A ghost's bed, and no need to worry, I didn't bleed on the sheets. I fell to the floor. My hand was the only contact with the bed when Death claimed my body."

She blew out a deep breath and tried to calm her pounding heart. "That's comforting."

"For you, maybe, but I'm dead, remember?"

If only she could. The trouble was, Ronnie kept forgetting that all-important fact. She kept seeing a man standing on her balcony, his tall, powerful form framed by the open French doors. She heard a man's voice describing a hot, humid night long, long ago when he'd been awakened in the wee morning hours and ambushed by a group of angry citizens led by the town minister.

"So who actually shot you?"

"The preacher himself."

"The preacher murdered you?"

"He was a father before he was a preacher. I'd deflowered his *virginal daughter and left her with child, or so he and the rest of the town thought."*

"You never told me why they thought such a thing."

"She made the accusation. *She said we spent one night together, the night of the town's annual harvest festival. There was a grand ball at a nearby plantation, where I supposedly swept her off her feet and into bed.*" He shook his head. "*I remember the ballroom being stuffed with people. Women, in particular. I remember many faces, but not hers.*"

"And the great Valentine Tremaine never forgets a woman's face."

He nodded.

"Or a name," she added, reminding him of his memory lapse a few days before.

He cast her a sharp glare. "*Unless I am severely distracted by scantily clad redheads bent on seduction.*"

She fought to hide her smile while he drew a deep breath and turned to stare over the balcony railing. "*I danced a few dances, kissed a delicious-looking woman in the garden, but otherwise—*"

"No Claire?"

"*Not that I can recall.*"

"And no flannel-wearing redheads?"

"*Thankfully, no.*"

"Then it's safe to say your memory was probably intact," she said. "What happened after the ball?"

"*I remember settling down to play cards in the library with the usual group, a few nearby plantation heads, men I knew through business dealings. I won a few hands, tossed down several drinks, and the rest is a blur. I awoke the next morning in a rundown cabin on the edge of my plantation.*"

"Alone?"

"*With the exception of one hellacious headache and a distinct impression on the sheets next to me where a woman had been.*"

"How do you know it was a woman?"

He gave her a heated look. "*The scent, chérie. I know a woman's scent. But, alas, I did not know the identity of the woman, and there was no evidence that she'd been a virgin.*"

"Evidence?"

"*Blood.*"

"Oh." She blushed, despite the fact that it was the nineties and she was a modern woman. Val made her feel so naïve with his vast experience. Worse, he made her feel hot. Bothered. Turned on. And with nothing more than a glance.

She cleared her throat. "Maybe it wasn't her."

"*That's what I told the preacher when he demanded the truth. That there was a chance I'd done the deed, but also a chance I had not, and that I could not recall.*"

"And then?"

"*He shot me in my bed.*" He said the words so matter-of-factly, as if the past didn't mean a thing.

It didn't, not to her anyway. She cared only about the future. Her future. Her career.

That's what she told herself, but she couldn't help the ache that stirred in her chest at the sight of him, the rigid set to his shoulders, the sadness that haunted his expression.

"*So how did you find out about my untimely demise?*" he asked after a long silent moment.

"At the archives in Baton Rouge. I did some research on Claire, and while I was there, I looked up your death certificate."

Hope lit his eyes as his gaze met hers. "*Claire? Did you find anything?*"

"A birth certificate. Val, there *was* a child born to a Claire Wilbur eight months to the day after your death."

"*Mine?*"

Disappointment welled inside her. "I'm sorry. There was no father listed. Just the mother."

He bolted to his feet and started to pace. "But I need to know. Merde! I have to know. How can I rest with something like that hanging over my head? I cannot. I simply cannot!"

"There's nothing you can do to make amends, Val. It was a long time ago. You can't let the guilt eat you up this way."

"Guilt?" He turned an incredulous gaze on her. "Is that what you think this is about?"

"Isn't it?"

"Bon Dieu, non!" He smiled. "It's hope, Veronique. Hope."

"You mean you want this child to be yours?"

His smile faded into serious contemplation. "Make no mistake, I regret the circumstances surrounding the conception, but a child. My child." Sheer joy chased the sadness from his rugged features. "I could never regret such a wondrous miracle. Tell me, was it a boy or a girl?"

"A girl."

"A daughter?" He closed his eyes as if relishing the information. "A daughter."

"I was the only son," he went on. "The last hope to carry on my father's name, but I failed. Until Claire. Maybe Claire." He shook his head, stark desperation creeping across his features. "My spirit cannot rest until I know whether or not I did, indeed, sire a child. My child." He stared at her. "Then I can cross over and finally be at peace. Then and only then."

The idea should have thrilled her. Val was temporary. Here today, gone tomorrow. Safe. Instead, the notion of his leaving left a dull ache in the pit of her stomach.

Because of her project. She couldn't let him go until she'd finished her paper, and despite the fact that they'd reached step twenty with all the flirting techniques and the ten different kisses, they still weren't even halfway to the Ultimate Fifty, and she had practically zero experiments to support what she'd learned.

She needed Val. In more ways than one, she added when he

stared at her lips a fraction too long and she felt that funny tingling in the pit of her stomach. Anticipation. Excitement. Hunger. Full-blown, desperate, I-want-you-here-and-now hunger.

"*So what do we do now?*" he asked.

She took a long, deep breath and fought for control of her rebellious hormones. "It's possible there are local records that might list Claire and/or Emma."

"*Emma?*" He smiled, saying the name again as if testing it. "*Emma. That's nice.*"

"I'll drive over to Heaven's Gate and see what I can find out next week. I've got Saturday morning off."

His gaze met hers. "*Thank you, Veronique.*" The words, so quiet and desperate, tugged at something deep, deep inside her, beneath the lust and the raging hormones.

She fought the feeling back down. "Don't say that."

"*Why not?*"

"Because this arrangement is mutually beneficial. I help you, you help me. This is strictly a business arrangement."

No sympathy. No compassion. No real feelings for a real man—make that *ghost*.

Just a ghost. A here-today, gone-tomorrow, no-strings-attached ghost.

"So what's on the agenda for tonight, Professor Love?"

A wicked grin spread across his handsome face, and Ronnie's blood rushed in anticipation. "*Kissing,*" he declared.

"But I thought we did kissing last night."

"*Oui, but tonight's the demonstration.*"

"This isn't what I had in mind," she said ten minutes later when Danny knocked on her door and Val said, "*Time for the demonstration.*"

"So what's the emergency?" Danny asked when she let him in.

"Emergency?"

"The message on my answering machine said you had an

emergency and I should come right over. I figured you were sick. You sounded really . . . funny. Your voice was deeper."

"I'm going to get you for this," she muttered under her breath.

"What did you say?"

She cleared her throat and lowered her tone. "I—I said I think I'm coming down with a cold."

"So what's the desperate emergency?"

"I, uh, ordered a pizza and I didn't want to eat by myself."

He cast her a puzzled glance. "Pizza? That's the emergency?"

"And I—I thought I heard a noise."

"And you called me?" He cast a wary glance around him and lowered his voice. "I'm not really cut out for this stuff, Ron. You should have called the police."

"It's okay. It was just . . . um, Pringles. Yeah, I found Pringles lurking around, but I'd already called you, so I thought I'd treat you to pizza, a reward for dragging you away from home in the middle of the night." She glanced at the clock. Half past midnight. "Hey, shouldn't you be at your midnight study session with Wanda?"

"I was, but then I left because I was supposed to be on my way to the vet. My dog's got the flu."

"You don't have a dog."

"I know."

"And I didn't know dogs could get the flu."

"Neither does Wanda. Lucky for you; otherwise you'd be eating pizza by yourself." He headed straight for her refrigerator, pulled out a carton of orange juice, and gulped straight from the carton. When he noticed her frown, he added, "I'll buy you a new one," before taking another huge gulp. "Geez, it's hot in here—or is it just me?"

"It's definitely you." She smiled. "You still haven't told her how you feel about her, have you?"

"Would I be taking my nonexistent dog to the vet if I had?"

"You know, Danny, she just might surprise you. Maybe she likes you, too, and doesn't know how to tell you."

"Maybe, and maybe not, and the maybe not's a helluva lot more possible than the maybe. So when's the pizza coming?" He flipped on the TV and flopped down in the recliner.

"What are you waiting for?" Val's deep whisper echoed in Ronnie's ears and she whirled to find him standing behind her.

"Get out of here!"

"He can't see me. Only those who believe in me can see me," he reminded her.

She turned back to find Danny's questioning gaze fixed on her. "Did you say something?" he asked.

"Uh, I said let me get you a beer."

"I didn't know you stocked beer."

"I, um, don't, but if I did, I would certainly get you one."

He looked puzzled. "That's nice of you. I guess."

"You're stalling," Val said. *"Stop wasting time and kiss him."*

"I can't kiss Danny. I don't even like him. I mean, I like him, but I don't *like* him. He's practically family."

"All the better," he murmured.

Or maybe it was wishful hearing on her part. She glanced at him. Not a hint of emotion shone in his deep blue eyes. Certainly not jealousy.

"You don't have to like this man," he added. *"Just kiss him, Veronique. It's an experiment."*

"I thought you didn't want me doing any more experiments."

"Danny is safe. You said so yourself."

"That's why I can't. He's my friend. I'd definitely be violating the safety issue."

"You'd rather be forced to search for a perfect stranger?"

"Actually, I'd settle for one stubborn tutor."

"Against the rules, chérie. *Now remember what I told you, and simply kiss him."*

Ronnie stared at Val with uncertainty for a long second, and something dangerously close to longing welled inside her. Longing? He was a ghost, for heaven's sake, and if he wasn't going to give her a demonstration, she *would* go elsewhere. After all, this was her project. Her grade. Her future.

Tamping down her insecurities, she turned and approached Danny.

"Ronnie, you need some—" Danny started, his sentence cut short when Ronnie leaned in, so close his warm breath fanned her lips. He jerked back an inch. "What are you doing?"

"Come here." She pulled him to his feet until they were toe to toe. "Close your eyes, all right?"

"Why?"

"I need your help for an experiment. Now close them. Please. I promise it won't hurt." At least, she didn't think it would. But since she hadn't kissed anyone since her fiancé, Raymond, and then it hadn't been half as detailed as what Val had described last night, she wasn't so sure.

He shrugged and his eyelids drifted closed. "Are you going to make me imagine another fantasy? Because if you are, I've got a really good one."

Ronnie took a deep breath and wet her lips. For all her determination, she hesitated. She was about to kiss a man—really kiss one for the very first time. Forget the pecks to her father's cheek, the chaste I'll-wait-till-we-get-married kisses Raymond had given her. This was the real thing.

"Stop stalling." Val's deep voice whispered through her head. She felt him next to her, surrounding her, it seemed, his lips a trembling vibration against her temple. *"Lean forward, open your mouth just as I described, and do what I told you."*

"Okay," she snapped. "Just hold your horses." I can do this, she told herself. I can, I can, I *can.*

"You can," Val assured her, then launched into a very descriptive explanation of everything he would do to her, if circumstances had been different. If he were a real man without a No Virgin policy.

"*Now kiss him,*" Val instructed.

She nodded, needing to kiss, to touch, after the enticing things Professor Love had murmured in her ear. This was in the interest of science, after all.

"*Now,*" he growled.

"Now," she said.

"Okay," Danny said. "The fantasy goes like this. We're in Wanda's room for this fantasy, just like before, and we're studying . . ."

Danny's vivid description of his latest erotic wish faded as Ronnie cracked one eye at Val to make sure he wasn't watching. This was embarrassing enough without an audience.

Her gaze collided with his. He stared at her, a strange look on his handsome face, and something shifted inside her. She felt the ache in her middle, the sizzle of blood through her veins, the anticipation. But none of it was directed at her kiss with Danny. She felt the strange emotions for Val.

". . . so she leans forward," Danny, went on, "and I feel the slow glide of silk on my arm—her hair. Man-o-man, it's soft."

Ronnie ignored the desperate urge to turn and lay one on Val, fixing her attention instead on Danny and leaning in.

". . . I've never felt anything so soft—"

Her lips touched his.

"What the . . . ?" He gasped and started to pull away, but she caught his face, holding his smooth cheeks beneath her hands, determined more than ever to do this. An experiment.

Danny tried to push her away. His fingers circled her wrists tightly, and then something happened. He stiffened, as if he meant to thrust her away, but then muscles relaxed, his grip loosened, and his lips parted.

And then he was the one doing the kissing.

His passionate response shocked her at first, then lulled her, his lips nibbling, coaxing, his hands trailing down her back, grazing the bumps of her spine and sending shivering tingles through her body.

Her tongue darted out, tangled with his in the slow thrust and glide Val had taught her. . . . *Val*.

She saw him in her mind's eye, felt his lips on hers, his hands touching her, pulling her close, closer . . .

But it was Danny's face she saw when she finally came up for air, her chest heaving, lips tingling.

He looked stunned, unmoving, blue eyes glazed. Shocked.

"Danny, I, um, sorry. I had to—" Wait a second. Blue?

She fixed her own eyes, but he'd already snapped his shut.

When they opened and focused, they were the same old brown they always were. As if they'd be anything else.

Blue. Wishful, diluted, desperate thinking.

Danny shook his head. "What just happened?"

"A kiss . . ." She'd *kissed* Danny. But that wasn't the problem. She'd liked kissing Danny. She'd loved it. Her head was spinning, her toes curling, her insides fumbling over one another. *That* was the problem.

"You have to go."

"But we were just getting to the part where I kiss her—"

"Go!" She steered him around and shoved him toward the door.

"What's wrong?"

"It's late and we both need to get to sleep."

"But I'm wide awake. I feel the best I've felt in a heck of a long time—"

"See ya." She slammed the door in his face, leaned back against the cool wood, and tried to slow her pounding heart.

And all because of one kiss. With Danny. *Danny*.

"I . . . it worked," she blurted when her eyes snapped open to find Val standing near the French doors, staring at her. "Your technique, um, was right on target." On target? Hell, she'd just shot a bull's-eye at a hundred paces. One more surefire step to add to her precious fifty.

So why wasn't she happy?

She was too busy being confused. Floored. Completely and totally baffled.

"*It worked, all right,*" Val grumbled, sounding about as pleased as she felt. Twin blue pools of liquid heat scorched her and her stomach went hollow. "*Too well, from the looks of things.*"

Guilt shot through her and she looked away. Guilt? Because she'd kissed Danny? Because she'd done it in front of Val? No, because she'd liked it in front of Val, the man of her dreams.

But he wasn't a man. He was a ghost, and he was fading right in front of her eyes even though it was barely two a.m.

"Val, something's wrong. You're fading."

"*I'm tired.*"

"But I thought you had enough spirit juice to keep going until three a.m."

"*Not tonight,*" he snapped. "*I'm retiring early. Sweet dreams.*" Before Ronnie could blink, Val faded completely, leaving her to wonder what had just happened.

Why Val had conked out before his time was up.

Why she was still buzzing from kissing *Danny*, of all people.

And why, oh why, she wanted to do it again. And again. And again.

Val tingled. From his head down to his transparent toes.

Which wasn't the problem in itself. A certain amount of tingling was to be expected after he'd concentrated so much energy and slipped inside Danny for those few moments of possession. Tingling, mind you. But Val was vibrating. Humming.

And all because of one kiss.

Her kiss.

He watched her move about the apartment. She picked up books, hung up stray clothes. She was upset, because no way would his Veronique willingly clean up when she should be climbing into bed to sleep. She didn't have time for cleaning, which was why he did it for her. To see that grateful look on her face, that small smile when she walked in and saw everything in its place.

She was upset, darting about the room grabbing at things, her gaze straying every once in a while, as if she expected to find him watching her.

Hell, he was, but she couldn't see him now, not when his spirit was so weak after the possession.

So shaken after the kiss.

She finally finished up and went into the bathroom. The door thudded behind her, and Val closed his eyes, thankful she'd taken the sweet, tempting scent of strawberries and cream with her.

He'd never had a fascination with strawberries. Never preferred the ripe scent. Until now.

Until her.

She'd tasted even better than she smelled, so rich and intoxicating, like a rich brandy that slid down a man's throat real slow and lazylike, seducing senses and making him crave more.

And he wanted more. More of her soft lips on his, nibbling, stroking, giving as good as they took, just as he'd taught her.

There was something inside her, an inborn passion that couldn't be learned or taught. He recognized it. It called to that same nature inside himself like a siren's song he couldn't resist or deny.

A damned *virgin*.

Hell, he concluded. He was stuck in bloody, fire-and-brimstone, torturous *hell*. He'd stayed in this life far too long, and now the Powers That Be were pulling him back over, tempting him the way they had the first time. When he'd been a man and he'd faced the same situation. He'd given in. Maybe. Probably.

Guilty or not, he'd paid the price. No one had given a damn whether or not he'd done the deed. They'd wanted justice, and they'd dealt out their own with the pull of a trigger, and Val had paid for his mistake with his life.

Veronique walked out of the bathroom at that moment,

wearing a long nightgown buttoned up to the throat. An innocent's nightgown. But as concealing as the white cloth might be, it didn't hide the dark shadow of her nipples, the enticing swell of her hips, and it didn't come anywhere close to covering her mouth. Full, sensuous lips made for kissing and other pleasurable activities.

She cast another searching glance around the room, climbed into bed, and curled beneath the blankets. Val simply sat nearby and watched her and for a few blissful moments, that was enough. Just to know she was there, nearby, and he had the pleasure of drinking his fill with his eyes, contented him and he felt a moment's reprieve from the lust gripping his soul.

That is, until her breathing grew deep and even and her clenched fingers abandoned the edge of the sheet. Relaxed in sleep, she rolled onto her back, her arms thrown over her head, her lips parted. A soft smile curved her mouth and he knew she dreamt of him.

She touched her nipple through the fabric, her fingertips working at the delicate tip until a soft, mewling sound crawled up her throat.

Lust speared through him. Powerful. Consuming. And he couldn't help himself. He inched closer to her and reached out to stroke her nipple himself. One touch and he could sate the desire scrambling his control. Just . . . one . . . touch . . .

His fingers stalled midway and curled into a fist.

Mon Dieu, hadn't he learned anything from that bullet?

Chapter Ten

This was not the film for Ronnie to be watching this early in the morning, not after the night she'd had.

". . . notice the heightened skin color as the stimulation increases . . ."

She'd had the dream again. The same exciting, infuriating dream that had haunted her as diligently as the ghost himself.

Her skin prickled as she remembered the slow glide of Val's hands on her body, skimming away clothing until she lay naked and panting and wanting. So much. Too much. But then, he was just a ghost, and it was just a dream.

Her nipples pebbled in memory of his fierce suckling, the playful nips of his teeth, his rasping tongue.

That's when last night's dream had taken a sharp detour from the orgasmic fantasy she'd come to expect and anticipate. Val had abandoned her nipple to lap at her skin, his tongue licking a sensual path *up* rather than down.

To her mouth.

He'd kissed her then, the taste of whiskey and warmth intoxicating her more than a dozen of her Aunt Mabel's rum balls. Her heart had revved like a race car at the starting line. His warm, rich scent had filled her nostrils. His muscles had tightened, rippling and flexing beneath her clinging hands. His hair-dusted chest had grazed her bare breasts.

Then she'd opened her eyes and seen . . . *Danny.*

Danny?

In the dream, she'd felt Val, but she'd seen Danny.

Okay, so last night had turned into more of a nightmare. An erotic, intensely arousing nightmare.

Now if she could just wake up.

". . . the increase in blood flow causes the preorgasmic flush . . ."

She tried to concentrate on taking notes. Calm, cool, indifferent notes about the various stages—countdown, as one of her classmates had dubbed it—that a woman's body goes through as it prepares for blast-off.

". . . breaths come more rapidly, more shallow, as excitement increases, accompanied by a feeling of lightheadedness, shivering . . ."

You ain't just whistling Dixie. Her pen shook from her trembling grip and she tightened her fingers.

Concentrate!

". . . the heart accelerates, pumping blood to the highly sensitive tissues, making them swell and blossom . . ."

And how, she thought as she shifted in her seat, fighting for a more comfortable position.

It's just a *film* and last night was . . .

What the hell was last night? The dream had been just a dream, but what about the part before that? The kiss where she'd felt Val, yet kissed Danny?

"There you have it," Guidry finally declared, flipping on the light switch and saving Ronnie from her disconcerting thoughts. "The levels leading up to sexual climax for the female. I hope everyone made adequate notes."

She took a deep breath and tried to calm her pounding heart and overly sensitized tissues. She wasn't sure about notes, but she'd just gleaned some firsthand knowledge. *Five, four, three, two . . . Houston, we have a problem.*

She drank in another deep draft of air that finally succeeded in calming her down. Geez, it was bad enough to get so excited over a dream, but to actually . . . to blast off . . . right here in the classroom . . . She might be a little sexually deprived, but she hadn't sunk that low.

Yet.

"We will have a quiz the next class period," Guidry went on in his boring, no-nonsense voice, despite the flushed faces of some of the females—stimulation level two, for the record—and decidedly stiff movements of the men—Ronnie wasn't sure about the level, since they hadn't reviewed male response. At least Ronnie wasn't the only person affected by the subject matter.

"The quiz will be followed by a film depicting the stimulation levels for the male."

"My kind of film," the woman next to Ronnie declared as she slapped her notebook closed and started packing away her things.

Guidry, who'd been busy working the projector, turned. His hard black gaze zeroed in on the woman. "Did you say something, Miss Wright?"

"I, um . . ."

"Do speak up." He waved his arms in a motion for her to continue. "And enlighten us all."

"I said I, um, am really looking forward to the film."

"And why would that be?"

The woman grinned. "Well, I've always been particularly interested in male stimulation."

"Have you, now?" Her enthusiastic nod met with several chuckles and a glare from Guidry. "Then you'll be more than eager to write a twenty-page study on the male sexual organs during each level of stimulation."

The woman's mouth dropped open. "*Twenty* pages?"

"Due at the beginning of the next class, and if you choose to argue the point, I will give you a demerit for every word that comes out of your mouth. Ten demerits equals an F for the semester, need I remind you?" The woman shook her head and Guidry snapped, "Class dismissed."

"The guy has no heart," the woman grumbled as she gathered up her book bag, "and no sense of humor, and a stick shoved so far up his butt, it would take a specialist to surgically remove the damned thing."

"They don't call him Iron Ball for nothing," a guy wearing blue jean shorts and a Hawaiian print shirt offered. "Cheer up, honey." The guy winked. "At least the subject matter's interesting, and I'd personally be willing to help you study."

"I bet you would. . . ."

The banter faded as Ronnie grabbed her book bag and hightailed it to her next class, pausing to lose two quarters in a vending machine in her search for a diet soda. Finally, sitting in the ice-cold lecture hall without any visual reminders of last night, she managed to calm her body down completely. No pounding heart, no rushing adrenaline, no tingling skin. Now, her mind was a different matter altogether.

She couldn't stop thinking, replaying the kiss, the dream, the Val fantasy versus the Danny reality.

Danny? Could she really and truly have been turned on by her buddy? Her pal? The closest thing she had to a brother?

Uh-uh. No way. No how.

Love-starved. That's what Ronnie decided by the time she reached the library for her evening shift. She'd ignored her social life for so long that when she'd finally taken the time to kiss a guy, even Danny, she'd been knocked clear out of her socks.

Any guy would have had the same effect and, just to prove it, Ronnie intended to conduct a few quick experiments. In the interest of science—she needed to try out Val's kissing techniques and accumulate documentation for her paper—and her own sanity.

Now all she needed was a few single males between the ages of eighteen and thirty-five.

She grabbed a cart of returned law books and headed for the second floor, her gaze scanning the aisles. No hot prospects. Just a gray-haired gentleman she recognized as one of the math professors, two female students, and an entire group of sixth graders on a field trip.

Oh, well. She had over four hours until her shift ended.

Two long, futile hours later, she shoved the last book into

place, pushed her empty cart down the P aisle, and ran smack-dab into a prime specimen.

He was tall, with short dark hair and brown eyes, and no wedding ring, she quickly determined after a glance at his left hand. So far, so good. Dressed in jeans, an oxford shirt, and loafers, he was college preppy all the way and not a day over twenty-five. Probably a law student, judging by his taste in books. She'd definitely hit pay dirt.

"Just relax, man," he told his companion, a long-haired *Wayne's World* reject dressed in worn jeans and a T-shirt. "I'll only be a minute and then we'll head on over to the wet T-shirt contest at the Keg."

Wet T-shirt contest?

He quickly slipped from top-grade soil to the smelly stuff her grandmother used to put on her roses, but beggars couldn't be choosers. While Ronnie might be insulted at his choice of leisure activities, she wasn't going to marry him, or anyone for that matter. She was just going to kiss the guy.

"I have to get this book for my contracts class—Umph!" His words ended in a grunt as Ronnie's cart hit him in the midsection with a little more force than she'd meant.

Okay, so she'd meant it.

"I'm so sorry," she purred. "I hope I didn't hurt you." She bent down, picked up the book he'd dropped, and handed it back to him.

"I think I'll live—" His words broke off as she planted one squarely on his surprised lips. His surfer friend let loose a loud wolf call and Ronnie blushed from the top of her head to the tips of her toes, but she'd come too far to pull away before she'd proven her point.

"Wow," the guy blurted when she finally ended the kiss. "That was something."

Nothing was more like it. No tingling or toe-curling or goose bumps dancing down her spine. A big fat zero.

"If that was your way of saying I'm sorry," he told her, "I'm up for another apology."

"Uh, no, I—I was just testing a new brand of lip gloss for the, um, engineering department." She smiled. "Yeah, that's it. Engineering. Special project. It's strawberry-flavored, all-natural, long-lasting, guaranteed to take a licking and keep on ticking."

His gaze narrowed and zeroed in on her mouth. "It doesn't even look like you're wearing lip gloss."

"It's one of those ultrasheer things you're not supposed to see. Just taste. It's going to revolutionize the cosmetics business. Well, I've taken up enough of your time. Gotta go."

"Hey, don't you want to know what I think? If I'm part of the sample, shouldn't you ask me questions or something?"

"Questions? Oh, yeah. Sure. So, um, what did you think?"

He grinned and licked his lips. "I'm not sure. Try me again."

"I'll take that as an undecided." She whipped the cart around and hightailed it around the corner. Lip gloss testing? Geez, you're a genius on your feet, Ron.

"What's wrong with you?" Delta asked when Ronnie burst into the snack room much later, after three more attractive, single, twenty-something guys and an equal number of kisses. "Are you coming down with something?"

"No." She retrieved a diet soda from the minifridge and tried to drown her disappointment in a rush of caffeine. Two long gulps and her heart was still pounding, her mortification factor at its peak, and disappointment . . . well, she'd shot clear off the scale on that one.

Chocolate. She needed chocolate.

Her fingers dove back inside the fridge for a piece of the fudge cake Delta had brought yesterday. She sliced off a hunk and grabbed a fork. Her taste buds launched into the "Hallelujah Chorus" at the first bite, temporarily easing the awful truth.

She'd fallen for Danny's kiss. *Danny*, of all people.

She inhaled several more bites.

"You look flushed," Delta pointed out as she stabbed a bite of the delicious-smelling food on her plate. "You're not catching the flu, are you?"

"I wouldn't be that lucky." If she'd been sick, she could have blamed some nasty little bacteria for sapping her common sense. A fever-induced delusion. She touched her forehead. Lukewarm. "Someone Upstairs is definitely out to get me." She eyed Delta. "Did you ever think you knew how you felt about someone, only to discover that what you thought you felt isn't even close to what you really feel?" She shook her head. "Am I making any sense?"

"Actually," Delta said, eyeing the plate in front of her, "you're making perfect sense."

"I am?"

The woman nodded and indicated her plate. "Chicken Florentine, courtesy of Cassius Gibbons." She took a bite and frowned.

"That bad?"

The woman swallowed and sighed. "That good, honey. I always knew the old guy could cook, but knowing it and tasting it's a whole different thing."

Ronnie thought of Danny's kiss. A mind-blowing meeting of lips that had her completely baffled, troubled, and totally freaked out. She closed her eyes as she replayed her recent experiments. Four good-looking men, an equal number of kisses, and diddly in the aftermath department.

This was not happening to her.

She licked her fork clean of all traces of chocolate frosting and rummaged in her pocket for change for the vending machine. She needed another quick fix. A candy bar. A big one.

Three pennies and one quarter. She dove into her purse next and managed to unearth one more quarter from the no-man's-land at the bottom.

"I guess I'll have to return his plate," Delta's voice followed

Ronnie as she hurried off down the hallway, money in hand. "Old, irritating codger or not, he did go out of his way."

Ronnie arrived at the ancient-looking machine. An array of sugar delights stared back at her from rows of slots, each protected by a circular wire that rotated when the corresponding button was pressed. She fed her quarters into the slot, hit the button for a Hershey's chocolate bar, and waited. And waited. A quick glance and she realized the candy had stalled; the edge hung on by a fraction of wrapper hooked to the circular wire.

The lip gloss story replayed in her head, along with her experiments, the disappointing results. . . .

She pounded the machine with one fist, but the candy didn't budge. She shoved her shoulder up against the metal edge and threw her weight into a fierce shove. The machine trembled and the chocolate bar hung on for dear life.

"Hey, lady. If you're hungry, you can have the rest of my cookie."

Ronnie glanced over her shoulder at a small blonde girl, one of the sixth graders visiting the library on a field trip. The kid held up a half-eaten cookie, and reality slapped Ronnie in the face.

What was she doing manhandling a candy bar machine?

She slumped back against the glass and closed her eyes. Her father's voice echoed in her head.

"Men and women are different, Veronica. Men think with their heads and women think with their hearts. That's why men make better providers and women make better nurturers. That's why both should stick to their traditional roles."

Ronnie had never believed him. She'd argued and fought against his old-fashioned, chauvinistic views on women. Now here she was about to bust into a candy machine because she was desperate for a chocolate rush. To soothe her feelings. Her desperate, confused, depraved *feelings*.

Calling all brain cells! Report for duty ASAP!

She took several deep, calming breaths, ignored the urge to snatch the child's cookie—a double chocolate chip, by the looks of it—and forced herself to think. Calm, cool logic. That's what she needed right now.

So she'd felt a spark with Danny? Of course she had. Not only had she been deprived of a really good kiss for all this time, but she'd been so worked up from Val's lesson, stimulated by his detailed instructions, aroused by his close proximity, frustrated by his lack of participation. At that moment, with her nerves buzzing, her hormones crying, she could have kissed Pringles and she would have felt the same rush.

Okay, so maybe she wouldn't have felt it with Pringles. The point was, any man would have had the same effect at that particular moment.

And she knew exactly how to prove it.

"Hey, Ronnie." Danny glanced up from his physics book just as Ronnie strode across the student lounge in the basement of the science building. "What are you doing here? You haven't had a science course in three ye—" His words drowned as she grabbed him by the collar, jerked him to his feet, and kissed him full on the mouth.

Ronnie? *Kissing* him?

While her mouth was soft and sweet, and she certainly had a way with a kiss, he couldn't bring himself to kiss her back. This was Ronnie, of all people, and hers weren't the lips from his fantasies.

She pulled away just as he started to. Thankfully. Because he and Ronnie were pals. Buds. He'd hate to have to get rough with her.

A smile split her face. "Nothing. I knew it. It was just the moment."

"Ronnie, I'm not sure what this is about, but we're just friends. You know that, right?"

"Is that what you think? Thank God, because after last night,

I didn't know if you thought what I thought, which was a pretty irrational, stupid thing to think. I mean, it was just one kiss under unusual circumstances."

"Last night?"

"Yeah. The kiss."

"What kiss—?"

"Danny?" The soft voice came from behind him.

He jerked around to see Wanda standing in the lounge door-way, her arms overloaded with books, a startled expression on her face that told him she'd witnessed the kiss.

Startled, as in affected, as in maybe, just maybe, finding an-other woman kissing him bothered her.

He wasn't sure why he didn't dismiss the thought. This was Wanda I-can-have-any-jock-I-want Deluca. Why would she care whether or not another woman kissed him? She wouldn't.

She did.

It was something in her eyes, a strange light that he'd never seen before, or maybe he'd just never noticed.

"I . . ." She licked her full, peach-tinted lips. "I didn't mean to catch you at a bad time. I thought since we didn't get a chance to meet last night—" she licked her lips again and heat shot straight to his jock "—you might quiz me a little while before my test."

"He's all yours." Ronnie started to turn away, but Danny grabbed her by the arm and swung her back around.

For the first time in his life, he didn't worry about what Wanda might think of him, good, bad, or not at all. He wanted to give her something to think about.

"Now, honey, don't get all mad," he said to Ronnie. "I told you, I'm sorry, but it's over."

She cast him a puzzled look. "What's over?"

"Us. You and me. *Over*." He gave Wanda a shrug. "I keep telling her to move on, but she can't seem to keep her hands off me."

"What are you talking . . . ?" Ronnie's words faded as Danny rolled his gaze toward Wanda and silently begged her to play along. Understanding lit her eyes. "Oh, *us*. You and me and the fact that I can't keep my hands off you even though I know it's over. *That's* what you're talking about."

"I never knew you two were going out," Wanda said.

"We weren't," Danny replied. "It was just sex."

His arm screamed as Ronnie took off a hunk of flesh with a discreet pinch that nearly made his knees buckle. He expected to see smoke blowing out of her ears, but instead she grinned up at him.

"Mind-blowing sex." She shivered. "I get chills just thinking about it. It's no wonder I'm lovesick. Sorry I disgraced myself again, Love Muffin, but I just can't stay away. You understand, don't you, Wanda? I mean, when a girl finds a man who has such strong hands and knows how to use them . . ." She shook her head and bit back a fake sob. "I can't even think about it, or I'm liable to burst into tears, and I've embarrassed myself enough for one day. I won't bother you again, Baby Cakes." Ronnie sighed dramatically, gave Danny one last look as if she were eyeing the last brownie before starting a fast. "Have a good life."

"So," Danny clapped his hands together once Ronnie had walked away with a big pretense of sighing and sobbing. He didn't miss the way Wanda stared at his hands. "About that quizzing . . ."

She shook her head, her gaze snapping to his. "What?"

"You wanted me to quiz you?"

"Oh, yeah." She handed him her book. "Kiss me. I mean, quiz me. Would you?"

"It would be my pleasure."

Ronnie felt much better.

So why didn't she *feel* better?

A faint pounding took up permanent residence in her temples for the rest of the day as she finished her classes and went back to the libary. She was standing in the middle of the L section when the shivering started.

"You are coming down with something," Delta said when she found Ronnie coughing in the back room, looking pale and drawn and ready to collapse. "I'll drive you home."

"No, I can walk," she insisted.

Big mistake.

She wasn't sure how she made it home, except that she had to stop twice because the ground tilted a little too much in certain spots and her vision failed her. She actually thought she saw Elvis on one particular street corner. Or maybe that was Hunk-a-hunk. Make that "Jailhouse Rock." No, "Heartbreak Hotel"—

Aw, who cares?

She stumbled into her apartment much, much later than usual. The throbbing did a furious Macarena against her temples and she was freezing despite the humid night air.

Val met her at the door. *"You're late—"* he started, then his gaze narrowed as he drank in her appearance. Worry lit his eyes. *"What's wrong?"*

"Nothing. I just need to sit down a few minutes."

Another thorough study and he frowned. *"I think you need to lie down."*

"I know what I need." She collapsed on a nearby chair. "I just need to sit here a few minutes, then I'll be fine."

He touched her forehead. *"You're sick."*

"I'm never sick. I don't have time to be sick. I have to study. I've got to read a chapter on tax credits and do our lesson and document today's experiments."

"What experiments?"

"Kissing experiments. I kissed four different subjects today." She blinked furiously against the haze infringing on her vision as she stared at Val. "Would you just stand still?"

"But I'm not moving—"

"Ronnie!" Danny's voice cut into Val's response. A loud

banging followed. "It's me. You'll never believe what just happened!"

Val speared her with a fierce look. *"Who did you kiss?"*

"Just a minute," she called out to Danny as she stumbled to the door.

"Who?" Val demanded, dogging her steps.

"It doesn't matter. I needed some evidence to support the lessons, and the technique worked perfectly, and I found out I wasn't nearly as affected by last night's kiss as I thought I was."

An expression dangerously close to pleasure crossed his handsome face. *"You were affected by last night's kiss?"*

"I thought I was, but I blew that theory out of the water, thank God." The last sentiment earned her a frown before she hauled open the door.

"Who were you talking to?" Danny asked.

She stared at the empty space where Val had been standing. "Um, that was the TV."

"The TV's off."

"Now, but it was on a few seconds ago. So what's your news?"

"It's about Wanda." His words stalled as his gaze swept her from head to toe. "Geez, Ron, you look awful."

"I feel even worse." She turned and plopped down on a kitchen chair. "So what's up?"

"Wanda's going out with me."

She grinned. "You really asked her out?"

He nodded. "I don't know how it happened. One second we were sitting there, and the next, it's coming out of my mouth. I wasn't even worried about her reaction, I just stared into her eyes and, bam, out it came."

"It's about time."

He grinned, before the expression faded into worry. "Look, about saying you and I were . . . you know. I just wanted to make her see me *that* way."

"Looks like it worked." She cleared her scratchy throat, which earned her a worried glance from Danny.

"You really look terrible."

"Delta sent me home early."

"Then I guess you didn't see this." He handed her a campus newspaper. "It's the evening issue."

She read the headline and her heart stalled.

KISSING BANDIT LOOSE IN DUPRÉ LIBRARY

"Four guys were attacked by this sex-crazed woman earlier today, during your shift. Did you see anything suspicious?"

"Sex-crazed? That's going overboard a bit, don't you think?"

"So you did see something?"

"N-no," she stammered, "I'm just saying these guys probably exaggerated." Her watery gaze scanned the column. "Listen to this . . . 'She wore a raincoat and flashed a complete frontal view before she pressed herself up against me, gyrated to some, silent beat, and kissed me.' Oh, please." She slapped the paper closed. "Give me a break." She didn't even own a raincoat. "In their dreams."

"What did you say?"

"I said, um, why didn't they scream? The library's full of people. If one of them had screamed, someone would have come to their rescue."

"They were too stunned, but the campus police are going to beef up security. If there's some crazed woman sneaking around, they'll find her." Danny flopped into a nearby chair and grabbed the remote.

"How comforting." The pounding in her temples increased and she leaned over to rest her head on her folded arms.

The television clicked on and *Jeopardy* blared in the background.

Pressing and gyrating. Right. First of all, none of the four had been nearly cute enough to inspire even a teensy bit of pressing, much less any gyrating. What a big load of overblown male bull . . .

Ronnie didn't realize she'd dozed off, until she felt strong hands at her neck, soothing, working magic as they rubbed and kneaded her sore muscles. Ah, Val.

Her eyes fluttered open and she half-turned to see Danny behind her. His gaze hooked with hers, intense and hot and deep, deep blue. . . . Blue? She snapped her eyes shut again. Danny did not have blue eyes, and Ronnie was sick. Feverish.

She relaxed. The hands soothed her aching muscles; she sighed and slipped deeper into a doze. Strong arms scooped her up, carried her to the bed, and tucked her in.

"*Sleep well*, Rouquin." The deep voice whispered through her head a second before sweet lips touched hers in a slow, lingering kiss that rocked her senses despite the fever.

Because of it, she reminded herself when her eyes opened and she saw Danny lean away from her and lick his lips.

Panic bolted through her, quickly swamped in a chill that gripped her body and forced her deeper into the covers. The fever, she told herself as she closed her eyes, her mouth still tingling from the kiss. Just the fever.

Chapter Eleven

Ronnie could have sworn it was Danny who tucked her into bed and kissed her goodnight. . . . Ugh, the kiss. It couldn't be. Not him. Not again.

It wasn't, she realized when she opened her eyes some time later and saw Val's concerned face.

Val.

No Danny. No brain scrambling. Just the imaginings of a wild fever.

Just *Val.*

He bathed her burning skin with a cool cloth, cradled her head, and urged her to drink. The smelly concoction burned down her throat and exploded a fireball in her stomach. The heat tempered to a pulsing warmth that swept through her body, gripped her nerves, and lulled her back to sleep.

Until she stirred again and he returned to repeat the process.

A dream.

The real thing, she realized when she finally opened her eyes and lifted her throbbing head.

He sat by her bedside, a bowl on the nightstand, a glass of some murky yellow mixture within arm's reach.

"What time is it?" she croaked.

"*Two a.m.*"

"Two?" She cast bleary eyes at the clock. She'd fallen asleep around one o'clock. "Geez, I feel like I've been sleeping forever—"

"*It's two a.m.—a full twenty-four hours later.*"

"*What?*" She bolted upright and wobbled.

Firm hands urged her back to the pillows. *"You're sick, Veronique. Lie down."*

"But my Friday classes—"

"You'll make them up." His fingers played across her cheek, strong yet gentle.

"But my professors. I never miss. They'll wonder—"

"I left a note on your door for your friend Danny and asked him to notify them of your absence."

"Danny?" She tried to draw his memory forth, but with Val so close, his warm scent filling her nostrils, his hands stroking down her bare arms, she couldn't think at all. Danny who?

"In the note, I also instructed him to call the CPA firm and the library. Now rest, chérie. You're sick."

"But," she sputtered. "But I can't be sick. I never get sick. I mean, I get colds and stuff, but nothing serious." She wiped at her teary eyes. "Nothing requiring bedrest."

"Complete bedrest."

She shook her head frantically. "I haven't been that sick since I had strep throat my senior year in high school."

"Then you've earned a rest. Now rest." He pushed her back into the pillows and she let him because her entire body was conspiring against her. Her eyes watered. Her head pounded. Her muscles cried. Her throat burned. Little match for her stubbornness.

She closed her eyes and tried not to panic. Okay, so she'd missed one day—a quiz and three lectures, three hours at the CPA firm and four hours at the library. It wasn't the end of the world. She could make up the quiz, borrow notes from classmates, double up at the library to compensate for missed wages, and she had sick days at the CPA firm, not that she'd ever used one—

"Drink," he said a moment before the glass touched her lips.

"Ugh," she sputtered as the sharp scent hit her. "It smells like burnt lemons."

"Don't smell it. Drink it."

She held her nose and swallowed several mouthfuls. "It tastes like burnt lemons," she said between choked coughs. "What was that?"

"*Something I mixed up. Guaranteed to cure what ails you.*"

A grin tugged at her lips despite her aching head. "Some nineteenth-century remedy from your past life?"

"*Actually, it's a twentieth-century liquid cold formula from your present life. I found the packet in the back of your medicine cabinet.*" He sniffed and wrinkled his nose. "*The remedies my grand-mère used to mix up smelled and tasted much better than this. Grand-mère Odile had a whiskey tonic that could cure a sore throat and put hair on your chest all in one sip.*"

"Just what I need—hair on my chest." She took another drink of the nasty cold remedy. "Your grandmother's name is Odile?"

"*Was,*" he corrected, putting the glass aside. "*She passed away when I was nineteen. She always wore yellow. A yellow dress, a yellow shawl, yellow daisies in her gray hair during the springtime. She came to look after me and my sisters when our parents died in a carriage accident. I was fourteen then.*"

"I'm sorry, Val."

He shrugged, the frown dissolving into a soft smile. "*It was a long time ago, and I still had my grandmother and my sisters.*" He winked. "*I grew up surrounded by the most beautiful women in Heaven's Gate.*"

"How many sisters do you have—I mean, *did* you have?"

"*I was the only boy out of six.*"

"And probably spoiled rotten. It's no wonder with all that feminine influence that you grew up so in tune with the female psyche." She settled back against the pillows and closed her burning eyes. "After five girls, I bet your father was happy when you came along."

"*Papa loved all his children equally, but he was pleased to see the name continue.*" A wistfulness filled his voice. "*A foolish dream.*" His expression closed and he held the glass to her lips again. "*You'd better drink some more.*"

The sour mixture tasted better the second time around, undoubtedly because the first few sips had permanently damaged her tastebuds. The throbbing in her head eased and she leaned back into the pillows. Ah, that felt better. "So what are—were—your sisters' names?" She had to stop thinking present tense. Val was the past. A *ghost*.

But talking to him, feeling him so close, he seemed so much more.

The fever, she told herself. Just the fever making her think crazy thoughts, like how nice it was just to sit and talk to someone without worrying about school or work or planning the next minute of her life.

"*Margaret, Elizabeth, Mary, Rebecca, and Nicole. Nicole was the youngest, two years my senior. I was the thorn in her side.*" A soft smile played at his lips. "*She was always mad at me. Because I'd slipped Willie into her lemonade, or under her bed, or next to her dinner plate. She hated Willie.*"

"Willie?"

"*My pet frog.*"

She grinned. "You must have loved her an awful lot."

"*Worship would be more appropriate, but I don't know that she ever realized it. I should have told her. I should have told them all. But, alas, one minute I was giving them hell, and the next they were off and married, having babies, and I was alone and in charge of the estate.*"

"I'm sure they knew, Val. You were their baby brother, and every girl knows that when a boy picks on you, he likes you. It's a fact of nature."

"*I still should have told them I loved them.*" A strange glimmer lit his eyes and something shifted inside her.

She knew the look so well. She'd worn it many times over the past eight years since she'd been on her own.

Longing.

Loneliness.

Regret.

Her gaze locked with his and an invisible connection flowed between them, an understanding. Val knew firsthand what it was like to be on his own. Alone. A century and a half without friends or family. Thinking about the past, wondering how things could have been different.

Her thoughts shifted to her father, to their bitter parting.

"You look sad." His attention riveted on her face. *"What is it?"*

"Nothing." She blinked back the sudden moisture in her eyes. "That stuff is making my eyes water."

"My senses are a hundred times more heightened than yours, and my eyes are not watering." He trailed a fingertip along her cheek and she closed her eyes, suddenly overwhelmed at the tenderness of it all. His gentle ministrations, his worried expression, the sincerity in his voice . . .

The cold remedy. That's why she was feeling the sudden urge to break into a pile of weepy tears and curl up in his arms.

"What are you thinking?"

She sniffled. "About my father."

"Tell me about him, chérie."

And she did. She wasn't sure why. She rarely talked about her father with anyone, including Jenny. But Val was different. He understood. A kindred spirit.

The cold remedy, she reminded herself. Drugs.

She grasped on to the last explanation and told him about growing up in a traditionalist household, the strict rules forced on her, the way she'd always felt less of a person because she'd been so limited by her father's old-fashioned view of women. She went on to tell him about her few and far-between dates in high school, nice clean-cut boys handpicked by her father, and about her engagement to Raymond.

"I'll never forget the look on my father's face when the minister asked if I would take Raymond and I said no." She closed her eyes. She could still see her father's shocked expression. His anger. His disappointment. All carefully concealed beneath a stern expression as he'd led her to the minister's chambers. She'd tried to explain her feelings, to make him understand, but he'd been too angry. Too set in his beliefs. And then he'd said the final words that had severed their relationship completely.

"If you walk out of here, you're no daughter of mine, Veronica Parrish. You're no daughter of mine!"

"So I walked away," she finished. "Because I didn't love Raymond, because my father didn't understand that, and most of all, because he didn't care. He wanted me to marry Raymond regardless."

"Marry a man you did not love?" Val muttered a few colorful phrases in French. *"Non, you could not do such a thing."*

"I know. But I've always wondered maybe, just maybe, if I'd made one final plea for my father's understanding, he might have taken his words back and maybe things would have turned out differently."

"Maybe," Val conceded. *"And maybe not."*

She sniffled. "Probably not. All the crying and begging I did in the first place didn't do anything but harden his resolve and prove him right. That women are ruled by emotion and men aren't."

"I could argue that one with you, chérie. *I have been known to act on pure emotion a time or two."* His comment coaxed a smile from her.

"Try three hundred and sixty-nine times—and that wasn't emotion, Valentine Tremaine. It was hormones." Her smiled faded. "I'm talking about the essence of who we are. My father believes that women think with their hearts, while men think with their heads."

"Perhaps he is right, to a certain extent. But I think the happiest person is the one who can acknowledge both. Who isn't afraid to act on his feelings, yet keeps his head when the situation calls for it."

"Like the ghost of a legendary lover who offers to give love lessons, but refuses any hands-on?"

"The generous but smart thing to do," he said, a stern frown creasing his face.

"Says you." She leaned back and closed her eyes as a lengthy silence settled around them.

"You did do the right thing," he finally said, his words quiet, heartfelt, comforting.

Her kindred spirit.

Spirit being the operative word, she reminded herself, fighting against the pull she felt toward Val. Something that went deeper than just physical lust Deeper . . .

Just a ghost and he wasn't *hers*. He was linked to the bed.

Her bed.

Okay, so technically, he was hers.

The thought pleased her a lot more than it should have.

She stifled another yawn, fought back the strange lethargy creeping through her, and fixed her gaze on her book bag, anything to distract her from the man sitting at her bedside.

"Why don't you hand me my schoolbooks? If I have to be in bed, I really should make the most of my time."

"You need to sleep."

"I've been sleeping."

"You're sick."

"I'm starting to feel better." Her throat didn't burn as fiercely and her head . . . the throbbing had faded to a faint tick and only when she opened her eyes really, really wide.

With them at half-mast, she felt all right.

"You've only been resting a few hours," Val pointed out.

"Twenty-four." She yawned again, her eyelids inching a little closer to shut out the light glowing on the nightstand. There, that was better. Not so bright. "They haven't made the cold that can beat this girl down. I'm like the Energizer bunny. I keep going and going and . . . going . . ." The words faded as her muscles relaxed and the warmth of the bed lulled her.

Or maybe it was Val's presence so close beside her, his fingertips brushing back the hair from her forehead, his deep, rumbling voice telling her about a mischievous little boy and his pet frog who wreaked havoc on five older sisters.

Either way, her eyes closed and she fell into a deep, restful sleep.

The best Ronnie Parrish had had in a long, long time because for the first time, she'd voiced aloud the fear that haunted her in the dead of night. The regret. And now she'd found peace.

Ronnie opened her eyes as the first rays of sunlight crept past the drapes. A quick glance at the clock and she smiled. She felt loads better and it was still early in the morning. Plenty of time for what she had in mind.

After showering and changing clothes, she ate a bowl of cereal and two slices of toast and drank juice, coffee, and two diet sodas. The food fed her depleted energy and the caffeine rush had her feeling fairly close to normal. Ready for a morning of research in Val's hometown. She had just enough time to make the two-and-a-half-hour drive, do some research, and head back to Lafayette in time for lunch with Jenny, then her afternoon shift at the library.

And if she was a little late . . .

She could make up the time later. She owed Val for nursing her back to health, for listening, for caring.

She forced the thought aside and concentrated on clearing away her breakfast dishes. She'd just turned to search for her book bag when her gaze fell to the bed.

A sliver of light worked its way past the drapes, hitting the white sheets at just the right angle to outline a shape on the bed. A faint, iridescent shadow of a man.

Val.

He was gloriously nude. A perfect male specimen. A prime opportunity for her to familiarize herself with the male body.

Sort of. He was see-through, after all, but with the light falling at such an angle, she could see every inch of him, from the glorious mane of hair on his head to his large feet tipped with long, tanned toes.

It wasn't Madame X's thirst for knowledge that drew her forward, however. It was her own sudden need to touch, to run her hands across his broad chest and feel the whisper-soft hair beneath her hands, the tightening of muscles, the strength.

She touched the shadow that was his shoulder. She didn't feel warm flesh as she had the first night he'd appeared to her, rather a vibrating heat that prickled her skin and pulsed from her fingertips through her body, skimming nerves and stirring them to life until she fairly vibrated herself. Ached. Burned.

As fiercely as the shadow at her fingertips.

He didn't open his eyes, but she knew he felt her touch. His muscles contracted, rippled, his lips parted on a gasp and her exploration grew more bold. She feathered fingertips over his hair-dusted abdomen and lower, to the cluster of silky hair surrounding the prominent shadow of his erection.

Erection?

Bold and beautiful, his penis jutted tall, twitching as she drew closer. So close. Heat burned her cheeks, but greater than her embarrassment was the sudden need to feel all of him.

Her fingers trailed the length of the satin-covered steel. A gasp broke from his lips and he arched, unconsciously begging for more. Lost in the moment, in the strange sensations coursing through her, she closed her eyes and wrapped her hand around him. He was so hard and hot and . . . *alive*.

But he wasn't.

The realization rocked her. Her eyes flew open and she snatched her hand away. He was a ghost and she was definitely losing her mind. Leftover fever madness. She felt fine, but the fever had fried a few major brain cells.

Her gaze stalled on him again, lingering on his face—his strong jaw, regal nose, sensuous lips that would have been a tad too large on most men, but on Val they simply added to his allure. For the first time, she noticed the faint hint of a scar near his temple, the small bump on the bridge of his nose, the three-inch-long, paper-thin scar going from just below his navel to his groin area. Imperfections. He certainly wasn't GQ handsome, though he did have the sort of hard, muscular body any underwear model would have killed for. His appeal really had little to do with his looks. There was just something about him. A confidence that glittered in his eyes and whispered that he knew all her secrets, that he wanted to know. A magnetism that made her look when she wanted nothing more than to look away. A charisma that drew her . . .

Of course he had charisma. That was probably standard issue for ghosts these days, and Ronnie wasn't falling for him. *It.* A *ghost.*

No way.

What she felt for Val was pure lust. Physical. Heat of the moment. Temporary.

Fragments of last night rushed at her, the strong hands bathing her face, the deep voice soothing her, the care and comfort that had felt so good, the understanding that had eased years of hurt.

She cradled his cheek, felt the warmth of his energy, and whispered, "Thank you." And then she turned away, but not before she saw the faint hint of a smile at his lips.

She did a double take, but the expression had disappeared, leaving her to wonder if she'd just imagined it.

Probably. Her imagination had been working overtime lately. Especially the night before last, when she'd imagined Danny's visit, him carrying her to bed, his kiss scrambling her senses. Right.

A hallucination brought on by the fever. She'd already proved beyond a doubt with that kiss in the lounge, a blah, non-toe-curling kiss, that there were no sparks between them.

Nada. Zip.

She drew the drapes tight and hurried about, straightening

up and checking to make sure all the burners on the stove were off and the toaster unplugged—

Her gaze snagged on a folded newspaper stuffed next to her TV, and her stomach did a somersault She knew, even before she picked up the paper and scanned the front page, what she would see.

A crude sketch of the Dupré Library's notorious kissing bandit stared back at her, right above the article she'd read two nights ago with Danny hanging over her shoulder.

He'd been real, *here*, and he'd kissed her, and she'd liked it. Again.

To make matters worse, she was a wanted woman.

Ugh.

Chapter Twelve

"I'm looking for Harvey Moulet." Ronnie stood at the circulation desk of Heaven's Gate's only library. "The lady over at the courthouse said I'd find him here."

"That would be Lucy. She knows everything about everybody, including where they have their lunch and what they eat. I'm having tuna on white." He sat behind the desk and held up a sandwich.

She grinned, remembering Lucy's spiel about Harvey's eating habits. "Then you're the man I'm looking for."

"And you are?"

"Veronica Parrish. I'm a student at USL and I'm doing a little research into a family tree."

He shook his head. "I don't recall any Parrishes in this area."

"Not my family tree. A friend of mine. He's busy and I offered to help him out. We've managed to trace all the way back to a particular woman. We found a birth certificate on her which lists her mother, but no father." She pulled out Emma's photocopied birth certificate and showed him.

"What about a marriage certificate? Did this—" he glanced down "—Emma get married? She might have listed her father on the marriage certificate."

"I checked at the archives building in Baton Rouge, but I didn't find one."

"That doesn't mean she didn't get married. Orleans Parish was one of the first in Louisiana to keep records, but it was something done on a voluntary basis and usually among the elite. There were births and deaths and marriages that were never recorded other than in personal diaries, Bibles, and the like."

"So how do I find her?"

"Let me see," he murmured, his gaze still studying the document. "She was born in 1849." He tugged off his glasses and looked up at her. "I'm working on a personal history of the Warren family which begins around this period. I'm doing the research, so I might as well keep an eye out for your Emma."

"I'd really appreciate that, because I'm really desperate to find something on her."

"I'm sure I'll turn something up." He grinned. "There isn't a person who's been born in the past two hundred years in Heaven's Gate that I can't find. My father was a historian and his grandfather before him, and they accumulated a massive collection of articles and documents and journals. Thanks to their hard work and a bit of my own, I was able to write this." He produced a book entitled, *Heaven's Gate: The Early Years*.

She gave him an apologetic glance. "Can't say as I've read it."

He grinned and reshelved the book. "It didn't exactly hit the *Times*. Give me a few days and I'll see what I can find out about your Emma Wilbur. So who's your friend tracing the tree?"

"His name is Tremaine. Va—Vince," she finished. "His family was originally from here."

"The Heaven's Gate Tremaines," Moulet supplied, pointing at one of the numerous paintings lining the wall. A huge plantation house surrounded by enormous, moss-draped trees. "The town rose up around their place, the biggest plantation in all of southeastern Louisiana up until the Civil War. Fell to ruin after that."

"Is there anything left of it?"

"Just a stretch of the prettiest country you've ever seen. Want to take a look? I'm knee-deep in work and I've got a field trip coming through here from the local elementary school in about a half hour, but I could draw you a map."

No. She had to be at the library in five hours and the drive would take half of that. Then there was her lunch date with Jenny.

"That would be great."

They exchanged phone numbers and Harvey promised to call the minute he uncovered anything helpful. Ronnie followed the map and drove the main road out of town. She turned off about three miles out, and followed a winding dirt road a quarter of a mile, as the map specified. The original town had been built around Heaven's Gate, but time and change had moved the hub farther west, leaving the original stretch near the outskirts.

A few more winding turns and she stopped. She found herself surrounded by huge oak trees covered in Spanish moss, stretches of green, green grass, and a feeling of peace unlike anything she'd ever felt before.

Beautiful. *Heaven on earth.* She smiled and walked around. In her mind's eye, she visualized the house from the painting, surrounded by trees. She tried to picture Val, running here and there, but she couldn't. Every time she closed her eyes, she saw him, but he was in bed. Her bed. His bed. Their bed.

Now where had that come from?

She walked around, spotted a few squirrels, and then gave up. She was heading back to her car when she smelled it.

Him.

Her gaze darted around but she saw only trees and the shimmering fog of Louisiana heat. She sniffed, and there it was. So clear and coaxing, teasing her nostrils and drawing her forward, through a cluster of trees. A few steps and she reached a clearing, and the source of the delicious smell.

A shimmering, sparkling river. The sharp scent of freshwater tinged with the smell of apples filled her nostrils. While apple season had come and gone, a few pieces of fruit littered the ground from some nearby trees, the smell faint but detectable.

Him.

She stood on the river bank and closed her eyes, and then it came. Crystal clear images. Val as a small boy, swinging from the trees, diving into the river, sitting on the bank with a pet frog. The vivid pictures flooded her mind, drifting so clear and easy through her head. A little boy. Then a teenager. Then a grown man stretched out on the bank, staring at a full moon overhead. Worrying and wondering. Sad.

The last image stayed with her all the way back to Lafayette and through her monthly lunch date with Jenny, no matter how she tried to push it aside and pretend that Val had never been anything more than he was right now.

"So tell me all about this man," Jenny said after they'd ordered lasagna and extra breadsticks at a small Italian restaurant near campus.

"He isn't exactly a man."

Jenny stopped in mid chew. "Maybe it's just my hearing. With two toddlers, I'm not used to all this quiet. Did you say, not exactly a man?"

"He's a . . . Well, he's a . . ."

"Don't say it, honey. He's a she. That's it, isn't it? That's why you've been living like a nun."

"Of course not. He's definitely all *he*, he's just . . . Well." She drew in a deep breath. "He's . . . uh, sort of different."

"As in, he's not the same color as you?"

"No."

"He's not the same religion?"

"No. He's . . . not exactly real. You see, he's the subject of my project for Guidry's class." Veronica knew she'd sunk to an all-time low by lying to Jenny, but how could she tell her friend, even her best friend, that her bed was haunted by the ghost of a legendary lover. Jenny would chalk that up to desperate hormones for sure, and be twice as worried.

"But I thought . . ."

"I know he sounded real when I told you about him, but I'm really getting into this project and sometimes I get a little carried away."

"You're coming to dinner at my house next week."

"I'm busy."

"Make time."

"Jenny, finals are in a few weeks. I've got this Guidry project. My diploma's on the line."

"Okay, but first thing after graduation, you're coming to my house for dinner and I plan on having at least three eligible friends of Matt's there, and you *will* have a lurid one-night stand with one of them if I have to set it up and oversee the damned thing myself."

"Yes, Mom."

"Speaking of moms, I've got a crate of strawberries overflowing in my trunk. Your mom dropped them by yesterday after I happened to mention I'd be seeing you today. Said she bought too many at the produce store and thought I might like them."

"But she knows you hate strawberries."

"And she knows you love them."

For the first time in a long time, Ronnie let herself remember something other than her father's bitter words. She thought of homemade strawberry pies, her father's favorite, and how she and her mother had baked several for every conceivable special occasion. The annual church bazaar. The Fourth of July. Her father's birthday. How watching her father enjoy the first bite, had always filled her with a strange sense of pride.

"Earth to Ronnie," Jenny said, waving a forkful of lasagna. "I vote you give your mom a break and call her."

"I always do. Last month when you brought me the canned cucumbers. The month before when you brought the peaches. The month before that when you brought pears. I call and say thanks, she says to make sure I eat right, then my dad asks who she's talking to. She says, 'Your daughter, Hank.' He asks, 'What daughter?' And that's the end of the phone call." Ronnie sighed and Jenny patted her hand.

"He misses you, Ronnie. I don't care what he says. He's hurting."

"He's mad, and unless I crawl home ready to be what he wants me to be, he'll never forgive me."

"As stubborn as your father is, I'd say you're right. But forever's an awful long time and I know he still loves you. They both do."

"I know that." Her mom's produce efforts, her father's belated pause before he said the dreaded words "What daughter?" They *did* still love her. "But sometimes love isn't enough."

"That's where you're wrong, honey. Love makes the world go 'round."

If only. But love wasn't enough to make her father eat his words, or her mother openly defy her husband to stay in touch with her only daughter personally, rather than using the vegetable excuse.

Love was . . . just love. Nice, but not powerful in the least. Not to overcome any and all odds. Not like people romanticized in songs and books and movies. In real life, love complicated rather than changed things, because the more you loved, the more you hurt.

"Speaking of which," Jenny said, grinning, and Ronnie knew she was about to get the monthly lecture on her nonexistent love life. "When are you going to give up the books for a few hours, find yourself a hunk, and have some wild, hot sex?"

"That's not love, it's lust."

"The next best thing. Hey," Jenny's face brightened. "You know what you need?"

"Money?"

"Try again."

"A great diet?"

"Strike two."

"Some peace and quiet so I can study?"

"Boring." Jenny made a face. "What you need is the Smile."

"I have a smile."

"Not *a* smile. *The* Smile. A surefire guarantee to a date. The next time you meet a cute guy, make eye contact and open your mouth like this." Jenny demonstrated. "When I'm in the mood, I give Matt the Smile."

"And that turns him on?"

"At least three guaranteed times."

"Three? But you've only got two . . ." She smiled. "You're pregnant."

"Four months. Can you believe I thought I was just eating too many cupcakes?" Jenny beamed. "The Smile never fails."

They hugged and Jenny spent the rest of lunch talking about her plans for the new baby.

"What do you think of Millicent for a girl or James for a boy?"

"They're both nice."

"I don't know. Matt's great-aunt is named Millicent and if I name the baby that, then my mom is liable to get upset that I didn't pick a name from my side of the family, but my only aunt's name is Gertrude and I'm not naming my daughter that. . . ."

Ronnie had listened to the name hunt for each of Jenny's first two and she'd always felt relieved not to have to make such a decision. She'd already made her choice. A career rather than baby.

But as she sat there, staring at the smile on Jenny's face, hearing the wistfulness in her voice, she actually started to wonder what she was missing.

Geez, not only were her hormones kicking up a ruckus, but her motherly instincts were stirring to life. She could practically hear her dad saying, "I told you, Veronica. If you had only listened. Obeyed. I *told* you. . . ."

Someone Upstairs was definitely out to get her.

"Where are you going, Norman Nathaniel Terribone?"

"To Buddy's. It's poker night," he told the blonde standing in the bedroom doorway, watching him lace up his tennis shoes.

"But you played cards last night and the night before."

"I'm on a winning streak, babe." He yanked on a new T-shirt and snatched up his car keys.

"But I miss you." Her soft voice echoed in his ears and he

halted in the doorway. "You're out every night, damn near all night. I'm getting lonely."

"I know," he said, sweeping a fingertip along the curve of her face. She was so soft and sexy and damned irresistible.

But that didn't seem to matter to Mac.

It would. Soon Mac would be standing up and taking notice of pretty Norma Renee and everything would be all right.

"I was hoping we could spend some time together." She rubbed up against him.

His breath caught and his attention centered on Mac lying so complacently against his thigh. Nothing. Not even a twinge, and Norma Renee was not only the love of his life, but a grade-A female.

"I was going to take a shower. You could join me. I'll wash your back," she gave him a sultry smile, "and your front."

He shook his head. "Not tonight, babe. I can't call it quits with the boys now. Stakes are high. I'm this close to winning the pot." He gave her a lingering kiss and ignored the guilt that niggled his gut.

A guy had to do what a guy had to do even if it did involve lying to his intended. Besides, Norman was doing this for the both of them, to bring them closer, to give Mac some damned incentive and Norma the husband she deserved. A good provider and a good lover. Working for his father at the restaurant, Norman had the first one licked. It was the second one he had to work on.

He headed outside, mentally counting deep breaths, just the way the doc had taught him. It was all about relaxing. Being stress-free.

But how could he be stress-free when the sight of Norma Renee taking her pleasure without him was eating him up inside?

He needed satisfaction, needed to work out his aggression in some physical way. That's what the doc had told him, and that's what he intended to do. He was *this* close.

Outside the house he shared with his sweet Norma Renee, he climbed into his T-Bird and started the engine. As usual, she purred like a newly stroked kitten. Norman pulled out his notebook from the glove compartment and his ax from beneath the seat. Tools of the trade.

He flipped on the radio, smiled as the King crooned "Love Me Tender," and headed for the Dupré Library. It was just about time for Veronica Parrish to get off work.

The minute Ronnie arrived home after her shift at the library, she had barely enough time to store her strawberries in the fridge before Suzanne knocked on her door. Jenny's wonderful news and all the talk about love and family had chipped away at Ronnie's defenses and she actually welcomed the twin terrors.

They really were adorable.

And so loving.

A tangle of arms smothered her in a fierce hug before she found herself freed as the kids turned their attention to her computer.

"Now, kids, don't touch that," Ronnie called out as they raced across the room, fascinated by the colorful screen and her spreadsheet. . . . Oh, God, her spreadsheet.

Eager fingers flew across her keyboard, her screen bleeped, then went dead, and Ronnie's heart stopped beating, which pretty much set the mood for the rest of the evening.

"Now, children. Leave Aunt Ronnie's stuff alone." Suzanne turned back to Ronnie. "Don't worry. They'll be out like lights in no time."

Right. Over the course of the next few hours, the twins had enough energy to turn sane, practical Ronnie into a screaming, hair-pulling woman who resorted to bribery to get the little angels to close their eyes.

"Ice cream," she vowed. "We'll go out for ice cream next Saturday if you just close your eyes for five minutes."

"With rainbow sprinkles?" Brandy asked, peeking from one eye.

"Yes."

"But I want chocolate sprinkles," Randy chimed in.

"You'll get chocolate and Brandy will get rainbow."

"How come she gets rainbow and I have to have chocolate?"

"I thought you wanted chocolate."

"I want chocolate," Brandy chimed in. "And rainbow."

"So do I."

"Then you'll both have rainbow and chocolate and Aunt Ronnie will have a lobotomy."

"What's a 'bonomy?" Brandy asked.

"Can I have one?" Randy begged.

"Sure you can," Ronnie muttered under her breath. "And Aunt Ronnie would be more than happy to give it to you." The bribes turned to threats, the threats to pleading, until Ronnie was simply too exhausted to think, much less form a coherent, convincing argument on why the twins should stop torturing her and please, *please* go to sleep. She closed her own eyes and tried to tune out the twins fighting over which cartoon character was the prettiest—Snow White or Pocahontas.

Ronnie was vaguely aware of the voices fading, the heavy weight of two small bodies as they collapsed onto her lap and vied for a comfortable position. Then quiet settled in. Blessed quiet . . .

It wasn't until the clock struck two a.m. that her eyelids fluttered open.

Through a sleepy daze, she saw Val sitting on the edge of the bed, a strange light in his eyes, a half-smile curving his sensuous lips. *"You've got the touch."*

She yawned. "The touch?" Her eyelids drifted partially closed, sleep lulling her back.

"A way with children. My father always said that you can tell how good a mother a woman will be by how she touches a child, any child. Soft but firm. You're going to make a good mother someday."

"Normally I'd say maybe, someday far, far into the future. But after tonight, I'm seriously considering having everything sewn up."

"Don't you like children?"

The question pricked at her conscience and she let out a deep sigh. "I like them all right, but later. Much later," she added as she glanced down and saw the fingerprints smudging her T-shirt.

"Why not now?"

"I intend to build a dynamite career first, and that takes time and effort and dedication if you intend to be successful, and I do."

"You would rather work than have a child?" At his incredulous expression, she frowned.

"Why is that so hard to believe?"

"Because—"

"—I'm a woman," she cut in, "and women are supposed to be content being barefoot and pregnant, cooking and cleaning. Women can do other things besides have children."

"Of course they can. Women are smart, beautiful, talented, and they have the ability to give mankind the greatest, most wondrous treasure of all. Why would they want to do anything else?"

"Because . . ." She seemed at a sudden loss for words. When he put it that way . . . "Because I just don't. I'm young and have more to offer the world." She glanced at the tangle of arms and legs across her lap. "Spitting up, sticky hands, and dirty diapers—no, thank you. I'll settle for running my own firm, worrying over employees and returns instead of kids and runny noses."

That's what she said, but Val didn't miss the way her hand absently stroked the little girl's golden hair, or the way her other hand curled around the little boy's arm protectively.

"Children are a blessing." He walked to the French doors and stared out at the surrounding landscape.

"You really think that, don't you?" The question, filled with surprise, carried to him on the soft breeze and he smiled.

"Not always, chérie. When I was young, I thought like most boys. Children were a far off responsibility that I hadn't the time or energy to deal with. I was much too busy getting into trouble. It is true what they say about never appreciating what you have until it is gone. I'd never wanted a child until I could not father one."

"What are you saying?"

"My parents weren't all that the carriage accident took from me. I was with them during the accident and I was hurt. One of the carriage rods pierced me in a very delicate area."

"I saw the scar."

He cut her a glance.

"When you were resting yesterday morning. I saw the scar."

"I healed, but I would never be whole again, that's what the doctor said. He told my gran that I would never be able to father a child because the rod damaged something inside me. It severed the wires, so to speak. I didn't believe him. I felt excitement, I still had an erection. How could I not be able to father a child? I was fourteen, and determined to prove him wrong. After all, I was the man of the house now. The only hope for the Tremaine name." His head dropped as he stared at the floor. "And I wanted a child. I wanted to be a loving father like my father had been, to continue his legacy. At first, I waited, determined to find the woman of my dreams the way my father had. Then all would be right." He shook his head. "I never found any one woman I felt that strongly about, and so I set my sights on simply fathering a child. I would then marry the woman who managed to conceive, and all would be right." He shook his head. "But nothing was ever right."

"So you've never been in love?"

"Non. Et tu?"

"Too busy."

"Perhaps you should slow down a bit."

"Slow down and get left behind. I've got bills to pay, studying to do, a diploma to earn. I don't have time for love. Most of all, I don't have the desire."

He turned and flashed her a grin. "*You're wrong on that count*, chérie. *You have a great deal of desire.*"

Too much, Val thought, noting her flushed cheeks, the way her lips parted on a soft gasp at his words. She brimmed with desire and it was all he could do to keep from crossing the distance to her, hauling her into his arms, and tasting just how much.

He shook away the sudden regret and forced his gaze back to the open French doors.

"I went to Heaven's Gate today." When he cut her a sharp glance, she shrugged. "I didn't find out anything interesting, but there's a local historian there who promised to keep an eye open. After I met with him, I drove out to the plantation.

"It's a beautiful stretch of land." Her voice softened. "I saw the river, the apple trees. I saw you, Val. It was the strangest thing. I closed my eyes, and there you were. In my head."

In my heart.

He could have sworn he heard the words. He would have, were it not for the emotion roiling inside him. The want. The need. Enough to make him imagine the damndest things.

"What happens when I find out the truth for you?" she asked after a long moment.

He didn't turn. He didn't trust himself to look at her as she was now, so soft and rumpled from sleep, the children in her arms. A picture that would haunt him for the eternity to come. "*I cross over into peace. Once I have the answer I seek, at the exact hour of my death, three a.m., I will make the journey to the other side. As I should have so long ago.*"

Silence fell around them then, disrupted only by the pounding of his own heart. Although she didn't ask any more of him, he felt her gaze burning into his back, questioning him, beckoning him.

Distance, he told himself. Emotional distance and he could

do this. He could tutor her and not make love to her, no matter how she did that little frowning thing with her eyebrows all wrinkled up, begging for his hands to soothe the expression away, or how her lips protruded in a slight pout, or how the fire flared in her eyes when she tossed a pillow at him.

The thing was, Val suddenly wasn't as worried about the making love part as he was about the falling in love.

Chapter Thirteen

"Shouldn't we be doing something a bit more . . . physical?" Ronnie asked the next night. "I mean, we mastered kissing so I thought we'd move on to touching. A little hand-holding. Something."

"*That's why you're the student and I'm the teacher,*" Val pointed out. "*How can you touch and be touched if you don't even know your heart's true desire?*" It sounded like a good argument, and heaven knew he needed one right now.

She was right. After the kiss they should have progressed to physical contact, to touching above the waist, then below, then . . .

He stiffened and frowned. "*You have to be in tune to your body.*"

"I'm already in tune to my body. How can I not be when there's so much of it?"

"*That's the sort of thinking that will stunt your progress. It's not about the way you look—*"

"—but the way you think. I know, I know." She glanced down. "But tell that to my hips."

He'd like nothing better.

He shook the thought away, his mouth drawing into a thin line. "*I want you to dig down, deep inside yourself, and discover what you truly yearn for.*" He gathered his control. *Deep* was not a word to be thinking of with a ripe beauty—this particular beauty—at his fingertips. "*Think of your wildest fantasy.*"

She gave him a suspicious glance before blowing out a deep breath that lifted her chest just enough to make him swallow.

"You're the boss."

"That I am. Now think."

Despite her initial reluctance, she didn't have to think very long before she poured out a very enticing, erotic fantasy, and Val wondered if maybe he hadn't made a big mistake.

He'd needed noncontact. Distance. Particularly after the kissing episode. But this . . . *Merde!* If this wasn't just as trying.

She sat on the edge of the bed, her eyes closed, head tilted back just enough to expose the smooth column of her throat. A soft smile tugged at the corners of her mouth as she described the most enticing fantasy featuring strawberries.

". . . a trickle of juice on my neck and lower. A drip-drop here." She pointed to one nipple straining against the soft fabric of her shirt. "And here." She pointed to the other. "And all the way—" her fingers swept down, down "—to right here—"

"Enough," he growled. *"That's quite enough for tonight."*

She smiled. "But I'm getting pretty good at this. I never would have thought about strawberries in that way, but after reading about that little episode with the grapes in one of your letters, I think I could definitely enjoy a few strawberries. By the way, who did you do that grape thing with?"

"Her name was . . ." He racked his brain for an answer. He knew the woman. He knew every woman. It was one of the traits that women liked most. No woman ever feared being forgotten by Valentine Tremaine. They were all important, every beautiful face, every heated moment. The grape episode had been one of his more pleasurable experiences. He'd always loved grapes and when she'd suggested it . . . What the blazes was her name?

"Who?" she prodded, and Val did the only thing a man in his position could do when a woman backed him into a corner and demanded the truth—he blurted the first lie that came to mind.

"Madonna." Madonna? While she had a pleasurable singing voice, she wasn't exactly his type.

What in *hell* was he thinking?

Every woman was his type. Blonde or brunette. Short, tall, thin, or voluptuous. The female race was his type, Madonna included, even if she could stand to gain a few pounds, and maybe try some hair color. A flaming, fiery red.

"Madonna? That name doesn't ring a bell. Was it a nickname? Did she use it in the letter?"

"You can't expect me to commit every signature to memory," he snapped, pacing to the window and back. *"Her name was Madonna and she loved grapes. That's the end of it."*

"But I thought you were the one who loved grapes. She said she suggested it because you—"

"What difference does it make?"

"You don't have to be so grumpy."

"I am not grumpy." He stomped a path to the French doors and opened them to a gust of humid Louisiana heat.

Just what he needed. More heat to suck the air from his lungs and make his head spin, his blood race, his body . . . *want.*

"The lesson is over."

"We just started."

"And we just finished."

"Look, Val, I need more than one fantasy on record for Miss X. She's a successful, mature woman who's looking for love. No way will Guidry buy that this woman only has one fantasy."

"It's late."

"It's barely two a.m." She closed her eyes and smiled like a child about to dig in to a platter of cookies. "Just listen to this. I've got another one that really rocks." She closed her eyes. "Okay, I'm standing in the shower, the water's streaming down, the glass is fogged. I can't see anything, but I feel everything." A soft smile parted her full lips. "Hands at my back, my hips, gliding around to touch my—"

"Enough." Her eyes snapped open again and collided with his. *"You'd be the death of me if I weren't already dead,"* he muttered, desperate to ignore the flush of her cheeks, the rosiness

creeping down her neck, disappearing beneath the neckline of her T-shirt. The longing in her eyes.

That drew him more than anything else. The gold heat that warmed him from the inside out and set him ablaze.

And he burned so damned hot.

Too hot because of what he was, what he'd become by his foolish passion and one fatal mistake.

Never again.

"You know, Val, you're supposed to be encouraging this. Some teacher you are."

He turned and snatched up her notebook. *"Here. Write the bloody fantasy down."* A few more lessons, a few more weeks, and this last trial would be over.

The truth would set him free from the desire gripping his soul and give his spirit peace.

Oddly enough, the thought didn't appeal nearly as much as it had before, not with Veronica's sweet breathing echoing in his ears, her scent fierce in his nostrils, her fantasies still vivid in his mind.

Strawberries and showers.

She was definitely learning well.

At the rate she was going, she was bound to lose her damned virginity and give him a grand send-off into the Afterlife.

As appealing as the thought was, it also bothered the hell out of him. It was a territorial thing, of course. He was tutoring her and so he didn't want her first time to be with just any clod without a clue as to how to handle such a passionate woman.

She needed an equal in her bed, a man who knew all there was to know about pleasuring a woman. A man who knew her deepest, sweetest desires, her fantasies . . .

Himself.

And he needed her, but worse was the fact that he *wanted* her, more than he'd ever wanted any woman before, and not for the sake of a child, but for his own.

The realization hit him as he watched her settle down at the kitchen table with her notebook, documenting Madame X's journey into the fantasy realm. She was covered from neck to feet in baggy clothes; her hair hung in a limp ponytail. She looked rumpled and tired and not the least bit provocative.

There was just something about the way she caught her full bottom lip as she eyed the paper, the soft whisper of her fingertips against her creamy cheek as she pushed a stray strand of hair back, the heavy-lidded gaze she cast his way as she contemplated her latest fantasy.

Bon Dieu, he wanted her!

More than an eternity of peace? For that's what he would trade should he act on his feelings before he discovered the truth about Claire's daughter. He would pay with his soul and doom his spirit to an eternity of longing, lusting, torture—

"Did you ever make love on a swing?" her voice cut into his damning thoughts.

"What?"

"A swing. I think it would be kind of exciting. You could start off slow, with a gentle rocking motion, then as things heat up, the swing moves faster and faster—"

"Write it down," he growled, gathering his determination and turning his attention to straightening up the bookshelves in the far corner.

"What about a picnic table?" Her voice followed him. "Outside? In the moonlight?"

He shoved several books into place. *"Just write."*

She wrote ten pages, a total of four fantasies, that sent her straight into a cold shower that did little to ease her discomfort. Clad in a thick robe, with a towel around her neck to catch the water from her still damp hair, she padded to her desk, slapped open a textbook, and managed to read the same sentence five times before she turned to Val.

"Why don't we do a quick refresher on the kiss?" She needed something, anything, even if it was only the sound of his voice.

He shot her a look that plainly said no.

"Fine," she muttered, tossing the towel she'd been using to dry her hair into her designated clothes corner, despite the fact that lately, with Val on the job, it looked as clean as the rest of her apartment.

"Damn, woman," Val muttered, bolting from his spot in front of the TV to retrieve the discarded towel. *"I cannot abide your living habits. Were you raised in a sty?"*

"A barn," she corrected, wadding up several sheets of notebook paper and tossing them on the floor for good measure. A childish act, she knew, but it looked as if making him mad was all the satisfaction she was going to get at the moment. "If you won't be my love slave," she muttered, "I'll settle for a slave slave."

The next night went much the same, with Ronnie writing down a few more fantasies that ultimately drove her straight into a cold shower. Afterward, while Val sat in front of the TV, completely oblivious to everything save a Spice Girls video, she sat in front of her computer and worked on a spreadsheet for her tax class.

Work, she told herself. She needed to calm down before she slid between the sheets; otherwise, she was liable to reach for Val despite the strict boundaries he'd established between them.

Her nerves still tingled from the erotic thoughts, her heart beat faster than it should have after a half hour and so much cold water her fingers and toes had shriveled.

She stiffened and forced her attention to the screen. Funny how if she squinted just so, the blaze of numbers looked dangerously close to a man's . . .

Hard up. That described her to a T, and it was no wonder, with a hunky, half-naked man—*ghost*, she reminded herself—tutoring her, tempting her.

Why the hell was he being so stubborn?

She cast a glare at him, noted the firm set of his mouth, the hard line of his jaw. His chest rose and fell easily, his attention completely focused. The rat.

Furniture wasn't the only thing they'd made solid back in the good old days.

Admiration crept through her. Val had a cast-iron will. He'd made up his mind about virgins, and he wasn't changing it.

That, or maybe he simply wasn't attracted to her.

She frowned. After one hundred and fifty years of celibacy? He should have been tempted by a nun.

She glanced down at her faded, loose-fitting jeans, her old T-shirt with the jelly stain—courtesy of the Hades twins—obliterating the w and the o in women do it better, so, of course it spelled men do it better.

First thing in the morning—into the trash.

Although she wasn't wearing a habit, in no way was she covering any more. Or less. Yet he still didn't pay her an added moment's attention.

Because he had convictions.

She smiled again. A man with convictions.

She frowned. A ghost, dimwit. A *ghost*.

With strict convictions.

Or an aversion to redheads. One in particular.

The frown returned.

Maybe he really wasn't attracted to her. Maybe the chemistry wasn't chemistry at all, but infatuation on her part. Wishful thinking because she wanted him.

He was so perfect, so safe, so . . . controlled.

Maybe.

Probably.

Definitely, she decided the next night when she asked him about his own fantasies. Strictly for comparison, of course. While she was hard up, she wasn't throwing herself at anyone who might not want her.

"My fantasies are inconsequential," he'd told her. "You should concentrate on your own if you intend to master steps twenty, twenty-one, and twenty-two." Which consisted of recognizing her heart's desire, manifesting that desire into her everyday life—she'd had a strawberry milkshake that morning—and discovering new fantasies.

Then he'd turned his attention to the music channel and a parade of big, buxom blondes.

Ronnie felt as though she'd just reached the front of the line only to have someone cut in front of her. She'd gone from kissing to fantasies. Physical to nonphysical. It had to be a step backward.

Not to Val. He kept insisting they were going full speed ahead, and he was the one with the three hundred and sixtynine glowing references, so he should know.

Added to her fantasy frustration was the fact that, although she lusted after Val, she couldn't shake the memory of Danny carrying her to bed when she'd been ill and kissing her forehead.

And curling her toes and inspiring her hormones into a rocking version of the "Hallelujah Chorus."

As much as she wanted to write the episode off as a hallucination, she couldn't. She'd felt the effect of that small kiss through a feverish fog.

But how could she have the hots for Danny when Val was the one starring in her dreams?

The question haunted her over the next few days, following her to school and work, lingering in her mind, ready to snatch her attention when she wasn't taking care to concentrate.

And even then.

She'd been smack-dab in the middle of a lecture, absorbed in taking fast and furious notes, when she'd become caught up in noticing the professor's blond hair. Thinking how that blond hair, with a little body and more length, would have resembled Val's silken mane.

This was the very reason she'd avoided dating, she thought as she stood behind the circulation desk and stamped a stack of due date cards. And relationships and, especially, sex. She didn't need distractions. How was she ever going to pass her classes if she couldn't concentrate? If she worried instead of studied?

If she kept thinking of Val and picturing him—six-feet-plus of hunky male with incredible blue eyes and a heart-stopping smile—

"What's wrong with you?" Delta's voice shattered her thoughts.

Ronnie glanced down to find herself this close to stamping the back of her hand. The stamper stalled an inch shy of trembling fingers.

"Uh, nothing. I—I ran out of cards. I'm fine. Really."

"Hmph," Delta snorted. "And I'm Kate Moss."

At just a pound this side of two hundred, Delta was definitely *not* Kate Moss.

"I've got finals in three weeks and a load of work between now and then."

"And *Sports Illustrated* just asked me to do the cover of their swimsuit issue."

Ronnie grinned. "I bet you'd sell a lot of issues."

Delta glared, then her expression softened and shifted to old Professor Gibbons sitting across the room, reading the evening issue of the campus newspaper, the *Beat*. "Well, maybe one."

Ronnie raised an eyebrow. "You and Professor Gibbons?"

"He's enamored with me, of course, but I'm just keeping him company."

"Is that what they call it now?"

"Listen here, missy, there is nothing between that old codger and me. We're just friends. He can really cook."

"I'll bet."

"In the kitchen."

"I've always wanted to try it in the kitchen." Or anywhere, lately.

"I was talking about cooking food. He stirs up a great shrimp creole, and that's all he stirs."

"You sure?"

"Even if he did stir up more, he's much too frail to handle someone as vivacious as me. Why, he'd probably have a heart attack before he could even break a sweat."

"He looks pretty sturdy."

"Yeah, well, looks can be deceiving." Delta narrowed her gaze. "You look a little peaked. You sure you're not having a relapse with that flu?"

If only. But flu was the last thing wrong with Ronnie. She was sexually frustrated and she needed relief.

The experiments.

She could always try out Val's techniques on a few target subjects and spend some of the energy simmering inside her.

She took a self-conscious glance around and pulled the baseball cap low on her forehead. Of course, she would have to be more careful. There were kissing bandit posters all over campus and Ronnie had taken to wearing her hair pulled up under a New Orleans Saints cap.

Not that there was even a Popsicle's chance in hell she would be mistaken for the bandit. The guys who'd initially reported the incident had embellished a little, and the reporter who'd done the story had embellished, and everyone who'd read it had embellished, and now the campus police were searching for a flame-haired vixen wearing a smile and nothing more, with captivating eyes and boobs that could double as twin beach balls.

She hunched down, plucking her shirt away from her chest, concealing the incriminating evidence beneath a tent of white cotton.

No more experiments, no matter how desperate. She would just have to bide her time and wait for Val. While he might not have any intention of taking her virginity, he was bound to get physical sooner or later. To demonstrate, if nothing else. After all, how many lessons could the fantasies take? Maybe two. Three at the most.

Six lessons later, Ronnie was penning her twenty-eighth fantasy while Val stared at the TV.

"I want my money back."

He didn't even spare her a glance. *"What are you talking about?"*

"This is getting old. When are we moving on to the next step?"

"Soon."

"How about now?"

"I'm the teacher."

"So teach and leave the TV alone."

He flicked the television off and glared at her. *"I can watch what I want. This isn't about me, it's about you—"*

"—about self-discovery, yada yada. How long did it take you to come up with that line of bull? Because at first I believed it, but enough's enough."

"Just write."

"No." She put the pen down and folded her arms. "You promised lessons, so give me lessons, or you can find out about Emma all by yourself."

Not that she would really desert him. She would never do such a thing. Because she needed him to finish her paper, she reminded herself. It certainly wasn't because she felt compassion for Val.

The only thing she felt at the moment was the sudden urge to rip his head off. That, or kiss him.

She slammed her notebook shut. "I'm not writing another word."

"Really?" He unfolded himself from the chair and stepped toward her.

"Really."

He reached her and stopped, hands on his hips as he towered over her and glared.

She held his gaze and tamped down the unease that swirled in her stomach. This was Val. Val who took care of her, picked up after her. Regardless of how predatory he suddenly looked.

Predatory? She drank in his ferocious expression, his eyebrows drawn together, his mouth a thin slash against his tanned face. Yes, sir, predatory.

She smiled.

He glared.

"*Have you ever heard the saying,* chérie, Do not wish too hard for something, you just may get it?"

"I should be so lucky."

His glare eased and she thought he was going to smile. His lips thinned just before she could actually classify his expression as a grin. He took on a thoughtful expression as his gaze swept over her, from her head to her toes. Wicked delight danced in the blue depths of his eyes.

"*You are in such a hurry to lose your virginity, I don't think you fully realize what it is you're hoping for.*"

"Then enlighten me."

"*Well,*" he circled her chair, coming up behind her, his hands closing over her shoulders just hard enough to communicate his superior strength. "*The breeching of a maidenhead,*" he murmured in her ear, "*is very painful,* chérie." His fingers tightened. "*Excruciating.*"

"Really?"

"*Indeed.*" He let go of her and circled her once more, as a hawk sizing up dinner. "*Truly unbearable.*"

"And how do you know? Have you had your maidenhead breeched?"

The question brought a frown to his face. Obviously, he wasn't the least bit pleased that she didn't cower in fear at his statement.

"*I just know,*" he declared.

"How?" she countered. "If Claire was your first virgin and you don't remember, you don't have any firsthand knowledge. Look, Val." She did some glaring of her own. "If you don't want to get physical with me, just come out and say it instead of beating around the bush, making up nonexistent steps, and then trying to scare me."

"*All right. I do not want to get physical with you.*"

His words pricked her ego and she stiffened. "Thanks a lot."

He gave her an exasperated look. "*You asked me, did you not?*"

"Yes, but you didn't have to be so blunt."

"*Meaning, I should lie?*"

"No." She huffed, staring moodily at her notebook. "Okay, so maybe a little."

"*Meaning you want me to lie.*"

"Not a full-blown lie. A teensy, weensy lie. For a good cause. Like, I'm wonderfully sexy, but you're just not in the mood, or you took a vow of celibacy for religious purposes, or you find me irresistible but you're still in love with someone from your past."

"*Those are all full-blown lies.*"

She shook her head. *Men.* "Thanks for pointing that out, Val. Would you mind helping me scrape what's left of my self-esteem off the floor?" Before he could reply, she rushed on, "Or maybe you'd like to stomp on it, do a little jig just to make sure there's nothing left." She nailed him with a stare. "What's so wrong with me, huh?" He opened his mouth, but she didn't give him the chance to answer. "Okay, so there's too much of me. That's it, isn't it? You don't do fat women."

He seemed at a momentary loss for words. "*You're not fat,*" he finally muttered. "*You are voluptuous.*"

"Same thing." She bolted to her feet and stalked toward him. "It's just a nice way of saying my thighs are too wide, my tummy pooches, I don't have legs up to here, and my boobs are way,

way too far out to there, and my butt is too wide. . . ." The words faded into a choked sob and she shook her head wildly. "Oh, great." She wiped frantically at her cheeks and turned away.

Crying. Of all the stupid, silly, . . . woman things to do. Her mother had cried during sappy movies and tender love songs, when Ronnie's goldfish had died, when her tulips had dried up. Her father had always shaken his head in that tolerant, condescending way that said . . . Women.

"So my thighs are wide," she blurted, trying to reason out the situation. Her head over her heart. "There are advantages to having wide thighs, and a big butt, and a tummy pooch. I don't have to worry about Playboy beating down my door for a centerfold, nor do I have to hold the guys off, which is a good thing because I don't have time for men in my life." She sniffled and choked back a sob.

"Don't cry, chérie."

"I am not crying."

"Yes, you are."

"No, I'm not."

"I can see you—" His words drowned under a loud bam bam as someone rapped on her door. "You misunderstood me," he added as she stomped toward the door.

"You find me repulsive. What's to misunderstand?"

"I do not find you repulsive."

"Then it must be virgins in general." The snap of a deadbolt punctuated her sentence as she hauled open the door.

"Who were you talking to—" Danny started, coming up short when he caught sight of a traitorous tear that squeezed past her lashes. "Whoa, are you—"

"No." She slapped the moisture away.

"—crying?" he finished. "You are. You're crying."

"I am not."

"What's wrong?"

She shook her head and went to rummage in the fridge.

When spiraling down the pit of self-loathing, it was best not to go it alone. She grabbed a container of chocolate pudding, then a carton of chocolate ice cream, whipped cream, two cupcakes, and a bottle of chocolate fudge syrup. Fuel for the long journey.

Val didn't find her attractive.

The truth beat at her brain and, after setting everything down on the counter, her trembling fingers dove back inside the fridge for a third cupcake. And some leftover chocolate-covered peanuts she'd picked up at the campus deli.

So what if he didn't like her? She didn't need him. She could find a nice, modern guy who liked full-figured women *and* virgins.

"Veronica." Danny's voice sounded right behind her as she ripped the lid off a container of pudding.

"What?" She shoveled in a mouthful of pudding, turned, and came nose to nose with him.

Her throat worked at the pudding, pulling it down in a hard swallow as his fierce blue gaze drilled into her. *Blue?*

Before she could give the sight another thought, he hauled her close, the container of pudding splattered at her feet, and he kissed her.

Chapter Fourteen

The sensation started at the tips of her toes. A tingling heat that sizzled through her like a live current running through brand new wire. She glowed. Vibrated. Hummed.

Danny.

She managed to crack one eye open and get an up close and personal view of the Big D. Then his tongue thrust deep, her knees trembled, and her mind shut down from temporary overload.

Common sense jumped ship and her senses took control of the wheel. She took a deep breath and inhaled the scent of him—a musky mingling of leather and male and the crispness of a cool river on a hot summer's day. Val. One hundred percent Va—Whoa, back up.

Danny, she reminded herself. *Danny.*

The name intruded into her thoughts and jerked her back to reality despite a really intoxicating kiss that tasted of whiskey and raw heat and . . . experience.

Lips coaxed and stroked, his tongue tasted and explored. Persuasively. Knowingly.

Danny?

She opened her eyes as her hands touched his chest and gave him a slight push.

His eyes opened and blazed a bright, brilliant blue.

Blue.

She closed her eyes. She was seeing things. That was it. Wishful thinking. She wanted Val and so she imagined his eyes staring at her, his lips kissing her. . . .

Her eyes snapped open in time to see the blue darken to a

rich brown. But that wasn't what sent her stumbling backward, shaking with shock and fear and . . . anger.

She watched as Val stepped from Danny's body, his spirit unfolding from the smaller man like a shadow stepping free.

Danny blinked and shook his head. "Ronnie? What's wrong? Did you hear the noise again?"

"W-what?" she stammered, shifting her gaze from Val to her very puzzled looking friend.

"The noise. You look as if you've just seen a ghost."

As if she were still seeing a ghost. A rotten, two-timing, sneaky, handsome ghost.

"And what's with all this pudding?" He bent to retrieve the forgotten container and scoop the contents back inside.

"You have to go to the bathroom," Val whispered as Danny straightened.

The man blinked. "Did you hear that?"

"What?"

"A voice." Danny dropped the pudding container into the sink. "Telling me I need to go to the bathroom."

"Must be your bladder."

"But I don't have to go."

"Yes, you do," Val whispered again.

Danny turned and stared straight at Val, but he didn't seem to see him. He turned the other way before swinging back around to Ronnie. "I guess maybe I do."

"Take your time," she called after him.

The door closed and she glared at Val. "It was you. You're the one who kissed me."

"It's not that I don't want to get physical," Val told her. *"I cannot. You must understand."*

"You *kissed* me," she went on, the sight of him stepping from Danny still vivid in her mind. Val had been the one kissing her, making her toes curl. Val.

"You are a virgin and I cannot deflower a virgin. It's against the rules."

"What rules?"

He started to answer, but the shrill ring of the telephone drowned him out. Ronnie made no move to pick it up.

"*Hello. This is Veronica . . .*" her recorded voice finally echoed over the answering machine.

"Still the same old boring message," Jenny said after the beep. "I know it's late, but Marcy has a cold and she's keeping me up and I know you keep late hours. So what do you think of Kyle for a boy or Kaylie for a girl? Matt has a second cousin named Kyle but I think we can get away with it. Call me and let me know." The machine clicked.

"*Someone is having a baby?*"

"Don't change the subject," she told Val. "It was you. Tonight, and that first night, when I kissed Danny. *You.*"

"*We must keep our distance,*" he said, his expression stern.

"Then why did you kiss me?"

"*My time here is temporary,*" he went on. "*I have to think about Emma, about the question haunting me. I cannot be distracted—*"

"Why?"

His gaze caught and held hers and she thought she saw longing. Then the emotion dove into the sparkling blue depths of his eyes and he shrugged. "*I did not want to see your valuable techniques wasted on inexperience.*"

"You were jealous."

He stiffened. "*I have never been jealous.*"

"You want me." She smiled and he frowned. "You do. You really do."

"*You are a woman. Of course I want you. I haven't been within a few feet of a woman in a long, long time, with the exception of that lawyer's assistant.*"

"What lawyer's assistant?"

"*She was cataloguing estate items when I was stuck in the warehouse. She had a certain fondness for my bed.*"

Her gaze narrowed. "Did you touch her?"

"*I intended to, but her fiancé disturbed us. Thankfully.*"

"Let me guess, you have a No Engaged Women policy as well as a No Virgin one."

"*Something like that.*"

"So what did she look like?"

"Très belle," he murmured. "*I think.*" He shook his head. "*That's irrelevant to the matter at hand.*"

"Which is," she grinned and said accusingly, "desperate or not, you *kissed* me. Not a butterfly kiss either. You demonstrated all ten kisses and then you did that lip-licking thing."

"*Merely a kiss—even all ten do not count as consummation, or haven't you learned anything these past few weeks?*"

They stared one another down, the tension building, the air charged with a sexual current that made the hair on the back of Ronnie's neck stand on end and her thighs tingle. He looked so calm and cool and completely unaffected that she suddenly wanted to strangle him.

She'd settle for shaking his composure.

"Actually," she smiled, her gaze hooking on the carton of ice cream she had left on the counter as an idea took root. "I've learned quite a bit, and I've developed quite an imagination. You're one heck of a teacher, Val." She grabbed the container and a spoon, and panic flashed in his eyes. "What's the matter? You look nervous." She scooped a spoonful of ice cream. "Surely big, macho, experienced you isn't afraid of a little ice cream." She eyed the chocolate delight before her tongue darted out to take a sensuous lick. She groaned as the sweetness exploded on her tongue. "Or maybe you're just afraid I won't give you any." She loaded another spoonful and eyed him. "Want a taste?"

"*You know I do not eat mortal food.*" His voice came out as little more than a hoarse whisper.

"I wasn't talking about the ice cream." She winked and touched her tongue provocatively to the decadent dessert before swallowing the bite.

With a long, deep, pleasurable groan, she gave up the spoon

for a larger one and scooped ice cream into a bowl, then reached for the fudge syrup. A huge drop dribbled down the side, slid over her fingers. She caught the thick sauce with her tongue. "Mmm," she murmured, licking the chocolate free of her skin and watching him swallow. Hard. "I think I've found my next fantasy."

"No more fantasies," he groaned.

"Ah, but I think this will be my best one yet." One determined to send him over the edge, because she was tired of waiting on Valentine Tremaine. She was frustrated and she wanted relief.

She scooped a dollop of sauce with the tip of her finger and slid it into her mouth. "Mmm," she murmured, suckling as she watched him. And he watched her. And the air around them sparked. "Ahhh," she pulled her glistening finger free. "I just love my sundaes with warm, thick fudge sauce." She scooped more sauce and suckled. Scooped and suckled. Scooped and—

"We'll move on to touching. Just—" he grabbed her hand and pulled it free of her mouth, his skin burning into hers *"—don't do that. Please don't do that."*

She arched an eyebrow at him. "Pretty please?"

He let her go abruptly. *"Damn woman, but you're maddening."*

"And you're stubborn."

"Infuriating."

"Bull-headed."

"Aggravating."

"A pain in the—" she started, but his voice cut her off.

"Truce," he growled. *"Let us call a truce and get on with tonight's lesson."*

"Touching," she declared triumphantly.

"Hand-holding," he corrected.

Hand-holding? That wasn't what she had in mind at all. "I'd rather have a sundae." She reached for the can of whipped cream. A press of the nozzle, and foamy sweetness squirted on top of the ice cream. "You know," she said, a smile tugging at her lips, "I've always wanted to try this stuff on more than just ice cream—"

"*Forget hand-holding.*" He snatched the can from her before she could demonstrate the "more." "*Real touching.*"

She put her hands on her hips and eyed him. "How real?"

"*We'll pick up where we left off after the kissing. Ear nibbling, then the neck lick, then . . .*" He swallowed. "*We'll move down from there.*"

"You mean move on."

His eyes gleamed with a wicked light. "*I mean* down."

"Oh." Heat flooded her cheeks despite the fact that this was what she'd been asking for. Hoping for.

Her gaze caught with Val's and she saw the heat simmering in his gaze, the desire, the want, the . . . hesitation.

She wanted to ask him why, but something in his eyes, a deep sadness, a fear, kept her from opening her mouth. The less she knew, the less she would care, and she couldn't care. Not real *caring.*

Lust. Just lust.

"You don't have to break your No Virgin rule, Val." What was she saying? That as much as she wanted him, she didn't want him to break a vow that obviously meant a great deal to him. "We're talking touching, not deflowering. I might be inexperienced, but I know enough to know there's a world of difference between the two."

"*Just touching?*"

"Touching," she reassured him. Before she could dwell on her sudden change of heart, Danny's loud singing voice carried from the bathroom. Ronnie's gaze shifted to the closed door. "No more using Danny. You're the tutor, so you do the nibbling and licking."

He nodded.

Worry furrowed her brow as Danny launched into a rather loud version of the Rolling Stones' "Start Me Up." "He's all right, isn't he? I mean, he lives for classical music."

"He still likes classical, he's just discovering his wild side."

"Danny doesn't have a wild side."

"He does now. One of the side effects of possession."

"Side effects? His head isn't going to start spinning around, is it?"

"More like twitching." An all-male grin curved Val's handsome face as he slid back into his sexy, charming self. "And growing and throbbing and—"

"I get the picture." Ronnie's cheeks flamed. "So this wild side is courtesy of your possession?"

He nodded, his smile fading into tired acceptance. "During the possession, I must suppress his spirit with my own. The entire process is very tiring for me, more so because when I exit his body, in my weakened state, it's impossible not to leave some of my energy behind."

"Like paying rent."

"In a way." He collapsed into a nearby chair. "I get the pleasure of a physical form, and he gets a boost of energy when I leave."

"Will he remember tonight? The kiss?"

"The kiss isn't his memory, love. It's mine." One Val wasn't likely to forget for a long, long time. Unfortunately.

Veronica smiled at him. "Because you want me."

"Because I am a dedicated teacher." He closed his eyes and tilted his head back, and then a pillow caught him in the chest.

His eyes snapped open and he frowned at her. "What was that for?"

Fire danced in her eyes. "For tricking me and for taking advantage of poor Danny."

"I saved you from the worst kiss of your life."

"It's a wonder your head isn't as big as that bed. You're so full of yourself."

Danny sang louder and Val barely suppressed the urge to cover his ears. "Actually, I'm not nearly as full as I usually am. Your friend is now enjoying my energy."

She cast another glance at the closed bathroom door, and a frown worried her brow anew when Danny launched into a very loud, very off-key version of George Michael's "I Want Your Sex." "So what's going to happen to him?"

"*Well*," Val said, settling back in the chair, arms folded over his chest, a cat-who-got-the-canary smile on his face, "I'd say about three or four inches."

Ten. Danny shook his head the next morning and stared down at the monster erection that had greeted him the moment he'd opened his eyes. He was a solid six and a half after a really good wet Wanda dream, maybe seven after a few hours of sitting beside her and smelling her perfume. But ten? And after a night of sound sleep?

He slapped the ruler onto the nightstand, grabbed the bottle of Excite and Energize, and stared at the ingredients. An all-natural herb and vitamin blend. No steroids or testosterone supplements. Nothing but good, old-fashioned Mother Nature.

As happy as he was at this morning's discovery, he was even happier when things calmed down a bit. After all, knowing the equipment worked properly and conducting a demonstration for his entire mechanical engineering class were two different things. It was enough to know he was capable.

The knowledge made him stand a little taller and put some strut into his walk. Danny Boudreax strutting?

Hell, stranger things could happen. Like Terry Lynn Wilhelm, the hottest babe in his physics class, could smile at him.

She smiled at him throughout the entire lecture, and approached him at the end of class to ask him out for coffee at the Student Union Building.

Coffee? Yes! No woman had ever asked him out for anything, except Bebe Larue, freshman year, who'd needed help on her biology project, then Janie Freeman, who'd asked him to be her lab partner in sophomore chemistry, and Wanda, who'd needed a tutor. But coffee? As in being seen together socially? As in *date*?

"Maybe some other time," he found himself saying, despite the sudden twitch in his groin area and his libido chanting *Go for it!*

He would, but not with Terry or any of the other women who made a point of smiling at him or saying hi or accidentally brushing up against him.

Tonight was his first date with Wanda. Probably a fluke on her part, but Danny intended to make the most of her moment of temporary insanity. As attractive as he found other women, as much as he enjoyed their sudden attention courtesy of his new vitamins, he only wanted one. Wanda.

The question was, did she want him?

She wanted his dessert.

He sat by and watched as Wanda took a bite of his chocolate-covered cheesecake.

"This is so good. I love cheesecake. Unfortunately, it loves me. My thighs anyway."

"I can see why." His gaze traveled to her pink miniskirt, carefully molding to her sleek legs.

"Are you flirting with me, Danny?"

"I'm just telling the truth. You've got great legs. Almost as great as your eyes."

"What did you say?"

"I said you have really great eyes. They . . . sparkle."

She actually blushed. Confident, every-man-wants-me Wanda blushed. "Nobody's ever said that to me before."

"I'm sorry."

"Don't be. What I mean is, most guys don't make it above the neck, if you know what I mean."

"I can't believe that. You're beautiful, but you're also intelligent. That's what shows in your eyes."

She smiled. "Say that again."

"Beautiful."

"No. The other part."

"Intelligent."

She closed her eyes as if savoring the word. "You know, I almost believe it when you say it."

"You should. It's true."

"You really think so?"

"I've always thought so. You're smart, Wanda. You just don't know it, and knowledge is power."

The smile she gave him was worth the hundred bucks he'd shelled out for dinner. It was worth the numberless nights he'd spent keeping his eyes open so he could drag himself over to her dorm room and play the devoted tutor. Just that smile, meant for him, only him, meant more than if she'd stripped herself naked, climbed onto his plate, and offered herself up as dessert.

Okay, so he wouldn't go that far. He was, after all, a guy, and he'd dreamt of her for too long to be content with a smile. But the night was young and Danny was determined.

He wanted her to want him more than those thick-necked jocks she dated. More than his chocolate-covered cheesecake.

More.

Every woman wanted Valentine Tremaine.

Val replayed that all-important fact throughout the evening while he waited for Ronnie to finish up her shift at the library. Last night, he'd managed to put off their first "touching" lesson thanks to her friend Danny, who'd been singing so loud that old Mr. Weatherby had knocked on the door to complain that the noise was making Pringles nervous.

By the time his sweet Veronica had managed to placate the old man and send her jubilant friend home, it had been nearly three a.m. Val had made the excuse—a very real excuse, after the draining possession—of being exhausted, and so the lesson had been put off until tonight.

He alternated between pacing the room, picking up after Veronica, and staring at the TV.

Every woman, he told himself again.

It was a fact of nature. Like the earth being round. The sky being blue. Ronnie's interest in him shouldn't be so . . . unsettling. Arousing. Exciting.

He'd spent a lifetime being the object of female attention, the fuel for their desire, the star of their fantasies, and never once had the knowledge affected him as it did now.

Of course, he hadn't been celibate for one hundred and fifty years back then. He'd been used to women wanting him and was grateful for it, intent on using it to his advantage. To make a precious child. He'd been merely determined back then. Not desperate, and deprived.

That had to account for his temporary memory loss, for the blurred images of his past. He tried to recall hot, erotic memories, and, while the situations came forth, he didn't see the women with whom he'd shared the pleasure. He saw Veronica Parrish.

In his bed.

Down by his river.

Stretched out on the velour seat of his carriage.

Sprawled on a bed of soft hay in his barn.

Standing in her miniature kitchen, eating an ice cream sundae as if she'd never tasted anything better.

Desperation. That was it, because no way could Valentine Tremaine, a man who'd slept with . . . How many had he slept with again?

A lot, he finally concluded after a few minutes of intense, futile contemplation. Numerous.

And he had proof. Dozens of letters, written by women whom he'd bedded, faces he couldn't remember, names that lingered just beyond his mind's recollection.

Still, no way could he, a man who'd shared pleasure with so many, be falling hard and fast, risking an eternity of peace, for one woman. One inexperienced, so-so attractive, infuriating as hell, stubborn as a mule, messy woman who actually thought ice cream a fitting substitute for pleasure.

Even if she was smart and dedicated and he admired her.

Even if she did have the touch with children.

Even if she wrinkled her brow in that certain way that made him ache to reach out and soothe her troubled expression.

Throughout many of his thirty-two years of life he'd been searching, planting his seed and perfecting his technique, and he'd never fallen in love with even the most generous of women, the most beautiful, the most seductive. There was no way he would accept that after a bullet and a century and a half as a ghost, he'd find *the* woman to share his life, his bed, his future with.

Not when he'd already lost two out of the three, and the bed he wouldn't have for much longer.

His sweet Veronica was on the trail to answering his last burning question, and as intelligent and resourceful as she was, he had no doubt she would find the answer. Then he would have freedom from the lust burning through him, making him think crazy thoughts.

Like how Veronica Parrish was the most perfect woman he'd ever met. She was beautiful with her flame-colored hair, her soft, soft skin. But it was more than her outside appearance that drew him. She had a strength about her, offset by an incredible tenderness. While she looked after herself, she was never too busy to help someone in need, be it her neighbor's cat, the twins. She was gentle, compassionate, caring . . . *perfect*.

Preposterous.

She was simply the last sip of brandy and he was a thirsty man. That was it, and as much as he wanted to take a great big gulp, he could limit himself to merely wetting his lips.

Just touching.

At least that's what Val told himself.

Now if he only truly believed it.

Ronnie picked up her pace and rounded the corner. The street-light cast flickering shadows on the pavement in front of her, but she wasn't frightened. She was anxious, despite her aching feet and a load of homework. Tonight was the night.

Ear nibbling and neck licking and then . . . down. The notion sent a shiver of anticipation through her.

Tonight—

Thunk.

The sound shattered her thoughts and she stopped, ears perked as she listened for the strange sound. Nothing. Just the distant murmur of cars, the hum of the street lamp, the faint laughter from a nightly sitcom drifting from a nearby television set. Her imagination.

She rubbed her arms to chase away the sudden goose bumps and started walking again.

Thunk thunk . . . The sound followed her around the corner as she left St. Mary's Street and turned onto University. Just a few more blocks—

She came to a staggering halt.

And so did the noise.

She turned, but saw only an empty sidewalk. A car zoomed by, with music blaring, and she took a deep breath. She was overreacting. Jumpy. It was no wonder. The kissing bandit search had escalated, with the fraternities on campus trying to top one another with reward offers. She'd even come face to face with the actual reporter who'd broken the story and was now doing a follow-up. Thankfully, her hair had been stuffed up under the baseball cap and the description of the bandit had been so exaggerated that Ronnie felt certain she hadn't aroused any suspicion.

Or had she?

She shook away the thought, gave herself a firm mental shake, and started walking.

By the time she reached her apartment, she almost believed it had been her imagination. She'd made the two blocks without any more noises or that strange prickling awareness, as if someone watched her.

The blaze of headlights caught her as a car veered into the parking lot across the street. She watched while Professor Guidry climbed from his Volvo, a stack of books in his hands, and headed for the front door of his building. Seconds later, he raced back out and headed for his car, undoubtedly on his way back to campus. Thursday nights were all-night grad sessions for the psychology department. Being the workaholic he was, he readily volunteered to supervise the various experiments, which covered topics ranging from sleep deprivation to hypnosis, and kept him out until the wee morning hours.

Even then, without a good night's sleep, he'd never been late to a Friday morning class. The guy wasn't human.

Ronnie caught the hello and goodbye before they had a chance to burst from her lips. She didn't need to attract his attention any more than necessary, even by being friendly. Better to lay low and wow him with a great paper. She turned back to her door, fit the key into the lock, and went inside.

Straight into an empty apartment.

"Val?"

"*Okay*," he said, stepping forward from the shadows, completely naked and aroused, a fierce look on his face. "*Take your clothes off and let's get this over with.*"

Chapter Fifteen

Ah, victory! her hormones crowed as adrenaline zinged through her veins. A rush of heat skimmed her nerves, her nipples pebbled, warmth flooded her thighs, and her hands trembled.

Or maybe the hand trembling was caused by the sudden fear niggling at her brain.

Fear? Of Val? A *ghost*?

He looked anything but a ghost standing not two feet away from her, his blue gaze burning like twin match flames, his tanned muscles bunched tight, rippling right before her eyes with every breath he took, every clench of his fists as he stood so fierce and warriorlike before her, his gloriously nude erection jutting out from a thatch of sand-colored hair.

So powerful. Masculine. Huge.

"Take off your clothes and let's get on with it."

At the deep growl of his voice, her gaze snapped back to his face, to his expression that reminded her of a sullen little boy being forced to drink a bottle of cod liver oil.

Or an experienced, sexy-as-sin lover about to settle for an inexperienced, so-so looking virgin.

You know for a fact that he wants you. He admitted it last night, the voice of reason insisted, but suddenly Ronnie couldn't hear anything above the frantic pounding of her own heart and Val's deep, rumbling voice.

"Go on. Take them off. Or would you like me to do it for you?"

Victory wasn't all it was cracked up to be. "Surely we can nibble ears with our clothes on."

"Yes, but it progresses from there."

Down. The word echoed in her head and her knees joined her trembling hands.

"Uh, maybe tonight isn't such a good night." Was that her voice?

"Take them off." He moved closer.

"No." She scooted back.

"Why not?"

Good question. "I've, uh, been thinking about what you originally said." Val stepped forward again and a picture of a lion stalking his dinner flashed in her head. She inched backward until her back flattened against the front door.

"Yes?" he prodded, and she realized she'd completely lost her train of thought.

"Well, I was, um, thinking about what you said . . . you know, that I should find a few subjects and try things out. . . ." Another step forward and she all but sank into the woodwork. "I—I think you're right."

"Since when?"

"Since, um, last night. I mean, you are the teacher and I am the student, and so we have a business relationship, despite the subject matter, and I wouldn't want anything to jeopardize that. So if you'll, um, just write everything down." Yes, writing was good. Great. "Like a study handout. I'll give the list a thorough reading and find somebody to try things out on myself. Somebody who's—"

"Real?" he cut in.

She'd been about to say "less intimidating," as in inexperienced, like herself, but if he thought his ghost status was turning her off, she wasn't going to argue.

She nodded. "Exactly."

"So it's not that you do not wish to touch, you simply do not wish to touch me, oui?" The confusion on his face turned to displeasure.

"Bingo."

"You expect me to believe such nonsense?" He actually smiled,

a wicked, gobble-you-up kind of smile that sent a wave of panic through her. Followed by a burst of anger.

The guy had such an ego, and no wonder, with his track record. But she wasn't another face to commit to memory, another name to add to the list. No sirree.

"You know, Val, I realize that you're not used to being turned down by a woman. I mean, they probably rip their panties off the minute they lay eyes on you—"

"*Bloomers,*" he cut in.

"What?"

"*Bloomers,*" he said again, the deep rumble of his voice effectively dousing her temper. "*Not panties.*"

"That's beside the point."

"*Which is?*"

That he was standing too close, scrambling her thoughts, and she couldn't breathe. "That I don't."

"*Don't what?*"

"Want to rip anything off." She inched to the side, creeping the few feet until her fingers closed around the bathroom doorknob as she sought the quickest escape from all that delicious male heat. "I'm going to take a shower." A cold one. Ice cold.

Before she could blurt out another lie, she bolted for the bathroom. Slamming the door, she slumped back against the wood and closed her eyes. What the hell was wrong with her? He was ready, willing, and able, and this was what she wanted.

What she'd dreamt of.

Him. Her. The two of them beefing up Madame X's personal account of life in the lust lane.

But not now. She was too startled by the past few moments, the way his nearness seemed to overload her senses and make her feel so many things—desire, desperation, fear. Not of pain and suffering, but of forgetting herself. Forgetting everything except him.

She forced the thought away, turned the shower on full

blast, and started stripping off her clothes. Her T-shirt hit the floor, jeans followed, until Ronnie stood only in her panties and bra.

The phone rang in the other room, but Ronnie had no intention of going after it. She couldn't face Val again. A very naked Val.

". . . think about Sophie or Roger?" Jenny's voice floated through the door. "Or Megan and Walter? Marcy's still got the cold and we're having a late night. Call me."

Ronnie checked the water temperature, turned the knob a notch colder, and reached for the hooks on her bra.

You're just tired, she told herself. *He caught you off guard.* The good old voice of reason. Always ready to jump in and save her when her heart started pounding a little too fast and her thoughts spiraled down the frantic drain. *You were spooked from the walk home. It only stands to reason that you would be startled by a completely naked man—make that ghost.* Which was the point exactly. He was a ghost. Just a ghost.

Harmless. Temporary. Perfect.

Her bra and panties hit the floor and she reached for the shower curtain.

"You're a poor liar."

She whirled, fingers clutching the plastic shower liner. Rings snapped, the shower rod groaned, and the curtain collapsed at her feet.

Val, wearing only a sinful, heart-stopping grin, stood inches away, his presence taking up every ounce of oxygen in her tiny bathroom. His expression had changed from stubborn acceptance to cool, wicked determination.

"I am not lying," she managed, despite the fact that she couldn't breathe.

"You do want to rip your bloomers off."

"Panties, and what makes you so sure?"

"Your body, chérie." His gaze zeroed in on her traitorous nipples like twin laser beams looking for a target.

She quickly folded her arms over her bare breasts. "Get out of here."

"Not until we finish our lesson." He stepped forward and she backed up.

"There is no lesson, I don't want you—"

"Didn't your maman warn you about telling lies, chérie?" He backed her up against the wall, pinning her in place by planting muscular arms on either side of her, his body blocking out everything save him.

"What are you doing?" she blurted when he dipped his head, his lips going to the sensitive shell of her ear.

"Step twenty-four."

"But I'm naked."

"And so am I."

"But . . ."

"Just relax." The words whispered over her ear and sent a wave of heat pulsing through her.

"What if I say no?"

He pulled back. His gaze locked with hers for a long, heated moment that made her tremble even more than his nearness. *"I shall stop."* He dipped his head again and this time she felt more than a warm rush of tingling breath. Warm lips nibbled and suckled at her ear, and fear bolted through her.

No! The word was there on the tip of her tongue. She opened her mouth, but all that escaped was a breathless, "Ahhhhhhh . . ."

"Does this please you, chérie?" drifted into her ear on a wave of sizzling breath and mind-blowing sensation.

Oh, yes. It pleased her, indeed. That was the problem. His tongue traced the outer shell of her ear before moving lower, to lave a tender path down her neck. He suckled a tiny bit of flesh into his mouth, teeth nipping just enough to send a shiver wiggling down her spine. She groaned.

Problem, a small voice reminded her. *Houston we have a big problem.*

Her eyes opened briefly as she felt the hard length of him nudge her stomach. Definitely a big problem. Huge.

The trouble was, Ronnie's body had overthrown her brain, and she was already in countdown mode. Short of something vital malfunctioning, she couldn't push Val away and murmur the one word that would put a stop to this . . . this . . . *this*.

"*Twenty-seven*," he murmured, doing the neck nibble/lick before he moved on, down to a tantalizing sweep of hot fingers around the tender sides of her breasts, his palms cupping their fullness—twenty-eight and twenty-nine.

Strong thumbs tweaked her nipples, rolled and massaged and brought them to painful awareness—thirty-one.

Wait a second. What happened to thirty?

Oh, yes. Thirty had been the delicate brush of fingertips against the budding crests, softly and reverently, as if Valentine Tremaine had never seen anything so beautiful, felt anything quite so soft, treasured anyone so much. . . .

As if.

He was Super Lover. The Doctor of Delight. Lord of Lust.

And she was losing it.

Get a grip, she told herself, fighting for her last ounce of control. Just say no—

Her denial disintegrated as warm lips closed over her aching nipple and sucked. Soft and teasing at first, then deep and insistent and oh so pleasurable.

". . . *thirty-three* . . ." came the deep, rumbling murmur from far, far away as he licked a path to her other breast to deliver the same sweet torment.

Her frantic heartbeat pounded in her ears, accompanied by the zing of blood through her veins, the chanting of long-deprived hormones. More, more, *more*!

Just touching, her brain reminded her. That's all they were doing. And quite well, she admitted as he suckled her long and hard and fierce, so fierce her entire body shook with the force of it.

"I . . . What step is this again?" She tried to remember, to slow her pounding heart by taking mental notes of every movement, from the tease of his fingertips up and down the sensitive sides of her breasts, to the way his long hair brushed across her in a sensual caress that prickled her skin and made her breath catch.

"Thirty-two?" she mumbled. "Or did we pass thirty-two?

He pulled away and her eyes snapped open to see him drop to his knees. His gaze burned into hers for a long, breathless moment. Her heart hit a speed bump, then revved forward, faster and faster, out of control.

It was the fire that danced in his blue, blue eyes that caused the reaction and promised more to come. *More.*

His eyes closed and his tongue flicked out as he traced her belly button before licking a delicious path lower. *Down.* Purposeful hands swept up the inside of her thigh as he lifted one leg and hooked it over his shoulder. One delicious fingertip grazed her slick, sensitive folds of flesh, and a strangled cry broke from her throat.

"Bon Dieu, *but you are perfect.*" His raw, gravelly voice filled her ears, rumbled over her ultrasensitive nerves. "*So warm and wet and tight.*" The discovery seemed to anger almost as much as it delighted him.

She could feel the turmoil raging inside him, then he slid a long, lean finger inside her slick passage and a moan curled up through her, from her belly to her throat, vibrating from the tip of her tongue.

A second finger joined the first, pushing deep, so deliciously deep. Her insides tightened in response, grasping at him, drawing him more fully inside as she marveled at the feel of a man's touch.

Her neck strained and her head snapped back as a tremor worked its way through her body. She caught sight of her reflection in the small bathroom mirror and felt a twinge of embarrassment at the provocative picture she made leaning against the wall, Val's strong, powerful body kneeling between her legs, his tanned skin a stark contrast with the paleness of her thigh draped over his broad shoulder.

Her lips were parted, her eyes at half-mast. Her breasts heaved with each frantic breath, her nipples still wet and ripe and red from his mouth.

Then Val rasped his tongue along the heart of her and she gasped. Her eyes shut as he murmured how sweet she tasted, the warmth of his breath stirring her before his lips joined in the loveplay.

"What number?" she managed to croak, doing her damndest to hold on to her last bit of sanity. Lessons, she reminded herself. This was a lesson in touching. Nothing more.

A warm chuckle teased her quivering flesh. *"Thirty-six,"* he murmured. *"I think."* Then he proceeded with a very thorough demonstration and Ronnie's mental note-taking faded as sensation after sensation rocked her.

Her body arched against his mouth, begging for more. More than his mouth and his tongue driving her wild. She wanted him. Strong and powerful, thrusting deep, deep inside her . . .

The insistent ring of the phone pushed past the pounding of her heart, the rush of blood through her veins. The sound continued, louder with each ring, before the machine finally picked it up.

"Hello. This is Veronica . . ."

Her voice on the machine faded into its boring monotone as the pressure in her body built. Heat spiraled inside her, hotter, hotter, fueling the want, the need, until she grasped Val's shoulders and begged for release.

"Please. I need you, Val. Over me, around me, inside me. *Please.*"

From the far-off distance, she heard Harvey Moulet's voice over her answering machine.

". . . I've got good news. Emma Wilbur married Michael Warren, of the Heaven's Gate Warrens."

Emma.

The name whispered through her head and quickly faded in the *bam, bam, bam* of her heart as the pressure built. Higher. Hotter—

Val stopped. He didn't move, didn't pull away, he simply stilled, anchoring her just this side of ecstasy.

"Please." She couldn't help herself. With his hot breath fanning her tenderest of spots, his hands burning into her bottom, holding her in place, his whisker-roughened face rasping the tender inside of her thigh, she was a slave to what she felt. To the man holding her. "Please," she said again.

"No." His voice was raw, pained, as if it took every ounce of control to deny her. It did. He trembled beneath her hands, his muscles bunched tight, as tight as she felt inside, like one of those windup toys coiled as tight as she could go with someone still holding the handle, keeping all that energy locked inside. If he let go, she'd go spinning off.

"Ma douce amie," he growled. *"I can't."*

He let go and stood, putting his back to her, his hands clenched at his sides, as if he fought so hard to keep from touching her.

But it wasn't the sight of him that sent a bolt of panic through her and forced her quivering legs to move. It was what he'd said. *Ma douce amie.* My sweet love.

She fled to the other room, grabbed a robe off a nearby chair, slipped into it, and, with trembling fingers, called Harvey back. Anything to distract and keep her from facing Val.

"I didn't make it to the phone in time," she explained, praying her voice didn't sound as shaky as she felt.

"Did you hear the message? I'm sorry to call so late but you said to call as soon as I found any new information." he said.

"It's okay but I'm afraid I didn't hear your message."

"Your Emma is Emma Warren. *The* Emma Warren. She's famous in Heaven's Gate."

"So it shouldn't be any trouble discovering the identity of her father, right?"

"Wrong, but at least we have several possibilities now. Emma

Warren was a prominent figure in the community. Chances are, she'll be listed in lots of the local records. Then there's the cemetery, the museum, the old newspaper archives. When can you drive up?"

"Let's see, it's Thursday. I've got class tomorrow, then work, but I could get away first thing Saturday morning."

"I'll meet you at eight a.m., and I'll do a little more checking between now and then."

"Thanks, Harvey."

"What are local historians for?"

She hung up and turned to find Val standing behind her. He'd put on his clothes, thankfully, but the fire still burned hotly in his blue eyes, mirroring her own raging feelings.

Lust . . . But it went beyond that.

Way, way beyond, because even more than Ronnie wanted him to make love to her, she wanted him to simply hold her in his arms and whisper those sweet words again and again.

Ma douce amie.

And that scared the daylights out of her.

It was all Val could do not to touch her, not to take her and finish what they'd started.

He licked his lips, savoring the ripe essence of her, prolonging the pleasure for just a few more moments. Enough to make him burn hotter, throb harder, not that he would act on any of it, no matter how he wanted to.

Or how much she wanted him to.

Despite the fear in her eyes and her sudden withdrawal from him, she still wanted him. She sat at the kitchen table, furiously documenting tonight's lesson as if she had no purpose, no desire, but to write.

Ah, but she wanted to do much more.

He could see it in the insistent push of her nipples against the fabric of her robe, in the flush that colored her pale skin a bright pink.

He felt it, an energy that crackled in the air, as fierce and potent as his own, drawing him to her.

He closed his eyes, his body trembling at the memory of her in his arms, the strength it had taken to pull away, to stop, especially after she'd asked him, begged him . . .

Peace, he reminded himself. He wanted an eternity of peace far more than he wanted Veronica Parrish.

The trouble was, with her so close, filling his nostrils, wetting his lips, her soft breaths echoing in his ears, her troubled frown stirring a tenderness he'd never known he possessed, it was all too easy to forget that all-important fact;

Even with his soul hanging in the balance.

"Where did you learn to do that?" Wanda's silky voice whispered over his skin and Danny smiled, staring down at her through the darkness. Despite the lack of light, he could still see her, her sweater pushed up, bra unsnapped, pale skin glowing in the moonlight.

"It's instinct." He wasn't sure why, but he knew every place to touch her, just how much pressure to use. He just knew.

Undoubtedly because he'd dreamt about this moment for so long. The two of them. On her couch. Doing more than simply sitting side by side, studying chemistry.

This *was* chemistry, and it was more potent than anything he'd ever imagined, and much, much easier.

"Say it again," she whispered, arching her full breast into the heat of his palm.

"You're smart," he murmured, punctuating the declaration with a reverent kiss to one tight nipple. "And beautiful. And God, you taste so good—"

"Wanda!" A loud rap on the door shattered the moment. "It's Tanya. I've got major trouble." She sniffled. "I've got a big date with Michael in a half hour and I can't decide between the red mini or the white sundress, and since you're so good when it comes to clothes . . ."

"I—I'm really busy," Wanda called out.

"With Danny?" A bubble of laughter followed. "Get real. You two can study later."

"But we're not . . ." For all her passion a moment ago, he saw the indecision on her face, the push-pull that he always sensed, as if she felt trapped between her friends and what they expected of her, and what she wanted. "Uh, yeah. Right."

"So pull your nose out of those books and answer the door. This is important."

"I'm coming," she called out, but she didn't move. Her anxious gaze went to him as if she waited for him to try to change her mind.

He could. He saw it in the longing in her soft blue eyes. Tonight he could have her, her friends be damned.

But tomorrow?

Danny gathered his self-control, marveling that he actually had any, pulled away, and righted her sweater. "Answer the door," he said when he'd slid the last button into place.

He turned the light on and reached for a nearby book.

Long, willowy fingers touched his arm. "Why?"

"I don't want you to lose face with your friends."

"Why?"

His gaze collided with hers. "Because it's important to you. They're important to you. When, if, it happens between us, I don't want you to have any regrets." And she would. Maybe not now, but later.

"I'm sorry," she whispered before bolting off the couch, righting her clothes and finger-combing her hair before pulling open the door. Though the apology was little consolation for the erection throbbing in his pants, hiding beneath an open chem book, the words eased the ache in his chest because he knew she meant it.

And that meant things weren't over between them.

Chapter Sixteen

"And there you have it, class, the phases of preorgasmic male stimulation."

For a lesson on male stimulation, Ronnie herself was quite stimulated.

Her gaze went to Guidry as he flipped on the lights and walked stiffly back to the podium. With his hair slicked back, his beady black eyes, his stern expression, and a necktie that appeared to be choking off the blood flow to his brain, he looked so sour it almost succeeded in dampening her inflamed senses. Unfortunately, the dream she'd had last night, preceded by a great big dose of reality, was still too vivid in her mind. Even the sight of unhappy, stuck-up Iron Ball couldn't cool her down.

"A reminder, people. Papers are due on the last day of class, two weeks from today. If I do not have your paper in my hand at the beginning of class, you automatically fail. No exceptions will be made."

Short of death, most professors would have said, but not Guidry. He, no doubt, would expect any student with the nerve to drop dead to have the hearse stop off on the way to the cemetery and deliver the treasured assignment, on time, into his cold hands. The guy needed a heart.

And Ronnie needed . . . *Val.*

Now where had that come from?

She certainly needed no such thing . . . person . . . *ghost.*

But somewhere along the line, Valentine Tremaine had turned into more than a ghost. She saw a man, felt a man. In her mind, he *was* a man. A man who took care of her when she was sick, who taunted and teased and kept her company. A man who scrambled her thoughts and made her yearn for marriage and babies and . . .

What the hell was she thinking?

She didn't want marriage and babies, and she certainly didn't want a man in her life. She was too busy studying, working, surviving.

Too afraid.

Who said that?

She forced the thought aside. She was not afraid of men.

Not of men. Of falling in love, stupid.

She stiffened. That either. Especially that. She simply didn't want to fall in love. She wanted a career first, foremost. More than she wanted Valentine Tremaine.

Her face heated at the thought of him and she clamped her legs together. Suddenly as determined as she'd been to seduce Val, she was even more hell-bent on avoiding him for the next two weeks. No more lessons. Madame X was only a few steps shy of the fifty. Ronnie could make up the rest. She would keep her distance, finish her paper, find out the truth about Emma, then give Val his walking papers. In the meantime, she had to concentrate.

She turned her attention, or at least tried, to school, and spent the rest of the morning rushing from class to class. After lunch, she headed to the accounting firm and spent four hours filing and answering phones. Then she headed back to campus for her shift at the library.

Not once did she think about Val, or what had happened.

No, it was more like a dozen times. Maybe two dozen. Just when she managed to forget him, his image popped into her head, his blue eyes vivid and intense, stirring so many things she'd never felt before.

That was the trouble. She *felt* too much where he was concerned. More than sympathy and admiration and compassion and lust. More.

* * *

"Are you all right?" Delta asked later that evening as they both stood behind the circulation desk and checked out books.

"Tired and stressed." Ronnie finished checking out one student and turned her attention to the next in line. "Finals start soon." She took a pile of books and flipped the top one open to the card pocket.

"Stress?" Delta gave her an I-don't-buy-that look. "And here I thought you looked so uptight because you were mooning over a man."

Try a ghost. "What makes you think I'm uptight?" She handed the stack of books back to the student.

"Well, you stamped the same book at least five times."

"Oh, no." She shook her head. "I don't know what's happening to me." But she did. She knew all too well and that's what had her so freaked out. She was falling for Val.

"It's okay." Delta sighed and glanced at the empty spot where Professor Gibbons usually sat every evening, reading his cooking magazine. "I completely forgot to pocket five cards a few minutes ago. Men," she muttered.

"Looks like Gibbons must be doing his reading at home."

Delta shrugged and turned to the next student. "It's a free country."

"So he *is* at home?" Ronnie pressed, grateful to be off the subject of her own love life and onto someone else's.

"I guess." At Ronnie's skeptical look, she shrugged. "Okay, he's at home, not that I've been spying on him."

"You drove by his house."

"I would never do any such thing." At Ronnie's knowing look, Delta shrugged. "I phoned him. He answered and I hung up."

"So how many times have you two gone out?"

"Four dinners and a lunch." Ronnie smiled, and Delta added, "Not that I'm keeping track. I mean, it's hard not to. The food is so memorable. Cass is a wonderful cook."

"Cass?"

"If I can eat the man's food, I can call him by his first name. It doesn't mean anything. I mean, he would like it to mean something. He wants more than good food and a little conversation, of course, but I'm not about to get serious with some over-the-hill Casanova even if he does cook a really divine chicken cordon bleu." ——————

"So you're snapping and growling because you miss the chicken, right?"

"I'm cranky because it's eight in the evening and I've been so busy, I haven't had time to eat. I need my nourishment, you know."

"Come on, Delta. You like the guy. Admit it."

"He's not a guy. He's a man. An old man."

"Who's really cute."

Delta seemed to soften. "Well, he does make me laugh, and we do like to watch Ted Koppel. And Letterman. Most men Cass's age like Leno; it's one of those loyalty things having to do with Johnny Carson that I still haven't figured out. But not Cass. He's a Letterman man all the way. And he likes Audrey Hepburn movies and Elvis . . ."

Speaking of Elvis.

Ronnie's gaze went to Mr. Heartbreak Hotel sitting in his usual spot in the reference section. He didn't spare her a glance, not that she wanted one. She pulled the baseball cap even lower and hunched over the circulation desk.

". . . and picnics and he's a Democrat." A big plus, Ronnie knew, because Delta's late husband had been not only a saint, but a Democratic saint. "And he likes to dance and he has all his own teeth."

"A definite plus," Ronnie agreed. "So why don't you *like* like him?"

"Because . . . Just because," she huffed, stuffing a card into a slot and shoving a book back toward a startled young man. "He's . . . old," she finally finished, but she didn't say the word with near as much distaste as she had before.

"From what you've told me, Cass seems very young at heart. In the prime of his life, teeth and all."

"Well," she conceded. "You'd certainly never be able to tell his age by the way he kisses."

"You've kissed him?"

"Well, uh, yes. Just a little peck. Nothing to write home about."

She grinned. "Admit it, Delta. You like him."

"Okay," she said with a deep sigh and a purse to her lips. "Maybe I do."

"Maybe?"

"Oh, all right, I do. But obviously he doesn't feel the same way." Her gaze went to his empty chair. "We sort of had a fight last night."

"Why?"

"Over the kiss. It surprised me. Not that he did it, but the fact that I liked it. A lot. Too damned much. Anyhow, I sort of threatened to chop off a certain part of his anatomy if he didn't start behaving like a gentleman. But I didn't mean it. I mean, I did at the time, but I didn't *really* mean it. Men are just too damned sensitive when it comes to their doohickeys."

"Did you tell him you were sorry?"

"Of course."

"And what did he say?"

"That maybe we should let things cool down a bit." She shook her head and frowned. "If he wants to cool down, fine, but this girl is not going to sit around waiting for him. I'm going out tonight." She eyed Ronnie. "You up for some after-work dessert at Jake's?"

Jake's was as famous as the House of Pies in the South, and always more packed because the twenty-four-hour café specialized in gourmet desserts, and Ronnie wasn't the only tired, overworked student who needed a daily sugar fix.

"They make a mean chocolate rum cake," Delta said, trying to tip the scales in her favor.

Ronnie could feel the fat cells expanding at the mere thought and she shook her head. "I've got a lot of studying to do. I have to get home." As the refusal rolled off her tongue, she thought about Val waiting for her, stretched out on the bed, so naked and handsome and tempting . . .

"Maybe one piece."

Jake's was packed, as usual. Ronnie and Delta took up residence at a table in the corner and shared their misery over two huge pieces of chocolate rum cake.

"Ronnie?" Danny's voice carried through the crowd and Ronnie's head snapped up to see him wind his way around several tables. When he reached their table, he exchange hellos with Delta, then turned to Ronnie. "What are you doing here?"

"Having dessert."

"You? But you don't drink."

She shoveled in the last bite of cake and licked her fork. "I'm not drinking, I'm eating."

He glanced at the second piece of rum-soaked cake waiting in the wings for her fork. "That definitely qualifies as both."

She grinned and reached for plate number two. "Want a bite?"

He shook his head. "I'm driving."

"You don't have a car."

"It's Wanda's car. She asked me to meet her here. We're supposed to study back at her place."

"Studying?" Delta raised her eyebrows. "Is that what they call it these days?"

"Unfortunately," Danny grumbled.

"What happened to your date the other night?" Ronnie asked.

"It started out great, we ended up back at her place, and then one of her friends showed up. End of date."

"Love sucks," Delta said, pouring a raspberry liquor sauce over her own monstrous piece of cake before shoveling a forkful into her mouth.

"Yeah." Ronnie took a bite out of her second piece of rum decadence. Or was that her third?

"Yeah." Danny eased into a seat beside Ronnie and glanced moodily at a table near the doorway where Wanda sat with a group of her friends—a few cheerleaders and some grade-A-looking hunks from the football team. He glanced at his watch.

"Are you taking medicine?" Ronnie asked.

"I've got a test at seven a.m. and we still have our nightly tutoring session."

"Then blow this off and go home without her," Ronnie told him. "You have to think about yourself."

"But it's calculus. Wanda's weak in calculus. Besides, this was kind of supposed to be our second date. We were going to have dessert before the studying."

"Here, honey," Delta said, waving a forkful of cake dripping with liquor sauce. "This will help."

Danny held up a hand. "I'm not really hungry."

The woman shrugged and shoved the bite into her own mouth. "It's not about hunger, sweetie," she said after she'd swallowed with a satisfied gulp. "It's about comfort."

"Yeah," Ronnie said, taking another bite. Her taste buds chanted in satisfaction almost as loud as her grumbling hormones.

Another bite and she closed her eyes at the rush of sweetness, followed by a hazy warmth that uncurled in her stomach and seeped outward. It wasn't as hot as the firestorm that had swept through her last night courtesy of Val, but at least she'd gone five minutes without wondering what he was doing.

Was he waiting for her?

Thinking about her?

She frowned and took another bite. A big bite.

Danny glanced behind him again, then turned back to his watch.

Ronnie pointed her fork at him. "Why don't you just go over there and tell her you're ready to go?"

"I don't want to bother her." He toyed with a napkin. "She's busy talking to her friends."

"She's busy following them out the door," Delta said, motioning to the front of the restaurant.

"What?" Danny's head whipped around in time to see Wanda wave at him and mouth a pink, pouty, "Sorry" before she disappeared. "Well, I'll be damned," he muttered. He shook his head and reached for Delta's fork.

The woman raised her eyebrows. "I thought you weren't hungry."

"I'm not." He shoveled in a forkful. "I'm miserable."

"Welcome to the club." Delta signaled the waitress and ordered another round of cake.

"Love sucks," Danny said, and all three raised their forks in a heartfelt salute.

Love did suck, not that Ronnie had to worry about that. She wasn't in love. She was in lust.

Lust, you got that?

No love. Not for this girl. No way, no how, forget it.

It was the cake making her think crazy thoughts like how she was actually anxious to see Val.

That's what she told herself as she stumbled home, her head buzzing, her taste buds still tingling from the sugar overload.

Outside her apartment, she fumbled with her key, a giggle passing her lips as her heart revved in anticipation.

Anticipation? More like rum cake. Three slices. Or was that four?

"Darned key," she mumbled, surprised at how thick her lips suddenly felt. And, geez, the floor had started to shake.

She jammed the metal into the lock. If only it would slide home. Then she could sit down, the floor wouldn't tremble so much, and maybe she could blink away this blasted fog glazing her eyes—

"Yikes," she shrieked as the door suddenly jerked open and she pitched straight into Val's embrace.

Strong arms closed around her. The scent of raw male and leather and fresh, ripe water snuck into her nostrils and infiltrated her brain before she could catch her breath, much less hold it. Heat scorched her fingertips where she splayed her hands against the hard wall of his chest.

Her head snapped up, her gaze collided with deep blue eyes.

"I . . ." The words tangled in her throat.

"You're all right." Relief filled his voice. *"I was terribly worried."*

"You were?" The very idea sent a spurt of joy through her. Her hands started creeping up, desperate to curl around behind his neck—

"The cake," she muttered, jerking away before she lost her sanity completely. Because no way could a man feel so warm, so right . . .

His relief seemed to give way to anger as he stared at her. *"Where the hell have you been?"*

Even the sight of his wrinkled forehead and his narrowed eyes did funny things to her insides. Made her feel jumpy and nervous and . . . *excited.* She shook her head frantically. "This isn't happening to me." Her words slurred together and his expression darkened.

"You've been drinking."

"Hah! That shows what you know. I've been eating."

A muscle ticked frantically in his jaw; his lips drew into a tight line. *"I was here worried sick, while you were out getting drunk. Drunk,"* he spat the word at her. *"You're drunk."*

"No, I'm not," she protested, despite the sudden churn of her stomach. "Not that it's any of your business. You're just cake."

"What?"

"Cake." She pounded a finger into his chest. "That's what's making me feel this way because no way am I falling for you." Was that her voice? Yes, it was, but it wasn't the voice of reason. It was the voice of a frustrated, half-drunk—her stomach vaulted again—make that *very* drunk woman who'd just consumed thousands of calories that were now making their way to her hips. Her stomach. Her butt . . . "Oh, God." Tears rushed to her already blurry eyes.

Valentine Tremaine had a surefire method for dealing with a crying woman. After all, he'd had years of practice at sliding his arms around a woman, soothing her, listening to her. Women loved men who kept their cool, stayed in control, and listened.

"*I was worried!*" he roared. "*Do you not have one responsible bone in your body?*" Before she could answer, he stalked her, backing her up until her back flattened against the wall. "*Hours,*" he growled. "*I've been waiting up for hours. I thought someone had slit your pretty little throat, or run you over with some bloody automobile. I thought you were dead!*"

"Good news." She sniffled and gave him a wobbly smile. "I'm not."

"*Not yet.*" He smiled, a dangerous, wicked smile meant to wipe the expression from her face. "*I get the pleasure of seeing to that myself.*"

Her smile faltered. "I . . ."

"*Yes?*"

"I . . ." She wet her trembling lips. "I—I think the rum cake is about to beat you to it." Then she stumbled past him in her haste to reach the bathroom. A few steps shy, she swayed to the side, her knees giving way.

Val caught her before she hit the ground and though he wanted nothing more than to throttle the life out of her, the pained expression on her face, the desperate way she clung to his neck, effectively doused his temper. For now.

Later, he told himself. Later he would kill her.

"Hurry," Ronnie managed to gasp before her stomach jumped and she clamped her lips shut against a wave of sickness.

The next thing she knew, she felt the cold tile of the floor beneath her legs. The cool rim met her fingertips.

It was a long while later, at least half a rum cake, before her stomach calmed down enough for her to wash her face and rinse out her mouth. Ronnie was this close to curling up on the floor rather than trying to get her trembling legs to cooperate, when Val picked her up and carried her to the bed.

He reached to help her out of her soiled T-shirt, but she slapped his hands away. He looked ready to argue, but then his gaze hooked on her lips, then her breasts, and he not only pushed her shirt back down, but yanked the cover up to add to her defenses.

Or his own.

"*Go to sleep*, Rouquin." He killed the light. Leather creaked as he settled into the recliner, always so intent on keeping his distance.

"I'm sorry," she mumbled, her eyes closed as she snuggled down into the covers and prayed for her stomach to keep its cool. "I didn't mean to worry you."

"*Just go to sleep*," he growled as if angry that she'd reminded him. But the fingertips that trailed over her cheek were anything but angry.

Fingertips? Yes, fingertips . . . He touched her softly, gently, and it felt so . . . right.

Her eyes snapped open, but she saw only the darkness hovering above her.

Imagination, she decided. That and all the rum-soaked cake she'd eaten. She turned onto her side and buried her fuzzy head in the pillows. Because no way, no how could she have done something so stupid, so irrational as to fall in love with a ghost. To fall in love, period.

She'd fallen in love.

Ronnie fought the truth throughout the next week by keeping Delta company after work each night and indulging her taste buds at Jake's. Danny joined them and the three drowned their troubles in virgin brownies and alcohol-free fudge cake.

Out of sight, out of mind, she kept telling herself. If she avoided Val long enough, she wouldn't be so enamored of him.

Right?

Wrong. The distance only served to wind her tighter and tighter. Frustration, she told herself. Deprived hormones. She needed a man, *man* being the operative word. If she weren't so sexually deprived, she wouldn't be yearning for Val. So, acting on this logic, she set her sights on finding herself a prime, grade-A male to indulge her hormones.

The past few weeks of love lessons had taught her well—she had two hot date prospects by the time Friday rolled around. But no matter how good-looking, how nice, how *real* both men were, neither could hold a candle to Val.

Unfortunately, he wasn't having the same thoughts about her. He rarely spared her a glance, as if he'd come to a few conclusions of his own about their relationship. Namely, that there was no relationship, and he intended to keep it that way.

Fine by her. She didn't want him distracting her, interfering in her life, turning her normal routine upside down. No, she certainly didn't want stubborn, egotistical Valentine Tremaine.

But need him . . . yes, she definitely needed him. Distracting her, interfering in her life, turning her normal routine upside down and inside out. She admitted as much to herself Tuesday night, a full week since she and Val had had their bathroom encounter, as she sat at Jake's and passed on chocolate Fudge Extravaganza in favor of chicken salad and an apple. She'd had her fill of caffeine and chocolate—proving beyond a doubt she'd gone off the deep end and traded her sanity for the forbidden *L* word.

Love.

She still couldn't believe it. She'd spent years avoiding love, intent on building something solid for herself. A successful career based on hard work because, in the end, just as she'd told Jenny, love wasn't enough.

It hadn't been enough to make her parents support their only daughter when she'd gone against their wishes and followed her own dreams.

And it certainly wasn't enough to change the inevitable. Val was leaving, headed for the Afterlife as soon as Harvey came through with some news on Emma. It was only a matter of time.

There would be no marriage and babies in their future. No big wedding, no nice house in the suburbs, no Lamaze classes or Little League or junior ballet lessons. No traditional family.

The funny thing was, Veronica Parrish had never wanted any of those things. Until now. Until Val.

Talk about *really* rotten luck.

The thought plagued her as she headed home around two in the morning. Val was in his usual spot in the recliner, his gaze fixed on the TV. She said hello, then headed straight to her computer and spent the next hour trying to work on her spreadsheets for her tax class. Trying, but not succeeding. Not with Val sitting so close, her feelings so ripe and new and totally inappropriate.

He was a *ghost*, for heaven's sake. They had no future. She shouldn't want a future. She didn't. She wanted her degree. Her career.

Forget about him, she told herself Wednesday morning as she sat in Guidry's class, after a sleepless night worrying and wondering and watching Val watch TV. She jotted down the notes Guidry gave about the female reproductive system, and forced herself to face reality. The future looked dismal, the relationship was hopeless . . . Duh, what relationship, Einstein?

Just *forget* him.

She fixed her gaze on the drawing on the chalkboard.

Ovaries.

Which reminded her of babies.

Which reminded her of Val.

So much for forgetting.

The only thing left was to acknowledge what she felt and deal with it.

She loved Val. While he might not return her feelings he *was* attracted to her. She saw proof when she caught him staring at her when he thought she wasn't looking. A simmering heat filled his gaze, a combination of longing and lust and love. . . .

If only.

But with the way her luck was playing out, she wasn't placing any bets that he returned her feelings. Still, he did feel *something* for her, and that gave her the courage she needed to take the initiative. She was a few steps shy of the Ultimate Fifty and the time had come for her to put all she'd learned to the test. Just to be sure, Ronnie spent Wednesday afternoon reviewing her notes and formulating a strategy. If Val thought she'd been bent on seduction before, he had a big surprise coming. That had been the inexperienced, I-barely-have-time-to-breathe-much-less-fall-in-love Ronnie. Now she was Madame Ronnie—ready and armed with knowledge and sex appeal—and a woman in love, and she was determined to make the most of the time she had left with Valentine Tremaine.

Starting tonight.

Chapter Seventeen

Despite what Val had said about dressing for success—namely, that it was unnecessary when a woman had it going on from the inside out—Ronnie stopped off at a local lingerie shop on her way between school and receptionist duty at Landry & Landry. While she didn't have any firsthand experience, she seriously doubted there was a man alive who could resist a woman clad in a black lace teddy, thigh-high black stockings, and a garter belt that read *Danger! Curves Ahead*. At least, that's what Paulette of Paulette's Pleasures guaranteed her as she plopped down her hard-earned babysitting money—putting up with the Hades twins for the past few years had finally paid off.

With her bag of X-rated goodies, she left the library that night when her shift ended at ten. By ten-thirty, she was begging Suzanne for the use of her bathroom on the pretense that Ronnie's didn't have any hot water. While Val wasn't at his solid best until midnight, he was still there, a shimmering, observant apparition, and Ronnie didn't want him to get a look at her until she was primed and ready.

She showered and changed, pulling on a pair of fuzzy slippers and a thick terry cloth robe that covered her from head to toe—as far as Suzanne knew she was just getting ready for bed. Then she spent a half hour reading to the twins, who were down with a cold and a fever—probably the same bug she'd had—before she kissed them goodnight and padded down the hall to her apartment at exactly midnight.

Perfect timing.

Her hand paused on the doorknob and she closed her eyes.

Step one. A sexy mindset. Just as Val had taught her, she

envisioned the dream and concentrated on the details. The scent of Val teasing her nostrils, the soft cotton sheet slithering down her bare legs, the touch of his warm fingertips on her body, gliding down . . .

Her breaths came quicker and her hands started to tremble. She wet her lips and opened her eyes. "Just do it," she told herself, and then she opened the door.

Two vital things registered in Val's brain when he saw Veronica framed in the open doorway. One, she was home early and two, she was definitely up to something.

When she ignored him completely, and proceeded straight to the stereo to pop in a CD, his suspicions escalated. He started to rise from the chair, but she turned on him, pinned him with a hot stare, and started to sway to the sultry tune drifting from the speakers.

He poised on the edge of the chair. "Shouldn't you be at Jake's?"

"It's final exam time." Despite the nervous light in her eyes, she slipped off her slippers and moved lightly trembling hands to the belt holding her robe in place and a wave of panic bolted through Val.

She was undressing. Right here. Right now. In front of him.

Get up, man! Get up and run for cover! But he couldn't move, couldn't breathe as white terry cloth pooled at her ankles, and left nothing to cover her but the skimpiest black lace underwear he'd ever seen, as sparse as any corset, and infinitely more revealing.

The black lace patterned her skin, making her look all the more pale and perfect. Thigh-high black stockings encased her long legs. A stretch of creamy white thigh started where the stockings ended, and stretched tantalizingly to where the black lace rode high on her hips. He saw the faintest whisper of red silk peeking through the black lace that covered the triangle between her legs before he forced his gaze up, where it snagged on her barely concealed breasts. Her puckered nipples pressed against the lace, pale pink shadows beneath the skimpy covering. His mouth went dry.

"Merde!" His voice was raw and choked. "You're not . . . that is, your clothes aren't . . ." He fought for words as she stood there, so close, so tempting. "Christ, where are your clothes?"

"These are clothes." She fingered one scanty shoulder strap of the black underwear. "Sort of. They cost as much as clothes, but they're a lot more uncomfortable." She smiled, her full lips parting just enough to make his groin tighten. "It's a good thing I won't be wearing them for long."

Funny, but it wasn't the sight of her half-naked body in all its pale perfection or her sultry promise that stalled the air in his lungs. It was the fierce gleam in her golden eyes. The look hit him like a shot of whiskey, fireballing through him, pinning him in place for a long, burning moment in which he couldn't move, much less think or breathe.

"Steps two through five," she murmured as she moved toward him. "How to entice a man with my eyes." She fixed her gaze on him, lowered her lashes, and gave a sultry wink. "And my mouth." She licked her full, pink lips. "My hands." She touched one hand to her throat, trailed a fingertip down her deep cleavage, over the skimpy material covering her lush breast, to tease one nipple. The tip hardened in response, protruding through the lace pattern. She gasped at the sensation and breathed, "Am I enticing you?"

Yes!

The answer echoed through his head, stirring his survival instincts, summoning the fear that lived and breathed inside of him.

"Y-you shouldn't," he managed. "Don't." Doubt chased determination across her features and he thought she might actually heed his words.

She didn't, and he realized, in a shattering instant, that he was more thankful than afraid.

He didn't want her to stop.

"I have to do this," was all she said as she thrust out her breasts, swayed a bit more to the music, and stepped toward him.

Fifteen breathless seconds later, after a seductive strip and tease that left her in nothing but skimpy panties and the sheerest black bra, Ronnie stood inches away. So close, he had but to reach out.

He needed to reach out. He wanted her so badly. Just one touch, he vowed to himself.

But he knew, deep inside, one touch wouldn't be enough. One would lead to more and she would lose her virginity, and he would lose his soul. His peace. *Everything.*

Her hands disappeared behind her, to the clasp of her bra, and he bolted to his feet.

"Don't!" He reached to stop her and she backed up.

She pinned him with a desperate look. "Just stay back. I'm doing this."

"No, you're not."

"Yes, I am." She worked frantically at the hooks as she stumbled backward. "This thing . . ." She gritted her teeth. "It's supposed to release—" she struggled "—at the flick of a finger. . . . I—" she gritted "—I think I want my money back.—*There*," she declared. Hooks popped, Ronnie smiled, and Val lunged forward.

"No!" His hands closed over the black lace cups, holding them in place and pinning her to the wall as the straps collapsed on her shoulders.

A moment of heart-pounding silence passed as Ronnie glanced down at his hands, then back up at his face. She burst into a fit of giggles.

"Why are you laughing?"

"Because you look so desperate not to see me naked, and if I don't laugh, I'm liable to cry."

His gaze went to his hands covering her chest, pinning the bra cups into place. A smile teased his lips before he became conscious of the heat of her skin through the skimpy covering the ripening of her nipples against his palms.

His eyes locked with hers and the humor drained from the moment. "Why, Rouquin? Why are you doing this to me?"

"Because I want you." She swallowed, some of her determination faltering beneath his searching gaze. "I want you to be the first."

The only, a voice whispered. Her voice. Inside his head, battling his defenses. *You.* The plea stirred something beyond fear, something that welled up inside him and swamped everything but the need to please this woman. *His* woman.

Ronnie watched the indecision play over his features before a distinct frown drew his mouth tight.

"*That was the worst striptease I have ever seen,*" he declared, pricking her ego and stirring her anger.

Her jealousy. "And I've bet you've seen plenty."

"*A fair share.*"

Her temper calmed beneath a wave of self-consciousness. "And mine was really the worst?"

"*It cannot begin to compare with the others.*" A slow, sensual smile slithered across his face. "*I loved it.*"

His words sang through her heart, feeding her determination. But she was still too new to the art of seduction to be completely convinced. "Love is an awful strong word. Maybe you just liked it."

"Loved," he assured her, so much feeling in the one word that it sent a spurt of heat through her. "*You are truly one of a kind.*"

He dropped his hands and the bra fell away, but he didn't look at her freed breasts. He looked at her face, her eyes, her mouth. "*Back to the lesson plan,* chérie. *Where were we? Oh, yes. You were about to review step ten. The kiss.*"

He bypassed the first nine kisses, steps ten through eighteen, and went straight for step nineteen. The full, open-mouthed French kiss.

His lips captured hers, his tongue plunged deep, stroking and coaxing until she joined him, her tongue tangling, giving as good as she got. And boy, did she get good.

Her toes curled, her nerves came alive, and a sizzling heat swept through her, starting where his lips touched hers and spreading outward in a search and destroy mission until she all but melted in his arms.

Her hands snaked around his neck, pulling him closer. Her aching breasts pressed against the soft material of his shirt, desperate to feel the heat of the man beneath.

And he burned so hot.

He felt every bit a real man, but there was something else. He vibrated. Everywhere she touched, she felt a prickling sensation, his energy alive and humming. The sensation stirred her nerves, set them to spinning until she felt as charged, as vibrant as the man touching her.

He splayed one hand at the base of her spine, pressing her closer while his other slipped inside her lace panties to cup her bottom and knead the soft flesh. He kissed and fondled her until she knew beyond a doubt that he'd loved her striptease.

That he wanted her.

That he meant to have her. Finally. Thankfully.

The knowledge sang through her and she broke the kiss long enough to slide her mouth along his stubbled jaw, to his ear, determined to do some reviewing of her own now that he was a ready and willing subject.

Steps twenty through twenty-eight consisted of fantasies, and Ronnie proceeded to whisper an enticing story about him and her and a tub full of strawberries and cream. Then she nibbled his earlobe and licked a delicious path down his neck, through a forest of silky hair. She suckled a brown male nipple, explored the rippled expanse of his abdomen as she moved into the thirties and proceeded *down*.

Eager fingers grazed the bulge beneath his pants and she felt a surge of female empowerment as he groaned long and low and deep. She dropped to her knees in front of him, just as he'd done with her the night in the bathroom.

She touched the waistband of his pants and slid the buttons free until his erection sprang hot and greedy toward her. A drop of pearly liquid beaded on the ripe purple head and she reached out, catching his essence and spreading it in a sensual stroke of her fingertip down the throbbing length of him, clear to the base surrounded by a thatch of sand-colored hair.

A throaty growl rumbled in his chest and she smiled before wrapping her hand around him. He arched into her touch, his iron-hard sex dark and forbidden against her long, pale fingers. Inviting. Like the fruit in the Garden of Eden, and she no stronger than Eve.

Her gaze trailed up, over a ridged abdomen, a broad, hair-dusted chest, a corded neck, the chiseled perfection of his face. His eyes burned as fierce as the center of a flame, so hot and bright and blue.

"*Don't,*" he said, but his gaze whispered something altogether different.

Ronnie couldn't help herself. She took him in her mouth, suckled and licked and gave him the pleasure he'd given her so freely the other night. His hands cradled her face, so delicate considering the tension gripping his body, carving every muscle until the veins in his forearms bulged.

He grew harder, hotter, heavier and she took all of him until he gasped and jerked back.

"*No.*" His hands closed over her shoulders, forcing her away.

He was stopping again. Desperation collided with a wave of disappointment and insecurity. "I didn't do anything wrong, did I—?"

The question ended as he drew her to her feet and crushed her to his chest, his lips claiming hers in a fierce kiss that sucked the air from her lungs.

Chest heaving, breathing harsh, he pulled away long enough

to murmur against her lips, "*I want to taste you*, chérie. *I want to pleasure you. I need to . . ."*

His words faded and he went rigid. Ronnie's eyes fluttered open to see him direct a murderous glare at the door behind her.

"What is it?" she gasped.

"*Someone's here.*"

Through the heat gripping her senses, the words registered, along with the faint thud of footsteps. She closed her eyes. "Not now." Of all the rotten timing. Her first instinct was to pretend she wasn't there. They could knock a little while, then go away.

But what if it was Suzanne? What if the twins had gotten worse? What if it was Mr. Weatherby? What if Pringles had had a relapse?

They'll live without you.

She pulled Val close and laid another kiss on him, and while the sheer contact of his lips on hers was enough to scramble her common sense, she still heard the creak of wood and felt the presence on the other side of the door.

She pulled away, drew in a deep draft of air. "Just give me a few seconds. I'll get rid of them," she vowed.

Val didn't say anything. His gaze swept her from head to toe, pausing at all the important places in between, then he shimmered and faded.

She retrieved her robe and turned to see the doorknob jiggle as someone tried to open it from the other side. Open it? The question registered as she shoved her arms into the sleeves, belted the waist, and stomped toward the door, but she was in too much of a hurry, too hungry, to wonder why whoever it was wasn't bothering to knock.

"This had better be life or death," she muttered as she hauled open the door.

In the blink of an eye, she came face to face with Mr. Hunk-a-hunk-a-burnin'-love. Only tonight he was "Mr. Viva Las Vegas."

And he held an ax in his hands.

Chapter Eighteen

Okay, this definitely involved life and death.

Her own.

"What are you doing here?" Viva Las Vegas demanded.

"I—I live here."

"I know that, but you're not supposed to be home." He frowned, yanked a spiral notebook from his pocket, and started flipping through it. "You're supposed to be with your friends at that dessert place."

"J-Jake's," she stammered, her gaze fixed on the ax, her heart shifting gears and nearly busting out of her chest.

"That's right. You're supposed to be at Jake's tonight. You've been there every night this past week. Six days in a row."

Her fear took a spur-of-the-moment vacation as his words registered in her head. *Jake's. Every night. Six days in a row.*

"How do you know where I've been . . . ?" The question faded as the pieces started to click together in her head. The numerous times she'd seen him around campus. The strange instances when she'd felt someone watching her.

"Y-you've been following me."

"It's called learning the subject's routine."

"My r-routine?"

"Where you go, what you do, et cetera." At her puzzled expression, he added, "Hey, I know the whole procedure, lady. Never miss an episode of *New York Undercover*." His eyes narrowed. "You're not supposed to be here," he said again as his fingers flexed around the ax handle. "Look, I'm sorry about this, but a guy's gotta do what a guy's gotta do." Ax raised, he stepped forward.

He was going to kill her. Right here. Right now. While she was wearing nothing but a shocked expression and a terry cloth robe. Her mouth opened, but nothing came out. Her gaze shot to the open doorway behind him. *Run!* her brain commanded, but in the face of death everything seemed to shut down. She couldn't scream, move, breathe, nothing.

She managed to clamp her eyes shut and pray. *Please forgive me for all my sins . . .*

The floor creaked.

. . . for every bad thing I've ever thought in my entire life . . .

His heavy breathing echoed in her ears.

. . . for lying to Jenny about that awful perm she got back in the eighth grade that I said was simply divine . . .

Footsteps sounded.

. . . for not making more time to help old people and small children, for watching that R movie on cable a few months back, for eating that double pint of rocky road when I know my body is a temple . . .

"Sorry," the guy grumbled again, closing the distance to her. The floor creaked, the ax hissed through the air and—

He moved past her. Whew. Thank God. No ax. No bloody murder—

Past her?

Her eyes popped open and she whirled to see Viva head for the bed. He raised the ax. The blade arced, flashing silver fire as it headed for one defenseless bedpost—

"No!" Her own voice blended with another female cry.

"Norman Nathaniel Presley!"

The ax poised and Ronnie whirled to see the woman standing in the open doorway. Six feet of luscious curves and a frown that made even Ronnie's heart pause in her chest.

"I knew it," the woman cried, her gaze pinning Ronnie in place. "You low-down, two-timing, snake in the grass. I knew you were cheating on me!"

"Cheating?" Norman actually looked relieved. "Is that what you think? Aw, I ain't here because of her, honey."

"Oh really?" She glared. "Tell that to your mama, buster, because I'm calling first thing when I get back home and telling her everything you've been up to."

"Now don't go flying off the handle. I'm telling the truth. I ain't here for her. I'm here for this." He motioned toward the bed.

Norma Renee's face went from angry to confused as she stared past him, blinking frantically and wiping at her tear-streaked face. "The bed. Oh, my lord, that's *the* bed."

"Not for long. I been waiting for this moment for weeks. I'm acting out. Just like the doc said."

She planted her hands on her hips and glared. "You mean to tell me you've been lying to me, telling me you're out playing cards with Buddy and Woodrow, making me think you're skirt chasing, when you're really bed chasing."

"Yep." He seemed pleased to have avoided the womanizing rap in favor of lying.

"Do you know how awful I felt when Buddy called me tonight and wanted to talk to you, and I said, he's at your house playing five-card stud, and he says, no he ain't? Stupid, that's how," she shouted before he could get a word in edgewise. "And mad. And upset. I cried for hours, then I decided if you were really fooling around, I had to see for myself."

"How'd you find me?"

"I drove around a few hours, then I spotted you at the Jiffy Mart taking a leak. Then I followed you." She shook her head. "Weeks of lies. *Weeks*, Norman Nathaniel. How could you?"

"I had to stake her out. I couldn't risk her being here when I made my move. I had to watch her, find out where she went, when she was gone, so I could pick the lock and do what I would have done if that security guard hadn't stopped me."

"You're the lawyer's assistant," Ronnie mumbled, remembering the story Val had told her about the near miss with the ax-wielding fiancé in the warehouse.

"Was." Norma Renee sniffled. "When the security guard reported that Norman, here, nearly chopped up a prime piece of estate furniture, I got fired." Tears poured down her face, leaving trails of black mascara in their wake.

"Now, honey, you didn't really like that job anyway."

"That wasn't the point. I got fired, I've never been fired. And then to find out my fiancé was cheating on me."

"I'm not cheating."

"But I didn't know that until just a few seconds ago."

"Now you do, so go on home, honey." He eyed the bed. "This is between me and *it*. I can practically feel the aggression draining away just looking at it, Norma. The doc's right about this. I know he is."

"Doc?" Ronnie asked, still trying to grasp the whole absurd scene unfolding in front of her.

"Our therapist," Norma Renee supplied. "Ever since Norman found me in that bed having a good time without him, he's been feeling guilty and jealous. Dr. Weiner suggested Norman act out his aggression on an inanimate object." She shot Norman a glance. "But I think any bed would do, Norman. It's symbolic."

"I thought about that and it's *this* bed that got me all worked up in the first place. It has to be this one." He raised the ax again.

"Stop!" Ronnie shouted. Okay, so he was an ax-wielding crazy man, but from the conversation going on, he was fast losing serial killer status and Ronnie wasn't about to see her hard-earned money go down the tube. "You can't do this. It's a bed, for Pete's sake. A defenseless bed. My bed." Val's bed. Not that he was anywhere in sight as the scene played out. But he was there. She felt a prickling awareness that soothed the fear inside her and made her stand taller. She glared at Norman, who pulled a wad of bills from his pocket.

"I'll pay for the damage, lady."

"Why didn't you just buy it in the first place?"

"I tried, but you got to the antique shop before me. That's where I got your name and address. From the bill of sale."

"Why didn't you just offer to buy it from me?"

"Would you have sold it to me?"

"No."

"That's why. It was a risk I couldn't take. I show up, offer you money, you turn me down. Later on the bed turns up destroyed, money left behind to pay for the damages. Who would you have suspected?"

"The guy who offered to buy it from me."

"Bingo, lady. You could have given a description of me to the police, my name, everything. I couldn't risk that."

"I can still give a description to the police, as well as your name and your girlfriend's, here."

The wrong thing to say to a man holding an ax, Ronnie realized when he tightened his grip and glared at her.

"We'll see about that," he started, but Norma cut him off.

"He isn't usually like this," she explained, her gaze pleading as Ronnie grabbed the phone. "Really he isn't. But he sort of has this problem—"

"Norma Renee!"

"That's why we're seeing the therapist. He told us that time sometimes heals these things and it's probably just stress that keeps him from getting it up—"

"Norma Renee!"

"What? You want to go to jail, because I can tell you right now, your mother will have a major cardiac arrest if you call her from the pokey." She cast pleading eyes on Ronnie. "His ma-ma's on the city council and crazy, ax-wielding sons won't look too good come reelection time. Anyhow, with Norman's prob-lem and us seeing the doctor and all, I wasn't exactly seeing sparklers in bed, if you know what I mean, much less a great big Roman candle. But then I sat down on that bed and it was like, *bam.* Fourth of July and New Year's Eve all rolled into one, and then Norman walks in and if it had been another man, he would have punched his lights out—that's what he did when Davey Joe Carver—that's my brother's best friend—tried to kiss me at the family Christmas party last year. My mama always throws these big spreads over in Shreveport—"

"Tell her our life story so there's no mistake when she reports it, why don't you?"

"Don't use that tone with me, Norman Nathaniel. You're the one who broke into this nice lady's apartment and is now acting like a crazy man. Anyhow—" she turned back to Ronnie "—Norman, here, sort of took me seeing fireworks as a personal affront to his manhood. I should have seen this coming, with him so insanely jealous and all."

"I have to get my feelings out," Norman said. "The doc said to act out, and I have to, honey. For us. Our future," he said, turning determined eyes on the bed. He lifted the ax.

Ronnie watched as Val materialized next to Norman and caught the ax midair. Wood splintered, the handle broke in two, and the man stumbled backward, eyes wide as he stared at the fallen ax.

"What the hell . . . ?" Norma's voice faded away as she, too, stared at the fallen ax.

"It's not a normal bed," Ronnie told them. "It's haunted."

"H-haunted?" Norman sputtered.

"That's right." Ronnie thought about calling the police at that moment, since she and Val seemed to have the upper hand, but considering the outrageous circumstances, she decided scaring the daylights out of Norman might be more efficient, and a lot more fun. Besides, she wasn't about to tolerate a police force combing every inch of her bed, or possibly confiscating it as evidence. "By a big, mean, bloodthirsty classical music lover who hates Elvis."

Norman's gaze dropped to his shirt, shifted back to the bed, then cut sideways to Ronnie. "You're making that up."

"Go on, then. Sing an Elvis song and see what happens."

"I-I think we should go. Now," Norma Renee said.

But Norman was already backing up, his eyes like saucers as he glanced past Ronnie toward the bed.

She turned and saw the source of his sudden distress. The pillow was rising off the bed, courtesy of a tanned arm attached to an equally tanned body, but Norman and Norma couldn't see that. They saw only the pillow.

"He doesn't like late-night visitors," Ronnie told them.

Both pairs of eyes stared past her in time to see a sheet rise off the bed, taking shape and form until it looked like a Halloween ghost minus the black eyehole cutouts.

They bolted for the door as if the Devil himself were chasing them.

Or a legendary lover covered in a sheet.

The door slammed and she turned on Val. "That wasn't nice."

He pulled the sheet off his head and grinned. *"But it was fun."*

A smile tugged at her lips as she bolted the door and slid the chain lock into place for good measure. "A lot of fun." She closed her eyes and touched a hand to her still pounding heart. "But for a few seconds there, I thought I was ground meat."

He came up behind her. Strong hands closed over her shoulders and kneaded the heavily knotted muscles. *"You need not have been afraid. I would never let anyone harm you."* His fingers tightened for the space of a heartbeat and she felt his desperation, his fear.

It mirrored her own when she'd seen Norman about to ax Val's treasured bed. His link. *Him.*

Lips nibbled at her neck as he slid his arms around her to untie the belt and cup her breasts. Thumbs grazed her nipples, brought them to throbbing life, and she tilted her head back into the cradle of his shoulder.

"Now, where were we, chérie?"

She touched his hands and slid them down to the part of her that burned the hottest. "Well, I think we were just about here."

"Mmm . . ." he murmured, his fingers pushing her panties down, ruffling the curls until his fingertip touched the slick folds between her legs. "And I was just about here."

"Val?"

"Mmm?"

"What would have happened if that security guard hadn't stopped Norman the first time?"

"He would have turned my bed into firewood." He nipped at her exposed shoulder and a tingle vibrated along her spine.

"I know that," she breathed. "But what would have happened to you?"

"With my link to this world destroyed, I would have been forced to cross over."

"To heaven? Is that what waits?"

"The Afterlife. An eternity of peace. That's what waits once I learn the truth." He plunged a fingertip deep inside her and she gasped, lost in the feeling for a long moment before she managed to find her voice.

"But if your bed is destroyed before you learn Emma's parentage?"

His hand stilled and his body went rigid, as if she'd just reminded him of something.

"Purgatory," he murmured after a long, silent second.

"Purgatory?"

"An eternity of restlessness, of longing, of loneliness. The place for questioning, tortured souls. For those foolish enough to make the same fatal mistake twice."

Fatal mistake. The words echoed in her head and she went stone still as the truth crystalized in her mind. Val's distaste for virgins. His reluctance to touch her. The way he'd stopped the first time despite the fact that she'd begged him to make love to her and he'd wanted to.

She jerked away from him and whirled to face him. "You

mean to tell me that if we . . . if you . . . because I'm a . . . Hell? You could go to hell?" He nodded and she shook her head. "How could you keep something like that from me? I never would've . . . Oh, my God, I almost . . . you almost . . . we almost . . . Hell, Val. Hell."

"A small price."

"Eternal damnation is a small price? We're talking forever. You could lose everything."

"Everything?" A bitter laugh passed his lips. "I thought so, too, chérie. But to lose everything, you must have something. I have nothing. Only bitter memories and past regrets. Nothing. But when I hold you . . ." A pained expression twisted his features. "Then I have something. Everything. You."

"What are you saying?"

"I try to imagine what things will be like for me once I learn the truth. An eternity of peace, but how will I rest, facing forever without you?" He shook his head. "Then I weigh the alternative. A moment in your arms and an eternity of restlessness." His gaze captured hers. "I could face a dozen forevers if I had one sweet memory of you to keep me company. Just one." His gaze fired hotter, brighter, and he moved toward her. "I could face anything, because I love you, Veronique." He reached for her. "I love you."

He loved her.

She tossed and turned that night, restless and frustrated, and determined to stay that way despite Val's efforts to seduce her once he'd made his declaration.

Ronnie had faced the second most difficult decision of her life then, and, just like the first time, she'd turned away, walked away.

Because she'd had to.

Not to preserve her own sense of self, but to save Val's soul. He loved her, and she loved him, and she couldn't, wouldn't doom him to an eternity of hell.

"Not touching you is hell," he'd told her. Even so, he'd backed off when she'd refused, a bleak look in his eyes, love warring with lust, the past with the present.

She tossed to the other side, buried her head in the pillow, and ignored the ache between her own legs. Inconsequential compared to the ache in her chest when she thought of how close Val had come to losing his soul.

Not once, but twice.

First with her damning seduction, then with Norman Nathaniel and his crazy intention to ax Val's bed.

Ronnie had since made up her mind to keep her clothes on. Meanwhile, she felt certain that Norman was scared witless and wouldn't be back to bother Val again. Just to be sure, she was planning on having Mr. Sams install an extra deadbolt, and, come morning, she was placing an anonymous call to Councilwoman Terribone to tell her her son had been caught spying on poor defenseless college women. That should take care of Norman Nathaniel for a little while.

Long enough for Ronnie to find out the truth and send Val into the Afterlife, which was exactly what she intended to do. She loved him, and while she couldn't express that love in a physical way, much less pledge to love, honor, and cherish till death do us part, she could give him peace.

She would, she promised herself the next morning as she forfeited her classes and work to make the three-hour drive to Heaven's Gate. She would find the truth and let Val go before anything else happened. Before Norman returned, and before she lost her selflessness and begged Valentine Tremaine to stay with her regardless of the consequences.

"*The* Emma Warren," Harvey said excitedly. "I never even considered the possibility."

"What's so special about Emma Warren?"

"She was a kind and generous woman. She funded a home for orphaned children that paved the way for modern-day shelters. She started the first town newspaper. She was always giving money to charity, helping those less fortunate. Because of her and her husband's support, this town went from a dried-up ghost town after the Civil War to a thriving, upper-class community by the turn of the century."

"So who's this legendary woman's father?"

"That I don't know. I have tons of research on her, but nothing that mentions her father. I don't think she even knew him, hence her sympathy for orphaned children. I've been to the cemetery, checked her headstone, the family mausoleum. I've picked through all my records. She even kept a diary." He shook his head. "But there's nothing on him."

"There has to be something. Does she have any descendants? Family members who might know something?"

He shook his head. "The only thing left of the Warrens is Sunnydale, the estate house where they lived. Preserved and cared for by the New Orleans Historical Society. It's open daily to tourists."

"A museum?" He nodded, and excitement bubbled inside Ronnie. "Maybe there's something there."

"Doubtful. I've been over every inch of the place. Other than some really great antiques, wonderful atmosphere, and a great lunch menu—they serve a daily Cajun brunch as part of the admission price—there's nothing helpful."

"I'd like to pay a visit anyway. Could you draw me a map?"

"I'll do one better. I'll show you."

Harvey was right. They served a fabulous brunch. Craw-fish salad. Shrimp étouffée. Crème brûlée. Her taste buds were happy and content as she walked through three stories of authentic period life, complete with a tour guide dressed as a Civil War-era Southern belle.

"I told you. There's nothing here," he said as the tour ended and they found themselves on the front steps of the main house.

She sat down and breathed a deep sigh, her gaze sweeping the immaculate lawn. Sunlight winked off a stone fountain a few feet away and Ronnie stared at the mirrorlike surface while Harvey went back inside to the gift shop to buy some homemade pecan pralines.

There had to be something. She knew it. She felt it deep inside, a sense of expectancy—

Her gaze stalled as she caught sight of a small white cottage partially hidden behind a deep grove of oak trees.

"Excuse me," she asked the Southern belle guide. "Who lives in that cottage?"

"No one, ma'am. It's part of the tour."

"Why didn't we get to see it?"

"It's been closed recently to have the floors redone. You wouldn't believe the wear and tear on hardwood floors with so many people in and out."

"Can I see it?"

She shook her head. "Sorry. It's off-limits." The woman started to walk away.

Ronnie stopped her. "What's the significance of the cottage?"

"It belonged to Miss Emma's momma. Spent her last days there."

Claire. Ronnie's heart was beating ninety to nothing by the time Harvey returned with the pecan pralines.

"Harvey." She steered him toward the cottage. "That cottage belonged to Emma's mother."

"So?" he asked around a mouthful of praline.

"So maybe there's something inside. Something that might clue us in."

"I've been inside. There's nothing."

"Let's check it out anyway."

"It's closed," he said as she started to haul him forward by the arm.

"We'll just look in the window."

Seconds later, Ronnie stood on tiptoes and stared through a window covered with lace sheers.

"See anything?" Harvey asked behind her.

She blinked and focused her eyes. "A table and chairs. A sewing machine. A hope chest. A Bible—"

"A Bible?" Harvey shoved her aside and peered into the window. "A Bible." He smiled.

"What's the big deal about a Bible . . . ?" Her words faded as she remembered something she'd read in one of the genealogy books. "People wrote family trees down in Bibles," she said, excitement pumping through her veins. "And dedications. And important names and dates."

"Bibles were the earliest form of records," Harvey said. "And while I've seen most everything there is that belonged to the Warrens, I haven't seen that book."

"Claire might have written down the father's name."

"*If* she knew the father's name," Harvey pointed out. "Maybe she didn't know. Maybe that's why Emma didn't know."

"Maybe. But it's still worth checking out, don't you think?"

"I'll go find the security guard and have him let us in."

"Can you do that?"

"I've been officially commissioned by the estate to write the Warren history. I have legal access to all documents."

"But I've been commissioned by the Warren estate," Harvey sputtered for the countless time to a very mean-looking security guard fifteen minutes later. The guard stood in front of the cottage door and barred any entrance.

"The cottage is closed for the next month," the man said.

"But I need to get inside now."

The guard shook his head. "Next month. Opens up the fifteenth."

"Sir," Ronnie said, stepping in when Harvey turned a beet-red color. "You don't understand. This man has legal access to what's inside, and we have to get inside today, just to look around a minute. We won't disturb anything."

"Next month."

"But we're here now."

The guard shook his head. "I've got my orders."

"Come on," Harvey said, grabbing Ronnie's hand.

"But we have to get inside—"

"We will."

"How?"

"I'll contact the estate lawyer, who will call someone at the historical society, who will send someone out here to seize the Bible and turn it over to me."

"And how long does all that take?"

"A few weeks."

"*Weeks?*"

"Three, tops. Either way, we'll get to it before the fifteenth of next month."

But Ronnie didn't intend to wait three weeks. She couldn't. What if Norman hadn't been scared away? Okay, chances were, he had been. But there was always the slight chance that he could come after the bed again, that maybe Ronnie wouldn't be there this time, that he would succeed and send Val straight to . . .

Then there was also the matter of her own lust, the way she melted when Val came near. What if he set his mind on seduction, consequences be damned, and she didn't stop him . . .

No! She was getting a look at that Bible even if she had to break into the cottage to do it.

"Let me see if I understand this. There is a Bible that may or may not contain the name of Emma's father sitting in a cottage that is off-limits to the public, and so you want to break inside and take a look?" Val asked later that evening. He was little more than a shadow, yet she could still see him, feel him.

"That sums it up."

He shook his head. *"You're insane."*

"I was thinking more along the lines of desperate, and I don't care what you say, I'm doing it."

"Then I shall go with you."

She'd expected a lot of things, but that hadn't been one of them. "And how do you plan to manage that? Oh, sure, I'll just load the bed into the backseat of my car and off we go."

"*I have an easier way in mind.*"

"And what would that be? In case you haven't noticed, you're a ghost, Val. Linked to this bed."

"*My spirit is.*"

"What's that supposed to mean?"

"*That my spirit cannot walk out of this apartment, but my body can.*"

"You don't have a body," she reminded him.

He motioned to the phone with a large, transparent hand. "*So find me one.*"

Chapter Nineteen

"I know this is going to sound crazy," Ronnie started to say after she'd steered Danny into the nearest seat the moment he arrived at her apartment. "I didn't believe it myself at first, but then I found the letters, and there he was, as plain as day."

"What are you talking about?"

"Remember when I asked you whether you believed in ghosts?"

"Because you saw a ghost and he talked to you."

"That's right. He's been talking to me for the past few weeks, tutoring me, to be more exact." She pulled out her notebook and showed it to him. "I've accumulated enough data for the Guidry paper thanks to Val."

"Val?"

"The ghost."

"Right."

"That's why I called you. You see, in order for him to tutor me, I sort of had to offer him a favor in return."

"You guys made a deal?"

"Right. Anyhow, I offered to find out the truth about this woman he supposedly had a fling with, way back when, that may or may not have resulted in a child."

"In return for love lessons?"

"Right."

"Right."

"Anyway, I think I might have found the one thing, a Bible, that might list who the father is—maybe or maybe not Val—and now all I need to do is to break into the Sunnydale Plantation Museum/Bed and Breakfast—they've closed part of the estate for remodeling and the security guard refused to let me in, otherwise, I wouldn't have to break the law. Except it's not really breaking the law since I don't want to steal anything and have no malicious intent."

"Technically, it's still breaking the law."

"Technically, yes, but not morally. Anyhow, I'll be doing the breaking, you'll just be entering."

"Come again?"

"And carrying."

"What are you talking about?"

She gave him a fierce stare and gripped his shoulders. "I need your body."

"Ronnie, I don't think we . . ." He pried her fingers loose and tried to inch away. "I mean, I like you and all, but not like that . . ."

"That's not what I'm talking about, stupid. You've been looking cuter lately, I'll give you that, but not that cute."

"Cuter? Me?"

"Yes, but that's beside the point. I need your body for the ghost. For Val. So he can come with me to the museum to get a look at Emma's family Bible."

"What are you talking about?"

"You volunteering your body. Val's spirit is linked to my bed and—"

"My *bed*," came a fierce voice.

Danny jerked back, his head snapping around. "Who said that?"

"You heard?" He nodded and she smiled. "That's good. It means you believe."

"In what?"

"The ghost. Val."

"You mean he's here?"

She glanced behind her to see Val pacing in front of the bed. "Right over there."

Danny's gaze followed the direction of Ronnie's finger. He blinked and shook his head. "I don't see anything."

"He doesn't completely believe," Val told her.

"Who the hell was that?" Danny asked, jerking his head around searchingly.

"I told you. It's Val."

"The ghost?"

"Yup."

"Right." He turned back to her, "Look, Ronnie, it's been great but I'm meeting Wanda at midnight and I've got a couple of hours of studying to do between now and then—" His words stalled as she gripped him by the collar.

"You can't walk out on me. We need you."

"Tell him about the possession," Val said.

"Possession?" Danny spun around to look behind him again. "What possession?"

"Val needs to use your body, to possess it, but since it's a forty-five-minute drive there, then back, and we have to allow for time in between for the breaking and entering, we're looking at two to three hours minimum. There's no way he can possess your body for that long unless you're willing, especially since it's only nine o'clock and his spirit isn't at its best until midnight. But he could do it if you agree—"

"You want me to let someone possess my body?"

"Just Val. He won't hurt anything. He didn't the last time."

"The last time?"

"When you . . . we . . . Last week," she finished, none too anxious to remind Danny about the kiss if he didn't remember. "When you were here. He possessed you for a few minutes, to help with a demonstration for my paper."

"He *possessed* me?"

"You don't have to sound so outraged. It was just for a little while, and after midnight. His spirit was strong, so he could suppress yours, but that was only for a few minutes. It's one thing to suppress a spirit for five minutes here, ten minutes there, when you're at your prime, and quite another to do it for several hours when you're weak. Right, Val?"

"*Exactly, ma belle.*"

At Danny's incredulous expression, she added, "He's French. So what do you say?"

"I say you've overworked yourself right into a nervous breakdown."

"I'm not crazy."

"Sure." He headed for the door again.

Ronnie reached out to stop him, but it was Val's hand that gripped his collar and hauled him backward.

"*I'm real,*" Val growled.

"Who said that?" Danny stared wildly about, stumbling backward by the force of a hand he couldn't see. "Who said that? Who's doing that?"

"A ghost," Ronnie told him.

"I don't believe in ghosts."

"*Even when the proof's got you by the collar?*" Val asked.

Danny's eyes widened as he flailed, pulling and tugging against the invisible hand.

"You can't get loose," Ronnie pointed out. "What's holding you if it isn't a ghost?"

"M-maybe you've got an electromagnetic force in your ceiling that's drawing me," he stammered. "Or there's a superconducting current flowing through your apart—"

"*Explain the ten inches,*" Val cut in, and Danny's struggles ceased. He went as white as a sheet.

"How do you know . . . ?" Danny's voice faded in a wave of shock as his head swiveled and his gaze fixed on Val. "Y-you're real. You're . . . that is, you're . . ."

"A *ghost,*" Val said. "*That's what we've been telling you.*"

"You're responsible for the ten inches?" Danny asked, and Val nodded.

"Ten inches?" Ronnie's puzzled glance shifted from Danny to Val. "What are you talking about?"

"His—" Val started, but Danny cut him off.

"It's a guy thing," he blurted out, before directing a worshipful look at Val. "So when do we leave?"

"How are you doing?" Ronnie cast a sideways glance at Danny.

"*You asked me that five minutes ago. And five minutes before that.*"

"And?"

"*And the answer is, I was perfectly fine then and I am perfectly fine now,*" Val growled. "*Are we almost there yet?*"

Ronnie made the last turn that led down the drive to the Sunnydale Plantation. "Just about. Though I thought we'd park down the road and go the rest on foot. Can you do that?"

He grinned, but it wasn't a Danny expression. It was pure Val, from the slight tilt of his lips to the bright blue of his eyes. Blue. She still couldn't believe it.

"You're sure you're up to it?"

"*I am not an invalid, Rouquin. It's a bit crowded in here, but quite comfortable.*"

"Can Danny hear me?"

"*He's resting, otherwise I wouldn't have the strength for this. It's still an hour shy of midnight. Thankfully, your friend is willing.*"

"Could you do that forever? Possess someone, I mean. If they were willing?" God, what was she thinking?

That she could get used to Val inside of Danny. Val inside anyone, as long as he was Val with those blue eyes and that wicked grin.

"*If they were willing, perhaps for a little while. But not indefinitely. Even a willing spirit can only sleep so long, then it would fight for control. It's human nature. Survival. Two spirits could never inhabit the same body. It isn't allowed.*"

"Like making the same fatal mistake twice?"

"*Exactly.*"

"The Hereafter sure has a lot of rules," she snapped as she pulled off to the side of the road just beyond a thick patch of trees that would effectively conceal her car from the road. "Okay, here's the plan," she started, but Val was already unfolding himself from the car.

"*Wait here,*" he growled.

"But you can't go in there by yourself."

"*I can and I will.*" He nailed her with a fierce stare. "*Regardless of the motive, this is illegal, Rouquin. I won't ask of you something this risky.*"

"You didn't ask. I volunteered."

"*Stay.*" He slammed the door and started walking.

"Not on your life," she muttered, sliding from behind the wheel.

She'd taken five steps before he whirled on her. "*What the Devil are you doing?*"

"Following you."

"*Go back to the car.*"

"You don't really want that."

"*Mais oui, I do.*"

"No, you don't."

"*Merde!*" He planted his hands on his hips. "*I do.*"

"But I have a plan. Do you have one?"

"*To walk in and look at that bible.*"

"You can't just walk in. The building is locked." She smiled. "But I cased the place earlier, and I know how we're going to get in."

"*How?*"

She sprinted ahead of him. "If I told you, you wouldn't need me."

"*Damn woman—*" he started, but Ronnie cut him off.

"I know, I know. I'd be the death of you, but you're already dead, which is why we're here. Come on."

"*I could have figured this out on my own,*" Val said as he reached inside the window he'd just broken and unlocked the latch. "*And you could have stayed in the car.*"

"And what would you do here in the dark?" She shined her pinlight flashlight in his face. "At least I had the forethought to bring a light. You should be grateful."

"*I'll be grateful if you stay put right here*," he said, hefting himself through the window. "*Outside*."

"If I stay, so does my flashlight."

Val took one look at the darkened room, then turned to glare at Ronnie and held out his hand to help her through the window.

"I knew you'd see the error of your stubbornness."

"*There's only one thing I want to see*," he said as he turned to survey the room. "*Where is it?*"

"There." Her heart thundered ahead and she had the insane urge to grab his arm, to beg him not to look.

Selfish, she told herself. And futile. She and Val couldn't go on the way they were. The connection between them was too powerful. They would come together eventually, and Val would lose his soul, and Ronnie would never forgive herself.

Peace was the only solution. The right one, she told herself despite the hesitation that gripped her when her flashlight fell on the bible.

Seconds later, they opened the book and Ronnie turned several pages until she found the family tree. A blaze of names glared back at her. "I knew it. It's all filled out." She scanned the page, the dread in her gut building. "Here's Emma." Her finger traced a path up to Claire's name. Her gaze shifted to the opposite branch. The father.

"*Nothing*," Val breathed. "*It's blank*." Was that relief she heard in his voice? Or her own wishful thinking? "*We shall not find the answer tonight*."

Which meant he was stuck here for a little while longer.

The realization thrilled as much as it frightened. Val in her bed for another night. Another week. Maybe another month.

Val tempting her, frustrating her.

Val smiling at her, keeping her company.

She sent up a silent thank-you, closed the bible, and put it back in its place. "Let's go home."

"*My fondest wish,*" a female voice chimed.

Ronnie whirled and realized she'd given thanks all too soon. Standing a few feet away was a petite woman with blonde hair and haunted blue eyes, dressed in an old-fashioned dress straight out of *Gone with the Wind*. Correction, not a woman but a *ghost*. The moonlight shone through the windows, shimmering through the woman's pale pink dress, giving her an ethereal glow.

"*Finally we meet,*" she told Val. "*I've been praying for it all this time, since the moment my body gave up the ghost. One hundred and twenty-five years staring at these cabin walls, reliving my past, regretting it, hoping with all hope that perhaps you, too, would yearn for the truth the way I yearn to tell it.*"

"Claire," Val breathed, and the woman nodded.

"The virgin," Ronnie blurted out. "Oh my God, you're the virgin!"

"*Once,*" the woman said, a sad smile curving her lips. "*A long, long time ago. Now I am simply a tortured spirit searching for my own peace, doomed to haunt this cabin where I passed on until I can set things right. I did a terrible thing telling my father about you, Val. I knew he would be angry, but I never thought he would go so far as to kill you.*"

"You should have come to me yourself. I would have married you and given the child my name, my home—everything."

"*Even a child that wasn't yours?*" At Val's incredulous expression, she went on, "*We were never together, Valentine Tremaine. You did little more than to speak a hello to me, much less take me to bed.*"

"But you told your father—"

"*I had to,*" she rushed on. "*I feared telling him the truth. He would have driven John away.*"

"John?" Val asked. "John Trudeau?"

Claire nodded. "*Emma's father.*"

"Did you know him?" Ronnie asked Val.

A grim expression drew his mouth tight. "*I played cards with him after the ball the night I supposedly deflowered Claire.*"

"*You also drank with him. A great deal of brandy,*" Claire said. "*Along with a potion he'd slipped into your drink. You became quite intoxicated and John steered you into his carriage to drive you home. Only he didn't take you home. You passed out and he left you in that cabin on the outskirts of your plantation. He tangled some of the sheet and separated some of my perfumes to make you believe a woman had been with you.*"

"*So I wasn't with a woman that night?*"

She shook her head. "*It was a ruse, to leave the question in your mind so you couldn't dispute my claim that you were the father of my child rather than John.*"

"Why didn't you tell the truth?" Ronnie asked.

"*She couldn't,*" Val said. "*John was married.*"

"*I know our love was wrong,*" Claire admitted. "*But at the time, it felt so right. I couldn't name John and destroy him. He was a God-fearing man. Decent. A true friend and devout member of my father's congregation. I went to him right away when I found out.*" A sad smile curved her lips. "*I suppose I hoped he would take me and we would run away together, but John was too good to do something so terrible to his family. His wife was terribly ill from the recent birth of their third child and he simply couldn't abandon her. She was weak, near death, and he had to look after the children. At first, he wanted me to do away with our child. He knew of this slave from a nearby plantation who could do that sort of thing, but I was afraid, and determined to have the babe. He tried to convince me, but I stood firm. This was my child, my babe. Finally John agreed and said we would find another way. He said if we named someone else as the father, our secret would be safe. I could have the child and later, once John's wife passed on, we could be together. Our child and John's three. One big, happy family.*"

"And you believed that?" Ronnie gave her an incredulous look.

"I wanted to believe it." Claire wiped at a silvery tear sliding down her face. "I realize now that John wasn't the man I thought." A laugh burst from her lips. "I realized long ago, but it was still too late to undo the tragedy that was already done."

"Why me?" Val asked. "Why did you choose me?"

"You had a reputation with women. You were a rake and a rogue. It was easy for my father to believe a lusty man such as you would seduce his daughter. And being an innocent, of course, I would have been too naïve to stop you."

"Thus absolving yourself of blame."

"Yes." She sniffled and wiped at her tears. "But make no mistake, I didn't do this for myself. I did it for John. To save him. I never told a soul he was the father, just as we agreed. I never even told Emma. She believed what everyone in this town believed. That I was taken advantage of by the most notorious rogue in Louisiana."

"What happened to John?" Ronnie asked.

"His wife survived. John took her and their children and moved before my babe was born. I never heard from him again." A pleading light filled her eyes as she faced Val. "I know now that John wasn't the man I thought. If he had been, he would never have encouraged me to do what I did. Not that he is at fault." She bowed her head for a moment. "I take full blame. I truly regret the wrong I have committed against you, so much that I have stayed here, forfeiting my peace for the chance to set things right."

"You lied," Val said, still trying to come to grips with Claire Wilbur's confession. A ruse. It had all been a ruse and he'd been the victim. Wrongly accused. Falsely persecuted.

Murdered.

Even more than death, he'd been tortured. "For a century and a half, I have worried, wondered, hoped." His gaze collided with Claire's. "All for naught. There was never even the slightest chance that I had fathered a child."

"I'm sorry. I, too, have endured a fate worse than death. My guilt. But now I have told the truth. I have admitted my wrong and set the record straight." She turned to stare at the silvery moon outside. "*It is almost time.*"

"Time?" Ronnie asked. "Time for what?"

"*To cross over. To peace.*" Her gaze went to the antique clock sitting on the mantel. "*In six minutes, at the exact time my heart gave out so long ago, I shall finally know peace.*" She settled into a nearby rocking chair. Wood creaked and grated as the chair started to rock.

"Val?" Veronica's soft voice pushed past the noise. Gentle fingers touched his arm. "We should get back. We promised Danny he would be back in time for his study session with Wanda."

He nodded, letting her lead him from the cabin, out into the night. They were halfway to the car when they heard the woman's voice.

Val whirled in time to see the shimmering light at the window of the cabin, the outline of a woman. Claire. The light grew brighter, blinding, before bursting into a million sparks. The tiny specks whirled and floated off into the night sky. The moon seemed to shimmer and brighten, luring the sparks, drawing them home. To the Afterlife. Peace.

What waited for Val in a precious few hours, once the clock struck three a.m. The time of his death. The time to cross over, now that he knew the truth.

Chapter Twenty

Ronnie and Val returned to her apartment, where Val promptly exited Danny's body.

"What are you thinking?" Ronnie asked once she'd told her friend thank you and sent him on his way.

Val, strong and solid now that midnight had come, stood in the open French doors and stared up at the night sky. He could already feel the strange pulling inside him, as if the moon were a magnet, calling and luring him.

"Are you angry?" she asked, coming up behind him.

"I was." He closed his eyes. "At being murdered, duped. But no more."

"Why not?"

He opened his eyes and stared up at the moon. But he didn't see the full ethereal ball. He saw Veronica, with her flame-colored hair and her pale-as-milk skin, and, despite the past and the future, and being robbed of both, Valentine Tremaine smiled.

"Claire did a terrible thing, but she did it for love. I wouldn't have understood the power of such a thing before, but I do now. Because of you." He turned on her, his gaze colliding with hers. "I cannot hate her, for I am grateful to her."

"Grateful?"

"Although I wanted to be Emma's father, I am thankful I wasn't." He shook his head. "I never thought I would feel such a thing. I wanted a child far more than I ever wanted a woman. Until now." He stepped toward her. "I didn't deflower Claire. I made no fatal mistake. My life was taken because of someone else's mistake, not my own."

The truth crystallized in Ronnie's mind and she realized what he was saying, that loving her wouldn't cost him his soul.

A bittersweet ache rushed through her. While the news brought her tremendous joy, it made her all the sadder.

"You still have to cross over." He nodded and a whirlwind of feeling rushed through her. Longing and desire and sadness and anger and . . . love. So fierce, she wanted to wrap her arms around him and never let go.

But she would have to.

Not yet, she reminded herself, suddenly determined to hold the moment, to treasure it for as long as possible and make as many memories as she could while she could. She wanted to make love with Val.

It had nothing to do with her paper and everything to do with the fact that she loved him, he loved her, and she wanted her first time to be with the man she loved.

She stepped toward him, but he turned away. "Val?"

"I know what you're thinking, chérie. It's all I have been thinking. All I want. But we can't"

"Why not? We still have three hours together, don't we?"

He nodded. "It's not the time. I cannot take what you're offering, no matter how much I want to. It wouldn't be fair. I have nothing to give you in return. Not my name, my wealth, my future. Nothing but a moment's pleasure."

He was right. His argument echoed everything Ronnie had told herself at one time, when she'd decided Val was the most logical choice to take her virginity. Nothing had changed, yet everything had changed.

He was still the best choice, but not because he was safe or temporary. She wanted him because he was the man she loved.

Ronnie didn't want him because he couldn't give her a future, she wanted him in spite of it. She loved him, and the feeling pushed her forward when fear and worry might have held her back.

"You're wrong, Val. You can give me more than a moment's

pleasure. You can give me a lifetime filled with sweet memories of this one night. This one precious night with the man I love."

He turned at her words. His gaze caught hers for a split second and she saw the fear and indecision. The anger and rage. The lust and love. So much love . . .

"Please," she murmured, and he hauled her into his arms and captured her mouth in a breathless kiss.

Desperation seemed to drive him for the first few moments of contact, then something happened. The kiss slowed, deepened as Val took the lead, giving instead of taking, stirring the heat inside her body until she was flushed and breathless and needy.

She whimpered and he swept her into his arms and carried her to the bed. He didn't release her right away; he simply held her, his mouth feasting on hers. Then he lowered her to her feet in a long, slow glide down the fierce heat of his hard, aroused body.

Ronnie wasn't sure what happened to their clothes. She remembered feeling him hot and throbbing beneath his breeches, her breasts pressed achingly against the lace of her bra. The next thing she knew, they were standing in a puddle of clothes. He drew her tight against him, kissing her deeply and thoroughly before stretching her out on the bed.

Skin met skin as he settled over her, blocking out everything except the sight and sound and smell and feel of him. His eyes glittered with liquid blue heat. Rasping breaths parted his sensual lips. The steamy scent of sex, heat, and aroused male filled the air. Muscle corded his body, flexing and bunching with every movement.

He kissed her again, slower this time, tasting and suckling her tongue until every nerve in her body came alive.

Strong hands roamed over her body, arousing every nerve, making her want and crave him in a way more intense than anything she'd ever felt before. Even the dream. This was Val touching her and loving her, in every sense of the word. She felt the emotion in the reverent way he cradled her breasts, teased her nipples. The way he kissed her neck and rasped his beard-stubbled cheek across her skin, as if he sought to mark her as his.

Then he slid down her sweat-dampened body, his lips closed over her nipple, and he suckled her with a fierce sweetness that actually brought tears to her eyes. His hand swept up the inside of her thigh and he cupped her heat. He trailed a fingertip along the slick, wet folds, before sliding one finger deep, deep inside.

She gasped, arching into his touch, taking as much as he could give while he whispered the sweetest encouragement, telling her how warm and wet she felt, how much he wanted her, urging her to come to him, to let herself go.

And she did, screaming his name as stars exploded behind her eyelids before everything went a shimmering black.

"*You are so beautiful.*" His soft murmur brought her back to life a moment before he settled himself between her parted thighs, his hardness probing the ultrasensitive spot between her legs.

She'd yearned for this moment since he'd first appeared to her, but for all her enthusiasm, she couldn't help the sudden fear that bolted through her. He was so hard, so hot, so huge. Her eyes snapped open.

This was *it*. The end of the line. Step fifty.

As if he sensed her doubts, he didn't plunge forward. Rather, he kissed her, his lips as soft and tender as his next words. "*I'll stop, chérie. I don't want to, but I will. For you.*" His gaze caught and held hers, and where she'd expected to see the self-assurance of an experienced lover, she saw a hint of uncertainty and dazed awe. "*Anything for you.*"

"No." Her hands grasped his buttocks when he started to pull away, urging him back until the tip of his erection nestled inside her. "I'm not having second thoughts. I'm just nervous. I don't know why I'm nervous. I know all the hows. Boy do I ever, after Guidry's class." She took a deep, steadying breath. "I know how everything's done, I'm just afraid you'll be disappointed. I mean, three hundred and sixty-nine women—"

"*And I cannot remember even one.*"

"But you bragged about your memory. That you knew every name, every face."

"*I did. Before I met you.*" He shook his head. "*It's the damndest thing, but try as I might, I haven't been able to draw forth one single, solitary name. Nor a face. Only you, Rouquin.*" Blue eyes drilled into her. "*You are all I see when I close my eyes, all I smell, all I feel. Just you.*"

"Really?"

He kissed the tip of her nose. "*My word as a gentleman.*"

"Mmm . . ." She wiggled, her hips drawing him a fraction deeper, feeling herself stretch. He sucked in a sharp breath. "You don't seem like much of a gentleman right now. Why don't you come a little closer and let me take a better look?"

He glanced down at his chest, at her breasts crushed beneath his weight. "*I don't think I can get any closer, chérie.*"

"Did I say closer? I meant deeper." She grasped his buttocks and spread her legs wider.

Val thrust fast and sure and so deep Ronnie felt as if he were splitting her in two. Then he stilled, his muscles bunched tight beneath her hands, his hard, thick length pulsing inside her.

"*Ssshhh,*" he murmured against her lips, licking at a tear that slid down her cheek. "*No more pain,*" he promised. "*Only pleasure. A lifetime,*" he vowed.

After several frantic heartbeats, the pain receded. Val moved his hips the tiniest bit and heat fluttered through her. She became increasingly aware of the delicious pressure of his sex inside her and she rotated her pelvis, giving him deeper access, begging him for more.

He flexed his buttocks and began to move slowly, penetrating deeply. His hands played over her body, touching and caressing, building the pressure inside her. He sucked and licked her nipples until she was panting and moaning and clinging to him.

This was going to kill her, she quickly decided as sensation spiraled along her nerve endings. Everything good in life turned lethal in the end. Chocolate—disastrous to her hips. Cheesecake—a cholesterol chisel picking at the walls of her arteries. This . . . ah, *this* . . . this was so good she was bound to die from the sheer pleasure of it.

The pressure built inside her, like a pot of water just put over the burner. The heat licked at her, pleasure bubbling through her in slow, trickling ripples. Then the bubbles grew in momentum as Val moved inside her, in and out, creating a dizzying friction until it was too much. The pressure too intense. She exploded, heat bursting through her as she cried his name and felt a joy unlike anything she'd ever experienced before.

Val felt her muscles tighten around him, milking him as the ecstasy gripped her. He plunged once, twice, thrice, burying himself to the hilt as he followed her over the edge. Time lost its importance and everything faded away as he held her in his arms and exploded inside her, their hearts thundering in perfect sync.

"*I have never known a woman like you,* Rouquin." Val lay on his side, his head propped on his elbow as he traced the tip of her breast as if he'd never seen one before. "*Never.*"

"You're one of a kind, yourself." She touched his jaw, traced the lines of his face, her breathing still raspy from their recent lovemaking, her body still buzzing from the flood of sensation. "I never thought I'd find someone that I would want to spend the rest of my life with." She closed her eyes against a sudden blur of tears. "I was so determined not to find someone, so convinced I wanted a career more than domestic bliss." She sniffled. "Now I'd sell my soul for a little house, a few kids, and a future growing old with you."

He cupped her face. "*Don't think past this moment,* chérie. *I'm here with you now. I'm here.*" His hands stroked her body as he sought to wipe the sadness from her face and give her as much happiness as he could. He parted her legs, sweeping a hand upward to cup her. "*I want to be here,*" he murmured, before he dipped his head and replaced his hand with his mouth.

A sob broke from her throat as he kissed and licked and tasted her sweetness. When Val slid up her body, her eyes were bright with passion rather than sadness. "*Shall we have another lesson, Rouquin?*"

She smiled. "I already know the fifty steps."

"*Then it's time we moved on to the fifty positions. One down and forty-nine to go.*"

"We don't have enough time." A stark expression gripped her face.

"*Perhaps not, but we'll enjoy the time we do have. Class is in session.*" He rolled over onto his back, pulling her astride him. The tip of his staff probed her passage. *Merde,* she was scorching hot. Drenched. Eager for him. He gripped her hips and pulled her down, embedding himself in one smooth, upward surge.

Her breath caught. Her palms flattened against his chest. Her eyes closed and she caught her bottom lip between her teeth, her body shuddering at the pure pleasure of their coupling.

He reached up to graze the throbbing tip of her breast with his knuckle and her eyelids fluttered open. Gone was the sadness, the worry, the fear. Desire glittered in her eyes. And love, so fierce and consuming that it cinched the air in his chest.

"I'm waiting, teacher," she breathed. "What next?"

"*Ride me,*" he said, his throat raw with feeling.

She started with a slow rise and fall that sent the blood pounding through his veins until he gripped her hips and urged her higher, faster, until she screamed his name, the tight muscles of her sheath convulsing around him. Val followed her, his release violent, potent, as he bucked beneath her, gripping her hips, anchoring her to him as he spilled himself deep inside her.

She collapsed atop him and he held her. And despite his fervent vow to hold the moment, he couldn't help but wonder how he would ever find the strength to let her go.

And then he wept, because, strength or not, he would have to.

It was nearly time.

Val stood at the open French doors and stared at the darkened street. Just this side of three a.m., there was little activity. The occasional bark of a dog, the passing blur of headlights as a car sped by.

The clock tick-tocked away and Val closed his eyes. Anger welled up inside him. But far greater than his resentment at finding his one true love when he had but a few blissful moments to give her, was the gratitude he felt at having found her at all. A lifetime he'd lived, and he'd never known the joy he'd felt in the past few weeks, the past few moments.

"Better to have loved and lost than never to have loved at all," Ronnie's voice whispered over his shoulder, and he turned to find her standing behind him, an oversized T-shirt molded to her lush, naked body. She sniffled and wiped at a tear that squeezed past her lashes. "I keep telling myself that."

"It is true, chérie." He pulled her into his arms and gave her a long, hungry kiss before settling her back against him, his arms circling her waist as they stared out at the street below.

Ronnie closed her hands over Val's, holding tight. As if by holding on to him, she could keep him here, in her arms, her life, for a few minutes longer.

Forever, her soul cried. Forever.

The clock ticked away in the background, each second thundering through her head, taunting her. She fought against the dread welling inside her, the sadness, and instead relished the feel of Val's warm arms, the solid strength behind her.

A blaze of headlights cut through the night as a car turned the corner and rolled down the street. Ronnie watched as Professor Guidry's Volvo rolled to a stop in his driveway. He gathered his books and climbed out of the car. Obviously a late night at the campus. Very late, but then, he was notorious for his dedication to the Thursday-night experiments.

She concentrated on the slap of his footsteps rather than on the clock, anything to distract her from the time, to keep her from turning and burying her head in the crook of Val's shoulder and begging him to stay.

It would do no good because leaving wasn't his choice, and she didn't want to make things any harder. He had to leave—

Cuckoo. The clock sounded just as Guidry's voice split open the silent night.

"Damn it!" the professor bellowed as his foot slipped on the steps and he pitched forward. Papers flew as he scrambled to catch his balance.

Cuckoo.

He recovered himself and jerked upright. His head smashed into the doorknob, he grunted, and his knees buckled.

"Prof—" Ronnie started to cry out, her voice drowned in the third and final *cuckoo.*

The noise faded into quiet, and Ronnie realized Val's arms were no longer around her, his strength was no longer at her back. She jerked around and saw nothing but her dimly lit apartment.

The clock had struck three a.m., and Val was gone.

Chapter Twenty-one

"No," Ronnie breathed, fighting the truth. It couldn't be! A coldness wrapped around her, tightened until she couldn't breathe. She struggled for air; her fingers clutched at the door as her knees buckled. *No!* her mind screamed over and over. *Don't let this be happening. Don't let it be real. Don't let him be gone. Please!*

She sank to the floor, her throat burning, tears streaming down her cheeks. *No!*

But all the denial in the world couldn't change anything. Val *was* gone, and Ronnie was alone.

The sound of doors slamming finally penetrated her misery and she turned in time to see the lights flick on next door to Guidry's house. Ronnie took one look at the professor's limp body sprawled on the front stoop and panic bolted through her, shoving aside the anger and despair long enough to force her to her feet.

Nine-one-one, her brain screamed. *Nine-one-one!*

A half hour later, standing near the curb wearing a T-shirt and sweatpants, Ronnie watched the paramedics load an unconscious Guidry into a waiting ambulance. He'd taken a nasty hit on the head and suffered a concussion, but at least he was alive.

The knowledge stuck in her mind as she walked back to her apartment. Once inside, however, she discarded any thoughts about Guidry's welfare. She simply stood there, staring at the chaos. The rumpled bed. Her discarded clothes lying here and there. Her books in disarray atop her desk. The entire place was a mess, the way it had been before Val had come into her life.

She sank down on the edge of the bed and touched the indentation where he'd lain. She could smell him, see him, but she couldn't *feel* him.

Her eyes blurred and she buried her head in the pillow. She wasn't sure how long she cried, great big sobbing gulps that echoed from her heart and gripped her entire body. It could have been minutes, hours. She only knew that when she managed to focus again, the bright morning sunshine streamed through the open French doors.

Ronnie was about to yank the doors and drapes closed and cocoon herself in misery, mindless that she had classes and work waiting for her, when her gaze fell to her nearly finished term paper due first thing Monday morning. *Fifty Steps to Ultimate Sexual Fulfillment by Veronica Parrish*.

She closed her eyes and relived her last few moments with Val, the lovemaking they'd shared, the joy. A deep-seated, overwhelming, *ultimate* joy that had little to do with sex and everything to do with the fact that she'd fallen helplessly, completely in love.

Before Ronnie could question what she was doing, she trashed her nearly completed paper, called in sick at the library, and sat down at her computer to write.

To set things right.

Ronnie spent all day Friday and Saturday writing and crying. She ignored the ringing phone, to the point that her answering machine overflowed and stopped picking up messages. The only person she talked to was Danny, and only to tell him she wasn't in the mood to talk. By Sunday morning, however, she'd finished the writing, so she spent the early morning hours baking and crying. Then driving and crying as she headed out to Covenant.

Home.

When Ronnie pulled into her parents' driveway, she killed the engine, took a deep breath, grabbed the still warm strawberry pie she'd made, and climbed out of her car.

Sometimes love isn't enough. Her own words echoed back through her head. She'd been right. Sometimes love wasn't enough. For her and Val, it hadn't been, but that's because forces much greater than stubbornness and fear had been calling the shots. Life-and-death forces that were beyond anyone's control.

Things were different with her parents. They were alive and breathing, and they did love her. And she loved them.

And that meant there was hope, and that love could be enough.

She ignored the logical part of her brain, which told her this was useless. That her folks would disown her all over again. That she was just inviting heartbreak.

But her heart was already broken, crumpled in tiny little pieces, and there wasn't too much that could make her feel worse.

Besides, she couldn't forget what Val had told her. That the happiest person listened to both her head and her heart. While Ronnie wasn't banking on happiness any time soon, she was through suppressing her feelings and running on reason alone.

She knocked.

A few seconds later, the door swung open. "Yes . . . ?" Her mother's voice faded. Shock chased surprise across the woman's features as she stared at Ronnie as if she were seeing a ghost.

If only.

Ronnie cleared her throat and fought for her suddenly shaky voice. "Hi, Mom."

"V-Veronica," her mother stammered. "You're here—"

"Janice? Who is it?" her father called from inside the house. "Is it Robert? I told him I would meet him at the golf course before ten o'clock tee-off. . . ." The words faded as her father appeared in the doorway. His expression went from exasperated to shocked as his gaze collided with his daughter's.

"I brought a pie," she explained after a moment of pressing silence. "A strawberry pie, made from the ones Mom sent me. Here." She handed him the pie.

He stared at the dessert as if it sported eyes and wore a Devout Democrat button, but he didn't chuck the pile of fruit and crust back into her face. Definitely a good sign.

"I'm graduating in a few weeks," she rushed on, eager to say what she'd come to say before she lost her nerve. "At least, I hope I am. There's one class that's a little iffy, but if I don't pass, I still have enough credits to go through the ceremony. Then I'll make the class up during the summer, or fall—whenever it's offered." She pulled an envelope from her pocket. "I'd really like you and Mom to be there."

He took the envelope, stared at it just the way he had regarded the pie. Then the door creaked and closed, and Ronnie found herself alone on the doorstep.

She simply stood there for a minute, marveling at how she didn't feel the need to run back to her car, to crawl beneath it. She'd faced them, faced her past, and even if they didn't come around right away, even if they never came around, at least she'd tried.

When she slid behind the wheel, she caught sight of her father through the kitchen window. He sat at the table, staring at the pie. Several seconds ticked past, but finally he lifted a knife and sliced into the dessert.

And for the first time since Val had left, Ronnie actually smiled. And then she cried.

"You look terrible," Delta told Ronnie when she reported for her shift at the library later that day.

"I feel it."

"Another flu bug."

"Something like that." Ronnie stashed her book bag under the counter and went to work behind the circulation desk.

She tossed the baseball cap she'd been wearing into a nearby trash can. The hunt was still on for the kissing bandit, but with the fraternities holding auditions for Miss Kiss of USL, there were plenty of women vying for the title and enough distraction that she could stop worrying.

Not that she even cared at the moment. The campus police could place her under arrest right now and she wouldn't so much as blink. The worst had already happened.

"Since you're sick, I won't ask you," Delta said.

"Ask me what?"

"To close up for me tonight. I mean, if you're feeling poorly, you probably want to get right home. I'll just tell Cass I can't make it—"

"Cass?"

"We're having dinner together."

"As in, you two finally kissed and made up?"

"Actually, it went a little beyond a kiss." Delta smiled. "For one who has so much snow on the roof, the man's got an inferno blazing in his cookstove."

"You sound happy." Ronnie smiled despite the ache gripping her chest. Two smiles in one day. She might not wither up and die, after all.

"I am." Delta's dreamy expression faded as she cast another worried glance at Ronnie. "But I'm not placing any bets on you. I'll close up."

"You go on to dinner. I'm fine," Ronnie said. At Delta's doubtful glance, she planted her hands on her hips and growled, "Go."

"If you're sure."

"I'm sure."

Delta beamed. "You're all heart, honey. Hi, Danny. Bye, Danny," she said as she passed the young man.

"What's gotten into her?"

"Love." Ronnie sighed. "If I can't have my own happy ending, it's nice to see someone else get hers."

"True, but I'd like to have one of my own." Danny's gaze followed Wanda as she exited the library with several of her friends.

"Move on," Ronnie told him.

"Speaking of moving on, from the looks of you, I'd say Val's gone."

She sniffled. "That bad, huh?"

"Your eyes are red and puffy. Your face is pale. I'd say you've cried a few buckets since the last time I saw you."

"More than a few. The only good thing is that I'm on the verge of dehydrating, which means no more tears."

"Hang in there." He touched a comforting hand to hers. "And if you need anything, you know where I am." His gaze shifted to the library door.

She nodded and watched him walk away, and then she cried. Again. So much for dehydration.

"Wanda, wait!" Danny called out as he caught up to her outside the library. "You got a sec?"

She excused herself from her friends, who walked on ahead.

"What's up?" she asked when he reached her.

"I wanted to talk to you."

"About what?"

"I thought . . . I thought maybe we—"

"Come on, Wanda," one of the women called out, effectively killing Danny's question. "The guys'll scarf down every slice of pizza if we don't get over there."

"Hold on," she called out. "Look, I've really got to go," she told Danny.

"But I thought maybe we could—"

"Wanda!" the woman called again.

"This can wait, can't it?" She didn't wait for a reply. She simply smiled that enticing smile and turned away to join her friends.

He started to walk away.

There was always tomorrow. A new day and fresh hope. Another tutoring session, maybe a few stolen kisses during one of her weaker moments. Maybe even another date. If he lucked out.

But Danny Boudreaux had never been lucky. He'd always had to work extra hard for the things in his life. When he'd wanted that brand-spanking-new bicycle back in elementary school, he'd cut ten yards in one Saturday afternoon to earn the money. He'd spent all four years of high school studying to win a scholarship, and every year of college with his nose to the grindstone to keep his GPA perfect and his future bright. If he wanted something, he went after it. Really went after it.

This time shouldn't have been any different, he admitted in a moment of staggering realization, as he watched the one woman he'd wanted for so long walk away from him. Again.

What the hell had he been doing all this time? He should have been pursuing Wanda with the same diligence he put into all his A's. Instead, he'd been sitting around, waiting. Waiting for her to notice how much he cared for her, to notice what a fine boyfriend he would make—loyal and hard-working with six-figure earning potential. Waiting for a miracle, because Wanda couldn't see past the surface—the not-so-muscular body, the glasses that made him look like a hoot owl. She couldn't see and, other than his small, spur-of-the-moment attempt to make her jealous by claiming Ronnie was his still enamored ex-girlfriend, he'd never done anything to really open Wanda's eyes.

Something snapped and he went after her. His fingers snaked around her wrist.

"It can't wait," he said, and then he hauled her into his arms and kissed her. In front of God and the overflow of students from the Student Union building. More importantly, in front of her friends, and he didn't feel a moment's hesitation. No fear that she'd slap his face and turn away, cancel their late-night tutoring sessions, and allow him no more contact with her whatsoever.

He didn't want to be her friend or her study buddy or her sometimes lover when no one was looking and she was in the mood and the planets were in perfect alignment. He wanted to be more.

Danny was through dreaming. He was a man of action. He always had been, he just hadn't realized it. But now . . . Thanks to Valentine Tremaine, he'd discovered a part of himself. His self-confidence when it came to women.

Her lips formed a tiny O at the first moment of contact, but then she softened, giving in to the insistent demand of his tongue. He kissed her deeply, the contact fueled by two years of lust and longing.

It ended as quickly as it had started, with Danny pulling back, letting go. She swayed, staring at him in a shocked daze, mindless of her friends, who made a very captive and vocal audience behind her.

Mindless of anyone except him.

He smiled, and *then* he walked away.

Monday dawned bright and sunny, with Ronnie still miserably hydrated. She blew her nose, dabbed her damp eyes, and slid into her seat in Guidry's class, her paper in hand.

The news of the professor's accident had spread like wildfire. Class had been canceled on Friday because of the accident and Ronnie half-expected one of the teacher's aides to fill in for Monday's class, particularly when she heard that the hospital had treated Guidry most of the weekend for his concussion.

"Just our luck, his head is as hard as his heart," a woman muttered and Ronnie turned, along with three dozen other students, to see Professor Guidry enter the classroom.

Her mouth dropped open and the air lodged in her throat as murmured amazement drifted through the class.

"Would you look at that?"

"Wow."

"That hit on the head must've done some permanent damage."

"What is that he's wearing?"

The "what" consisted of a white T-shirt that hugged a broad chest and well-muscled arms, a pair of snug, faded Levi's, and worn cowboy boots.

"Who knew Guidry was hiding a body like that under his lab coat?"

"Check out his butt."

"I never knew Guidry had a butt."

"Everybody has a butt."

"Not one shaped like that."

Mmm, Ronnie thought. He did have a good butt.

Oh, God. What was she thinking? Val had been gone less than seventy-two hours and she was checking out another man's butt. What was wrong with her?

She was witnessing a historic event, that's what, because Iron Ball Guidry had transformed from the Nutty Professor into the Marlboro Man, and the result was . . . incredible.

"And his hair. He's got real hair."

The thick black locks hung loose, rather than being combed back in his usual severe style. His hair brushed the tops of his shoulders, falling around his face, making him almost attractive.

Okay, very attractive.

But it wasn't just the way he looked that had changed. It was everything about him. His walk, the swagger of his hips as he moved in front of the blackboard to write the day's lesson plan. His movements—the way he held the chalk, shifted his weight. He had a certain confidence, an air of control. Just like . . .

Impossible. The wishful, desperate thinking of a heartbroken woman. She shook away the strange thoughts and focused on the blackboard.

"All right!" The cheers went up as Guidry printed in nice, neat letters: CLASS DISMISSED! The chalk hit the tray and he dusted off his hands while a buzz went through the lecture hall. Chairs creaked as everyone rushed to clear out before he changed his mind.

"Term papers," he called out, his voice a bit deeper than usual. With a strange, throaty accent . . .

Ridiculous. She shook away her damning thoughts and watched the mountain of papers slowly bury his desk. Adding hers to the stack, she hefted her book bag onto her shoulder and turned to leave.

"Miss Parrish. If you'll grant me a moment, I would like to speak with you."

Grant me a moment?

The strange phrasing echoed through her head, quickly fading in a wave of dread as he motioned her into a desk near the podium and picked her paper out of the stack.

"I have been waiting a long time for this."

For the chance to fail her, and she had no doubt he would once he read the very detailed account of Madame X, a woman looking for fulfillment, who found it not in erotic loveplay, but in the deep emotion she felt for a certain man, the longing, the devotion, the love. . . . Guidry saw everything in scientific, black-and-white, emotionless terms. He would surely laugh at her romantic portrayal of sexual fulfillment—that there is none without love. Love is the last and final step. The ultimate.

A surefire ticket to an F.

Ronnie braced herself as Guidry scanned her paper. Minutes ticked by as he read. Her stomach jumped, but she took deep breaths and fixed her attention on a tiny crack in the desk. She traced it from corner to corner and back before he finally finished. Pages rustled as he put the papers back in order and marked something in red in the top corner.

"What happened to Madame X?" he murmured as he laid the paper on the desk. "There's no mention of her anywhere here. Wasn't she your subject?"

"How do you know about Madame X . . . ?" Her words faded

as her attention shot to the A+ scribbled on her paper. Her head snapped up and her gaze collided with his.

"I know her . . . personally. Intimately." Bright blue eyes twinkled back at her and a smile that was pure charm—pure Val—stopped her broken heart and started the pieces to mend. "I've missed you, *Rouquin*."

"Oh my God," she gasped. "It *is* you. *You*." The knowledge sank in, filling her with a warmth that seeped through her body and salved the hurt. "But how?" Even as the question passed her lips, she already knew the answer.

Guidry hadn't suffered just a concussion. He'd passed on, and somehow, someway, Val had inherited his body.

"I was wronged, *chérie*," Val explained, "murdered before my time, robbed of so many years. Fate gave me a second chance with your Professor Guidry, here."

"It really is you." She reached out, her fingertips trailing over the small bandage at his temple, the curve of his jaw, the slope of his nose. Guidry's, and yet, when she tried to picture the professor, she didn't see the man who stood before her. This man with his charming smile and flashing blue eyes was Valentine Tremaine.

"Being a brunet will take some getting used to. I had quite a fright when I woke up in the hospital after sleeping for over twenty-four hours. I took one look in the mirror, let loose a howl, and the nurses came running." He cupped her face in his warm hands. "I wanted to run straight to you, *chérie*, to tell you, but I couldn't. The hospital didn't release me until the doctor gave his approval late yesterday, and I've spent the past twenty-four hours trying to adjust to a new body, a new life. I'm no longer Valentine Tremaine." When she started to shake her head, he added, "I am. Inside where it counts, but it's the outside that's giving me a great deal of trouble. Outside, I am Professor Mark Guidry, only child of Doris and John Guidry, both deceased. I've got atrocious taste in clothes and I drive the most revolting automobile, a subject we won't even go into, since I have never driven anything faster than a carriage and the Volvo's front end is now proof."

"You had a wreck?"

"On my way home from the hospital, but I'm fine." I grinned. "More than fine. I'm alive, with a second chance at life, love, children."

Hope blossomed inside her as the reality of what he was saying hit her. "You mean . . . ?"

"I've got a splitting headache, but otherwise, everything else is in perfect working order, or so the doctor assured me. But I am most anxious to put this new body to the test What do you say, *chérie*? Will you help me? Love me? Marry me?"

"Yes, yes, and *yes!*" She threw herself into his arms a held tight. Ronnie wasn't letting him go ever again.

"You know," she told him after a long, lingering kiss that curled her toes and melted her insides and made her think of babies. Lots and lots of babies. Maybe even a pair of her very own Hades twins. "There just may be justice in the world, after all."

"How's that?"

"Well, I can't think of a better profession for a legendary lover than professor of human sexuality."

"Neither can I, *mon coeur*. Neither can I."

Epilogue

"Your friend Danny is awfully cute," the woman sitting next to Ronnie, an acquaintance from one of her business classes, told her as they watched Danny skirt the bleachers in the Cajun Dome, wave to Ronnie, then sit down next to Delta and Cassius Gibbons, who also smiled and waved.

"I'm having a get-together at my place after graduation. He'll be there," Ronnie told the woman. She thought briefly about talking Danny up, mentioning his major and his earning potential as he'd done so many times to her about his friends. But the thing was, he didn't need it. The woman was interested regardless. A lot of women were interested, and Danny Boudreaux was now having the time of his life. "Why don't you stop by?" she asked.

The brunette smiled, "I'd love to."

Ronnie caught Danny's gaze and gave him a thumbs-up sign as she waited for the dean of the business college to call her name. Her gaze shifted to a nearby row of bleachers where Val sat between her parents and Jenny.

A camera flashed as her mother snapped a picture and beamed. Her father didn't look as happy. Still, he'd come of his own free will and when she'd hugged him earlier, he'd actually hugged her back for a brief, sweet moment.

Another camera flashed as Jenny snapped a shot, waved wildly, then lowered herself back to her seat, a hand placed protectively on her slightly rounded stomach.

Through the thin black graduation gown, Ronnie felt her own tummy, still flat and soft. But not for long. A grin tugged at her lips. While she didn't know for sure, she had a feeling, and if there was one thing Valentine Tremaine had taught her, it was to trust her feelings.

She glanced up and caught Val's gaze, felt the heat of his blue eyes, the love communicated in them, and she said another silent thank you to the Powers That Be for giving him a second chance. For giving them both one.

"Veronica Parrish Guidry," the dean called out, and Ronnie took her turn walking across the stage, toward the rest of her life. Filled with a career and a husband and a family, and pure bliss.

Who said a woman couldn't have it all?

". . . so we're thinking about Jackson for a boy and Felice for a girl," Jenny told Veronica's mother before her attention shifted back to the stage. "Doesn't Ronnie look great?" She nudged Veronica's father, who muttered a grudging agreement.

But great didn't begin to describe the woman who smiled up at Val from a sea of faces, the woman who stood out and held his eye with a bewitching intensity so he saw no other but her. She was beautiful, exquisite, everything a woman should be and so much more, and he was completely, utterly, hopelessly in love with her.

There was just something about the softness of her skin, the shine of her hair, the warm musky scent that was hers and hers alone, the way she walked and talked and smiled and did other, more *relevant* things.

Ah, yes. This woman. *His* woman.

She came in only one size and shape; medium height with a delectable bosom not too small, not too large. She was his red-headed temptress, his golden-eyed siren. She could be shy as a summer shower and bold as a clap of thunder, and Val adored her regardless. *Because.*

Yes, Val loved this woman, *his* woman, his wife, and she loved him. And the future looked very bright indeed!

KIMBERLY RAYE

Slippery When Wet

The Flag Is Up

Jaycee Anderson is the first female to take the NASCAR Sprint Cup circuit by storm, and after finishing fourth overall last season, she has her eyes on the prize: knocking Rory Canyon out of the number three spot. She'll do anything to see the job done, too, even transform herself from a tomboy into a glamour queen if that's what it takes to get sponsorship and the edge. Rory's the kind of infuriating chauvinist who's just begging to get the pants beat off him by a woman — on the track, at least; Jaycee's fairly sure he's never had to beg anywhere else. Not with the millions of female fans who buy his shirts and caps and posters. Rory's just the type who gets Jaycee's own pistons pumping, her wheels spinning, and her engine burning oil. With their past, she's surprised they haven't already seen a smashup that ended in flames. But this track they're running has some deadly curves . . . and it's getting more slippery by the minute.

ISBN 13: 978-0-505-52773-8

Tammy Kane

BREATH OF FIRE

"A fantastic new world of dragons!"
—Jade Lee, *USA Today* Bestselling Author of *Dragonbound*

When the dragon came to claim him, Karl knew his great plan had gone horribly wrong. If he had known the creature was real, he wouldn't have scoffed at the villagers…and he *certainly* wouldn't have been so quick to let them chain him to a rock. Mattaen Initiates trained as warriors, but no man could defeat a dragon.

"My name is Elera daughter of Shane. And you, Initiate, are my virgin prize."

She had vanquished the beast and named her price: one night with the virgin sacrifice she'd saved. He'd taken a vow of chastity, but Karl still had a man's needs—and Elera's sultry curves made him ache to taste his first woman. With a scorching kiss she shattered his defenses…and led him into a world of deception and seduction, where he'd be forced to choose between the brotherhood that had raised him and the woman whose courage set his heart on fire.

ISBN 13: 978-0-505-52816-2

Tracy Madison

A Stroke of Magic

You know how freaky it is, to expect one taste and get another? Imagine picking up a can of tepid ginger ale and taking a swig of delicious, icy cold peppermint tea. Alice Raymond did just that. And though the tea is exactly what she wants, she bought herself a soda.

ONE STROKE OF MAGIC,
AND EVERYTHING HAS CHANGED

No, Alice's life isn't exactly paint-by-numbers. After breaking things off with her lying, stealing, bum of an ex, she discovered she's pregnant. Motherhood was definitely on her "someday" wish list, but a baby means less time for her art and no time for recent hallucinations that include this switcharoo with the tea. She has to impress her new boss, the ridiculously long-lashed, smoky-eyed Ethan Gallagher, and she has to deal with her family, who have started rambling about gypsy curses. Only a soul-deep bond with the right man can save her and her child? As if being single wasn't pressure enough!

Available July 2009!   ISBN 13: 978-0-505-52811-7

Marjorie Liu

Long ago, shape-shifters were plentiful, soaring through the sky as crows, racing across African veldts as cheetahs, raging furious as dragons atop the Himalayas. Like gods, they reigned supreme. But even gods have laws, and those laws, when broken, destroy.

Zoufalství. Epätoivo. Asa. Three words in three very different languages, and yet Soria understands. Like all members of Dirk & Steele, she has a gift, and hers is communication: That was why she was chosen to address the stranger. Strong as a lion, quick as a serpent, Karr is his name, and in his day he was king. But he is a son of strife, a creature of tragedy. As fire consumed all he loved, so an icy sleep has been his atonement. Now, against his will, he has awoken. *Zoufalství. Epätoivo. Asa.* In English, the word is despair. But Soria knows the words for love.

THE Fire King

A DIRK & STEELE NOVEL

ISBN 13: 978-0-8439-5940-6

MELANIE JACKSON

Author of *Night Visitor* and *The Selkie*

A ghostly hound stalks Noltland Castle. For years, such appearances have signaled doom for the clan Balfour, and there is little reason to believe this time will be any different. Wasn't their laird cut down while defending the Scottish king, leaving a boy to take a man's place?

Frances Balfour has done all she can, using guts and guile to keep her cousin safe in his new lairdship, but enemies encroach from all sides, and now the secluded isle of Orkney is beset from within. A stranger has arrived, and his green gaze promises to strip every secret bare. The newcomer is a swordsman, a seducer and a sometimes spy for the English king, but for all that, he seems a friend. And Colin Mortlock can see into the Night Side, that spectral world between life and death. He shall be the destruction of all Frances loves—or her salvation.

The Night Side

ISBN 13: 978-0-505-52804-9

✂ ☐ YES!

Sign me up for the Love Spell Book Club and send my FREE BOOKS! If I choose to stay in the club, I will pay only $8.50* each month, a savings of $6.48!

NAME: _____

ADDRESS: _____

TELEPHONE: _____

EMAIL: _____

☐ I want to pay by credit card.

☐ **VISA**   ☐ **MasterCard.**   ☐ **DISCOVER**

ACCOUNT #: _____

EXPIRATION DATE: _____

SIGNATURE: _____

Mail this page along with $2.00 shipping and handling to:
Love Spell Book Club
PO Box 6640
Wayne, PA 19087
Or fax (must include credit card information) to:
610-995-9274
You can also sign up online at www.dorchesterpub.com.

*Plus $2.00 for shipping. Offer open to residents of the U.S. and Canada only. Canadian residents please call 1-800-481-9191 for pricing information. If under 18, a parent or guardian must sign. Terms, prices and conditions subject to change. Subscription subject to acceptance. Dorchester Publishing reserves the right to reject any order or cancel any subscription.